SWEET

There beneath the b... came to her, his muscles rippling as he knelt over her, his eyes a tiger's eyes: hungry, predatory, a mirror to the desire that flared within the depths of his soul.

His battle-worn hands cupped her face. Smothering her gasp, his kiss locked her between him and the burning sands. At first Bellina resisted, but then she gave in, curiously excited by his invasion. It spread a languid weakness, thrilled every fiber of her being, and made her want to give in entirely to his will.

He forced away from his mind the fact that she did not belong to his world, his life, and that he could have no claim on her. For now there was no denying that the power he wielded with his love would hold her captive for as long as he willed it.

Drawn by the mystery of the forbidden, she was like a bird flying closer and closer to the desert sun. She was sure Surek could feel the effect his caresses had upon her. As he drank of her sweetness, she knew her desire was a thirst that only his body could quench.

THE BEST IN HISTORICAL ROMANCES

TIME-KEPT PROMISES   (2422, $3.95)
by Constance O'Day Flannery
Sean O'Mara froze when he saw his wife Christina standing before him. She had vanished and the news had been written about in all of the papers—he had even been charged with her murder! But now he had living proof of his innocence, and Sean was not about to let her get away. No matter that the woman was claiming to be someone named Kristine; she still caused his blood to boil.

PASSION'S PRISONER   (2573, $3.95)
by Casey Stewart
When Cassandra Lansing put on men's clothing and entered the Rawlings saloon she didn't expect to lose anything—in fact she was sure that she would win back her prized horse Rapscallion that her grandfather lost in a card game. She almost got a smug satisfaction at the thought of fooling the gamblers into believing that she was a man. But once she caught a glimpse of the virile Josh Rawlings, Cassandra wanted to be the woman in his embrace!

ANGEL HEART   (2426, $3.95)
by Victoria Thompson
Ever since Angelica's father died, Harlan Snyder had been angling to get his hands on her ranch, the Diamond R. And now, just when she had an important government contract to fulfill, she couldn't find a single cowhand to hire—all because of Snyder's threats. It was only a matter of time before the legendary gunfighter Kid Collins turned up on her doorstep, badly wounded. Angelica assessed his firmly muscled physique and stared into his startling blue eyes. Beneath all that blood and dirt he was the handsomest man she had ever seen, and the one person who could help beat Snyder at his own game.

SLAVE OF MY HEART

ANN LYNN

ZEBRA BOOKS
KENSINGTON PUBLISHING CORP.

ZEBRA BOOKS

are published by

Kensington Publishing Corp.
475 Park Avenue South
New York, NY 10016

First printing: January, 1990

Printed in the United States of America

To J.W.G.,
mentor and friend,
for all your support.

And to Mom and Dad
for always encouraging creativity.

One

Under a sky so low that churches' spires stabbed into murky clouds thick with a month's explusion of cannon fire and burning ships, a young Venetian girl, foreign to Constantinople, carefully threaded her way through the crumbling city. She took a lace handkerchief from a fold in her skirt, and wiped the soot from her face. After looking at the cloth disdainfully, she shoved it back into her dress. Smoke covered everything. It reminded her of the fog that silently drew a curtain over Venice. It blackened the sun and seeped through invisible cracks, slowly devouring breathable air. The only light now was the yellow haze of fire light reflected off the belly of the sky.

At the moment, finding her father and their survival were enough for Bellina to think about, but she couldn't help cursing the reasons for her predicament.

Everything had looked so promising until now. Born into the elite merchant class, she enjoyed all the privileges wealth and position afforded—dresses of shimmering silks, exotic perfumes, servants who ran her father's house and pampered her, and a father who could not deny her a single wish, even if it was to sail with him to the richest port in the world, Constantinople.

Since she could remember, all she had ever wanted to do was to sail with her father and Miquel. Dear sweet Miquel, her father's captain and her only friend. It was from Miquel, that she had learned the secrets of the sea and how to tie knots better than she could wield a needle and thread. How her Aunt Claudia and her cousins Flavia and Devota had been shocked when she demonstrated on the gold braid swag adorning the music room's lengthy drapes! Her father had agreed to take her with him to Constantinople when she agreed that upon her return she would marry the Conte Aurelian Sordici. The Conte, she knew, would lock her in a tower with all his other riches, so she had been determined to have one last adventure. An adventure that had now become a nightmare.

Now as she leaned against the city's wall, peering into the waters of the Golden Horn, her lips were set with determination. Her dark green eyes reflected a sea churned by two raging forces that sucked innocents like herself in its whirlpool of destruction. Her back stiffened and she raised her head to challenge anyone who would destroy the life she had known.

"Giovanni is dead!" she heard someone shriek, and it was repeated like a death knell, leaping from one to another. Giovanni dead? Giovanni, their only hope of winning the ongoing battle with the Ottomans? Their brave leader upon whom all of their faith had rested? She clasped a hand tightly over her mouth. She felt a little bit of her confidence dissolve. "I must find father," she thought. "With Miquel, he will get us home."

Gathering her skirts, she clawed upstream against the wave of people, avoiding the bodies that littered the streets, and taking care that her footing was secure lest the same fate befall her. She headed for Hagia Sophia. At last the basilica rose like a huge mountain, its domed roof arching towards the heavens. She entered, believing in her childish mind, that if one could only stay within its sheltering beauty, the horrors of war could never touch you. Even the atmosphere had a special quality: heady and ethereal, a balm to tortured nerves. Its ceiling rounded above her, encircled by a ring of arched windows and decorated with glittering mosaics, creating an illusion of unreality. Every pew was filled, even the aisles, and, as if governed by only one mind, the people murmured their desperate prayers. A hasty futile search revealed what she already knew: her father was not here. She would stay just long enough to regain her breath.

Lighting a candle, she gazed into the tiny flickering light and offered a prayer. Yet as much as she tried, she failed to feel in its depths the power of all that was holy and cherished, and could only picture the burning ships that dotted the Golden Horn; in all-too-real testimony to the destructive forces of the Ottomans.

Only a month before, her father had let her climb

up to a sheltered niche in the wall around Constantinople. Upon the waters before her a line of three hundred fifty—no it must have been no more than three hundred battle-ravaged and half-charred vessels—stood between them and the sultan's forces. She shuddered. Somehow though, as her father had pointed out to her, the tiny clumps of men commanded by the Grand Duke Notaros skillfully deflected many of the flaming arrows that spanned the bay and controlled the fires that sprouted upon their decks. If Notaros could last a few more days, the Ottomans would be repulsed, her father told her. Their lack of powder, the scarcity of timber, and an army of unruly men would prove to be strong weaknesses.

"They are not seamen," he assured her, "They have only eighteen galleys, poorly equipped, and the rest of the fleet is a motley collection of rafts and dinghies. Besides," he brushed back a lock of black hair that the sea breeze released from the knot of hair that crowned her head, "It would be impossible for the infidels to scale this wall, even if they first could climb out of the one-hundred-cubic-foot ravine below."

So she was falsely reassured by the sturdy six-mile-long wall that ran double thickness from shore to shore, and by the deep moat that skirted along its bottom. By day the Ottomans filled the moat with timber, hogs' heads, rocks, and dead men, in an effort to bridge the gap between land and wall; by night the defenders had to clear away the debris. Though the sultan's initial plan was foiled by their diligence, the wall had begun to show signs of distress from the battery of cannon fire, and was itself crumbling into the moat.

Bellina watched the pool of melted wax extinguish her candle, and she lit another with trembling fingers. All would be fine. She would find her father and her duenna, Rosa. Miquel would sail them back to Venice. The city would fall, of course, she knew that, but it didn't have to destroy her life, too. She wouldn't let it!

Turning to a towering set of double doors, Bellina left the basilica and forced herself into the swell of people, her will hardened by a single purpose. As she searched every passing face, hoping for one familiar visage among the thousands, reason began to slip away, and the assurance she felt moments before turned to anger and frustration. Frantically, she struggled like a drowning man as people pulled her along. She clenched her teeth and battled her way to a small niche between two houses, just to catch her breath and clamp a lid upon the rising panic which threatened to envelop her.

"If I become as witless as my duenna, Rosa, I will never find Papa," she told her waning courage. How could that bothersome duenna have failed her now? Now, when Papa had not returned to their apartments all day, and the city threatened to split at its seams? Why were those people running around like fools when they could be fighting the Osmanlis?

When the statue of the patron saint of Constantinople had fallen, smashing into unrecognizable fragments, and then the Turkish ships had made their way into the harbor, it had been too much for her duenna. "It is an evil omen." Rosa had

11

gasped, "We are lost! All is lost. May God forgive us." Her voice had quickly edged towards hysteria.

Later, Bellina had begged Rosa to come with her and find Papa, but it was no use. Her childhood pillar of strength had crumbled like a sand fortress under an oncoming wave. She had finally been forced to leave the woman with her black pearl rosary clutched between her trembling fingers, praying to a God who had turned his blessing away from them.

A faceless man jarred her from her resting spot as he shoved his way past, clawing like a frightened cat. She let the mob push her towards the gate of Saint Romanus, since it was where she had decided to go.

Had it really been only a few days ago that her father had bragged how he and others had stung the flanks of the Turkish army from the gate's walls? "Hah!" she scowled pessimistically. "Like a bee pestering a bull no doubt."

Had she actually begged her father to visit this cursed city? Why hadn't she listened to his protests? An unbidden sob touched her lips. Why was she so stubborn? Where was her father?

Her green eyes turned stormy as she carefully searched each face. Many of them were able-bodied men able to fight, ignoring the church bells that tolled in desperation, calling them to their posts. She recognized them as Giovanni's men. Leaderless, they would never go back. "Thank God the Greeks were not as foolish a lot," she thought. "Or they all might as well just open the gates and invite the sultan in."

Suddenly, a familiar dark bushy head popped up before her, using his sausagelike arm as a battering ram. "Papa, wait!" she screamed, her blood thundering through her head, but he continued onward not hearing.

Like a weasel she flattened her body against the rough wooden houses, pressing through the crowd, trying not to lose sight of him. "Oh wait!" she bleated. "Papa!" And then with a relieved sigh, she saw him turn to her. But the kindly face she expected turned out to be the snarling pock-marked face of a stranger.

She stopped in her tracks, her mind shrieking as her thoughts suddenly spun dizzily. Her father had to be here. Never would she even consider the chances against finding him in the same part of the city today. He *had* to be here!

Scanning the northern wall, her eyes fell upon the gate; the moonlight played games with the shadows at its edges. Why, its patterns almost formed the shape of a horse's head. Horse's head? Horse's body! She screamed soundlessly, shocked and disbelieving as the mounted Turks spilled through the demolished gate of Saint Romanus. She froze on the very spot she stood and could not tear her eyes from those furies which surely seemed to be escaping from hell itself.

They came swift and deadly. As easily as wheat before the scythe, the people fell under flashing scimitars before they had time to take one step towards shelter. Howls, hungry for blood, bubbled from their demon lips; encouraging terror to have a free hand. Bellina watched in horror as a trickle of thick red fluid inched down the cobblestones until it surrounded her slippered feet. Still she stood, breath suspended, body cold.

A sharp staccato clatter beat in time with her pounding heart and came to a deadening silence beside her. Slowly she turned her head to see a long slender-legged mare who bared her teeth against a restraining bit. Her mouth dropped open, for above her back a blood-slimed wraith—holding a dripping scimitar in mid-sweep—formed from the murky shadows. As a blaze of light from a passing raider's torch bathed his in crimson, Bellina gasped when she beheld two jet black eyes, holding her own gaze in their iron clasp. Surely with those demon orbs he was a messenger from Satan himself, ready to dispatch her soul down into the Stygian darkness of the underworld. Those eyes so queerly feline jolted her from her trance, and suddenly, as the blood surged into her limbs, she darted down the road for an alley.

The walls of the building-lined passageway threatened to swallow her into their infinity. She fled silently, never daring to look back, twisting down nameless streets and heading unconciously towards the apartments where she and her father dwelled. As the familiar building appeared in the distance ahead, she felt a surge of excitement and new hope. If only she could get to her room, everything would somehow pass. She never should have left the house!

Then, unbelievably, her father was standing in the doorway, the relief in his face obvious in the light of the lantern he held. The sound of joy that rang from her throat encompassed all the words she wanted to say to him.

But the sound ended, strangled, as she watched his face contort. A javelin's shaft had impaled him to the wooden door. His bulging eyes gazed vacantly at her.

14

His hands grasped the javelin's shaft for one fragment of time, until with one last shudder, he hung lifeless. The brief spot of light was lost to the darkness as the lantern crashed to the stone. "No!" she screamed, the walls echoing her anguish. "No, no, no, NO!"

She looked up suddenly as she felt another presence. Lurking in the shadows was the dark horseman, his luminous eyes searching for her. Softly she backed away, but it was too late; she had been seen. With a shriek of anguish, she fled. Labored gasps of breath tore from her throat. Her lungs were afire and her ears pounded with each echoing clap of a hoof. She ran through an inferno, dodging gruesome phantoms in the man-made hell, stumbling over lifeless appendages and slipping in their blood. Her damp slippers flopped resentfully along with each stride, until, in disgust, she tore them from her feet and braved the cobblestones barefoot. It was not long before her soles were shredded, leaving bloody tracks. Glancing back with foreboding, the moonlight revealed to her an evergaining pursuer. The fetid odor of both man and horse assailed her flaring nostrils. In one last effort she stretched her stride longer.

A covered lantern softly beamed over a door not too far away. Frantically groping, grasping its glowing brass handle, she turned and desperately tugged at the barrier to the sanctuary. Just as it opened, her breath rushed out of her explosively as she was crushed in an iron embrace. He hauled her up with careless ease, like the sailors on her father's merchant ships hauled bundles of fabric upon the deck, and she was unceremoniously flung across his saddle. Bellina struggled despite her position: head down, the sharp edge of the pommel digging into her stomach, and the ground below jumping dizzily. Her head banged against leather, her blood rushed hot to her face, and in a sudden spasm, she gasped for breath, but no air came. Only darkness descended, weighing down her flailing limbs, numbing every thought and fear, until there was just cold nothingness.

Two

Bellina spiraled weightlessly down into the depths of her mind like a leaf; spinning endlessly into eternity where time and war did not exist. What a safe haven of nothingness; a place secure from the joys and agonies of life. Certain that death had claimed her, her mind reached into the heavy mists, searching for the welcome embrace of her long dead mother. "The plague. It must have taken me just like Mamma," she vaguely guessed, as the apparition of a wasting woman lying on a huge feather bed, sinking further into its softness on the passing of each day, appeared before her.

Her mother lifted one hand, once so white and animated but now so deathly gray, and beckoned her. Drawing closer, Bellina watched in horror. While the drummer's roll thundered, lightning stabbed again and again. "No!" she screamed, but her mother was no longer there to comfort her.

"No," she began to say; yet he hadn't heard and soon a hundred whirled about; dragging her with

17

them, crushing and trampling in time to the krummhorn and drums. Oh God, she thought, I'll be trampled. Pulling her hand from the fox's grasp, she pounded at them all.

"Bellina, take my hand and follow," a familiar voice called to her.

Miquel! Oh, it is Miquel, she silently cried in relief when his wooly black curls announced him among the mob.

"Did you know the moon is full tonight?" he smiled a knowing smile. "Your duenna won't miss you. I've sent that gossip Flavia to keep her ear."

Why was Miquel here? Didn't he know the Conte would be happy to find any excuse to bury a Sordici dagger into his chest?

A moan surfaced from her lips, and consciousness for one brief second almost overpowered the sluggish blackness that soaked her mind. Instead, weakness pulled her back, forcing all the fears, doubts, and joys of the past years to flood her mind as it wandered, searching for a path to reality or peace.

"Bellina!" She heard her duenna call in scolding tones. The round face of Rosa peered into every sheltered nook, searching. "Bellina Magela!" she snorted, and Bellina crouched lower behind the brush where she hid. The round face wavered, grew bright, and as Bellina watched, a few clouds faded across it.

"A full moon!" her heart sang, and by its light she could see Miquel slowly pick his way up the hillside with nervous glances backward. When he found her at their pre-arranged spot, he clasped her to him in shy eagerness and, much to her shock, kissed her right there beneath the watching moon!

A fearful buzzing lanced her thoughts. Somewhere Father Masalia's carefully lowered voice dealt out prayers of penance for her sins, as Papa laughed away Aunt Claudia's protests.

"Seventeen, Papa," Bellina cried, "I'm seventeen, and that is old enough to go to Constantinople. I'll never have this chance again!"

"Misereatur tui omnipotens Deus, et dismissis peccatis tuis . . ." Father Masalia droned on. Bellina's hands flew to her ears.

"Do you know where she was?" Rosa demanded.

"Domine!" Claudia shrieked. "You would take a child into a city of barbarians? If Francesca was alive, she would *never* allow her daughter to do *half* the things she gets away with."

"You forget yourself, sister." Her father's gray eyes turned dark.

Their angry voices clashed, attacking and straining in a violent discord that rose to a sharp crescendo and ate away at the fog that clouded everything. Phantoms streamed through the bolted gate, and Bellina saw her father disappear into the madness. "Don't leave me here!" she screamed.

Bellina's eyes flew open with startling abruptness. Slowly, her head cleared, aided by the savory aroma of broth. It tickled her nose, arousing her other senses, making her aware of a hungry, hurting body. Her bruised, throbbing feet assured her she was very much alive. Wrinkling her nose, she squinted, trying to bring her eyes to focus upon the faint shadow above her. Gradually, the fuzzy outline sharpened and the father she had expected transformed into a much younger man who sat across from her in rigid watchfulness. He looked as if carved from stone; a hard figure of a man, his penetrating eyes surveying her without expression. With a shudder, she realized that these very eyes had peered from the mounted specter of that cursed night, and with that brutal reminder, a stricken heart knew her father was lost to her forever. Her hand reached unconsciously to the heart-shaped necklace around her neck. At least it had not been stolen—yet.

The spirited girl under his gaze reminded him of the sister he had not seen in four years. Surek thought he had successfully blocked her memory from his mind, until this waif appeared in the tumultuous shadows of Constantinople. Teva would be about her age, and she too would refuse to whimper like a scared pup under the same circumstances. But there the resemblance ended. This girl was pale as the moon, with hair black as night, and thin as a reed compared to Teva. Like himself, Teva was part Mongol, inheriting rich skin, almond eyes, and a strong frame. He thought of her tending his father. Then he thought of this one; parted from her family, separated from her country—for she was obviously not of Constantinople—all because of two warring empires.

Bellina sat up with a start and would have fled, but he was suddenly there, pushing her gently back, smiling reassuringly into her eyes.

"There is no need to be frightened, little one," he told her in a strangely accented voice. "You are safe here."

She watched the face beneath the turban, the beard

and moustache making it unreadable. Despite the gentleness of his words, she backed away as far as she could. "You!" she cried, her voice accusing. "You were there."

He turned his head away and let the silence between them thicken until she thought it would smother her. Reaching to the table behind him, picking up a bowl of steamy broth, he offered it to her. "It will give you strength."

She looked fleetingly at the richness of the carpets and furnishings and back to him in his battle-worn clothes. "Where am I?"

He abruptly lowered the bowl. "I am Surek—"

"That tells me a lot! Where am I?"

"I am Surek Harum Edib, captain of the Spahiglani. This is my tent, and these are my possessions." His arm waved through the air, encompassing the whole of the tent.

"And what of me? Am I another possession?"

"Is that what you think?" His eyes met hers piercingly, and once again he pushed the bowl towards her.

"Yes!" she cried, striking the bowl from his hands. The soup washed down his boots to stain the carpet. "I do not want your poison!"

He grabbed her wrist. "Poison? You foolish child. I should be so ungracious as you, and ask who *is* this beggarly creature who insults my hospitality and does not even realize how fortunate she is. Would you rather be in that wounded city selling your body for food? That is what you would be doing before long, if I had not picked you up."

With a snarl she pulled her hand away, "I would

21

sooner die. You didn't save my neck for my benefit. Do you think me naive enough not to know when I've been abducted?"

He gave a grunt and mentally updated her age by two years. The child he had been watching in her haunted sleep had metamorphasized into a harpy. He was wrong—she was unlike Teva. Teva would have more sense than to insult her savior. Her words, harsh and accusing, pursued him.

"One of your men murdered my father, and that makes you as guilty as if you had flung that javelin yourself. And I'm supposed to kiss your feet in gratitude? Ha!" Her voice lowered dangerously and her eyes were as murky as a storm-tossed sea, "Touch me again, and you will not soon forget my wrath."

Allah give me patience, he silently prayed. How can one so young and beautiful be so arrogant? He stood abruptly with a bitter laugh. "Who are you? Do you not realize that I could cut your mocking tongue from your mouth, or run you through, and no one would think twice?" He paced the span of the tent. The scimitar at his side caught the sunlight that filtered through the tent and radiated menacing flashes upon the pillows around her. "Are you so eager for death? You, whose eyes leaped with fear when I first saw you?"

He stopped, and his eyes, like two pits of impenetrable black, pulled at her, and she could not stop the fingers of fear that traced her spine. He let his fingers follow the gold chain around her neck until they stopped upon the heart pendant. When he surrendered it, letting it fall to her chest, she clasped a hand possessively over it. Now it was her only possession, her only link to Venice, but most of all, it was a gift from her father.

"You must be of a handsome dowry, my dear, to be embellished in gold. Let's see . . ." he studied her intently. "By your dress you are no peasant, but you have none of the manners of royalty. Your father was with you in Constantinople, and you are obviously foreign. Ah hah! A Genoese merchant and his daughter!"

Bellina stiffened. "I am Bellina Magela D'Rosallini—a Venetian!"

"Well, Bellina, obviously you are alien to this part of the world. What fool is responsible for bringing you here, where a child does not belong?"

"My father was no fool, and I'm not a child. He knew the streets and people of Constantinople like the lines in his hand. And he has made his fortune in proof of that!"

"Perhaps he was wise in business, but in raising a daughter I find his talents lacking. You do not even have a civil tongue in your head."

"Who are you to judge, butcherer of innocent women and children? I will see you pay for your atrocities." Her eyes followed the curved blade and then met his, sharp as any dagger.

"I hardly call Constantine's armies children. I have never murdered a child . . . or a woman," he said, glaring at her. "But there is always a first time."

"What do you want of me?" she said flatly, brushing aside his words.

He threw his hands up in disgust, "I do not want you, and am quickly regretting my hasty actions!" What *did* he want of her? What was he thinking of

23

when he lifted this child from the street and brought her here, he asked himself. He was pretending to be two people for too long, and it was taking its toll. Never before was he so careless as to let emotions rule his decisions. It was time to give up this dual role and return to Muscovy, before he died with his father believing him to be a traitor. He doubted that Prince Stivanovich on his own would clear his name as promised and admit to spying on the Ottoman Empire. He would have to wait for the right moment, and until then, he would continue to play a dangerous game.

"You ought to regret them, for you will be hung for my abduction and the atrocities committed on the people of Constantinople. When the Emperor Constantine recovers his troops, you will be crawling at my feet begging for mercy."

As if she had hit him, he felt his face burning. "Constantine!" he spat in disgust, "Constantine is lost! He charged into the sultan's army like a mad dog, waving a sword and proclaiming 'long live the Roman Empire.' He hasn't been found—nor will ever, I fear. And your Great Duke Giustiani Logo has fled with his treachery and ambition. The Genoese have long since placed themselves at the Fatih's disposal." He smiled devilishly as his words stabbed her without mercy. "And without their aid, Mehmet would not have been so successful in passing his galleys through ten miles of thicket to the hills of Pera."

He sat back, his arms crossed behind his head, and raised an eyebrow in mock surprise. "You did not know that your neighbors were instrumental in the flight of our galleys that sailed into the harbor to bypass so efficiently your Imperial brigantines?"

"NO!" she shouted, "That can not be true!"

"Yes," he told her. "So it seems, my sparrow, as fate would have it, you will be the one to kneel at *my* feet like the city of Constantinople kneels to Moslem rule. The sultan has moved into the Emperor's palace and has declared Constantinople a state of Islam in the name of Allah. No one is more alone or at anyone's mercy than you, so take care."

It was the wrong thing to say, shouted in a flash of anger, he realized that as soon as he saw her face. Like one dazed by opium, she sat ashen, bravado lost, hands trembling, staring at him with eyes that spoke of hope lost and the pain of a part of her life ending.

"You lie, you lie, curse your soul to a living agony!" she choked, tears finally falling down her cheeks. With sudden desperation she scanned the tent. It was like a maze divided by drapery. She was a gnat caught in a beautiful web and the spider sat there across from her. All was so futile. A shiver racked her body uncontrollably and his hand reached out to comfort. Like a falcon never trained to the wrist, she leaped at him, the destroyer of what hope she had still clung to. Blood congealed under her nails as she raked his face.

"Wait," he yelled, grabbing her wrists. He was met by a sharp kick in the shin, followed quickly by another. He clutched her tightly. "Will you listen?"

"Release me!" she shrieked, and no sooner was the cry out then she sank her teeth into one bronzed arm. With a bellow, he quickly let her go, propelling her dizzily against the table, the china it held shattering across the floor. He pressed his left hand over the wound to still its throbbing.

"This I need?" He stepped over the shards of glass. "I brought no timid sparrow into my nest, but a sparrow hawk who claws and bites the hand that would feed her!"

In response she knocked his turban off, sending it spinning through the air, and with an outraged cry she grasped his hair and wrenched. Peeling back her fingers, he gripped her by the waist when she struggled, and soon both fell tangled on the floor. His weight full upon her, she lay immobile and gasping for air.

"No one will harm you here!" He told her again, "On my life, I promise this to you before Allah as my witness." He felt the wild tremor of her heart beneath his chest, so like a captive bird. Would she prove as fragile? He brushed a hand gently across her hair and she flinched. Her breath came in gasps as if she were sobbing, but no sound came.

"Now," he murmured, "will you eat something? But I warn you, if you throw it on the floor again, it will be the last I'll ever offer you." He stood up, wincing as he moved his right arm, and offered his other hand to her. She rose scorning it, silently sitting down amongst the pillows. He brought a plate of cheese and crusty bread and a small brown boy who picked up the broken glass. She ate woodenly and he sat watching, ignoring the red that stained his shirt where she had wounded him. She watched it spread; seeping down the arm in an ever widening circle and searching her heart for any remorse, found none. Seeing her staring, he smiled.

"No doubt you are rejoicing on your luck in nicking me? But I think not, you do not look so cruel. Forgive my temper, I should not have been so callous and told you so suddenly about the city." He paused, when she gave no acknowledgment to his words, he continued, "But surely you had guessed? Its fate, like ours, was decided a lifetime ago, despite you or our sultan. Allah knows. Only Allah."

She bit back a retort. Instead she handed him a piece of bread which he took, adding a slab of cheese.

"Why?" she asked tonelessly.

"Why what?" He filled two glasses.

"Why are you doing this? Why did you take so much trouble 'rescuing' me out of the many you killed last night? Just to return me later? What am I to you?"

He stopped chewing and met her defiant eyes. "Perhaps because I remember my sister, once as young and arrogant as you. And as beautiful. Perhaps because I am not a monster, despite what you think. I did not start this war. I only serve my sultan and Allah." His eyes darkened, "Besides, do you think you will sit in this tent all day, while I wait on you like a slave? You will earn your keep." He saw her features harden and her fingers clench around the bread. "No, not as you are thinking; mending, washing, cooking, and so on. Allah! Give me patience to live with one so untrusting!"

"Live with you?" she stammered.

"Of course! Did you think to have this tent to yourself, and me sleep with the horses? You'll have your own pallet. And I assure you, you are safer here with me than with any of my men. Why, they eat little children for breakfast!"

She turned her head away in disbelief and despair at his words and mockery. Her throat tightened painfully. Her voice was like a leaf whispering in a winter wind. "I will die here."

"That I find hard to believe." He took the last piece of cheese and laughed, "You, my dear, are a survivor."

Three

Bellina never woke before Surek. She yawned, hearing the scrape of his knife against his plate, and knew that if she did not talk to him now, he would be gone for the day.

During the first days after she had left the half-oval mark of her teeth on his arm, they had studied each other like two strange cats, saying few words if any, each carefully defensive. But then as her curiosity peaked and fear lessened, she watched him with great interest, for he was, to her, strange. As if leprosy had spotted her hands, he avoided her, returning to the tent only to sleep, as promised, in the far corner. Did he really have no interest in her? She was wary to the ways of men; did he never lust for her? Indeed it was maddening, she thought. Not that she would welcome his interest, but he made her feel as ugly as the water spiders that clung to the walkways of the canals. No, of her beauty she was certain. What kept him away then? Her sharp tongue, no doubt. However, he deserved all she had said. She regretted nothing, well, almost nothing. She was sorry for biting him. As if he had been bitten by a viper, it had become infected almost immediately, swelling horribly.

She heard him push aside the bowl and the rasp of a sword as it slid from its sheath. Yes, if she did not hurry, she thought, pulling on the tunic he had given her in place of her bloodied gown, she would never see him this day. She pushed aside the drape partition and he turned, startled, his eyes piercing her. Behind the beard and moustache, his lips were a firm grim line, yet still her voice came steady.

"When you are gone, the guards will not let me go outside. It is my understanding that I am not a prisoner here."

"You are not a prisoner here, but still you must go by my rules. It is for your own protection. Do you think I have the time to watch my men and you all day? Before I'd know it, you'd be running to me, blaming one of my men for assaulting you. A Spahiglani camp is no place for a woman."

"But still I am here, and through no fault of mine." She met his eyes pleading. "Can I not go out for just a little while? I'm going mad in here! You're seldom around, there's no one to talk to, and there is nothing for me to do."

"No." He wiped an oiled cloth against his jambiyyah and placed it back in its sheath.

"You could send a janissary with me."

"Do you think they are nursemaids?" His eyes deepened to the blackness of coal as they glared warningly, "Are you set to giving orders? I said no; that is the end of this discussion." He lifted up a

30

goatskin pouch and slung it over his shoulder. "I am riding into Constantinople today and will be gone for a few days. There are clothes to be sent here for mending, which should occupy your time until my return. My comrades can not express the overwhelming gratitude they feel for your 'uncomplaining' services. It leaves their hands free for more important matters." His lips drew into a mocking smile that teased the anger from her, intensifying her fiery beauty.

Bellina gulped back a rising lump in her throat. "You and your men can wear your clothes till the seat of your pants show through! I'm sick of needlework! Sick of polishing your brass lanterns! Sick of looking at these ugly pillows and drapery that makes this place a suffocating maze."

He looked at her flushed face, responding flatly, "Very well. Then you may stay here and do nothing, if you wish." And then he left, pausing to speak to the janissaries who patrolled outside in that strange guttural language she found so hard to learn. But still, even with her poor knowledge of it, she knew exactly who he was talking of.

She sat down abruptly and studied the mound of clothes left from yesterday and envisioned it consumed suddenly in flames. "Wouldn't that please your men, Surek?" she said under her breath. But instead she wearily lifted her body, moving to the tent's opening. Surek was already on a horse. Whirling the beast around on its haunches, he let the horse have its head. Feeling her presence behind them, the sentries closed together, blocking Surek and any thoughts of escape from her mind.

31

"Kurahsak ur'dei!" She shouted at their stiff backs in their language, but they stood like carved wood figures, showing no effect from her insults. She paced the length of her enclosure like a caged panther, holding the heart-shaped locket in her hand.

How could anyone remain sane when their whole existence dangled on the whim of a dispassionate tyrant? She circled the tent until she began to feel dizzy. The sun beat down from above, turning the air hot and sticky. She laid across her pallet and stared for the hundredth time at Surek's collection of tins, painted with the tiger that also tipped his scimitar. She never heard the bowl of yogurt and dates being placed on the table, but the next time she turned her head, it was there. And she let it stay there untouched, growing warm.

"Oh that sun, that cursed sun," she moaned as the heat became stifling and the day wore on. It now cast a radiating sphere upon the backside of the tent. She blinked at it venomously. Then suddenly a smile spread across her face as an idea bloomed in her mind. Of course! Why hadn't she thought of it before? If the fabric of the tent was thin . . . Frantically she searched through her box among threads and needles, it was nowhere to be found. She lifted up pillows, opened containers, even pulled up the corners of the rugs, but could not find the scissors. She sat down frustrated. Hadn't she seen them sitting there upon a nest of thread? Once again she picked through the box, then, carrying it to her pallet, she dumped the contents out. There, tangled amongst thread, metal flashed. She grabbed them, as if once found they would sprout wings to fly away, and squeezing in between the back wall and her bed, she carefully cut the fabric where it met the ground. Once a small slit was made, she peeked out. Before her stretched a plain, brush growing sporadically like hair upon a mangy dog. No trees, no men, but still she heard the laughter of Surek's men close by and apprehensions poked at her desire to venture out. Surek would be gone for a long while, she thought, so he would not catch her. And if anyone else caught her, what difference would that make? All they could do was make her go back to the confines of this prison. Besides, she did not intend to get caught dressed as she was in men's clothes. All she needed was a turban to wind around her hair, so she retrieved a length of fabric from the mending. Without further hesitation she banished remaining doubts, disguised herself, and, wiggling through the slice in the tent, crawled out into the open. But in her enthusiasm she had been careless, for a wide-eyed slave stared at her from under the basket he carried. She gave him a grim smile. "May the brightness of the day bless you," she said in greeting. But what she really wanted to do was get to her knees and plead. Yet the slave was as flustered as she. At her words his face took on a stricken look and, before she knew it, he was upon the ground rambling words quicker than she could translate. Oh God, she thought, someone else is going to come with all his noise and I don't even know what he's saying. And then it became apparent to her that the slave was embarrassed, and no doubt her form of address had been socially incorrect. What did he, a slave, care if she, dressed as a Spahiglani, liked to crawl out of slits in tents? It was not his lot in life to question. She almost laughed as relief filled her with bravado. Well, she never did quite pay attention when her father tried teaching her this barbaric language.

"Go!" She ordered him in a voice low and threatening, and as easy as that he was gone. Bellina gathered her courage and walked purposefully from behind the tents to the far end of the camp where the horses were roped off. There, with the heat of the day at its highest and the flies swarming in heavy masses, she would be least likely to encounter anyone else.

The camp was deserted of Spahiglani. Only slaves worked beneath the merciless sun, as the horsemen slept the heat away in their tents. Janissaries with not much to do bunched around her tent with the two who normally stood guard, their laughter rising to accompany her footsteps as she crossed to the horses. After an eternity she slipped under the rope and lost herself among the beasts, still staying a safe distance from them. They eyed her strangely, shifting. Fear began to grip her as she imagined herself crushed beneath their large splayed hoofs.

"Boy, what are you doing near the horses!" The harsh voice from behind startled an unwilling gasp, and before she could say anything, she was pulled sharply around to face him. He was only a boy himself, a few years from manhood, but he frowned sternly at her. "You're the queerest-looking boy I've ever seen."

He squinted into her face and surveyed her feminine form from top to bottom. He spoke again, then stopped when he saw her blank look. He said slowly, "You are the Captain's little slave girl, no?"

Laughing at the red that crept across her cheeks, he added, "And what a coincidence to find you out here just after the Captain has left."

Dismay at discovery evaporated her exhilaration, like dew beneath a relentless sun. "I just wanted to breathe fresh air again, and it's so lonely in there," she stammered.

His eyes brightened with mischief as he made the most of her plight. "My silence is not for free you know."

Her heart plunged as Surek's words of that morning buzzed in her head. No, he was just a boy, surely . . . She backed from him, her eyes wide.

His white teeth flashed against his brown skin. "Just don't let the Captain find out, and you can help me tend the horses."

A rush of air escaped her in relief. "Fine, that will be fine."

"You any good with horses, slave girl?"

"Bellina. And I'm no slave girl."

"Whatever," he replied, and he motioned to a horse that stood apart from the others, all the weight of his hindquarters shifted to one leg. "See him? Take him to the stream and stand that sore fetlock in the water for—"

"But I've never handled a horse before!"

"Just as I thought. Now what good are you going to be to me?"

"Well, you could teach me."

"Me? Naqu, tender of the herd, teach *you?*" He eyed her, "Well, we'll see. At any rate you could at least help me remove the burrs from their coats. They'll be grazing and paying you no heed, and you won't have to lead them around. Just watch out for that one—he's a nipper."

She followed to where he pointed and her mouth dropped open. There amongst the herd was a thick-lipped, horselike creature whose back rose like a mountain. "What is that?"

Naqu laughed at her dismayed face. "Haven't you ever seen a camel before?"

"It is seldom you see horses in Venice, let alone a camel."

He tried the foreign word upon his tongue, "Venice?"

"There the paths are water; our horses boats. There I do not have to worry about whether I will be bit or trampled."

He listened spellbound as she told him of her home. She let him journey through her memories to another life, rich in comforts, strange in customs. His eyes burned when she told him how her grandfather Bernadino had finally ended their feud with the Malestrano family one rainy night, with the tip of his secreted dagger. She spoke of gypsies, carnivals, and merchant fairs that drew white-haired people from the north. He listened to her until the sun slipped down and more and more men left the comforts of their tents to finish jobs undone. Abruptly she stopped.

"I must go, or risk being discovered."

Naqu yawned, breaking from his trance. "You can go only if you promise to come tomorrow."

She smiled. "I will."

"And I will accompany you back, so it seems less suspicious."

"I was very fortunate to meet up with you, Naqu, and nobody else," she suddenly admitted.

"I know," he replied flatly.

They met no difficulties making their way to the back of the tents, but once there, it was a long time until it was clear for her to wriggle back in. Outside she heard Naqu walk away whistling. Ah, boys are the same all over, she mused. She sat down contented, picked up a cambric shirt from the pile, and darned a sword's slice through its weave. She could not help wonder if the unfortunate soldier who had worn it had been restored his wholeness as simply as the shirt. Men were such fools. If women ruled, she was sure none of this hopeless warring would have come about. Her mother had practiced the best philosophy: let people live as they wish; it is not anyone's place to judge or hinder. She reflected on this and hoped that Surek would not hinder in any way her return home.

The next days went all too quickly, and she encountered no difficulty during her excursions. Lazily, Naqu would listen to tales, all work forgotten until Bellina had to prod him into action. She, herself, learned to like the giant beasts, if not entirely trust them.

It all ended quite abruptly: as silently as a cat one night, Surek returned. She did not see him from where she sat, her needle flashing under the flame of a nearby tallow lamp. With a sigh, she stood to push remaining clothes into a corner where no one would trip over them. There, out of the corner of her eye, she saw him half in shadows reclining against a pillow, quietly observing her. She jumped. He took the roll

37

of shimmery green cloth that rested next to him.

"This is from the city and I've paid good silver for it. I hope you like it." He offered it to her and she took it uncomprehending. "Here," he helped her spread it out. Like the trails of fireflies, gold thread spiraled intricate paths through the weave.

"It is beautiful," Bellina murmured, afraid to touch it.

Surek's mouth curved at one end. "That is in appreciation for all the mending you have done, and to make decent clothing befitting a girl. My men's clothes do not become you."

She thanked him, swallowing back the bitter taste of guilt, for she had not done as much mending as she could have. She felt his eyes burning upon her.

"Have you eaten yet, my lord?" she said hurriedly to keep the nervousness that crept up her spine at bay.

"My lord is it? You have mellowed since I've been gone. Indeed, tent life seems to agree with you, your color has improved tremendously."

He leaned closer, peering at her sun-tanned face. "If I did not know better, I would have thought . . . No . . ."

Fear leaped into Bellina's face, but he sat back again and the look of puzzlement faded. He sighed, "Yes, I have had a bit to eat from my pouch already." He stood wearily, grasping the pillow in one hand, pulling the cover away and off of his pallet.

"You aren't going to sleep already, are you?"

"After all that arguing with the sultan these past days, I am tired enough to sleep two days."

"Sultan!" Bellina moved nearer to Surek. "You actually saw Mehmet II? The Conqueror? And you argued with him?"

Surek laughed at her surprise. "Yes, I argued and survived. Now, let me go to sleep before I expire from exhaustion."

Reluctantly, she went to her own side and he untied the drape, letting it fall between them. It was late, she had to admit, removing all garments until only a thin underlayer of cotton remained. She laid across the pallet and listened as Surek pulled his boots off.

"What did you argue about?" she suddenly asked.

He snorted in disbelief. "Girl, you have no manners." He let silence drag between them as he struggled, cursing his swollen feet. "Never mind. It may be of interest to you anyway, and then perhaps you'll let me sleep?"

A boot hit against the table, rattling the tins stacked there. "Put simply, I, among other advisors, convinced him of the need to resume trade with the Christian city-states. We can not replace our lost warships without their timber."

"Including Venice?" she almost shouted.

"Yes, Venice is weeping for trade. Now go to sleep."

Sleep! How could she sleep? Her whole body nearly hummed with joy. It would be soon now! Soon she would hear the lap of water outside her home, instead of the sand that the wind ground against this tent. Had she misjudged Surek? All she had said, all the curses she had rained upon him and his descendants, the scars of that healing bite wound . . . He was different from the others. If he had attacked her tooth and nail, she would never have let him live to see those wounds healed. Instead, he brought her gifts. She turned restlessly upon the pallet. Perhaps this all was some well-planned trick to lower her guard, make her cooperative? But still . . . I must talk with him in the morning, she thought. We both have let our tempers and the tragedies of that nightmare in Constantinople hold us puppets to our rulers' hate.

However, by the time she woke the next day, he was gone, and the morning passed slowly without his return. She was cutting out the green material when she heard Naqu hissing at the slit behind her bed.

"Not today," she whispered.

She heard him groan. "Come on, Bellina, you said you would tell me about the storm on the sea and how you almost lost the first mate." Sensing her hesitation, he added, "Maybe I'll let you ride today."

"Some other time, I have too much to do."

"You are cruel," she heard him whine. His words touched a sore spot after the guilt that had built up as she lay tossing in her bed last night.

"Alright, but have you seen your captain?"

"No, he rode out at dawn."

"Very well, I'll be with you in a moment."

The day was beautiful with the humidity of the previous week gone. It was perfect for learning to ride. Visions of Spahiglani flying along on their horses, set free from the limitations of their slow human forms, made it difficult for her mind to stay on what she told Naqu. As soon as she finished with first mate Giovanni and the storm that forced the *Portia Regalia* to seek port, she suggested that they commence with the horses before it was time for her

40

to return. Naqu was by no means anxious to see her bouncing along erratically on a horse's back. That had lost its humor long ago. He particularly didn't want to go chasing around some reluctant mount from among the herd. Noticing Bellina's enthusiasm, he made his decision.

"Alright, Bellina, the choice is yours among the packhorses. You've seen me catch them, now this time let's see you."

Scanning the herd, she settled on Temur, who possessively grazed a choice spot of scrubby grass near the stream. His flanks were flecked in gray. Hardly the dream of the Spahiglani, but after all, there was a lot to learn before she would be riding anything more fiery. With apprehension she approached him. Uncaring, he continued to snatch clumps of grass, mashing them between stained teeth until she made a grab for the rope around his head. Easily, he danced away. The second time Bellina was quicker. Catching him, she pulled while he, standing as firm as a staked tent before a pushing wind, refused to budge. "There must be a better way," she panted, jerking harder.

From the top of the hill, Naqu stood watching, his lips thinning into a grin. Then, with a sudden chill, he saw her move to the back of the horse, set on pushing him from the rear. "Stop!" he yelled as he ran towards her with waving hands, but before he could intervene the irritated Temur squealed and shot one hind leg out. By the time Naqu reached Bellina, she was sprawled across the ground, gasping. As she tried to rise, he roughly pushed her back, his voice sharp. "Never, never go behind a horse like that again! Look at this, now what am I to do?"

He placed his hand against her middle and she cried out. That was it, he thought grimly, there was no mistaking the grating he felt beneath his hand. "For sure Surek will want to know how this came about. By Allah, may that horse find his way to the sultan's table. This rib is broken!"

"Don't blame the horse," she labored.

"Shut up! Because of your stupidity *I'll* find myself on the sultan's table. You're lucky that hoof missed your head."

Hot tears streaked her cheeks and a painful lump closed her throat as she reflected on her existence. Was there ever to be a feeling of worth in her life? She had encouraged this boy in deceiving his master where she had not the right, and now look at what had happened. Whatever she seemed to do turned against her and hurt others. If she had not flung herself at her father in a tantrum, begging to go with him to the East, she would now be in Venice. Even her very presence seemed to aggravate Surek. Now she had brought trouble for Naqu through her own ignorance and selfishness.

Naqu took his own shirt off and ripped it furiously into strips. "Stop squirming," he snapped as he untied her shirt. "You're no longer a little rich girl in Venice. I have to bind this rib, or too much movement on your part and you'll have a speared lung."

She felt the air upon her bare chest and felt her nipples grow hard. From under his sandy lashes Naqu studied the rise and fall of her breasts. She had the slender grace of a boy, yet was as voluptuous as befitted a sultan's most treasured concubine. Abruptly, he lowered his eyes to the livid hoof print before she noticed his attention and wound the bandages around her. He should be as lucky, he thought, to be captain of the Spahiglani and have this one to warm his bed. Never would she seem the same girl to him from this day on.

Bellina frowned as she watched Naqu, feeling terribly exposed to the world. Was that lust that sparked his eyes? Foolish girl, she chastised herself. Naqu is a friend, and friends were too scarce to begin accusing them blindly. Besides, he was only a boy. She jerked away as his arm brushed against one nipple.

He smiled innocently, "Sorry." Quickly tying the ends of the bandage in a knot, he helped her on with her shirt. "Can you walk back by yourself? It would look suspicious if I were seen carrying you."

"It's alright. I'll manage. Don't worry, I won't mention all you've done for me. If I'm found out, it will be my problem alone."

"Keep that bandage on until the new moon, and for your sake hope our captain stays ignorant." He helped her up and watched as she slowly made her way back. "I'll cover for you. Just keep walking as if nothing happened and don't stop."

Once inside the tent, after the agony of squeezing through the slit, she tried in vain to settle into a comfortable position on her bed. Perhaps sleep would lull the pain away. But despite her attempts, her mind was assaulted with nightmares of Surek's reaction to her deception. How would Naqu fare in the face of his anger? Ah, she never should have involved him. How could she have taken such a chance without even once thinking of the consequences?

Returning in the darkness, Surek was puzzled that the lamps were not kept burning for his return. Trying to navigate his way, his feet became entangled in the mending he had left before his departure. They had not been touched. Upon finally finding a lamp, he spied Bellina half-sitting, propped up awkwardly with pillows, asleep. As the light glanced off her face, her eyes opened.

"You're back," she mumbled.

"There was no light lit for me." He peered closer at her face, "Are you sick?"

His words were like cold water in her face. "No, I forgot to keep them burning."

"And you forgot to work the clothes?" Placing the lamp safely out of reach, his voice came low and stern. "Alright, did that fool Naqu have you on a horse too strong for you?"

He saw her mouth drop open in shock. "Did you think my guards are so inept? I was simply tolerating your disobedience, since your jaunts outside seemed a balm to your temper."

Bellina watched his face for anger but it remained expressionless. "Naqu had nothing to do with this. When I couldn't budge Temur, I approached the horse from behind and shoved him. He kicked me in the side."

"Ho, it seems Temur has made you pay well enough for your deceit." She winced at his words. "And Naqu is receiving his just payment as he worries about me discovering the truth, eh, my

44

hawk? Let me see the injury."

She stiffened. "There is no need. One rib was broken, that is all. Naqu has already tied it up."

"Very well, Naqu has bandaged my horses' legs well enough." She shivered as he leaned closer, drawing her into his eyes. "It is well you learn how to master a horse. Once that rib heals, I myself will teach you the right way. You will ride as well as any Mongol."

She stared wide-eyed, soundless, expecting reprisal but frightened at this new turn. At times he said the strangest things for an Ottoman. Ride as well as a Mongol, she puzzled.

His laughter, loud and burning, mocked her. "No words?" he prodded, while lazily he lit his pipe. "Bellina, this is most amazing. You are halfway tolerable this way." And as he brought the tip of the pipe to his lips, a pillow caught him full in the face.

Four

Before the sun had a chance to bake away the mist that clung affectionately to the tents, Surek's voice was heard calling for his horse, Kayaska, to be caught, his saddle brought, and Bellina to be out before he dragged her lazy body from the bed. Naqu gave him Kayaska's lead and inwardly Surek smiled at the waxed saddle and watched the youth bow in humbleness that came awkwardly.

"Master, I beg your forgiveness," Naqu whined. "Have you yet thought how I may mend my misdeeds?"

"Away with you," Surek boomed. "When the time is right, you will know." Adjusting Kayaska's bit he caught a grin stretched between the ears of one of his men. "And what amuses you, Ahmir?"

"Oh, nothing, my captain, but the fact that you are serious about teaching this woman to ride."

"Next she'll be riding with the Spahiglani," Surek heard, recognizing the deep voice of his most adroit horseman, and he turned, one brow raised.

"You sound jealous, Ismeran. Do you wish me to teach you also?"

And with that reply he heard them begin to tease Ismeran mercilessly, forcing brash boasts, and they soon drifted away to prove them, jesting, mocking, their voices puffed with bravado. Surek pulled Kayaska's girth tighter and dodged her teeth as she swung her head around at him.

"So you are as reluctant at this early workout as Bellina, eh, my pet? It is about time you two met; you are both uncannily alike."

He rubbed the mare's forelock affectionately and glanced impatiently back at the tent. "Bellina!" he shouted. Where was that girl? "If you do not come out, I'm—"

She stepped from the tent reluctantly, her hair in a tight black braid that fell like a rope down her back and her legs bared from the knees in the costume he had provided her. She met his impatience with a defiant tilt of her chin. "My side still hurts."

"And if I listened to you, it would still be hurting a year from now. You need to get out."

He watched her step forward unenthusiastically and excitement jumped along his spine. She is as fine-legged as Kayaska and as spirited, he thought, continuing the comparison in his mind.

"Come," he murmured huskily. "Surely you are not afraid? I would not have thought that one encounter with a horse would cure you of your desire to be outdoors."

She flashed a sharp look at his amused expression, then focused on a mare that danced sideways, stomping the ground into a cloud of dust. "This is no

47

packhorse. Surely you do not mean to put me on her!"

"You might as well begin on a horse worth its feed—or else you learn nothing. Come now!" he barked at Kayaska and she stilled, trembling.

Without giving her any moment for protest, he threw Bellina onto the horse's back, then mounted behind her. His arms encircled her to pick up the reins and she felt the hardness of his chest pressed against her. "Now, my hands. See how the reins are held? Not tightly, but not so loose that you cannot feel the contact with the horse's mouth."

She felt his words brush against her ear, but they were lost to her as her heart began to flutter like a startled bird. "Your knees exert pressure so you can keep your seat," he continued. She heard him gently soothe the mare who calmed, attentive to his voice. Bellina smiled. He called the horse pet, love, beauty, and touched a hand to her withers. Bellina found herself laughing.

They spent the morning circling the camp with Bellina first watching his hands, feeling his legs behind hers, and then taking the reins herself for brief moments, until eventually he dismounted to let her go it alone. By that time they all thirsted for something to drink and she followed Surek to the stream, leading Kayaska. "She is a beautiful horse," Bellina said wistfully, watching the doe-eyed creature put her muzzle to the water.

Surek slapped the mare's rump affectionately. "You are looking at the best in all the land. Even Mehmet has had an eye on her, although he knows that anyone who would dare make an offer might

48

find the curve of my blade his answer."

Upstream from Kayaska, he dipped cupped hands into the water and held them out to Bellina. At first she hesitated, but then with an indifferent shrug she drank from them. An odd light glowed deep within the blackness of his eyes. He was so strange: gentle and harsh, civilized and barbaric, young yet aged by scars and the weary sorrow she had seen when he looked upon the braggadocio that painted the faces of his young warriors. He was at contrast with those around him, hardly belonging to this chaotic empire bound together by a fanatic religious zeal. He was the riddle to be answered.

She brushed back the loose strands of her hair as he dipped his hands for himself, and she looked northward where he rode so often.

Spots of cypress huddled together for comfort against the harshness of the land. There were hills that rolled in the distance like water until they joined the skyline. She sat along the bank to rest her aching muscles. "Is it far, Constantinople?"

Surek pulled Kayaska's greedy head from the water and then sat alongside of Bellina. "If you have a swift mount and a cool sun, a day and a half will see you there."

She sighed, "It is hard to believe it is so close to so empty a plain."

"Empty?" He smiled but it did not reach his eyes and he pointed, "There, a horse's breath away behind those hills, camp the Anatolians. And not far from there, the bulk of the sultan's soldiers await his words. This land crawls with the activity of a young and vibrant empire."

"Please, I don't want to talk of it," she said, the peace of the stream suddenly altered.

"Ah," he murmured almost to himself. "How those words play mirror to the attitude of those who Mehmet has conquered. Perhaps, if they had not chosen to close their minds so long to the wolf's head that snapped at their backs . . ." Although his voice was soft, something wakened in Bellina's mind.

"You sound almost resentful," she said, searching his eyes for something hidden, but his face revealed nothing.

Suddenly, he stood up. "The heat thickens. Do you wish to go back before it turns you as red as a pomegranate?"

She stretched her legs lazily. "No, let it bake these tired muscles a bit longer, for I swear if I get up to walk now, they will buckle weakly."

She saw the glint in his eye, the smile beneath his beard, and still she did not expect it. All she knew was that he lifted her up like a child and, holding her in his arms, laughed at the shock that flashed across her face.

"What are you doing," she gasped.

"Why helping your poor tired legs, of course." He stared into her widened eyes.

"Put me down! I am no child to be carried!" she sputtered, but he wasn't paying heed.

"You are a child—one playing a dangerous game of being a woman."

A child! How dare he call her that! She glared at him, trying to control the red haze that swept through her. Painfully, she bit back a stinging retort, for she knew it would only add fuel to his argument.

50

He pushed her up on Kayaska and mounted; they turned towards the crescent of tents.

Silently she raged as they rode at a leisurely walk. Weren't there many men—young and old alike—who had appreciated her slender but well-curved figure? Or had they been more impressed with the wealth that came with her? *The devil take you, Surek,* she seethed, *I'll soon be eighteen and should have been married long ago.* What did he know anyway?

As they neared the camp, his men crowded around smiling up at her with mockery. This she had become used to, but in her present frame of mind it touched on raw nerves. Naqu emerged from the bunch to grab Kayaska's head. His smile was genuine and she was glad he held no grudge against her. Although his life had gone harder since Surek had revealed his knowledge of their deception, he showed himself indeed a true friend.

Surek dismounted and extended his hand to Bellina. Recklessly, just to convince her damaged ego, she smiled at him. It was her most provocative smile: lower lip extended to accentuate its fullness, upper curving slightly to reveal even, white teeth. Her eyes sparkled, her eyebrows arched, and her breath came quickly, making her well-endowed bosom rise attractively. Surek looked into those eyes, the color of a restless sea, and he laughed.

Yes! Laughed! She trembled in her rage. This was hardly funny; she was dead serious. How dare he question her femininity. She shunned his hand viciously and jumped to the ground, almost falling. Furious, she entered the tent and turned to confront him. But he was not there behind her. Had he denied her even this?

She picked up the shimmery green cloth that was an almost completed gown, and taking up her needle, an idea flashed before her. He would learn that she was indeed a woman, she vowed.

It was not until dusk that he returned, hungry and jovial, his mood well lightened by the light banter he had had with his men. He noticed the drape partition right away and figured Bellina had been exhausted and so had retired. He called to the guard and requested that his dinner be brought. Then, as he stretched, untied his sash and pulled his shirt off, he saw a movement on the edge of his vision.

There, dressed in the regal fabric, the gold thread melting like lava flow through the weave, was Bellina. It clung seductively to her breasts, her waist, and her hips. She smiled as his eyes deepened. Like a trained concubine, she sat at his feet.

"I thank you for this morning," she told him smoothly, her cheeks flushed.

He reached out and lifted one dark curl from her shoulder. She was the most beautiful succubus. Her hair fanned over her shoulders, a dark web of curls contrasting with the creamy tan of her sun-kissed skin. An uncipherable spark glowed within the restless green of her eyes. His hand let fall the tiny curl and slipped around her waist, pulling her tight against his chest, and then his mouth hungrily claimed hers. Taken by surprise, never expecting to lose control, she hung stunned in his embrace. She felt a strange languidness spreading through her legs, felt his furred chest against her own, his tongue push against her mouth, demanding, and then its

52

sensuous probing as her lips parted. He pulled at one shoulder of the gown and pressed his hand against her bared breast, its nipple stiffening beneath his palm. She trembled and sighed her satisfaction and pulled him closer.

He clasped her tightly. So tightly that she couldn't move, and her breath rushed out of her. She felt the pounding of his heart. Slowly he loosened his hold and grasping her chin, he lifted it until she gazed into his eyes. It was like looking into a well which no one could fathom. "Bellina," he murmured, his voice rasping in his throat, "you play a dangerous game."

She blinked, uncomprehending as her thoughts swirled. He let her go and stood, turning away. How could he have let this happen, he silently raged, placing a hand against his forehead.

"Kadi," he heard the deep rumble of his guard call, from outside the flap of the tent.

"Yes, what is it?" he snapped, pulling the flap aside.

"Kadi, did you not hear the horses? A messenger from our most esteemed sultan has arrived, and asks to speak with you."

With a last glance at Bellina as she sat stiffly upon the floor, he left. *Without a word*, she thought, *without one last bit of warmth to ease this chill which creeps into my heart.*

That night she slept fitfully. Indeed, hardly at all. The minutes dragged like hours, a night which had no end. Her ears listened for Surek's boots muffled against the carpets, but he never came. Her heart ached with a terrible sickness and she could not shut Surek's image from her mind or the strange excitement of his touch. Had she sensed a gentleness in his caress, had she felt his heart beat to her excited rhythm, had she trembled for his touch, had she, had she? Her head pounded as her blood rushed. Why had he stopped? Why had she not pushed him away right from the very beginning? Angrily, she kicked away the damp sheet that clung to her in suffocating folds. Where was he that he stayed away all night? She rose, feeling crushed beneath the stuffiness of the tent. Climbing over Surek's empty pallet, she moved towards the flap and raised it, letting the night breezes evaporate the perspiration that beaded across her forehead.

Around the pit in the center of camp, a spartan fire glowed off the faces of Surek, the janissaries who played sentry to their tent, and a stranger. Surek's laughter carried to her on the wind. The stranger's smile grew serious.

"Surek, you think I jest. I assure you the offer was made in all seriousness. Word of her beauty is a constant foxtail in the sultan's ear. I'm afraid he must have her."

"Ten? Twenty thousand in gold would not buy her! Besides, who is to say our most respected sultan would be pleased with what he got? She bites, you know."

Bellina's hand flew to her mouth before her cry of stunned disbelief betrayed her. They were talking about her!

"Ah, that is no vice, but only a showing of spirit!" the stranger said admiringly. "Just what our sultan is looking for. I'll offer eighteen thousand, and that is robbery. Robbery of your sultan! You know he could

54

just demand her, you'd best not anger him. Tell me, is she a good breeder?"

"That is yet to be proven, but I have no doubts. Twenty-five thousand perhaps I'll consider it."

Bellina could stand no more. She ran to her bed, her face afire. *He's going to sell me,* she sobbed. She clenched her pillow in her fists, knuckles white, and bit back a scream. And she had actually begun to trust him. Bastardo!

She felt a pain constrict her chest and anguish made her shiver. She couldn't stay here, not after this, and she had no time to lose. For the first time in a long while, she felt panic rear its ugly head. Suppose they did not even wait until morning before they packed her off to their sultan? She had to act quickly. She dressed, curling her hair beneath one of Surek's turbans, and spying his jambiyyah upon the table, clenched it in her hand. She slipped through her slit, and like a shadow moved among the tents over to the horses. They were like dark mountains, asleep where they stood. She murmured their names as she passed so as not to startle them. Half-feeling her way amongst the sleek coats, she finally found Kayaska. Like two wraiths, they moved through the herd soundlessly. She sawed at the rope of the enclosure with the blade and led the mare through. Having no saddle, no bridle, and no time to get them, she sliced the rope to an acceptable length and split it into a pliable thickness. It made a makeshift bitless bridle that would have to do. Kayaska chafed at its roughness.

Bellina stroked the mare's muzzle, walking as far away from the camp as they could, so their passage would not be betrayed by noisy hoofbeats. However, time was her enemy. She knew that soon Surek would be finding a deserted tent. Glancing back towards the camp, she was only able to make out the dull glow of the campfire. She wrapped one hand tightly in Kayaska's mane and pulled herself with luck and determination onto the horse's back. She had best keep her seat, she thought gloomily, for that fall could never be repeated again. Turning towards the north, she hung precariously and kicked Kayaska to a bounce.

The Bashaw glared at the man who sat across from him, twisting the end of his beard, meeting his eyes challengingly. He didn't care if this arrogant fool was Captain of the Spahiglani, he didn't have the right. A haughty sneer turned his lip. "What you ask is ridiculous—no, unheard of! Twenty-five thousand! No horse is worth that," he spit.

Surek's eyes flashed with amusement. It had gone as he had wished. "Kayaska is worth that to me. I am grieved the sultan does not appreciate her true worth."

"You will come to regret this, Captain," he cried in rage, jumping to his feet.

"Naqu! Will you please bring the Bashaw his horse, for I believe he is ready to leave us."

Once the sound of the Bashaw's horse faded in the distance, Surek relaxed. One of these days he was not going to be able to prevent it, and Kayaska would be added to Mehmet's stables. He kicked sand onto the coals, burying them. Well, at least this unpleasant conversation had enlightened him to one thing: a few enterprising merchants from Europe had resumed trade. The news saddened him, but he also realized it was for the better, he would find a ship to place Bellina on. He had promised that, once, so long ago. Maybe she didn't have family left in Venice, but surely there were friends.

He walked back to his tent, oblivious that the stars were shimmering with a brightness seldom seen. Suppose he had stayed with her more often, or for a few more months, then perhaps she would grow to love this country and not want to leave. But after today . . . things were getting out of hand, it was time. A gentle humid breeze caressed his troubled forehead, but the humming of a million insects seemed to press in from all sides. He lifted the flap to his tent.

The moment he entered he knew something was wrong. His jambiyyah was gone from where he had left it, and an overturned pillow sat accusingly in the middle of the floor. He pulled aside a drape and found Bellina's cover strewn half on the bed, half on the carpet.

"Kielb! Topar!" The severity of his tone brought the two janissaries running. He turned and faced them, anger freezing his features. "She's gone."

Stricken, the two janissaries yelled at the sleeping soldiers, and soon the whole camp crawled with men. It was not long before they found the cut in the rope, the horses scattered.

"Incompetent fools!" Surek raged. "No one bothers to stand watch anymore? Allah prevent me from impaling the whole lot of you upon your own swords! You bask in the light of past glories and neglect to perform the simplest of duties! Naqu find Kayaska. I will find the girl. The rest of you retrieve your horses before they are food for the jackals."

When Naqu returned, he faced Surek with another horse. His voice came, tremulous, "She probably took Kayaska; she is not to be found."

"By the prophet's beard," Surek cried, "she will regret this!" And he mounted, plunging into the night.

Bellina's path was not difficult to pick up; it pointed towards Constantinople. Foolish girl, he cursed. What was she trying to do? Perish in the wilds? Get raped and murdered by renegades? Hadn't he shown every kindness possible to the girl? She had no reason to do this.

He gave the stallion his head and his legs stretched out, eating up the ground before them. Thank Allah for a bright moon, he thought, without it they would be crawling, straining for signs of her tracks. At least she was only traveling at a trot. Did she think he would let her off so easily? Not even bother to track her down? If she did, she had a thing or two to learn about her place in his life. Curse her, she was his, whether she liked it or not—the spoils of war, to do with what he pleased. His lips thinned into a grim smile. He would present her with a better surprise than the one he had planned earlier. Before the coming of the morning, he vowed, she would be in his hands, and what pleasure it would give him to see her face. To humble that spoiled brat would almost be reward enough for his troubles.

White foam dripped from the stallion's mouth and

spotted his chest and flanks. Surfacing from his thoughts and guiltily realizing he was pushing the horse too hard, he reined him to a trot, gradually slowing down to a walk. No use ruining a good horse for that insolent Venetian, he growled to himself. She would be his soon enough.

The foam dried to a sticky film, dulling the once glossy coat. The stars faded until they disappeared altogether in the blaze of a new day. The horse struggled on, the weight of his rider sinking his hoofs deep into the sand.

As thirst began to tease him, Surek was regretting his rash neglect at leaving without even a drop of water for himself or his mount. As the midday sun burned through his caffa blouse, streams of sweat stained and melted it to his skin. As the heat increased his discomfort, his temper flared in concordance. Shielding his eyes against the glare, he scanned the broken branches on the scrub brush. Impatiently he quickened the pace.

Before long he spied a slow-moving dot on the horizon. Without question he knew it was Bellina. No other creature in its right mind would be out in this relentless sun. There she struggled, her image wavering in the heat that radiated from the broiled ground. Like a demon up from the depths of hell, he kicked the stallion to speed and bore down on her.

Bellina heard him before she saw him. With a cry she urged Kayaska faster, clinging to her neck in a struggle to stay on. As Surek neared, he put his fingers to his mouth, letting a shrill whistle cut the air. Kayaska laid her ears back, flung her head high and halted, her haunches dragging the ground.

Bellina flew over her head into the burning sand. With a shriek she dove for Kayaska's dangling rope, yet the mare whirled away traitorously, fleeing towards her master. Bellina gasped as the black stallion closed the distance rapidly, then scrambled to her feet to face the inevitable.

Surek's stallion slid to a halt beside her, and from his back his master looked down, his face a mask of rage. Bellina braced herself for the bite of his voice but he spoke not a word, and somehow, that terrified her more.

"I'm not going back," she cried into his silence.

Nudging the stallion closer, Surek made a grab. She dove to the ground and he missed. As she leaped to her feet, he could see her face bore the expression of a hunted animal. Good! It was what he wanted to see. When he reeled the stallion around, she circled with him adeptly, keeping him from getting a hold on her. With a curse, he flung himself to the ground, sending her running from his near grasp. She stumbled, half-crawled, half-ran, not quite getting to her feet, when his body fell upon hers, crushing her to the ground and grinding her face into the sand. He flung her over and skewered her with his eyes. "What do you think you're doing?" he rasped through clenched teeth, "Am I so abhorrent to you that you seek the comfort of a hostile land? Go willingly into the arms of bandits and nomads who would sell you for less than two goats and a hen?"

She cringed as his fingers dug painfully into her arms. "And you wouldn't?" She turned her face away, knowing that if she met his demanding stare all would be lost to a flood of tears and self-pity. He seized her trembling chin and forced her to face him.

"Have I treated you so badly? Tell me! Do you starve for a meal? Perhaps you dress in rags and sleep in the rain like our animals? Or maybe I abuse you— force my attentions on you?" The light in his eyes dimmed until they became an alarming inky void. With paralyzed limbs she lay beneath him, caught in his gaze, his words pounding inside her head. Her breath caught in her throat.

"Speak!" he suddenly yelled, making her jerk at his harshness. "I would like to hear your reasons, for you must have at least one. You would not want to disappoint me."

She swallowed convulsively and her voice was strained.

"I cannot hear you," Surek demanded. "What, the sultan? What does he have to do with this!"

Anger overshadowed her fear at what he said. "Curse you, Surek," she croaked. "Will you stop playing games? I know of your plans to sell me, like some bargain picked off the streets!"

His mouth tightened, "Has this sun fried your brains? You speak in riddles that have no substance."

"And I suppose twenty-five thousand in gold has no substance? I tire of *your* games, Surek. You've caught me, let's get this over with. But I promise you, your sultan will live to curse your name, for I do not only bite. I will make his life and yours a living hell."

Comprehension pushed the wild fury from Surek's face. To Bellina's surprise he rolled off of her, and for a long time he stared at the clouds that shifted above. Then a strange sound started in his throat, half-strangled, half-choked, until nothing would stop it, and laughter erupted from him, shaking his whole body and twisting his face. Finally it died to a groan of mirth. He looked into Bellina's puzzled face. "And I suppose you heard the part about being a good breeder?" She nodded, her eyes smoldering, and he coughed, fighting against the laugh still caught in his throat. "Didn't your parents ever tell you never to eavesdrop? Bellina, that was Kayaska we were discussing, not you. Mehmet doesn't even know you exist! Nor would he pay that much gold for an odalisque!"

Her mouth sagged and she felt as if she would die. Oh God, was this some cruel trick of Surek's making? No, she knew it for the truth.

"Bellina, you hurt me to the quick. Have you no trust for anyone?" he asked, and she turned over to face the sand rather than those accusing eyes.

"I don't know what to say. I did not mean to eavesdrop, I just couldn't fall asleep, and . . . Oh!" A sob burst from her, despite the girl's attempts to clamp it back. Her shoulders shook wretchedly.

Surek lifted her face from the sand and pressed her to him. "It is all right, it was only a misunderstanding. We're both still here, aren't we? Only our pride has been stepped on." He brushed back her hair and she clung to him. One tear of silver fell down her cheek and he kissed it away. She was so beautiful, so tragically beautiful. He kissed her again, her throat, the curve of her shoulder, and then her lips met his— softly, fleetingly, like the wings of a butterfly. And then she kissed him again, lingering, drawing him closer to her.

In gentleness, his battle-worn hands cupped her face, then brushed her hair back and, following the curve of her shoulders, clasped her firmly against him. His mouth was hungry upon hers; his tongue a sudden demanding probe. At first, Bellina drew back, but then gave in, curiously excited by his invasion. It spread a languid weakness, thrilled every fiber of her being, and made her want to give up entirely to his will. "Surek," she whispered, her breath a caress upon his ear, "I love you."

A soft rumble came from his throat as he held her, never wanting to let go, forcing away from his mind the fact that he could have no claim on her. There was no room in his thoughts to admit that she did not wish to belong to his world, his life.

He loosened her shirt and slipped a hand against her breast, gently stroking. "Bellina," he called and she shivered to hear the longing and passion her name could hold. Her buttons fell away as if they themselves took pity upon the lovers and would not hinder. She felt the roughness of his hands cup her breasts and draw them to his lips. His tongue caressed each of her swollen nipples in turn, first circling, then flicking against their hardened crests until Bellina squirmed, her breath coming in little gasps. His hands found her buttock and pressed her against him, but he was finding it difficult to be slow and gentle. His teeth held a nipple captive, then he sucked deeply until a moan came from Bellina's lips.

A flame of mutual desire shot through her and sparked an uncontrollable wave of passion. The beating of her heart quickened as blood pulsed through every vein. She was sure Surek could feel the effect his caresses had upon her. There would be no denying it, the power he wielded with his love would hold her captive for as long as he willed it. She felt fire leap across wherever he touched. It flickered up her spine, between her legs, until she thought she would go mad. She clutched at him, but he drew away and shed his clothes and spread his saddle cloth upon the sand.

There beneath the burning truth of the sun, he came to her, a Sun-God in his own right, bronzed, passion licking through his veins as he stood boldly above her. His muscles rippled as he knelt over her, his eyes a tiger's eyes, hungry, predatory, a mirror to the desire that flared within the depths of his soul.

Bellina's lips parted with anticipation. She felt as though she were living a dream. When his mouth claimed hers, his tongue probed the soft wetness inside. As he drank of her sweetness, he knew his desire was a thirst that only her body could quench. Surek ran his hand from her breast along the curve of her side, until he reached the drawstring which fastened her pants. With adept fingers that seemed only to brush against her stomach, he slid the loosened pants down over rounded hips. A flicker of resistance moved Bellina to reach for his hand, but she could not push it away. Something else was taking over her body. It had started with a tingling shiver, but now it was a deep need that demanded satisfaction. A quiver shook her body as Surek's hand trailed up her inner thigh and rested upon the warm crevice between her legs. Smothering her gasp, his kiss locked her between him and the burning sands. While he plunged his finger deep within her body,

64

Bellina moaned, feeling her soul soar to new and dangerous heights. Drawn by the mystery of the forbidden, she was like a bird flying closer and closer to the desert sun. As he probed deeper, his thumb kneaded at her bud of pleasure until she thought she'd go mad.

"Don't stop!" Bellina cried as his hand spread her legs even wider before him, and drove his hardened flesh deep into her softness, taking away the last remnant of a child. With each stab of ecstasy into the throbbing core of her body, Bellina flew higher, sure her heart would burst. Greedily her hips met his thrusts, for she wanted to fill her entire being with the power of him. Her breath was ragged, her hands clasped his buttock to her, and suddenly, as if time fragmented, her entire being was consumed in fire. It spread upward overtaking all thought and reason, exploding in her brain like a thousand bits of light. Dimly, she heard Surek cry out, his hot seed spilling into her in one more violent thrust. Together they came, body and spirits melting for one glorious moment.

It seemed a long time before she could breathe again. They fell back exhausted, tangled, the gift of love continuing to set their insides glowing. Bellina's hand rested against Surek's cheek. Gone was the hate that had burned in her heart, driven away before their passion. For the time being, the restless world around them no longer existed. Here, they had found their own peace.

Five

Although the summer was more than half ended, the hot dryness of the Shamal wind continued to harass, threatening to dry the feeble stream that supplied their water. The Spahiglani, tired of their boasts and their endless mock battles, grew restless, their good humor disappearing as rapidly as the water. They were anxious to be off, impatient to serve their sultan, and confident that if given the chance, the empire of Trebizond, Rhodes, Cyprus, and eventually Venice and Genoa—and who could imagine what else—would fall before their onslaught. They were undefeatable, and they were also stuck here, forced to await their sultan's desires.

Ismeran was dispatched again for news, and once again he returned, his face revealing the sultan's message before his tongue ever did. As he entered the heart of the camp, his mount's sides heaving spastically, and his mouth set in a grim line, the horsemen crowded around him, hoping that the news from his lips would perchance deny his eyes.

Respectfully they gave way as Surek moved forward.

"So, Ismeran," he breathed through clenched teeth, "what says our sultan this time?"

"The time has not come," Ismeran growled, and the Spahiglani grumbled.

Secretly Surek smiled. It meant at least that they would remain at camp until the end of autumn, perhaps longer. It gave him a short time longer to enjoy Bellina's company before Mehmet would decide his fleet was well enough replenished. However, he quickly told himself, before that time came and the uneasy trade was once again broken, she would have to be on a Venice-bound ship.

He left his men to their shared misery and found Bellina in the tent. "Ismeran has returned," he told her, watching her hand stop suddenly as she looked up.

"And what does he say of trade?"

Was there also expectation and hope written on that face? Was there remorse, no hesitation at leaving him? Surek wondered. Ever since that day when they had let their passions override distrust and heal their wounds, he had wondered if she could ever . . . No. Why was he indulging in this insane train of thought? She wanted to return. It would be impossible for her to stay much longer, once Mehmet made his move, and Surek was in no position to be tied down. Already he was courting the displeasure of his men the longer she stayed. And displeasure led to disrespect. He sat upon the floor next to her, his lips gently meeting hers.

"Surek!" she protested, pushing him away. "You did not answer my question. Have you word of the trade ships?"

"The word is that although a few have dared resume trade, the number is small indeed. I'm afraid their captains are still quite nervous and, under those circumstances, they would be too quick to begin a fray at the slightest provocation. It's best we wait," he told her, neglecting to add that Mehmet had strictly forbidden any attacks upon merchant vessels no matter how justified.

Bellina sat back frowning. "Another delay? Sometimes I wonder if I'll ever go home." With a sadness that startled her, Surek got to his feet.

"Is that all you dwell upon? Going home? Does my promise mean nothing to you?"

She stared at him, trying to comprehend the reason for the anger in his voice. As she replayed her words in her mind, she realized just how callous and ungrateful they sounded. "No, I do not only think of going home. I also think of you coming with me. You have come to mean a lot to me, and I have found you a man of honor. But can you not understand the part of me that wastes away in this foreign land?"

"Yes, I can. More than you think I do," he whispered into her ear, and she felt his strong arms encircle her, causing her to feel light-headed.

"Do not patronize me," she murmured sulkily.

"Patronize you?" he questioned bitterly, "I do not. I assure you, my feet wish to feel the crunch of crisp morning snow as much as you wish for the swell of a Venetian wave beneath you. This endless desert of late makes me weary."

She tried to read his eyes, struck by his odd exclamation, but he held her close. In a whirl of confusion, her thoughts tumbled trying to make sense of it. "Snow?" she finally sputtered. "There isn't any snow here."

"I know," he said, looking deep into her eyes, then squeezing her tightly.

"Surek!" She wanted to pursue a thousand questions coming to mind. What place was he talking of? Did it mean he wasn't an Ottoman? She wanted to know of his childhood, his parents, every incident in the life of this man she had come to love, but he buried his lips in the tangle of her hair.

Smoothly he moved to the nape of her neck and trailed kisses to her shoulder, her back, as far as her tunic would let him. Like water dripping from a cup, she lost her thoughts and protests one by one until she waited, ready for him to fill her emptiness.

"You are too beautiful," he murmured almost to himself, stroking the satiny skin of her neck, the peak of her breast where it strained against her clothes. There he lingered to give a playful pinch that sent a tremor of desire down her spine. His hand passed suggestively over her belly to rest below.

"I have a better way to spend our time than with mere words," he said into her ear, his breath causing a shiver. His touch was fire, his touch was paralyzing, his touch was a drug that sparked her senses and robbed her will. She didn't even hear the soft rustle of their clothes as he unfastened them and let them fall. His hands held her waist, crushing her against the hard naked length of him and his stiff manhood prodding her belly, his mouth hungry upon hers. His tongue and hands moved with a mind of their own; darting, licking, probing, stroking; down her shoulders, across her breast to a rosebud nipple, tracing her hips, and sliding down the long whiteness of her legs. She was being devoured, helplessly, wondrously devoured!

He was on his knees before her, as if in worship, his hands clasping her buttock, his mouth eager against her moist parted legs. She moaned, her knees growing weak as his tongue darted deep inside her. Her fingers woven in his hair, she pulled him closer, glorying in the sparks and delicious shudders he sent through her body. He sought and found her tiny center of esctasy, flickering his hot tongue against it until she let out a cry and sank to the rug beneath them, pulling him with her. Their pallet was only a few feet away but neither of them cared as they tumbled, limbs entwined. He played her like a song, ringing every possible note of passion she had. He pulled her on top of him, spiking his swollen manhood deep within her with a low growl. With his encouraging hands firm upon her hips, she slid the length of him, exalting in the fire they both built. It was his turn to groan as she rode him faster and faster, letting the heat build until it consumed them in a flash.

She couldn't hold back a cry as she felt him explode into her. Spasms of pleasure wracked her body until, exhausted, she fell back against his chest. Weakly they cradled in each other's arms, their ragged breath slowly calming to a peaceful sleep.

They were rudely awakened as the guard from outside announced the arrival of a mounted party wearing the red and gold that marked them as a retinue from Mehmet II. With a curse, Surek dressed.

70

Bellina heard Ismeran hail the visitor, his usual mocking voice puffed with respect and ceremony.

"What is it, do you think?" Bellina questioned, fearful that some battle, somewhere, had begun and would now be shattering the contentment she had just found.

"Stay put." He commanded as she began to rise. "Under no circumstances do I want you to show yourself. Mehmet's informers will get one look at you and that is all I'll need." He strapped on his scimitar and left her, confused and curious at his words. She walked softly to the tent's flap and knelt, strained to catch the angry discourse that ensued. "Greetings, Amanullah Bashaw," Surek growled. "I did not think you would come to visit us again so soon. Is our sultan well?"

"You well know why I am here, Captain Edib, and I assure you our sultan has never felt better. However, there is one thorn in his side. Among his peerless stable of horses that Allah himself would envy, there is one stall unfilled. There he would place the silver mare that all whisper can outrace Shaitan."

"Outrace the devil!" Surek laughed incredulously, but his eyes were black and dangerous. "I did not think our esteemed sultan let exaggerated gossip bother him."

"I did not come here to engage in unpleasant disagreements. The matter is quite beyond you or me, Surek." He tossed a leather pouch and Surek caught it more by reflex than desire. The Bashaw looked into the Spahiglani captain's eyes. How he detested the arrogance in those eyes. Never had he liked this one. Always he had thought Mehmet let too much value

71

and power rest upon this cur. He, Amanullah, did not trust him, and he was seldom wrong.

Watching Surek fling aside the pouch without opening it, the Bashaw smiled. "Do you not want to count it? It is not your twenty-five thousand in gold, but it is more than thirty in jewels."

"Your sultan is most generous."

The reply held a biting tone of sarcasm. Amanullah stiffened, one hand clenching uncontrollably. "*My* sultan? Don't you mean *our* sultan? Indeed I agree with you: he is unexcelled in generosity. If I had been he, your insolent tongue would be a lifeless flag in your severed head upon the palace gate."

Inflamed resentment at the Bashaw's words showed only too plainly in Surek's men. Here and there metal slid against metal sheaths, and with gradual but noticeable movement they approached.

Amanullah was not a foolish man. "Shall we approach the horses?" he said contemptuously with a nod of his head. "Our sultan is anxious that I and the mare return with haste, and he is most tired with these games of yours, Captain."

"Yes, let us get this over with, for I grow tired of you," Surek snarled and Amanullah was uncomfortably aware of the black rage that stiffened the captain's shoulders and expression. "Indeed, tired but interested. In fact, Bashaw, you could say these few conversations I have had with you will be remembered for a long time to come. I do believe I will never forget you and can hardly wait for the next time we meet. Without *them*," Surek added, nodding toward the well-armed and mounted Bashi Bazouks that surrounded Amanullah.

The Bashaw felt a chill creep over him at the venom the captain's voice held. Here was one who would prove a worthy adversary. "And without them," Amanullah said, waving his hand at Surek's men.

"Indeed, that is the only way I'll have it," Surek answered coolly, watching the Bashaw shift in his saddle, and with a clipped angry stride, he turned towards the herd.

Once the Bashaw and his men had left with Kayaska led behind, a red-and-gold-tasseled halter around her head, Surek was unapproachable. His men, well used to his black moods, avoided him. Bellina, too, followed their example. Once again she sought the company of Naqu and left Surek alone as he set about training the black stallion to his needs.

"And what does the Bashaw have to fear?" Bellina laughed, "That coward is too close to the sultan's protective arm to have any fears, if you ask me."

"I can tell you do not know our Captain."

Bellina frowned. "Explain yourself!"

"Once," Naqu drawled, "he had a man buried to his chin beneath that burning sand, and let him stay there till his face was covered with sun blisters and he was too weak to scream his agony. All that because the poor soul had sold him a milkless goat."

"What nonsense do you tell?" Bellina protested. "He would never have done that."

"Wouldn't he?" Naqu leaned against a scrubby tree and held her with his eyes. "He will hunt that Bashaw like the seven jinns and get him, too. Of course, he will never be suspected. There are too many nomads who could be conveniently accused if

73

the right evidence is left." He paused to savor her horrified look. "And it will be."

Bellina felt a chill sweep through her, for despite what she would have liked to believe, she had sensed the underlying violence that Surek kept so tightly controlled.

"And," Naqu continued, eyeing Bellina thoughtfully, "I would not want to be you. For what better exchange for Kayaska could he offer our much admiring sultan than your beauty? You would be the peerless jewel to buy back our captain's peerless Kayaska, who after all, would serve him better on the battlefield."

"Alright, Naqu," Bellina flared, her eyes taking on the same angry brilliance Surek's had these days past. "Maybe your bitterness springs from the extra chores you earned in our deception, but you have no right to go about spouting these lies! Surek has been more than kind to me. He is a man of honor and has even promised to place me on a merchant vessel, Venice-bound. He is incapable of doing what you accuse him of."

Naqu grew quiet and cast his eyes to the ground. "Bellina, I have known both our captain and sultan since I was seven—a long time ago. It is not my wish to dissolve your hopes or your trust. You love him, what a pity." He shook his head and looked away, "You are like a sister to me and I cannot see you hurt. Tell me, has your passage been arranged on such a ship?"

Bellina's mouth drew a defiant line. "No, but that is only because it is too dangerous yet. I must be patient."

74

"Unsafe? And I do not have to ask who told you that. Haven't you heard the sultan has forbidden, under penalty of death, any attacks upon a merchant vessel?" He threw up his hands, "Of course you haven't heard, you are not there to hear what our messengers say when they return. We need timber. What do you think would happen to trade if there were any messy incidents?"

"I think you are jealous, Naqu. Jealous and resentful. You had better change the subject or I'm leaving."

Naqu sighed. "Very well, but my only wish is to open your eyes. You do not know this land and these men as I do. Please think on what I have said for your own sake."

I won't think of it, Bellina thought, for I know it all to be lies. But she did think of it, all that day and the next. It was like a needle that was there to jab her whenever she turned. Finally one evening, she tried to approach the subject with Surek; yet he was in such a glowering silence that she didn't get far and dropped all conversation, retiring to their now shared bed. He smoked on his nargileh, lost in some thought that troubled him, and it wasn't until late that he joined her.

Feeling his arms wrap around her protectively, his head nestle in her hair, a terrible ache, a longing too strong to ignore filled her being. A smile faintly curved her lips. He is the flame—a flame of this fiery land. And I am but a moth who is helplessly drawn to him. She turned, her eyes two pools of desire meeting his troubled ones. They studied each other's faces as if they were lovers reunited after a time of searching.

Their lips drew together in a long kiss that committed the final joining of their love.

Slipping into a shallow sleep, Bellina dreamed of moths and searing light, of dancing about flames while they drew upon her soul. Embracing its warmth, she fell into the heat to be devoured. She heard the crackling of fire and felt curled smokey fingers wrap around her throat and body in a suffocating hold. A bright light pierced her eyelids as if the sun was shining.

"Bellina!" The loud voice jostled her awake with its urgency.

"Surek?" she asked fuzzily.

"Listen to me! Some of the tents are on fire and it's spreading rapidly. Wait by the stream where the horses have been tethered. You can help to calm them. Stay there, it'll be safe." He fled from the tent, swearing at someone's carelessness to extinguish a lamp or campfire.

Huge flames towered, whipping the sky with ferocity, their heat turning a warm night into one immense oven. Eyes tearing, his nose covered with his shirt against the smoke, he struggled to be heard over the roar in an effort to organize his men. One tent collapsed just after Kielb ran out, but one unfortunate man followed him engulfed in fire—a living torch.

"Water!" Kielb screamed, but Surek knew from the sickening stench of burning flesh that no amount of water could save the man now. He sent the rest of his men to salvage what remained of the tents. A long chain was formed, leading from the stream to the campsite and the water was sloshed from one to another, quickly yet carefully. Every drop was precious. Others beat out the flames with carpets. How futile this all is, Surek despaired. With the wind rising up to whip the flames higher, it was no use. The camp was engulfed, beyond saving, and it would be a mere pile of ashes before dawn. Dodging fragments of burning tent, he promised himself that the cause of this calamity would be uncovered. Bellina watched from the bank as flames licked the sky in frenzied fury. As each tent collapsed to the ground it released a soft surrendering sigh into the early dawn. How could such a thing have started? Thank God the horses were safe—and Surek, she breathed with relief as she watched him with the wounded. After a while, the brilliant dancing motion of the fire hypnotized her so that it was all she was aware of. A light touch to her arm made her jump. "Naqu! Thank heavens you're alright."

"I am riding into Constantinople for the captain," he panted hurriedly as he glanced furtively around. "You can ride with me. There I know a merchant who will take you to Venice aboard his ship. Do you want to go?"

"Do I want to go!" she cried, but deep within her the words echoed. Do I want to go? Do I? She found no sure answer, only confusion. "I've been dreaming of this since the beginning," she said, more to herself than Naqu. Here, reason told her, here there may be his love—and even that could be questioned—but here there was also no future and a surplus of dangers.

"Come on," Naqu cried. "There is no time for delay! This will probably be your only chance to get back home; he has no intentions of returning you. If

77

you stopped lying to yourself, you would know what I said before was the truth. He may want you now, but one day he'll tire of you."

Yes, Bellina reluctantly agreed, it was true. She had known that when he evaded her questions. Although she couldn't understand his reasons for doing so, it made her uncomfortable. Would he go back on his word? She thought not, but could she really take the chance? Did she truly know him? If he tired of her, she would have nowhere to turn in this foreign land.

"Your master would not take kindly to you spiriting me away," Bellina said doubtfully.

"It is alright," Naqu said quickly, pulling her with him as he talked, "He'll never know. After the tale I tell him, he will be sifting the ashes for your remains. Here, give me your locket."

Her eyes turned resentful and she clutched the locket protectively.

"Come on," Naqu urged sternly, "We have no time to waste arguing. It will serve to convince him you're gone forever, and he'll forget you as quickly as the others."

Her face paled. "Others?" The thought of Surek holding someone else had never occurred to her. Of course there were others. How could she have been so naive to think there was any other feeling for her besides his lust? She was a convenient bedmate to pass the inactivity of these past weeks. That is why he was keeping her. She would leave this place to the devil who seemed to have already claimed it. Numbly, she handed the locket over to Naqu.

With a satisfied nod, he stuffed it away and pulled

her hurriedly. As he lifted her to his horse, she shivered at the fleeting look of cruelty that passed over his face like a dark shadow. She shrugged it off as merely the play of light upon him. In a flash he was up behind her, his arms so tight around her that her breath came stiffly.

They rode only a short distance before a dark shadow on horseback approached them from a small blind of brush. "Naqu," Bellina whispered fearfully.

He dismounted and greeted the shadow in a language she couldn't understand. He pointed at her and the man nodded with a smile that failed to soften the harshness of his face. Bellina smiled back at him, more in apprehension than in greeting. There was something strange happening but she couldn't understand what prompted the cold fear that settled in her stomach. This is silly, she thought scoldingly, Naqu would never let that man harm me.

With a wave of his hand that ended their conversation, Naqu returned to her, with the man behind. "Bellina we will eat now before our long ride," he told her with a smooth smile that she had never seen. "A long journey is more bearable on a full stomach."

As he helped her down, she felt the wandering eyes of their companion and met his rude surveillance with her own hard stare. Naqu nodded towards him. "This is Rashid, he will accompany us into Constantinople. It is safer to travel in numbers. There are unscrupulous nomadic tribes who would . . . never mind. I see I am upsetting you with this talk."

The wandering desert tribes did not bother Bellina as much as Rashid, for he looked to her to be more unsavory than any nomad she could imagine meeting. She sat as far away from his fetid stench as possible. Never had she seen or smelled anyone so filthy. He pushed food into his mouth with hands blackened by what seemed like a century's collection of dirt. Rashid flashed an occasional smile, showing two rows of black and broken teeth. His ruddy face glistened with grease as he intently devoured the last of a rancid piece of lamb. As far as she was concerned, she would have little to do with this repulsive beast.

Becoming anxious to be on their way, she gave Naqu a questioning glance that he read instantly. Pulling a goatskin pouch from his saddle, he uncorked it and gave it to her. "Drink this, for the sun will draw the water from your body. Then we'll go."

Pressing the sack to her lips she tasted the cooling but bitter liquid. "What is this? It's not water, it's horrible."

"It is *gundaiya*, a drink made with herbs that is better than water for travel in the heat of the day."

She took another gulp but couldn't help making a face. As Naqu spoke of the day's journey she found herself squinting to see him. She swayed and was steadied by a supporting arm. There are only two of them she told herself, yet many people swirled before her. With a cry, she clutched at the sudden cramp of her stomach. The figures thinned, became transparent as they danced around her, swaying back and forth in dizzy profusion, gradually fading into the blackness that crept about the edges of her vision. "Naqu!" she tried to call, but her throat constricted with dryness and closed finally with the swelling of her tongue. Their laughing voices echoed, then disappeared into the void that finally claimed her.

Naqu caught her in his arms and, satisfied she was completely unconscious, wrapped her in a bolt of green velvet and tossed this bundle over the back of Rashid's horse, securing everything with a leather thong. "Don't forget the parchment goes with the girl. It would be unfortunate for you if the bearer of this little gift is unknown. And don't think of claiming the credit for yourself. Should my parcel be harmed in any way before delivery, I will have Surek Harum Edib trailing you to the end of the earth."

Rashid spat to the ground at Naqu's feet, his spittle dripping down the soft leather of his boot. "If you're so worried about your precious bundle, why don't you deliver her personally!"

"I told you, I have to tie up loose ends at camp. And what do you think Surek will think, finding me and the girl gone after that fire? I'm no fool like you!"

"Don't be so sure of that, Naqu. What is to stop me from killing you here, eh?"

"Enough dinars to satisfy even you. But you'll not get another until she's in the sultan's hands—alive and well."

"And a lot of gold it better be. It wasn't easy lugging that fat whore all the way from Constantinople, sticking her inside Surek's tent, and then rushing back here. Why my horse is ruined, I tell you! I'd like to hear how big you'd talk if they discover her body before your little fire covers everything up."

"Stop complaining. I'm sure you had your fun before you slit her throat."

A smile twisted Rashid's puffy lips as he thought of the ecstasy of the writhing, bleeding body under

81

his, and the pleading screams that still sounded in his ears. "Ahh, she was a plump one—not like this one here. I prefer a trifle more meat, so don't worry, the sultan can have her. But Naqu, if you fall back on your word, I will collect my due, even after delivery, and it will be the sultan tailing you to the end of the earth. And perhaps Surek, too."

They glared at each other with suspicion and loathing until Rashid kicked his horse into a gallop and disappeared in a rising cloud of dust. Naqu turned his horse around, sending her in the direction of the smoke-filled sky. A pleased look spread over him as he mentally reviewed the success of his plan. The fire had been easy, and Bellina was, as ever, predictably eager. Rashid could be satisfied with enough gold, but Naqu was not a rich man and could not afford Rashid's greed. "Humph! Rashid," he thought, "the burr up a horse's ass. Once that little surprise gift is delivered, I will once again be in the sultan's good graces. Rashid!" He spat. "You'll have your payment—a long golden visit with Allah!"

Cautiously, he approached the still-smoldering grounds and was relieved to see Surek and the others attentively shoveling sand onto the hot embers. Slithering through the now-settled horses, he worked his way to the rubble that was once Surek's tent. There, he let the delicate gold chain slip through his fingers to silently fall into the bed of powdery black ashes. The heart sparkled against the blackness with gentle touches of sunlight. Naqu sank inconspicuously into hard labor.

"Naqu!" Surek shouted as he spied him nearby sifting through some debris. "Come here and help move some of this." They struggled with removing charred timbers from the heap of rubble until they were able to pull out what could still be salvaged. Throwing aside a damaged flagon, Surek wiped the sweat from his sooty brow and looked up at the rising sun. "It is almost noon; I sent Bellina over to the horses hours ago. What has she been up to?"

"I did not see her there, Captain, she must be somewhere else, but if it pleases you, I will check."

Tired and dirty, he answered with a note of irritation as he readied himself for another problem. "No, I'll find her. See to it that the men get water, Ismeran." Ismeran nodded, keeping his thoughts of disapproval to himself. It was no good having the Venetian girl here.

Swearing under his breath, Surek stormed through what was left of their camp. What could she be up to now? After taking a count of the herd, he was satisfied she had not tried running away again, but was puzzled at her disappearance. If she had run, which he doubted, it would have had to be on foot, and even she wasn't that foolish.

Naqu's voice slit his thoughts. "Captain Edib! Kadi!" The boy stopped, out of breath, and rambled unintelligibly.

"Speak slowly. How can I understand you!" Surek snapped.

"Captain, her necklace was found in the ashes of your tent."

Almost before he could finish, Surek was racing back with Naqu at his heels. This cannot be, his mind anguished. She left the tent; she was safe by the stream's edge. But he remembered that in his haste he

83

had not noticed if she had gone to safety; he had just assumed she would.

Naqu showed him the spot where the gold locket lay shining in the sunlight. Stooping to pick it up, he noticed that the clasp was unlatched. It was the one thing she clung to fiercely, never taking it off. It was her link to the past, and now it lay opened as if symbolically releasing her from a life she hated. "Naqu," he said flatly, "get help and rake through all this. Report back to me." As he somberly walked away, his face became a mask showing no trace of the loss and emptiness he felt inside.

Later, when Naqu showed him the charred remains of her body, he fell into a silence that no one dared to disturb. He grasped the locket as if it were a live part of her and studied the filigree flowers until the golden image was etched in his memory. Nothing could erase the thought of her from his mind: she would haunt him forever. Never would he be able to kiss another woman without tasting the sweetness of Bellina, or feeling the hammer of her heart when he held her. Closing his eyes, he shut out the stars, the glowing embers, and the shadows of the sleeping soldiers around him, but he could not shut out the golden heart.

Six

Camillus Santari Poletti studied the flickering candle before him and tried to force away the horrible scenes that flashed through his head. Ever since news of the Turkish attack on Constantinople had arrived in Venice, he could not live with the torment of his fears. The news if it could be called that was two months old. Two months! While he, Camillus, was relaxing with his family, his wife's only brother, poor Gerardo, was probably lying on those blood-drenched streets, his life's blood joining the rivers of others. And Bellina—no, he did not want to dwell on it. How could Gerardo have been so insane as to go to that unsettled part of the world! And with his young daughter no less! He could have sent Miquel Campanello; there was not a better man or sailor in the whole of Venice. The choosing of some brocades and silks could have been trusted to him!

His fist smashed the top of the secretary and the struggling flame flickered his anguished profile upon the wall. No, he knew the reason. Despite Gerardo's many years, the call of the sea and adventure still tugged at his heartstrings. However, there was no excuse in bringing Bellina. To lose Gerardo was cruel enough, but the loss of two so dear to his heart was beyond bearing.

"I must not think this way!" he angrily muttered, furious at the funereal current of thought that refused to stop flowing in his head. There had been a handful of survivors, surely God had spared them. There was a possibility that they were alive, his mind reasoned, but his heart did not accept. If they were alive and captives under those infidels, he would rather have them dead.

He was disturbed by a faint tapping at the study door and he wearily opened it, letting Anna place a tray laden with wine and bread upon the circular table that bordered the fireplace. He returned to the dark corner of the room, not wanting her to see the tears that stained his face. "Messer Poletti," the girl murmured with a bob of respect, "Conte Sordici has arrived."

No sooner had she spoken then a tall, well-dressed man, his stride showing impatience, pushed through the doorway. "Messer Poletti, I came as soon as was possible. I still can't believe it! Bellina's father never even told me he was going to take her to that godforsaken country! I for one, never would have let him, had I known."

Camillus sat down heavily on a chair close by the fire. "Aurelian, stop raving and listen, for my heart is heavy and I am not up to listening to you." He ignored the man's darkening eyes. "I realize Messer

D'Rosallini had promised Bellina to you this summer, but that does not give you the right to dictate to a father what he does with his daughter. Besides, you are never around. Instead of gallivanting around the countryside, you should have taken a stronger interest in your future wife!"

"Let us lay aside our differences for once, Uncle." He took a seat, carefully smoothing his threadbare velvet clothes, as if the polished wood chair would rub it vindictively just because he was a Sordici. He smiled, poorly concealing the poison of his manner. "You called me here because of news of Bellina, I trust, not to judge the journeys I have to make in the interest of my business."

"Business? Ha!" Camillus turned his head away from him in disgust and gazed upon the smoldering logs in the fireplace. "No, I have no news of Gerardo or my niece. They are both very dear to me."

His hand trembled as he poured the ruby wine. "And I will not rest until I know for certain what has happened to them. I hope you feel the same."

Aurelian waved aside the crystal goblet that was offered him. "Of course, I do. Is there any doubt?" His eyes snapped his challenge.

Camillus leaned forward, meeting the challenge. "Then if you do, leave with Miquel Campanello in three days hence and join him in searching for them. He has been to that cursed city before and knows it well. It is dangerous, I know. If I was younger, I would not stay behind here to be of no use at all." As tears glassed his eyes, he desperately struggled to compose himself. "I would turn over every grain of earth in that cruel land until they or their sun-bleached bones were in my arms!"

Although Aurelian had always known Camillus was a soft, weak, old man, he was sickened by his lack of control. Rising with disgust, he left him to himself and crossed the complaining floor to where a thick-paned window looked out upon the black waters of the canal. The light from a scimitar moon danced upon the waves, and every once in a while illuminated a paddling traveler, anxious to reach home. It was a peaceful night, for almost everyone was safe in their home, readying for the morrow—the start of the merchant fairs. Ony the rhythmic slap of a wave or swish of a paddle disturbed the calm. But Camillus's bent figure was mirrored upon the pane, and Aurelian's thoughts were not on the beauty of a summer night in Venice.

Aurelian's future had been so hopeful, so full of promise, when fate had blessed him with a wealthy merchant happy to marry his equally wealthy daughter to him, a man of title, if a bit lacking in funds. And the girl was as delicate as a springtime blossom. So what if she was not as cultured and subdued as he would have desired. But now this! Because of a father who lacks a brain, and a foolish girl's whim, his whole life had taken a complete turn—downhill. If he had any sense, he'd forget Bellina and marry the Duchess of Saguerno. However, her dowry left a lot to be desired and the thought of making love to that fat cow nauseated him. He'd rather take his chances searching for Bellina.

He turned, tapping a finger restlessly against his thigh. "Camillus, I sympathize with you, for both of them are as dear to me as my own family. Tell Miquel I will join him no matter what dangers are involved. Only please, set my mind at ease—if I find Bellina alive and her father (may the heavens forbid!) no longer belongs to this world, will you honor the agreement he made with me for his daughter's hand?"

"Of course, of course, if God so wills Gerardo's death! Just find her and bring her home. But remember, she is not yet prepared for her father's plans for you. Speak none of this to her; I would tell her myself as an uncle should." He sighed wearily, but was comforted that every effort for the discovery of his niece and his wife's brother would be made. "Please, Aurelian, leave me to rest. I have never felt so aged in my whole life."

"As you wish. Miquel, I trust, will see to securing a ship?"

The old man nodded and Aurelian left with a flat smile.

It was a dreary morning when the *Portia Regalia*'s sails puffed with a brisk northern wind and set out for a distant and hostile land. The small caravel held twenty-four seamen, captained by a sun-bronzed man who ran his well-disciplined crew with ease and flair. It also held a pompous, slightly impoverished aristocrat and his much abused servant, below decks sick from the rough seas.

To Miquel, this was a blessing beyond all hoping. Although he had known Aurelian for only one day, he somehow was convinced beyond any doubt that all would find life easier if he remained out of sight and hearing. It was hard to believe that Bellina's father could have planned giving her to such a buffoon.

The ship heaved upon each wave and the rigging slapped against the masts. Dear Bellina, how could her life have gotten so tangled up? For a moment Miquel allowed himself the luxury of a backward look into the past, back to a gentler place and time. How carefree he and Bellina had been then! They left no rock unturned, no flowers unpicked, and no prank undone, he mused. What a couple of urchins! They had both enjoyed each other's company so much they had been branded loners. But how fortunate they had been in finding each other to frolic together over the hillsides outside Verona and explore the canals of Venice in his rickety boat.

He could not stop the heat that rose in his cheeks when he reflected on how their friendship had turned to the fire of first love. When on a summer retreat into the country, he had coaxed her into the lush green meadows that only the sheep roamed, and there had tasted the forbidden joys of a kiss. After that day his father had made sure that he was kept busy with the D'Rosallini galleys that spent time in distant ports. "Do you think yourself the doge of Venice?" his father had yelled, twisting his nose. "You are my son, the whelp of a servant, and no suitor of Bellina. You repay Messer D'Rosallini's kindnesses by kissing his daughter? Aie!"

Miquel combed his fingers through his curly mop.

Somehow Bellina's duenna must have been behind it all, he later thought. They had been forced to go separate ways—until now. And what an unfortunate set of circumstances this was!

Distantly, he heard Aurelian complaining to his servant to place another wet cloth on his forehead. Poor Marco, he was as ill as his master, and he had to additionally suffer Aurelian's every whim and whine. A seagull shrieked above and Miquel almost felt it was scolding him for wasting the day away in daydreams. What was past, was past, but now for the present he would do all in his power to find Messer D'Rosallini and his daughter.

When he turned from the railing he almost bumped into the green face of Aurelian. The conte pressed a limp cloth to his forehead, pathetically. "Captain, tell your men to turn back, this dreadful rocking is certain to be the death of me."

"Nonsense!" Miquel could not believe he had heard correctly. "No one ever died from seasickness; we are not going back. Go below and don't concentrate on the motion."

Aurelian grabbed Miquel's shirt with a fierceness that surprised Miquel. "I said we're going back!"

"So you did," Miquel growled, "but I say we are not. And since I have been entrusted by Messer Poletti as well as Messer D'Rosallini to captain their ships, I get my way!"

He struck Aurelian's fist from his shirt and let two of the crew pull him back to his bunk. Aurelian rained obscenities upon them all, but his struggles were too weak to matter.

Miquel retreated to his cabin to write down the incident and the day's events. Silently he prayed that God would grant him the patience to suffer Aurelian until this quest was through. A devoted husband-to-be, he was not. If Miquel could help it, and if Bellina was found—as somehow he believed she would be—he would see to it that Aurelian never married her.

Seven

When the *Portia Regalia*'s hull scraped against the dock of Port Solomon, it was enough to send the high-strung conte into a panic. Sweat began to bead his brow almost instantly as he frantically searched for his doublet and stockings.

"We must surely have been besieged by pirates! I never should have allowed myself to be convinced into going on this insane voyage! The idea that Camillus would even *suggest* that a man of my standing should . . . Humph! Marco! Where is that boy? Marco!" His almost-feminine voice shrilled continuously until a timid knock was heard at his door. "Marco is that you?"

His voice came unsure and quivering, "Yes, my Conte, it is Marco."

"Well come in!" Aurelian boomed. "What the devil took you so long? Don't you have ears, boy? What's happening anyway?"

The boy rushed to aid the flustered conte, who in his haste had became tangled in his own clothing.

93

Aurelian forgot his breeding and expelled a gust of curses in the common dialect.

"We have docked at Port Solomon, master. It will please you to set foot on land once again?"

"Finally!" Grabbing a diamond and ruby pin from the boy's trembling fingers, he fastened a flounce of lace that graced his thick neck. "Let me do this, you fool. I can manage from here; you'd no doubt stick me with it. That peasant who calls himself Capitano can't even dock a ship properly. Nearly knocked me out of bed! I always told D'Rosallini he was no good," he continued as he fussed with his brocade doublet. "Now, go get me something to eat—from shore. I'm so sick of those dried slivers of mutton our capitano has been so stingy to part with. It's a wonder I'm still alive!"

Like his master, Marco agreed that it was indeed good to see land again, and he too favored the thought of a hearty breakfast and the feel of firm earth beneath his feet. When he reached topside, all hands were busy winding thick ropes around new pylons that stood next to their blackened counterparts—vivid reminders of the battle of Constantinople.

After the caravel was securely anchored, Miquel gave his handful of men a long list of cautions before disembarking. Most had heard this speech before, and to Miquel's comfort, they were not complete strangers to the city. "Remember," he had warned them, "this is no longer the city it once was. We are more foreign now than ever before, and unfortunately do not rule over her. She is a Moslem state, part of the Ottoman Empire. Remember this—the war is

94

still fresh in the minds of many, so watch your tongues, or you may find yourselves chained to the city's wall, left for the birds to pick your bones."

There was little concern in Miquel's mind that his crew would not heed his words. News of Mehmet II and the atrocious tales of his force had swept Venice like a raging fire to bring a fear that made even the bravest of men cringe. And there was no doubt that this was Mehmet's city now.

As Miquel looked to shore, he acknowledged the long arduous task of finding his master Gerardo D'Rosallini and his daughter Bellina Magela. When he should have been full of hope, he felt nothing but despair as he looked into the thick populace that worked along the docks and crowded the streets. Yet, he could not think of them as dead. Gerardo D'Rosallini, who had been like a father to him, and Bellina, his secret love, couldn't be dead. They were somewhere in Constantinople, and he would find them, even if it took months.

"Capitano?" Marco's voice sneaked into his thoughts. "Would you like me to bring you some food? That is, if you are not leaving yourself."

"No, I'm not leaving yet, and it would be greatly appreciated if you brought back something more edible than our rations."

"Conte Sordici's thoughts, also, Capitano."

"No doubt."

Marco was gleeful as he attempted to skip down the wood planking on legs that were still in tune to the rhythm of the waves that had rocked them for so many weeks. Sooner than Miquel expected, Marco returned, toting a sack that bulged with their breakfast.

"Give me that sack!"

The conte picked at the stringy meat gingerly until his hunger got the best of him, then he ate as ravenously as Miquel and Marco.

By midday Miquel was anxious to begin his search, but was delayed by the pompous conte. The captain's boots clicked away the minutes as he paced, imagining Aurelian primping before his looking glass. If it had been up to him, Aurelian would be sitting in a stuffed chair, sipping orange water, and crying endlessly to Camillus over his lost love. And for sure that was precisely what Aurelian would prefer, had it not been for his fear of losing the D'Rosallini wealth. If the conte did not think Camillus might retract the marriage agreement between himself and Bellina, he would not have gone on what he called "this cursed journey into the lair of a demoniacal monster." It sickened Miquel that wealth was the conte's sole motivation. Why didn't Messer D'Rosallini see through Aurelian's intentions before promising his only daughter?

"Miquel, uh, Capitano, I see you are ready to begin our sorrowful job of searching for my poor intended and, of course, her father. Who knows what has happened to them at the hands of those infidels."

"Those infidels are our hosts, like it or not. Guard your tongue, for I have no wish to be their permanent guest. Let's be on our way, we've lost precious time." Miquel looked at Aurelian's silk slippers, "Really, Conte, nobody here cares what you look like. I think you're forgetting why we're here."

"I think you're forgetting who you are talking

96

to, Capitano."

As he tossed back a strand of greasy hair, Aurelian left for shore with a flounce. "Just because we are forced to explore this place and mingle with who knows what manner of beasts, doesn't mean we must lower ourselves to their pitiful standards. I, for one, have no intentions of becoming involved with the lower class here or anywhere else. And dearest Bellina, just the memory of her voice rings in my heart like a tiny crystal bell. How could you insinuate I've forgotten her, when my whole being aches for that angelica? Why she's my light, my life, my—"

Miquel couldn't contain himself any longer. "And what do you propose to do with her fortune? Perhaps gamble it away like your father did with his, leaving your heir to seek a wealthy bride—even if she's an untitled one?" It gave him satisfaction to see the conte's spine stiffen like rigging in a storm.

"You will regret that remark one day. You forget that once I am married to Bellina, I become your master as well as hers."

Miquel could not imagine his free-spirited Bellina subordinate to anyone, and suddenly felt as though he might be rescuing her only to deliver her into slavery. What fate could be worse than being married to one such as Conte Aurelian Sordici?

The two would have vanished into the crowd unnoticed if it wasn't for the elaborately dressed conte. Dockworkers paused, resting on barrels or heavy bales as they eyed this curiosity. Before they were a hundred lengths from the *Portia Regalia*, Aurelian's complaints began.

97

"My feet are *killing* me. Don't tell me you intend to comb the city in one day?"

"If you hadn't worn court slippers, your feet would be fine, so don't complain to me about them. If you're so tired, go back."

"And let you tell Camillus I took no active part in finding his niece? Certainly not!"

Miquel gave an indifferent shrug. "There's a market near the center of the city where we can get water from one of the merchants, and an inn where you can rest during the afternoon heat. I will search the eastern part of the city. You do as you wish." Miquel then left the flabbergasted Conte on his own and disappeared into the city.

As he approached the city's nucleus, Miquel noticed the debris, a reminder of the horror that had taken place months before. It was also apparent that the recent occupation of Ottomans was slowly changing the city. The colorful cathedrals—now white-washed mosques—appeared as ghosts of a past regime. However, the city was being repaired. Donkeys and oxen strained under the weight of their loads, while slaves, as sullen-looking as the animals, pulled on ropes attached to pulleys and hoisted large stones to the top of a nearby structure. Whips cracked in the still air, punctuated by human moans and the raucous protests of beasts.

A panorama of striped and solid-colored canvas panels covered each merchant's display of goods. Bolts of fine silks, brocades, and damask flowed over tabletops in a waterfall of color and texture. The air was permeated with the odors of fish, spices, burning incense, human and animal sweat, and newly tanned leather: the combination was so stunning to the senses that it was impossible to distinguish one from the other. An old woman fanned flies from sticky honey cakes with a dried oxtail, and beside her Miquel found a huge clay vessel he hoped contained water. Miquel pointed to the jug, "Water?" The woman nodded her head. Parting with a coin, he dipped a ladle into the jug and drew the cool water to his lips.

"Have you seen a man like me in the bazaar with a young woman?" He asked in a voice cracked with desperate hope. The woman just looked at him, then turned away, more concerned with the flies that hovered and lighted on the honey cakes. "A pretty girl, with hair like that." Miquel pointed to the woman's black silk robes. "And eyes," first laying a finger aside his eye, then lifting a polished bracelet and tapping on its green stones. She held her hand out. Miquel dropped a coin into her palm, but she shook her head and would not be satisfied until two more followed. Depositing the money, she turned away again to turn her attention on a promising customer. Miquel sighed and walked on, hoping to find someone who would understand him. He stuffed the unwanted bracelet into a pocket.

After an endless day of searching, it was not too soon when the tall-masted galleons and caravels loomed before them like the gates of heaven. Miquel laboriously climbed the gangplank, disappointment shadowing on his face. His crew kept a respectful silence. Giovanni reluctantly followed Miquel to his cabin. He stood almost at attention while Miquel tore off his boots. Crossing one leg over the next, he massaged the arch of one foot.

"Giovanni, it is as hopeless as finding the doge's gold ring in the canal."

"Capitano, it is only one day," Giovanni offered hopefully.

"Yes," Miquel sighed, "one day. It will take months of days, I fear." He stretched his legs. "Now, what is it? I can sense it is not pleasant, so spill it out."

His first mate cleared his throat. "There has been some trouble in the bazaar. It seems the Conte caused some commotion . . ."

"With his insults, no doubt."

"He was accused of stealing from one of the merchants, a row ensued—you can imagine!"

Miquel stilled. "Were soldiers . . . ?"

"No, the Conte did get back without being followed, he says. It was only moments before you arrived, so time will tell."

"I should have kept my eye on him!" Miquel stood and paced the narrow length of his cabin. "Send him here."

In moments, Aurelian looked into Miquel's blazing eyes. "Well," Miquel drawled, challenging an explanation from the Conte.

"Well, just look at this!" Aurelian burst out, showing his torn stockings, "A disgrace when a man is cheated by a mere peasant and then becomes a fugitive himself. What sort of city is this? Where is the justice? If we were in Venice, the condottiere would have that thief in irons by now. But no, here I am—the victim of a crime—and I, Conte Aurelian Sordici, am forced to run through the streets in fear of my life because some . . . Oh, I can't bear to relive the humiliation."

"You're lucky to live at all," Miquel steamed under a tight lid of self-control. "Conte Sordici, for your own safety, I find it necessary to confine you to ship. If you are recognized ashore, I fear for your life. Crimes are not dealt with lightly here, and I will not have my ship and crew put in danger."

"Crime! What crime? The only crime I'm aware of is that thieving merchant goes unpunished for insulting a nobleman."

"On the contrary, Conte, you have insulted him, and caused him to lose a day, as well as some of his goods. How can I find Bellina if we are all in prison?"

Aurelian sobered. "Capitano, it is not necessary for you to confine me to this ship. A man in my position often is the object of lower-class jealousies. I therefore will leave this search in the hands of those best qualified to deal with them. Good day, Capitano."

With Aurelian out of his cabin, Miquel sat on the edge of a wide chair and filled another glass with port. Before long the bottle was more empty than full and his head fell to the desktop as the ship pitched, his thoughts lost to a swirling cloud that ended in darkness.

After the fourteenth day in Constantinople, Miquel returned to the *Portia Regalia*, again discouraged. He had been directed to every stocky mustached man living in the city, only to find disappointment. He began to think that Gerardo D'Rosallini was either dead or laboring as a slave somewhere outside of the city. He feared the worst for Bellina. He was at a loss of what to do. Yet, how could he give up with the saddened face of Camillus still fresh in his memory?

Aurelian was there to greet him as usual, probing with his ferret eyes, watchful for anything Miquel might be trying to hide from him. But Miquel and his small band of men filed past the waiting conte. Not to be ignored, he marched along with them.

"Well, Capitano, don't tell me you have come up with nothing again?"

"Conte, it's been a long day. If you'll excuse me . . ."

"You'll not dismiss me so lightly, Capitano. It's been an equally long day for me aboard this ship with nothing to do but stare at the sea and get sick from it. How long do you intend on staying here?"

"Until we find them. That is our duty."

"Bah, duty. It's time to go back to Venice and find someone who knows what they are doing. I refuse to stay on this ship and idle away another day while you scurry about the city."

"Aurelian, let's understand this—I am not one of your servants. On this ship you answer to me, and unless you wish to take up permanent residence in this city, you will adhere to my command!" Miquel punctuated his response with the slam of his cabin door and then sent for his first mate, Giovanni.

Giovanni couldn't believe his ears! The captain was actually sending him to a slave auction! Not that he minded, but it was so unlike the Capitano that it worried him. Never had he seen Miquel so pre-occupied with his thoughts, and just when he thought all was well, the Capitano sends him to choose a girl for none other than the Conte! What use the Conte would have for her he didn't know, and Miquel was obviously worse off than Giovanni thought.

Miquel's first mate whistled lightly as he bounded down the street, his oil lamp swinging at his side, lighting a path before him. Giovanni's size drew stares of disbelief from those who lurked in the shadows of buildings, and although his lamp did catch the gleam of metal in one man's hand, Giovanni walked on in peace.

It was not hard to find the building Miquel had described: the sweet musty smoke from countless pipes seeped from beneath a door, leaving an eerie cloud which spread across the street in long thin fingers. The high whine of music mixed with the rumble of conversation. Giovanni pushed his way in and settled down with an appreciative eye.

The next morning Miquel congratulated Giovanni on his good choice, assuring him that the slave girl was sure to keep Aurelian out of their hair. The captain left his ship with more confidence than he had felt in weeks and continued his search by engaging the service of a Serb who agreed to add him to his produce wagon. The old man welcomed the coins that jingled in his pocket, for travelers were scarce since the arrival of Mehmet II. He would also now have a strong youth to help with the wagon's load. They bounced along a road so rutted and decaying that at times it was safer to detour along the fields.

"What business do you have outside of Constantinople? You don't look like a farmer, though strong you are," questioned the man as his eyes raked over Miquel.

"I'm looking for a friend lost since the battle."

"Sadly, that is the tale of many. I've lost my own sons to the sultan. One day they were loading the wagon for market and along come some of his soldiers and enlist my boys in the service of the Empire. What could I do? What can *you* do? Nothing, I tell you, nothing," he concluded with finality and slumped into silence.

Miquel was not about to give up until he had searched the countryside. Perhaps Bellina and her father had retreated to the hills and had been taken in by some farmer. Now it seemed to him that was more likely than staying in the city, and with this thought, his hopes were revived.

The cart rocked back and forth, lulling the exhausted Miquel into a half-sleep. While he dozed, he failed to see the splayed ears or note the quivering muzzle of the donkey as he stopped and stood statue-still on the hillside. The farmer frowned and reached for his switch. Despite the hail of whippings, the donkey couldn't move the wagon from a scramble of petrified tracks and rocks. Its wheels creaked for a moment before one split rim snapped under the strain, sending produce and occupants to the ground. Cabbages tumbled around knocking together, becoming speckled with bits of yellow grain that spilled from one of the split burlap sacks. A squealing donkey kicked furiously and struggled to get to his feet. Miquel, dazed, crawled to the gray-haired man who lay motionless beneath the cart.

Only after unharnessing the donkey was Miquel able to push the wagon over, freeing the Serb. A thick ooze of scarlet seeped into the ground from the poor man's head, and when Miquel gently turned it, rock poked up. His ribs jabbed up brokenly to mirror the cart's edge.

One by one, Miquel piled a pyramid of rocks over the Serb's body until a monument to his kindness stood on the gnarled hill. After burying the man, Miquel mounted the donkey and continued alone. He hoped to find a traveler during the day to check his direction, and prayed for a clear night. However, nightfall came with a sky so clouded that the stars were invisible. "I have the luck of a jinn-haunted man," he thought sarcastically.

After hobbling the donkey for the third starless night, Miquel wrapped himself in his tattered blanket and tried to sleep. Morning came slowly and painfully as his stomach cramped with hunger and his throat begged for water. He envied the animal as he watched him cropping the sprigs of vegetation that sprung up from between the rocks, but knew that before long he too would perish without water.

Miquel's mind began to wander and brought him back to the *Portia Regalia* as the little donkey plodded along the deserted countryside. Giovanni will take care of the crew, he thought, and see them safely to Venice and Aurelian, Aurelian . . .

His eyes blinked several times to clear the fog that masked the spectral forms hovering over him. They were surrounded by darkness, their faces levitating spiritually in the fuzziness of his vision.

"Aurelian?" he questioned in his confusion. He

was sure one of the faces was Aurelian's, but Aurelian was on the *Portia Regalia*. He had told him to stay there. What would he be doing here? He fought to reason clearly as he struggled to gain control of his senses. Puzzled over the second face that moved closer to him, Miquel tried to reach out as the man lifted him from the ground, but he fell back unconscious.

"Brother Lucian, help me carry this poor soul to the wagon. It is my guess he hasn't had water for a few days, and in this heat, even a camel couldn't survive without it. Ugh! He is a heavy one. Brother, if you'd just get that leg over, we'll have him in. That's good." The two monks struggled to get Miquel into their wagon.

"When Abbot Amadeus hears we have left a good barrel and replaced it with this stranger—who could be an escaped slave—and haven't even delivered our wine and oil, he will be most displeased with us, Brother John."

"Prayer, Frater, how will he know of the keg? I would rather think he would be happy that a life was exchanged for a mere empty barrel."

"Humph!"

Miquel heard a deep voice, no more than a whisper, floated from a dark corner in a small room.

"Well, well, well. You have finally decided to join us."

A shaft of dim light cut its way through an arched window so narrow, it seemed more of a crack in the stone masonry than a window. It was impossible for him to distinguish anything but the small portion of space the thread of light had illuminated.

Miquel's memory failed. The marketplace was the

last he could remember. He concluded that the dark cubby hole was part of a dungeon; there was no other answer. Aurelian and the pursuing soldiers loomed before him like a nightmare.

The man who spoke to him blended into the stone wall, appearing like one of the stacked blocks that imprisoned them. Slowly, the bulky form rose and partially stood in the beam of light that sliced the room in half until it ended as a spot of liquid yellow. Miquel squinted to make out the features of his cellmate.

Strangely, the man appeared to him as a saint, standing as he was with his arms draped in cloth and rays of light disseminating from behind him. Miquel found himself too weak to raise himself from the pallet that supported him.

"Please, don't get up; you are still weak. We had feared it was going to be the Lord's wish to take you, but I see He is not ready for you yet—or maybe you are not ready for him yet?"

The heavy-set man glided across the floor and ponderously lowered his frame to rest at the foot of Miquel's bed. "I am Brother John. Through your delirium you have told us many things in the past weeks that weigh heavily upon you. But you have not mentioned your name. Unless it is Aurelian? You seem to have mistaken Brother Lucian for this Aurelian fellow and . . ." He chuckled as he recalled an incident he found particularly amusing, but then turned serious as he chastised himself for taking pleasure in another man's unfortunate predicament. He remembered that tonight he should say a few more prayers for his soul.

"As I was saying," he continued, his calloused hands illustrating each word as he spoke, "it was Brother Lucian's turn to sit with you through the night. Well, after being here only a short while, he barged out in a fury covered with gruel. Do you remember? I thought not. Well, God will forgive you; I'm sure it was the fever. It's said the devil can possess a body too weak to resist and causes all kinds of havoc. After that, poor Lucian swore we brought Satan into the monastery and refused to set foot in here again."

Miquel took an immediate liking to the jolly monk who sat with him. "I assure you, Brother, I'm only possessed by love."

"Ah, that could be as driving a force as Satan himself!"

"My name is Miquel Campanello, capitano of the *Portia Regalia*, a merchant ship from Venice."

"You are indeed far from your ship, Capitano."

"How far are we from Constantinople, Frater?"

"A week's ride. That is by a donkey pulling twelve barrels of wine and oil, and only if you're not detained by roaming janissaries. We seldom make the trip anymore; it's getting too risky. Before we only had to fear being robbed, now the sultan's men roam the countryside checking this and that. It's a relief the sultan hasn't banned Christianity! But the beautiful cathedrals! You should see what's become of them! I'm saddened that such beauty has come to be whitewashed. All the mosaics, the chalices of gold—melted down, encaustics, everything hidden now and forever under white. They are now worshipping a pagan god in our house of the Lord.

Can you imagine that!"

It did not concern Miquel which god was being worshipped in the old cathedrals, only that it had been weeks since he had left Giovanni in charge of his ship. He could only imagine the worst. They probably thought he was dead, and had returned to Venice.

"Your donkey, Capitano, seems to be more adapted to the terrain than you are. He has made friends with Angelina, our donkey, who is more of a devil than an angel. I think the two have made a marriage, so we have much to thank your little visit for."

Miquel held his head in his hands in despair, hardly hearing the monk at all. "Frater, I hate to impose on your goodness more than I already have, but do you think you could spare some provisions for my journey back to the city? It is important that I return as soon as possible."

"What could be so important? You are not ready for such a trip yet. All the riches in the East will still be in the marketplace months, years, from now. I think it best if you stay a little longer. Besides, if you could just see your donkey and Angelina, you would not have the heart to separate the two lovers."

"Brother John, I appreciate your concern, but I feel fine. I cannot stress enough the importance of my return. It is not for any treasure of gold, silver, or cloth, but for two people who are as close to me as if their blood flowed in my veins."

"Ah, I see." The monk's voice was compassionate and filled with understanding as he spoke. "My son, so many good people—Serbs, Greeks, Venetians, and

Ottomans alike—have met their end in this senseless war for the world's marketplace. For fear of their lives, some of Emperor Constantine's supporters have fled into the hills, but were sooner or later captured. Our monastery was subjected to many searches. Others stowed away on ships that sailed to ports unknown to them. And then there were those who fell into the hands of profiteers and the slave souk. Go home. God will deliver them in his own time if they are alive. But you will meet your own end if you are not careful, and what would become of your remaining family then?"

Miquel sighed, weary and despairing. Counting the months that had already passed, he had to face the cold facts and agree with the Frater that perhaps he attempted an impossible feat. But he knew his heart would never give up hope. He could not accept that his strong-willed Bellina was dead. Not her—she was a survivor. He frowned as his choices formed in his mind.

"Brother John, it would be an honor if you could stand me for a few more days. After all, I have combed Constantinople, but I have much of the hills yet to search, and with your knowledge of this area and a few prayers, who knows?"

The despair that filled Miquel was the same despair that Bellina began to feel as Rashid relentlessly pushed her through the desert. They moved further away from camp, their trail soon to be lost in the shifting sands. Each time Bellina turned to check the disappearing tracks, Rashid grinned sadistically.

As much as Rashid made her skin crawl, thoughts of Naqu stoked a fire of hate to a blaze. How could she have been so fooled? She didn't care to ask Rashid what she was worth to him. She thought it must have been a nice bit of gold, since he forced her to ride in front of him instead of dragging her behind his mount. She suffered through his groping hands and the stench of his body and thought she would have preferred to walk. To pass the time from sunrise to sunset, she imagined what Surek would do to Naqu and Rashid when he found them out.

Meanwhile, many miles away, Surek was pacing in his makeshift tent, reviewing their last night together, the words they exchanged, their love-making, the fire, Naqu's helpfulness, the rubble, and more of Naqu's help. For a lazy servant, Naqu was certainly working very hard of late. So diligent was he, that he became suspect in Surek's mind. Surek pulled out the gold heart—the gold heart that should have melted in the intense fire—its filigree still beautiful and the delicate chain flowing undamaged through his fingers. He wondered who put the locket in the ash for him to find. And he wondered just how devious Bellina could be.

Eight

Giovanni paced like a panther, his muscles flexing under the thinness of his shirt. The restlessness of the crew was as thick as the whitecaps that showed on the sea. And who could blame them, when they had left their families so long alone at home? As it was, with every new day, Aurelian looked better and better as a puppet captain and mutiny was not far from their lips.

Where was Miquel? Did everyone who ventured into this land mysteriously disappear? They searched for Messer D'Rosallini and Bellina and now Miquel.

Giovanni leaned against the mizzen and stared at the grooves in the deck. He would not return to Venice without his captain, even if it took a year of waiting. However, a missive had to be sent to Messer Poletti that they were alive and still searching.

Aurelian approached him from the bow, and by the time he was in sight, it was too late for Giovanni to avoid him.

"Giovanni!" he hailed in a patronizing whine.

"It's getting unbearably tedious bobbing up and down in this godforsaken port. We've exhausted our welcome. As for the capitano, we could continue to search for him and still come up with nothing." Met with silence, Aurelian took a stiff stance and continued to bombard Giovanni with angry words.

"Since appealing to your common sense has gone nowhere, I am now ordering you, as your superior, to set sail promptly for Venice!"

"Is that right?" His patience stretched to its limit, Giovanni drew his sword and confiscated Aurelian's with one quick movement. "We are going nowhere until Capitano Campanello orders it, and that is on his authority. Take this man to his cabin at once, and see he remains there for the duration of our stay."

Giovanni drew sharp stares from the two men who sat close by. For an eternity they continued to pull waxed cord through the sail they mended.

"Santaro! Paolo! If I repeat myself, neither of you will find yourself on this ship when it *does* go home."

Santaro gave a disdainful grunt, but he came slowly to his feet and grabbed the conte by the arm.

Giovanni got to his feet. So, Aurelian's seeds of dissension, well fertilized by homesickness, were beginning to grow. He returned Paolo's glare. "Get your belongings and wages and be off before the sun sets."

"With gladness, almighty leader," the man said, throwing the sail upon the deck.

Giovanni turned away and could not help looking to the city with wistfulness. It was as busy as ever with seamen and merchants and the inevitable clutch of

113

slum girls who winked at passersby. There was the occasional glimpse of a yellow-booted janissary; the bellow of an angry boy chasing a stray with a fat turnover in its mouth; the colorful beat of birds in their cages as they were loaded upon the *Dorothia*. There was no Miquel.

The *Santa Dorothia* seemed to sink even lower as they piled birds and rugs and fat barrels into her hold. As she nodded heavily with each rolling wave, Giovanni's eyes sparked with hope. Yes! Perhaps it was possible!

Leaning over, he visually crossed the span that separated the caravel and galleon, searching for the captain among the men. Marco approached and leaned over next to Giovanni, following his gaze. "That ship will get two days out and split her sides."

Marco broke a piece of the bread he carried and threw it to the sea; from the air came the cries of seagulls. A gull swooped from a yardarm, glided skillfully through the rigging that crisscrossed the powder blue sky, and finally alighted on a roll of water.

"What do you have, a whole loaf of our good bread under that cape, boy?" Giovanni grinned.

Marco smiled, shaking his head, tossing from his eyes some of his brown hair that was now streaked with gold. "Isn't it amazing?"

"The whole world's amazing," Giovanni replied, absently.

"No, the birds. Look how they soar to such heights! They float on the air as easily as the *Portia Regalia* rides the waves. If we could fly like that, and had eyes as sharp as theirs, we could span the whole

114

Ottoman Empire in one day and find Captain Campanello and the D'Rosallinis."

"Humph. That's nonsense—the whimsy of a child. Since you have nothing to do but dream and play, as soon as I spy the *Santa Dorothia*'s capitano, I want you to tell Conte Sordici to pack his belongings."

Soon after, Giovanni saw the stocky, bearded captain and hailed, "Capitano, you look ready to sail!"

"God willing, if the last of these barrels ever get secured below. Aiiie! Idiots, take care with that!" The captain gestured wildly at his men.

"Would you be setting sail in the morning then?" Giovanni prodded.

"If the wind is with us, as soon as we can." The captain squinted at Giovanni, "What is it to you?"

"If you could spare some space for an extra passenger, it would be helpful to me and possibly advantageous to you."

The captain's face twisted in a sardonic smile. "Would it now? Do you think me mad? We're in danger of sinking already; the last thing I need is extra baggage!"

"Wait! He may be useful to you."

"I have all the hands I need."

"His name is Conte Aurelian Sordici."

The captain turned, a touch of interest showing in the arch of his brows, and Giovanni's tenseness fell away. He turned his gold ring thoughtfully as he considered the advantages of aiding a grateful, desperate, wealthy conte. He eyed Giovanni, puffing up pompously. "Conte Sordici, you say? Couldn't he

115

tell that tub of yours wasn't meant to make a voyage such as this one? Well, perhaps I can help the conte. Tell him to be ready to leave by dawn."

A broad smile widened Giovanni's face. "Done, Capitano. He'll be most appreciative."

Now that Aurelian would soon be on his way, Giovanni felt more at ease. Without the constant prodding to leave for Venice, the crew might be content for a few more weeks. However, Giovanni knew that if Miquel didn't return soon, he would be forced to turn the *Portia Regalia* for home.

That morning the little donkey cart juggled Brother John, Lucian, and Miquel as it bounced down the hillside, leaving the peaks of Pera behind. As they approached Constantinople, Miquel's nostrils flared at the occasional salty smell that was carried on a flirtatious puff of air.

"Did you smell it that time, Frater?"

"Again?" Brother John laughed. "No. I guess it has to take a true seaman to smell the sea from this distance."

Without taking his concentration from the path ahead, Lucian added grimly, "How'd you get lost in the first place with a nose like that?"

After three weeks of searching the countryside and accepting the hospitality of those that lived outside the monastery, Miquel was ready to return to Venice. The monks had promised to inquire about the D'Rosallinis in their occasional dealings with outsiders. With this assurance, Miquel could return, knowing he had done everything possible. Where he had failed, perhaps the people who lived here would succeed.

The three travelers filled their stomachs with monk's bread and warmed the crisp night with the little wine Brother John had packed. The next morning, Brother John gave the land a satisfied survey. "Hopefully we'll be in Constantinople soon, but who knows? This donkey sets the pace. If she wants to go, she goes, if not . . . Well, then we rest."

Lucian was the last to clamber into the little cart, squeezing Miquel between layers of brown wool. The wool pricked at his exposed skin, bristling his annoyance with the fidgeting monk, whose movements were a constant reminder that the seat was made for two.

Miquel longed for the soothing rock of his ship. He had as much as he could take of sharp jolts every time a wheel hit a stone or rut. "If we reach the *Portia Regalia* soon, we'll be able to set sail today," he said, noting the direction of the wind. "Frater, I see why you limit your journeys, and I don't think it's because of the soldiers or thieves. I fear that when I get up, the seat of my pants will be worn threadbare." Brother John chuckled but Brother Lucian settled his mouth into a tight line and ignored them both.

Miquel was alert and scanning the landscape ahead for a rooftop or dome of a cathedral. Soon their cart was passing some of the peasants' huts that could be seen from Port Solomon. Miquel remembered looking up to the rolling hills that seemed to flow one into the other like massive green waves, their symmetry broken by the occasional whitewashed homes that were scattered about like tiny white pebbles. Now he was among them, wondering if at this moment Giovanni was gazing into the hills from

117

the *Portia Regalia.*

The last mile seemed longer to Miquel than all the rest combined, especially when they entered the bazaars and were caught in the busy dealings of city life.

The streets were crowded and the air stagnant. He felt they would never move through the suffocating crowds. A brown-skinned boy prodded his oxen along, yet the obstructing cart moved at a slow pace despite the urging of the brother's olive branch switch. The monk managed to maneuver around the oxen only to be detained further along their route by a man carrying a large chest upon his hunched back. The cart was forced to a standstill by a sea of curly furred sheep.

"There is one rule of the street you should not forget," the robust monk sighed, "and that is never, for any reason, stop, or you'll be stuck in that spot all day."

A blind beggar grabbed at Miquel's sleeve, not releasing it until he pressed his last coin into the man's bony hand. The sad wail of a rude flute floated down from one of the balconies that hung over the street.

Soon Miquel could see masts poking into the sky and searched for signs of his own ship. There she was, just as he had left her, tied and secure, and with a load of silk being lowered into her hold besides. How could he have doubted Giovanni?

Miquel almost toppled the cart in his jubilance as he popped up waving to an astonished Giovanni. "There she is, Brothers! The *Portia Regalia!*"

"You see, I knew they would wait for their Capitano."

Giovanni hopped neatly from ship to shore, despite the restless tugging of the caravel against her anchor. "Capitano!" he shouted, "You pup. Where have you been?"

"I've been living with the good brothers in a monastery."

His first mate gave a snort. "A monastery! You? Ha! You'd do your mother proud, rest her soul. And all along I thought you were bedding every woman in the hills. Excuse me, Brothers."

Miquel gave him a thump upon his broad back. "So, Aurelian hasn't sobered you in the past weeks."

"Aaaagh, him! I'd like to leave him here, but," he added gleefully, "instead I set him sailing on the *Santa Dorothia* two days ago."

"At least all is not bad news my friend." Miquel's voice was heavy with despair at not finding the D'Rosallinis. A silence that suspended time made Giovanni shift his weight from one heavy boot to the other. "Well," Miquel finally sighed, "It is time to set sail. I know all must be anxious to return."

Giovanni gave him a sideways look and rolled his eyes heavenward. "That is true enough. I have seen it in everyone's eyes, but except for a few, they have kept their wishes to themselves and will abide by whatever their captain decides."

"They are good men, Giovanni, that is why it is not fair to keep them here any longer. I have exhausted every possibility, and there was not even a clue as to what happened to the D'Rosallinis. It is time."

"Surely you have not given up hope, Capitano?"

"I will never give up hoping, but for now . . ." He paused sadly, searching for words, but Brother John,

119

never at a loss, interrupted.

"Forgive me for my intrusion but, when God permits, your friends will be found. My brothers and I will keep them in our prayers, and in our own way, we will be here searching with our eyes and ears."

"And it is only that promise that gives me the strength to leave here," Miquel said as he embraced the monk. "Thank you."

They watched the monks disappear, swallowed by the sea of people, and then boarded the *Portia Regalia* with plans to set sail.

Nine

Streams of gray smoke still grew from the smoldering ashes of the Spahiglani camp, dulling a fireball sun that climbed over the eastern horizon. Ever more suspicious of Naqu's eager helpfulness and his theories on Bellina's fate, Surek dispatched Ismeran with orders not only to track the Bashaw, but to look for any other trails that led from the camp. He paced impatiently, crushing chunks of ash beneath his boots, while he waited for Ismeran's return. The blade of the scimitar that hung from his waist flashed angrily and served as a warning to those who might approach him in his blackest of moods. His mare, stolen by those who would favor the sultan with a most prized gift, and the possible defection of Bellina heated his thoughts. Squinting into the sun, he saw the wavering image of a horse and rider bounding over already steaming ground, a cloud of sand billowing around the animal's legs.

Even as Ismeran dismounted, a small, brown boy caught the stallion's reins and pulled him away to be

121

watered. Revealing parched lips, Ismeran yanked off the white cloth that wrapped his face. "Captain, I fear your suspicions are correct. There are two trails that lead from here. The Bashaw, there," he drew his hand from beneath his sleeve and pointed to where two separated groves of brush poked the horizon. "And another, over there."

Ismeran stood before his master in silence, dreading Surek's reaction to his news. He breathed heavily, watching him grip the handle of his sword, straining the skin over his knuckles. Nervously, he stepped back and bowed deeply before what was a volcano about to erupt. Surek commanded in a taut voice. "Get the camels. The horses will not last in the noon sun."

Naqu could not avoid Surek's piercing stare cast down from the mountainous back of a Bactrian camel. He feared his fate if Surek met with Rashid. His plan would too quickly spill from Rashid's lips like piss from a camel. Naqu thought it wise not to be in camp when the captain returned. He waited until a cloud of dust devoured the ten riders and then took his own departure.

The party of camels did not penetrate far into the desert before the trail of craters the horses left behind disappeared. However, it was enough to give Surek a direction and clue to the riders' destination. The vast desert spread before him like melted butter. Only a fool—or someone who knew the desert well—would venture into it. If Bellina was fool enough she would be dead by now, and he did not take her for that much of a fool, but she was desperate enough to leave if someone had tempted her enough. A horse would not get far. Whoever was helping her would meet with others for a fresh mount or they would travel with one of the desert tribes. If they met with nomads, she would be lost to him. He stopped to confer with Ismeran, and he, too, thought they would join one of the desert tribes.

"You think I am a fool to go to all this trouble for a woman, Ismeran?" Surek asked, squinting in the sun, trying to detect any speck of movement on the horizon.

"No, Master. I would do the same, but . . . when I found her, I would not love her."

Surek was surprised that Ismeran had been so bold to speak this way. Even through his silence, Surek had always known how he felt about Bellina. Ismeran would have had his revenge for being made a fool of by a woman.

As if reading Surek's thoughts, Ismeran replied, "It is not the way of your people."

Surek flashed a warning at his horseman. "My people are those that serve the sultan." It was dangerous for Ismeran to know so much, thought Surek. Ismeran was getting suspicious of his loyalties and would keep a close watch on him. In turn, Surek would take guard.

The sun was relentless, and so was Surek's determination to find Bellina. His temper began to match the broiling temperatures. When he got her, he would follow Ismeran's suggestions.

*　　　*　　　*

Bellina winced as another fire ant stung her skin with its bite. Rashid had tied her to a stick of a tree after he caught her crawling away from their resting place. It was foolish of her to attempt such a thoughtless escape, and now, unable to brush them away, she had to endure the ants. Rashid grinned at her with a checkerboard smile before settling on the cloth he had spread beneath him. It did not take him long to slip into a deep sleep, once he was sure she could not get away.

Before long, the spot of shade around Bellina began to shrink, exposing her legs to the burning rays of the sun. Would he never wake up? she wondered as her skin turned from pink to red. Where was Surek? And why was this pig so confident that he could sleep in the open like this, she anguished. Then she felt a vibration in the ground beneath her. Her hopes of being rescued from this foul beast were now more than a prayer. Those were horses pounding the ground and they were coming closer. She begged the saints that Rashid would not wake but he did, with a start that rose him quickly from his bed. He slid his dagger through the rope that bound her to the tree, but she planted her feet in the sand as he tried to pull her to his mount.

"Come here, bitch! You are more trouble than— Ugh!" Rashid folded in pain from the swift and unexpected knee jammed between his legs. Before he could grab her, Bellina was already a yard away.

Rashid viewed the frenzied approach of riders rising over the peak of a mountain of white sand. A quick glance at Bellina convinced him it would be best to leave her here than lose time battling with her.

No amount of gold was worth his life. With only a moment of hesitation, he climbed upon his mount, kicked it furiously, and hoped no one would think he was worth the chase. It wasn't long before his thoughts were dashed. Two of the riders had veered from the group and began to eat up the distance between them and Rashid.

Bellina's flight across the sand was soon slowed by its sinking softness. She could not give up. She would not let Rashid have her to sell into slavery. The pounding rhythm came closer still. She was losing ground and would have to face him too exhausted to fight. Unable to carry her further, her legs buckled and then collapsed beneath her weight. She held her head in her hands as the pounding grew louder. When it stopped, she heard the heavy breathing of animals all around her. She looked up in disbelief at the humped creatures that caged her with their legs. Their riders, wrapped in white muslin, looked like mummies come to life. All forms of swords hung from their waists, each sparkling with the slightest movement.

One rider stood out among the others. He was cloaked in black and approached her as deliberately as a spector seeking a soul for the devil. His camel stopped a few yards from her and kneeled at a touch from his rider's crop. The ominous-looking figure steadily stalked her. With the hot wind struggling to escape from the folds of his black caftan, she thought he looked like a great winged bird ready to claim its prey. The closer he came, the quicker her heart beat. Though the sun had dulled her thinking, there was something familiar about the dark figure. He towered above her, looking down on her crouched form with eyes as sharp as the sword that gleamed at his side.

"Surek," she breathed in relief. She pressed her face against the soft leather boots and waited for him to carry her in his arms once more to safety. But instead, she felt a crushing grip enclose her arm. She was pulled with a jerk from her knees to face the dark scowl of a stranger. He held both wrists in one hand and lifted her to her toes. He stared into her confused face with a look so penetrating and cold that in spite of the desert heat, she shivered. This was the spector from the ravaged streets of Constantinople, not the Surek she had come to know in the past months. There was not a trace of the gentleness he had shown her, only a vengeful anger.

With long, deliberate strides, Surek led his captive to the coffee-colored camel kneeling in the sand. So as not to fuel his wrath, Bellina obediently threw one leg over the beast and settled into a sculpted blanket without saying a word.

"Ismeran, find the Bashaw and return Kayaska to me. And the fool who fled from us—there is no need to return him." Bellina flinched at the tone of cruel vindictiveness and the smile of Ismeran who would enjoy dealing out Surek's command. Two other men joined Ismeran and trotted off in the direction of Rashid and the janisarries who no doubt had caught up with the scoundrel.

Though silent, Bellina's thoughts whipped into a rage, interrupted only by her struggle to remain seated on the camel's hilly back. What right had he to be angry with her? As though she had betrayed him!

126

Did he think she would leave willingly with a desert rat like Rashid? Whatever his thoughts, she was surely going to vent hers when they were alone.

The ride back to camp seemed as though it would never end. When they finally stopped to rest, Bellina thought her legs would never be closer together than a foot. "Saints above! This man means to torture me as much as he can," she complained to herself, not being able to bear the silence any longer. Her complaints were answered by one of Surek's pointed glares.

Noticing Bellina's face was a mask of red, Surek untied the sash from his waist and approached her with it. She stood stoically, her jaw set firmly in defiance. "I am not fool enough to run from you in the middle of this desert. I do not think it is necessary to tie me with that cloth."

"I did not ask what you thought," he coldly replied as he wrapped her head and face with the sash. "Your cohort, whoever he is, did not take care in protecting your alabaster Venetian skin from our 'barbarian sun.'"

"Cohort!" Her muffled voice protested. "How could you think . . . So that is why you're acting as if your last horse was stolen," she sputtered like a dying fire.

Turning on his heels, he left her standing alone, to simmer in the sun if she liked. He would not give her the satisfaction of an argument before his men. No, he would wait until they were back in camp.

Ten

After a few sharp commands from Surek, Bellina was nearly dragged from their camel by two janissaries and was cannoned into one of the camp's tents. Too drained from riding in the desert sun to stand, she merely sat upon the Persian carpet to survey her surroundings. The new accommodations were apparently acquired from one of Surek's lieutenants. It was not as spacious as the old tent, but displayed rich crimson, gold, and blue carpets which were hung around the perimeter of the tent and spread over the floor. Elaborately etched lanterns descended from every corner, their soft veil of light filtered over a scattering of pillows.

Before Bellina could catch her breath, two sun-baked slaves entered, struggling with a massive copper tub. Bellina's skin was so dry she ached to sink to her chin in water and soak for a week. The sight of the boys sloshing buckets of cool water over the tub's rim was enough to make her heart soften and forgive Surek for his temper. She removed her sandals and untwisted the sash from around her head, causing a waterfall of hair to spill over her shoulders. At that moment a shard of light sliced through the tent, at its beginning, a silhouette of a man posed for a moment. When the opening closed, erasing daylight, she let her eyes focus until she could see him clearly.

Recognizing Surek, a smile began to curve her lips, but the impulse was soon stifled. She could detect a contained anger in the way his muscles moved when he approached her. He walked around her like a tiger circling its prey before the attack. As much as she feared the savage in him, she would not cower under those glaring eyes. She stood to face him. Without a word, or removing his own eyes from hers, he unwrapped the black cloth from his face. In all his fury he was incredibly handsome. His features were as if carved from smooth sandstone. A black beard and tanned skin accented his masculinity. Bellina felt drawn to him and intrigued by the danger. She wanted to embrace him at that moment, but stood still in rigid defiance.

He tossed his caftan aside, revealing almost European britches that stretched across the broadness of his thighs. Bellina could not help her lowered gaze. He removed his white caffa slowly, opening it to his waist. She felt the shallow quickness of her breath as she longed for his touch, but was at the same time fearful of what fueled his passion. She knew she should flee from him as he undressed before her, but like one mesmerized by the hypnotic sway of a cobra, she could not move.

Surek's lips thinned into a faint smile as he noted the agony he caused her. He planned to tame her fiery belligerence so she would never leave him again. He would make her want him above everyone and everything.

When Surek sank into the cool oasis within the copper walls of the tub, Bellina could no longer remain silent. All the fury in her escaped like the jinn from Aladdin's lamp.

"You are a barbarian!" She shrieked incredulously. "To drag me through that inferno like an errant slave. To order your men to throw me around like a sack of meal; not to mention to have had to endure the likes of that, that *nomad* dragging me about!" she huffed until she was almost out of breath, mindless of how beautiful she looked to him, standing with her legs apart and her delicate hands spread over her hips. Her shirt strained and parted to reveal an untanned portion of breast.

"That was your very unwise decision, Bellina," he smoothly replied through an infuriatingly smug grin. "Did you expect the likes of him to set you off sailing for Venice? Believe me, you are better off here." He paused, giving her a hard look. "As long as you don't try to deceive me again."

Bellina seethed as she watched him squeeze water from a large sea sponge. So he thinks I arranged the fire, well, let him go to blazes then, she cursed silently.

The trickle of water drew her attention to the bath. Knowing how she craved water gave him a weapon to

130

taunt her with. If she was to rile him now, she would die of thirst. Trying to curb her sharp tongue, she moved closer to the tub and let her fingers dip into the cool liquid. "In my country, a gentleman would have offered a lady a private bath."

"You're not in your country, Bellina, and you said yourself that I'm a barbarian, so why should I offer you a bath?" He leaned over to cup his hand under her chin. His eyes followed a rivulet of water trail down her neck and between her breasts. "In my country, the women bathe the men."

Bellina's eyes sparked with anger as she snapped her hand from the water. She began to rise, but her move was anticipated by Surek. He wrapped his fingers around her forearm and pulled her toward him. The edge of the tub seemed to slice through her stomach as he held her there. Bellina pushed against its rim with her free arm in an attempt to escape being pulled in. She felt his warm breath run over her skin as he nibbled at her neck. His hand caressed and glided across her shoulder, coaxing her shirt over her shoulders. Ivory breasts fell from the opened shirt. She could feel her nipples touch the soft curls covering his chest. Her grip weakened and she was pulled further over the tub. A last attempt to regain her composure was suppressed by the hypnotic effect of his caresses. His teeth gently grazed her neck, then she felt the warm wetness of his tongue trace the inside of her ear, a tingling spread down her spine to her toes.

Surek felt her lose control under the spell of his expert lovemaking. She was his if he wanted her, and

131

there was little she could do about it. His hand ran over her shoulder and across her chest to fondle the breasts that hung over him. He felt a surge in his loins that needed to be satisfied. Crushing her against him, he pulled her over the tub's rim and into the water.

With a resounding splash, Bellina was rudely awakened from the erotic trance. Pushing Surek back, she thrashed wildly, trying to untangle her legs from pants that now clung around her knees. Water from the tub flowed over the sides as she wrestled with him. With help from him, her pants were removed, leaving her legs free, and a most vulnerable part exposed. Bellina tried to stand but slipped back into the water and Surek's embrace. He put his full weight upon her, pressing her to the back of the tub. She could feel the presence of his manhood between her legs as his mouth covered hers in a kiss that crushed her lips against her teeth. She felt his hands follow the curve of her back and spread over the roundness of her buttocks. Her only escape was to sink beneath the water. She dunked her head and managed to end his embrace. Her folly amused Surek so he leaned back and bellowed so that she felt quite foolish.

"How long did you expect to remain under water? Are my kisses so horrid you would sooner drown?" She looked like a sea nymph to him as she shook the water from her hair.

"Let me out of this tub!" she demanded as soon as her breath returned.

"Not until we bathe, love." His white teeth flashed

and his eyes glittered with mischievous intent. He longed to feel his fingers slip over every inch of her body, and he would hold her there until his desire was granted.

"You are a barbarian!" Bellina turned her back to him in exasperation.

Eleven

Bellina woke from a deep sleep with a start. A hoopla of gruff voices assaulted her. It began as a low drone, increasing in volume as the sound crept inside, penetrating the canvas of her dreams. Her thoughts drifted from the commotion outside the tent. How different from those mornings in Venice when she was afforded the luxury of a down-stuffed bed and coverlet. She tried to imagine sinking into the center of such a cloud. There were no abrupt awakenings then, the days were so predictable, except for the time Conte Sordici "accidentally" entered her room. How could father have fancied him so, she wondered. Then she toyed with the idea of which would be worse, being sent to a marriage to one she detested, or to remain here to be tormented by Surek's ever-changing moods. She smiled to herself. Maybe she should be happy to have escaped a certain marriage to a pompous fool.

Her smile disappeared when she stretched and rubbed against the rough sheet that covered her. The raw pain of burned skin brought back memories of the day before. She moaned to herself while trying not to let anything touch the blaze of fire that ran over her. In the midst of her agony, Surek lifted the flap of tent and studied her. His expression was not of concern but of mild amusement.

"In your country, one would say that God has punished you."

"Perhaps he has," she retorted sharply. "It seems I have burned somewhat and am here with the devil himself." She glowered at his patronizing smile. "You're in a jolly mood."

He flipped a silver-handled dagger from his boot, thrust its point into the flesh of an orange, and took pleasure in shaving the skin from the fruit. "That I am. Thievery has been avenged, Kayaska has returned."

"Do you always get what you want?" Bellina challenged him.

"Always." He let his eyes touch her intimately. "Eventually."

Quickly Bellina changed the subject, not wanting to hear the details of Kayaska's return. She was sure the Bashaw, who had devised his own plan to steal the mare and present it to the sultan, had been dealt with harshly before his imminent death.

"Well, I'd like some water. Do I always have to beg for water?" She threw her words at him testily.

Surek curled his fingers in her hair and twisted it around the back of his hand until the tension pulled her head back. His face was so close to hers, she felt the warmth of his breath as he spoke.

"Beg? No, but water is scarce, so it demands a high

135

price. Besides, water will not cool your skin."

She stepped back from him when he released her. "And you must have something in mind that will cool my skin?"

"Indeed, it will cool your bad temper, too," he laughed.

"Hah! My bad temper! Are you intending to send me back to Venice? For that is what will soften my temper."

It infuriated her to have him bargain with her so smugly. Yet she knew that if he held her in his arms, she would all too quickly fall victim to his every wish. He had the power to erase all memory and longing for Venice with one kiss, but she would not let him that close to her again, for fear he would discover her weakness.

"Very well, Bellina. I'll not argue with you this morning. Your meals will be sent to you. I will not see you until tomorrow. If you wish to suffer all day and night with that burn, then so be it." He gave her no more than ten seconds to reply, then turned to leave.

"Surek," her voice choked with the effort it took to speak. "All right."

A demoniacal grin cut across his face, causing her knees to come apart. "Take your clothes off."

"I will not!" She had already regretted accepting his help.

"Bellina," he slowly rolled her name over his tongue, showing a strained patience. "I told you I would not banter with you."

"Go away. I've changed my mind."

"Since you have been such a fool, you no longer

136

have the privilege of making any decisions concerning your well-being. Now do as I say. Or I will take them off myself!"

Bellina bit her lip as she peeled away the muslin shirt under Surek's stare. Her pants were slower to come off, but he did not mind the delay. She looked like a vision rising from the pile of white cloth folded around her feet. His eyes raked over her body in a long, slow, sweep that spared no inch of skin, no curve or mound of soft flesh. He felt the effect of her beauty pulse through his veins and swell his manhood like the tide under the spell of a full moon. He lifted her mane of hair in his hands and let it fall between his fingers. She was frozen before him like a frightened rabbit, as if her stillness would somehow make her invisible to the enemy. Is that how she saw him? If so, she would make a formidable, yet delightful, foe to conquer. He let a hand drop to her shoulder and trail along the curve of her back, delighting in the smoothness of her skin.

Bellina thought that her legs would betray her and buckle at any moment, and then she would collapse in front of him. How could she let his touch command her? She swayed against her will, but was quickly engulfed in Surek's arms. He drew her body against his and crushed her so tightly to him that she could hardly breath. Her senses were overwhelmed by his closeness. The heavy scent of musk and spice was like a drug that calmed her spirit and sent her mind swirling in a whirlwind of desire. The coarseness of his clothes rubbed against her nakedness, sending ripples of goose bumps over her skin. She flushed at the thought that he could feel the hardness of her nipples pressed against his chest and wriggled protesting in his embrace. Her squirming only provoked a tighter hold that threatened to break her ribs.

"You're hurting me," she protested weakly.

"If you behave, I will only give you pleasure," he promised in a throaty voice. "Now sit here, so I can have a better look at those burns."

Bellina obeyed as he scrutinized the red skin of her arms and ankles and the bronze mask that ran over her cheeks and nose. She watched silently as he unflasked a slender-necked carafe and ceremoniously poured some of its contents into the bowl of his hand. Even though he kneeled next to her, he had to lower his head to look into her eyes. A smile stretched across his face as he noted her tenseness.

"You look as though I'm going to beat you. Which I should," he added as he lightly brushed his oiled fingers over her face. Bellina closed her eyes so as not to sink into the black depths of his eyes, now so close to hers. "Ismeran would have me bury you up to this lovely neck," he continued, while tracing his fingers from behind her ears, down the length of her neck, and finally encircling it.

He rotated his fingers in small massaging circles, moving up her neck and then down to her shoulders and across the base of her throat. Bellina felt his touch slip lightly across her skin as he rubbed the soothing oil over her chest. Her anxiety peaked when she realized he would surely feel the rapid beating of her heart under his hand.

He lowered his head and pressed his lips to the softened skin of her neck, branding her with his kiss.

138

When she instinctively backed away from him, he caught her shoulders in his hands and held her tightly. She suffered in rigid silence, wishing he would stop, but wanting more. Her heart beat so furiously, the pounding sound filled her ears. He gently caught her earlobe between his teeth, then nipped her skin in a burning path to her heart.

To his satisfaction, she could not suppress a low gasp nor the shiver he felt run through her. "Why do you fight me so, and deny yourself pleasure? It was not so long ago you were the child playing the woman. Now you are afraid to cross over that boundary." His lips continued to savor the sweet taste of her skin as he breathed his words to her with hot puffs of breath that warmed her soul with desire. "Your heart beats like that of a captive bird."

Bellina tore his hand from her heart and summoned enough stamina to angrily snap at the bemused captain. "Because you are keeping me captive. You have horses and camels. Take me to Constantinople. Put me on a vessel for Venice. You are always reminding me how much trouble I am. My uncle will pay you for your trouble."

"It's all so simple to you." He looked at her with disdain. "Is that what you said to the desert rat who I found you with? Haven't you learned from that?" He laughed at her naivete. "A beautiful woman traveling alone. Just imagine the impossibility of that! Indeed, I am only protecting you. Which is not an easy task. Besides, the sultan would pay more for you than your uncle could—if I was interested in gold."

Bellina held her retort and stiffened under the expanse of his calloused palm as it slid up and down her arm, relieving the fiery burn of her skin.

"If you don't stop squirming, I'll have to stake you to the ground—as has been recommended!"

His touch raised goose flesh that spread over her in a blush that made the whiteness of her breasts and abdomen glow like the sand under the salmon-colored rays of a setting sun. There was no hiding the effects of his touch in light of her nakedness. The coarseness of his hand slipped over and around her full breasts and rubbed her nipples until they stiffened and peaked under his palm. He lowered his head and buried his face in the soft cleft of flesh and relished the smell and taste of her. His hands flared over her hips as he planted a row of searing nibbles down the center of her belly to the triangle of matted hair between her thighs.

Bellina was spinning in a whirlpool of desire. Unable to climb from the cyclone that held her within its spinning walls, she fell deeper and deeper into its swirling center. She tried to recover her senses when Surek straightened to pour some more of the scented oil into his hand, but she was not as quick in her halfhearted retreat as he was in pulling her back to him.

"Your ankles are as red as the banners that fly over this tent." He sounded so cool, she thought, while her heart pounded and her flesh steamed from his touch.

She feared if she did not please him, he would sell her as he said he could. But if she did, she would be no better than an odalisque, and that she would *not* become. Her troubled thoughts were gradually dulled by the erotic effect of his hands as he kneaded

140

droplets of oil over her ankles and feet, then her calves, and around her knees.

"How do you feel?" He asked her, smiling, so satisfied with himself.

Bellina lifted her chin and pulled her knees up tightly. "Your oil is quite amazing. I think you've gotten all the spots, thank you."

Before she could rise, he placed a hand on her shoulder and leaned his weight into her, forcing her to fall back into a mound of pillows. "I think not," he whispered huskily into her ear, sending a shiver down her spine.

The force of his chest pressed against hers and pinned her to the floor. She tried to free her legs as she pushed her palms against his wide chest, but only provoked a low chuckle. He lowered a heavy leg across hers to still their thrashing. His full lips bruised hers, crushing a whimper of protest into the back of her throat. His knee edged along her inner thigh, prying her legs apart. The texture of the cloth stretched over his knee rubbed sensuously against her skin, sending a wave of excitement coursing through her. He surrounded her shoulders in one sweep of his arm, holding her tightly, forcing the hardness of her nipples into his opened shirt.

Reaching down to the soft inside of her thigh, his fingertips revolved in ever-increasing circles of pleasure. Moving higher, his hand reached between her legs and slowly caressed the moist folds of skin. Bellina felt her hips move rhythmically against her will as he explored her intimately.

She no longer rejected his closeness, but drew him to her and accepted the touch of his tongue over her

141

lips. She seeped deeper into the depths of passion, she lost all sensibility until the presence of another brought her back to reality.

When Ismeran cleared his throat, Surek turned to give the gloating lieutenant a glare of disapproval for his lack of discretion. "I beg your forgiveness, Captain, but as you commanded, Kayaska is ready."

Surek stood and dismissed him, but not before Ismeran could throw a look of contempt at Bellina. Incensed, Bellina turned her anger on Surek.

"You are barbarians! In Venice one would have at least *knocked!*"

Surek's laugh rumbled through the tent at her silly remark. "Ismeran should have announced himself, but maybe he did try," he said, while tying a black sash around his middle and thrusting a curved sword securely in its sheath. He grabbed her tilted chin and sunk his black eyes so deeply into hers, she was almost once again under his spell. "But we will soon change that fact, my dear, and become civilized to please you. I will leave this with you." He placed the carafe in her hands. "And when I return we will begin where we left off."

Bellina shot her hand under his, forcing it away. A move she quickly regretted when he wound her hair into his hand and pulled her to her feet.

"Like the city, Bellina, you too shall come to me."

Twelve

After a day and a half of riding with only occasional stops for rest, Surek met the lone rider as the setting sun plunged the desert into chilly darkness. The man was ragged like a beggar, but the intelligence that lit his eyes, his cultured if accented Arabic, and his quality mount, all belied his appearance.

"This will be the last time here," Surek said. "It's getting too risky for me, and I may be changing my location anyway."

"Mehmet?" the man questioned.

"No, no," Surek shook his head. "A subordinate of mine who, unfortunately, is too efficient. And too loyal to his sultan. He would not hesitate one minute if he had any suspicions."

The man's lips curled in a disdainful frown. "Send the bothersome asp on an errand into the desert—to me."

Surek shook his head, "That won't be necessary."

The sharp little eyes studied Surek carefully.

"Listen, Captain," he said, exaggerating his title. "Don't ever acquire these people as friends, for that would indeed be a fatal mistake. Enough of this! What do you have for me?"

"Mehmet plans no action as of now, and I doubt if there will be any in the near future," Surek replied. "For now there is the city with his new mosque and a new palace to take his attentions. Also he is eager for trade to be reestablished. Once that happens and his stores have been replenished, the Spahiglani will ride again."

"To Muscovy?"

Surek met the demanding eyes, "That is the best possibility."

"How many? And where?"

Kayaska shifted and Surek placed a calming hand on her neck. "I have no knowledge as of yet."

The man arched his brows, "Well! We must find that out, now, mustn't we?"

"Listen, Markenov," Surek growled, "When I know, you will, and no sooner."

"It's just that it's been so long," the little man said, "and you've given me so little."

Surek's eyes flashed, "To move faster would evoke suspicion and cost lives. Muscovite lives."

"You have changed, Captain," Markenov spat. "You've been too long a captain of the Spahiglani." He turned his horse sharply to leave, but paused adding, "Or perhaps it's this girl I've heard of. Nothing like a woman to soften a man's senses or loyalties."

Surek put Markenov's remarks behind him. They had never liked each other: they only served a common cause. However, Surek could not help but feel a certain amount of surprise that Markenov had heard of Bellina. One of his spies must be planted in the Spahiglani troop. That would be like him. Surek would furnish the information and Markenov would claim credit. It would be more difficult, but next time Surek would get the word through to Muscovy in his own way.

Surek paused once more in his travels and shared water with Kayaska, his thoughts turning too easily to Bellina. She had become such a thorn in his side. He had ranted in anger that he would conquer her, but in truth, she was profoundly affecting him so much it was disturbing. Away from her his mind was consumed by her image, and it was hard to bring his thoughts to bear on the difficulties his responsibilities brought. In the sun's glare he closed his eyes and could almost feel her soft skin and smell her sweet hair. Despite all—Markenov, Ismeran, the crazy twists and turns of fate, and most of all Bellina herself—he would someday make her entirely, totally his. Maybe then his heart would know peace.

Bellina could feel the desert heat increase with each circle of the tent she paced. Another day. Another day to listen through the tent as the Spahiglani went about their duties, to sweat, to think, and to do absolutely nothing. He was not supposed to be gone this long. It wouldn't be half as boring if she could at least have Surek here to spar with. Instead, her mind took her through a jumble of memories, creating two conflicting desires: a longing for home and an ache to feel Surek's arms around her. How could she betray her feelings and actually desire him?

He had been gone now three days. Surely not a long time, but enough so that she was starting to mumble to herself as she oiled one of Kayaska's bridles. It was unfair that he should be able to leave this camp whenever and for however long he wanted, leaving her to endure long days and endless nights that held nothing but torturous thoughts. She began to feel the resentment swell and peak like a wave about to crash against a rock.

Each day she had the same heated sun broiling the tiny tent, the same insects to bat at, and the same slaves to bring her meals. Trying to converse with them was like trying to pry a few words from Ismeran, who she knew spoke her language. Silence was all they afforded her. They saved their small talk, arguments, and curses for each other. The only excitement to break this lull of monotonous existence was the morning she poured a sleeping snake from her water pitcher. Her screams brought a small army of Spahiglani to her side, only to witness the last bit of tail disappear under the tent. From their departing scowls, she was certain no one would rush to her aid again.

Far worse than the days were the nights, when even the camp outside lay in cold stillness and she had only her thin blanket for comfort. How she wished she could hear Surek's breath next to her ear as he slept upon the pallet. She would stretch out expecting to touch him, meeting only the chill of an empty sheet. It was then that she felt the most alone and neglected. The feelings he evoked made her hate him with a passion that was as great as her desire for him.

On the fourth day, Bellina put the bridle aside, her embroidery aside, and told the slaves she was fasting. Before her stood Surek's collection of boxes, saved from the fire, each day looked at and walked around, but never noticed with interest until now. Perhaps she should give them a closer look, she told herself, shrugging off any guilt about prying. There had to be something their contents would reveal to help her pass her idle time. Perhaps a tablet to write on or even a book!

Carefully she lifted the first lid and prodded a finger into his possessions. There was a turban's length of scarlet silk curled at the top, and under that a bejeweled ribbon sitting next to a plain if unusually shaped stone. More fabric, clothes no doubt, and then the empty bottom. She replaced the lid, slid the box to the floor, and opened the one beneath it. This one hid a ceremonial sword carefully cased, a polished cup and brush, a roll of felt, and a leather satchel that revealed a pair of worn boots. She sniffed in disgust. What was he saving those for? She fingered the roll of felt, met a lump, and carefully unwrapped it. It held a wooden square, hinged on one edge, elaborately carved and highlighted with gilt. Opened, it revealed a woman's face, beautifully delicate, offset by a rush of curls as dark as Bellina's own hair. The artist had skillfully captured a mischievous glint in her wide and expressive eyes, and an almost concealed smile. Part of a blue and cream gown, not too different from the ones Bellina had worn in Venice, was included with detailed

147

brush strokes. Below the image Bellina read "Beloved Tatiana." Bellina's mind jumped. Who was she? Why wasn't she dressed in a caftan and veiled like most Moslem wives? If this was a wife! She turned it over looking for more clues—a date or a place.

Suddenly the miniature was snatched out of her hand. So absorbed in thought she had not heard a presence near her.

"Do you never cease to search out trouble?" Surek's eyes narrowed as he snapped the wooden picture closed and began wrapping it up in the felt. "There is nothing here that concerns you," he growled.

"I was looking for a book, or parchment to write on," Bellina stumbled.

"You didn't stop to think that you were prying where you shouldn't! Allah! I find you *gyaours* an undisciplined and unmannerly lot. I can't even trust you alone for a few days." He closed the box with a thud, arranging them the way they were.

Bellina felt the heat in her face but could say nothing. It hurt that he labeled her with the insulting name she often heard the others call the foreigners. She watched through blurred vision as he laid his scimitar upon a hassock and unwrapped his turban. One of the slaves called and entered with their midday meal, but Bellina didn't take much notice. She tried to catch Surek's eyes.

"I was looking for a book or something to do. I stare at the sides of this oven all day, every day, and I am going mad!" She protested vainly, her voice starting to edge with anger.

"Didn't I leave you that bridle to polish?" he

countered. "And later I'll bring you down to the stream to wash our clothes if you want."

Now she was really angry. "What do you think I have a mind of? Sand? Do you think all I need is your chores and life will be a merry adventure? In Venice—"

"I know, I know," his hand went up in defense. "You lived a life of luxury, your every whim fulfilled by an eager father, and every night you danced at masked balls and dined on delicacies from around the world in wonderful, magical Venice! Here you are my slave to do with as I please. Remember that! Come, sit, and eat!"

Her guilt at prying burned away in a sudden flash of hate and jealousy. Her hands twitched at her side, her anger bubbling with no way for release. This damned tent, she couldn't even retreat to release furious tears.

"And don't get any ideas about throwing your food again," he growled, "or you'll be busier than you ever dreamed washing down this tent."

"Who is that girl in the miniature?" Bellina cried. "Another one you 'saved' only to imprison?"

Surek snorted in disgust, "It's none of your concern."

"Where is she?" She continued relentlessly, ignoring the throbbing vein at his temple that warned of an explosion of anger. "Abandoned, once you tired of her? Sold off in the bazaars?"

Surek grabbed her and pulled her down sharply next to him. "Eat! And not another word."

They finished their meal silent and resentful, and afterward when he pushed the trays back and stretched upon his pallet to nap away the strain of travel, Bellina rose to seek her own.

"Stay," Surek spoke gently this time, beckoning her.

Stiffly she sat back down. He pulled her into his arms and, despite her reluctance, nuzzled her neck. "I'm sorry," he murmured into her ear, "I know this camp doesn't have much to offer you, but you must make the best of it. And you shouldn't be snooping in my belongings. I don't have anything of use to you anyway."

Bellina said nothing, which was unlike her. Surek felt the wetness of tears against his face. This was bothering her more than he thought. But what could he do? It was dangerous for her to leave this tent too often. After all, she was one woman among two hundred seventy-six soldiers who were as hot, bored, and edgy as she. They would welcome any chance to create a bit of excitement, and Bellina was too much of a temptation. And the last time she was looking for a diversion she ended up breaking a rib. Surek sighed and held her close.

It was several days later, after another dry heated day, that Surek returned to the tent and tossed a bundle to Bellina. "Try that on," he said to the quizzical arch of her brows.

Her heart leaped with curiosity; anything new was welcome. It was so soft. A new fabric from the city perhaps? Surek would probably like her in a new gown. The satchel jerked open as her eager fingers broke the knot and a foul odor hit her nostrils. She pulled out the dirty trousers and tunic of a Spahig-lani slave.

150

She glared at Surek. "I don't view this as a jest but a cruel insult. If you think for one moment that I am going to wear—" Then her eyes lit up. "Unless we are going riding!"

Surek was laughing, "Put them on. I want to see if they fit. I'm not jesting. Don't forget the sandals on the bottom." In a moment she was dressed. "What an eye I have," Surek said, taking in her appearance, "A perfect fit. You should be able to pass for one of my boys once we hide your hair. Tomorrow we'll steal a few moments and go to the bazaar."

The breath she had been holding sputtered out, "Oh! The bazaar! Do you mean in Constantinople?" She raced on, "Of course! That's probably the closest one."

Surek studied her. "We will go only if you promise to obey me in all matters, for in the city your life will depend on it."

"Of course! Oh, thank you!" She bounced and hugged him, touched that he had made such an effort on her behalf, and laughed when his nose wrinkled. Mischievously, she pulled his face down and kissed him deeply, sensuously, and pressed her body against him. Despite her masculine garb, she felt very much like a woman, and she was pleased when she felt him become hard and rigid with longing.

"Take these dirty things off," he said impatiently.

She kissed him again and turned to their pallet.

"No," he murmured, "here."

She trembled, paused, then lifted the tunic over her head. It strained over her full breasts, releasing them reluctantly. Surek's hands caught them and kneaded her hard nipples between his fingers.

"Only I will know what you'll be hiding beneath those rags," he said, and he pulled down her trousers, tossing them far, then pulled Bellina down with him. As she lay on top of him, his insistent member nudging against her thighs, she felt a tingling heat and weakness spread, a desire that pushed all other thoughts, questioning or hesitant, from her mind. She found her fingers loosening his clothes, pulling them off. Their eyes met, each drinking in the other's love while their bodies strained to get closer.

"Oh Bellina," Surek cried with longing, "I need you now!" He kissed her mouth, her neck, her breasts.

"And I, you," she answered, guiding his hand to her most hidden spot. She moaned as he caressed her there with rhythmic gentle touches.

Eagerly she found and grasped his hardness in her hand, her eyes closed to heighten her other senses, and he gasped. "Come to me." And she did, feeling that first piercing with a joyous shudder, an ecstasy of closeness that was almost unbearable. She slid up and down his hot shaft, taking it in as deeply as she could. With a moan Surek grasped her hips, and pulling her down even further, stabbed into her forcefully. Bellina felt he filled her entire being as he never had before and with a shudder and a cry she found a golden release of desire, a love so deep it hurt. Forgotten were the arguments of yesterday for a brief suspended moment, while their hungry souls and bodies possessed each other, silencing their harried dreams and persistent nightmares.

Afterward, they both lay exhausted, she still on top of him, her face next to his, her arm cradling his head. Already she could hear his breathing slow.

Their lovemaking had brought to her heart the greatest joy of her life, but also her greatest sorrow. She knew she was his prized possession. Often she had heard the remarks of Ismeran, and she also knew what her common sense told her—she didn't have a place in a military camp and she couldn't stay here forever. And men as passionate as Surek didn't stay long with one woman. Sooner or later there would be someone else, and her value would be less dear. She didn't plan on meeting that day, certainly not as a prisoner, and her mind was a constant warring of dreamed escapes and the desire for the one man she would ever love.

Bellina kissed Surek's forehead lightly. Sleep had removed the sternness in his face and now only gentleness remained. "Tomorrow," she thought, feeling as if a knife twisted in her heart, "I will leave you, Surek, for in the rush of Constantinople, I will certainly see my chance." Her mind was made up even if her heart refused to follow.

Thirteen

Surek woke her early, before light had touched the
endless sand, for the day promised to be as hot as
those before it. Ismeran let two horses out of the dark.
Surek, of course, rode Kayaska. With hostile eyes,
Ismeran handed the reins of a little roach-backed
mare to Bellina and then turned his back on her.

"Captain, safe journey, all is secure with me." He
saluted and Surek acknowledged.

"We will return before dusk. Until then, Ismeran."

Bellina struggled onto the mare's back, her feet
clumsily finding their stirrups. Surek had already
moved Kayaska forward, but Bellina's first kick was
met with a roll of the mare's eyes and a fling of her
head. By this time Surek had doubled back, a grin
spreading over his face, and wordlessly he smacked
the miserable beast on the rump as he passed. With a
jolting leap forward, Bellina was following, but the
mare quickly settled back into an easy plod.

"Of all the Spahiglani horses," Bellina shouted at
his back, "couldn't Ismeran find me one that
moves?"

"He was following my orders," Surek laughed. "I wanted a safe horse for the city for you. You don't want to get thrown in the noisy confusion of the bazaar, do you?"

Bellina snorted, "At this speed we will never get there." And I can forget about using this horse in any escape, she added silently, and wondered if Surek could read minds.

"Here!" Surek said, reining next to her and handing over a small leather pouch, "as my servant you will keep track of my money. If I decide on a purchase at the bazaar, you will settle with the merchant. When a slave haggles, the prices drop a lot quicker than they would for Captain Edib."

Bellina weighed the heavy little bag in her hand. Was that why he wanted her with him? So he could get better prices? Perhaps he had arranged it all just for that alone. But she knew the falseness of the thought, for Surek had many other slaves. Still, she told herself, he doesn't love me. I'm better off getting away from this all.

"And of course," Surek said, giving her a smile and interrupting her thoughts, "If you see anything you want, don't hesitate—within reason, that is."

He's buying my affection, her mind raged. But of course he isn't, her heart answered, for he already had it. However, didn't he say he would conquer her like Constantinople? Was she to be no more than a concubine, now to be pampered? She had been much too willing last night, caught up in the fiery passion his body always stirred in her.

"No," Bellina said with a sharp edge in her voice. "I need nothing from you!" As Surek's eyes darkened, she continued, "After all, I'm just a slave, aren't

155

I? I wouldn't want to place myself above any of the others. I cannot accept anything from you until I'm free."

"Suit yourself," Surek said, his indifference hurting more than angry words, and he left her alone with her plodding mare.

After a while they entered the city, pushing through the myriad of people towards the bazaar. "See?" Surek said, waving a hand to encompass the whole seething, noisy bustle, "Nothing has changed. It is more vibrant than ever."

"The world has changed," Bellina said sadly, "So of course, it is different. It's changed in its heart."

"You mean *your* world has changed. And I think not because of a war that is past. You are still at war with yourself."

Surek did not like the way this day was going, nor could he understand it. Bellina had been so passionate, so willing the night before, and he knew she had looked forward to today. He thought he had calmed the turbulence in her, but something had set her off again.

The colorful tented maze of streets ahead and the raucous clash of merchants calling announced the bazaar. Here Bellina almost felt at home, for she had spent many hours with her father picking through the wares for what could be sent back to Venice for a profit. It was a feast for the senses: spices and teas scented the way as they baked in their barrels beneath the sun, brightly hued fabrics from all corners of the orient splashed across their tables, an oud maker played a lively tune, flies buzzed, metal smiths pounded, and, as always, the customers and merchants shouted at each other, often in several languages. It was a place of contrasts, for rich and poor alike walked these streets piled with a bounty of unrelated items of ranging quality. It was also a place where anything could be found, be it rare silks, trained camels, or freedom. Many a slave had escaped in the chaos of the bazaar—and many had died for it.

Surek tied Bellina's horse to Kayaska's saddle and slowly picked a path. It wasn't long before they faced a table crowded with costly treasures: maps and parchments and a couple of books—priceless beyond belief. Surek dismounted and picked up one book under the merchant's watchful gaze. He was acutely aware of Bellina's interest as he thumbed through it.

"Lovely illuminations," he said, "but I have no use whatsoever for it. Do you see anything we need?" he glanced at Bellina.

"No," Bellina said, reluctantly.

He later picked up a little flute, fingered brocades and satins, even carried a caged songbird over to her, to look up and each time ask, "Do you think we need this?"

He plays games with me, she seethed. I should have known this trip was arranged for his enjoyment, not mine.

Surek smiled to himself. Nothing was going to ruin this day for him, even Bellina's strange mood, for he knew exactly what he was going to buy her. He thought of the man he had spoken to a few weeks back. He had driven a hard bargain, but the house was worth it. It would be a place Bellina could call home, just far enough from the desert and the hectic city, but close enough to be convenient. He would show it to her after the bazaar, and once she knew of his plans, he was certain she would be content. The atmosphere of the camp antagonized her and Ismeran was right, it was no place for a woman. There was an uncertainty about Mehmet, for he could be unpredictable.

Bellina saw the rest of the day through a wavering haze of anger. He laughs at my expense, she told herself, but I will have the last laugh in the end.

If she leaped from the mare she could lose herself in the crowd easily enough, but her slave garb would brand her. Surely someone would snatch her up and detain her. A diversion was needed, but what?

She eyed Kayaska. If she could untie her horse and prick Kayaska, the mare would flee down the street, creating all sorts of havoc with many people probably straining to catch and claim her. That would surely get Surek's attention.

Yet before she could follow her thoughts with action, Surek left one of the booths and mounted Kayaska again. "Are you hungry yet?" he asked her.

"My appetite is little," she said, "By all means, eat if you wish."

"I plan to," he said, turning onto another street, "but first, there is an Arab I wish to settle a matter with."

They turned onto the wrong street at the wrong time, for down it came a covered gilded litter escorted by many tall armored eunuchs. People rushed to make way, carefully averting their eyes. This was Mehmet's sultana, or at the very least a royal concubine, and for any male to peer behind the curtains or even appear interested was met with instant death from a eunuch's scimitar. No questions asked, no answers sought.

"Damn!" Surek growled, "I wish they'd stay at the palace. Down here and don't look." He pulled Bellina from her horse. She followed the procession with her ears. Little bells tinkled, eunuchs huffed, and every now and then she heard a soft feminine giggle. "The sultana," someone whispered, and it spread like fire through the crowd. Bellina's curiosity was almost unbearable as the litter drew near and, as if sensing this, Surek tightened his hold on her.

"Captain Edib!" a silken voice called. Surek winced, recognizing the voice of Sultana Jamil. He turned, his eyes lowered. "Your Majesty," he replied. "It is good to hear your lovely voice again."

"And what a fortune to see you, Captain," Jamil purred. "It has been many seasons since last we had the pleasure to share our banquets with you."

The lady's overly familiar tone irked Bellina until she could stand it no longer, if Surek could look, why not she?

She had begun to turn slowly, a small movement unnoticed, she thought, until she heard Surek shout. She was thrown to the ground as he dove at her. Her hair raised as she felt the rush of a scimitar's blade as it sent her turban flying into the street, and people screamed, expecting a head to fall. Her scalp stung, blood dripped, but Bellina dispelled her shock with a rush of adrenalin and saw her chance.

She let momentum roll her body further, then sprung to her feet, already mixing with the scattering crowd. Rudely she pushed through two women blocking the doorway to a butcher shop.

159

"Evil jinn!" One of the women grabbed at her, falling back, and screamed, "There go my cheeses!"

Surek's head poked high above the people, hearing her voice, and rushed to follow.

Now she was trapped, not seeing another door in a panicked sweep of the store. The butcher watched her, cleaver in hand. "Out," he barked, jerking the knife at a door blocked by hanging carcasses. "I don't want any trouble here." Before his last word was out she was through the door—but Surek was quickly behind.

"No!" Bellina gasped, dodging his grasp. She zigzagged down the alleyway like a hare.

"Bellina!" Surek called, his voice alive with anger, "Stop or you'll get yourself killed!"

"Wait a minute, little slave," the old man said, catching her as she accidentally ran into him.

"Let me go!" Bellina screamed, kicking him, and at his startled yelp she leaped away. Another shop, out another door, she crossed the street, glanced behind anxiously, and couldn't see Surek. Her hair flew about her shoulders in a tangled mess; her lungs were on fire. She entered a tent that protected a wide collection of rugs in several piles. Some were hung to show their excellent weave. Bellina paused among these, trying to slow her gasps for air. Through the opening of the tent she saw Surek talking to a woman on the street and she was pointing towards the tent.

Bellina cursed as she saw Surek coming her way and hurried out the other side. The alley it opened into was deserted of people but wagons lined the street, some loaded with produce. She crouched behind one of the wagons and stifled a gasp as Surek pushed roughly out of the tent. Angrily his eyes scanned the road. Bellina tightened ever lower into a ball. He crossed the street and turned, his senses eager for a clue, shielded the sun from his eyes, and looked again. A door of one of the shops opened, and two boys carried out a basin, dumping its rancid contents into the gutter. They argued as they worked, occasionally giving the other a rough push.

Bellina moved carefully, keeping her eye on Surek as he started questioning the boys. She had to get out of here before he found her, for he *would* find her if she stayed where she was. But to run from cover now would bring his wrath instantly upon her. The wagon she crouched behind held barrels while a few of them were still unloaded, waiting on the street. Could she squeeze between them on the wagon? The space was too narrow. She turned her attention to the unloaded kegs, trying to pry the top of one open. It shifted as she turned it, coming off easily to release the pungent smell of olives, but it was empty. She closed it, quickly deciding the barrel was too large to climb easily into. Instead, she turned her attention to the wagon and its stacks of barrels. Lightly she wrapped a knuckle on them. They all seemed hollow.

Surek was still talking, gesturing sharply, so she quickly removed a lid and crawled into a barrel with the help of the wagon. The lid she shifted awkwardly until it fell back into position and effectively shut out all light and most noise. Her heart pounded in her ears, her fingers clutched tightly at the lid, afraid it would soon be ripped away, and her thoughts raced in a tumble with her emotions.

161

She could hear steps approaching. With a sudden jar, a barrel was thrown against hers, then another. Then a laugh.

"That was the best price ever! Eh, Brother? It makes me want to buy a fattened pig to roast, just to celebrate!"

"Why do you suppose a Spahiglani is talking to old Etan's boys?" a second voice asked.

"I always knew they'd get into trouble," replied the other. "Let's get out of here. I don't want to be drawn into anything. Ho, Angelina." The wagon jerked forward and was making a tight turn to leave the alley when Surek strode towards them.

"Have either of you seen a girl with black hair, dressed in the trousers and tunic of a slave?"

Brother John shook his head, "We have just come from bargaining with Atul Zaborah for an unrelieved hour. We've seen no one but him."

Surek turned from them, after slowly scanning the wagon, and uttered an oath. Bellina jumped as his fist smacked her barrel angrily. "When I find that girl, I will shackle those damned itchy legs of hers to a stake! Two stakes," he corrected.

Bellina felt the wagon move again, but it was a while before she let her fingers loosen on the lid and felt her breathing relax. She felt as if she were going to be ill. Surek was gone. But once discovered, would these men return her? She shuddered, for the thought of Surek getting his hands on her this time chilled her soul. There was no doubt in her mind that he would shackle her—or worse. She had seen the same crazed flash of anger in him when Kayaska was taken.

She had Surek's leather pouch. Perhaps these men

could be bribed. Perhaps enough would be left to buy her way onto a ship. At the very least, she needed to get out of the smelly and shabby clothes Surek had given her to wear and find something appropriate.

The wagon pitched and bucked. Bellina's legs cramped painfully, and her head hurt more. Now she felt the gash in her scalp where the scimitar had grazed her. It wasn't deep and it had clotted almost immediately, matting her hair. The voices of the two men came loosely to her, blocked for the most part by the jogging of the barrels. After awhile sleep snuck up and dragged her into its depths.

She awoke, rolling, then coming to a crashing stop. Other barrels had followed, ramming into hers with a bone-jarring smack.

"I thought we carried six full kegs to Atul," one of the men said, puzzled. "A keg here feels full."

"Of course we did Brother John, you're just getting weak is all."

"In a pig's eye! Over here. I'm opening it, help me right it."

Bellina felt her muscles tighten as the lid to her barrel was pried off.

"Ho! Brother Adrian! It's that runaway the Spahiglani captain was looking for."

Brother Adrian backed away with lips thinned in disgust. "Well, you can't stay in there, girl. Off with you! I just hope our next batch of oil doesn't go rancid. I'll have to leach that barrel myself."

"Hush," Brother John said coolly to Adrian. "Let me help you out, give me your hand." He pulled her out and she stood on wobbly legs. Adjusting her eyes to the gentle light of dusk, she found herself on the

163

grounds of a monastery standing before the two monks.

"Where am I? How far are we from the city?" she asked.

"Far enough away for that captain never to guess where you are," the rotund friar laughed. "You must be famished. How about a bath and a hot meal?"

Brother Adrian glowered. "I don't think we should get involved in this. After all, a slave is property. If we aid her, it's as good as stealing."

"I'm not a slave!" Bellina said, turning piercing eyes upon him. "That captain has held me prisoner. I'm no one's slave. I don't even belong in this wretched, heathen place! And I'm leaving and going home!" She surprised herself by bursting into tears.

Brother John engulfed her in a generous hug. The warmth of his brown robe was comforting. "Sure you're going home, and I'll do all I can to help you. Where's home, little one?"

"Venice," she sniffled.

Adrian snorted, "Another one! They all come from Venice!"

"Don't mind Brother Adrian," Brother John said, patting her. "Journeys always make him crabby. We just delivered a nice young lad from your country. Captain of a ship, he was! And I'm sure he'd take you back to your land."

"I can pay," Bellina offered.

"He's leaving before dawn, though, if the wind is right."

"I'm not making that trip again," Adrian said with a snort and turned, stamping away from them.

Brother John gave her a pat on her shoulder,

164

"We'll have to leave almost immediately. Angelina will know the way in the dark. Just a quick bite, but I'm afraid you'll have to forgo your bath, my child."

"Bellina," she said. "You may call me Bellina."

Brother John's mouth dropped, "Holy Mary, mother of God!" He stared, walking a slow circle. "Of course! You're the one he was looking for."

She was confused, her mind still on Surek.

"Now I see it." The friar almost shouted in glee, scrutinizing her, "Bellina Magela D'Rossalini. That ship can't leave without you."

And when he told Bellina about Miquel and his search, she felt her knees buckling and she slumped to the ground.

Fourteen

It was a bright and clear morning, the sea sparkled with the brilliance of a multitude of gems, as if someone had spilled the contents of the world's riches upon her. Jib sails fluttering in farewell, the *Portia Regalia* silently drifted over the bed of jewels and left Port Solomon.

Miquel thought it a miracle when the monk had returned with Bellina a few days before. Throwing himself into the task of preparing to sail, his thoughts were free of Bellina, directed only to overseeing last-minute mending of canvas, stocking of supplies for the long journey, and tarring between the dry planks that baked and spread apart in the sun.

Bellina leaned against the rail and welcomed a shower of salty mist. Sunlight played in the spray, sending little rainbows of color through the air. Miquel thought the marriage of spray and light made her look eerily transparent. To assure himself that she was real, his hand reached out to feel the warmth that lay beneath her damp, glistening skin.

It was a boyhood fantasy of his to think of marrying her. Yet even if her father would have permitted it, a home in Venice could not have contained him for long. He knew she could only be in his dreams.

She caught his hand between hers, stirring him from his thoughts, and pressed his calloused fingertips to her lips.

"Oh, Miquel, I still can't believe I am truly safe. Constantinople is now just a speck soon to be devoured completely by this ocean."

"True, soon we will be embraced by the light of San Marco, and you will be delivered unharmed to a family which, no doubt, has been grieving these past months."

She wrapped her arms around his neck, just as she had as a child when her father had stolen her away to the docks. Only now she was far from the child who chased the ship's cats from stern to bow while her father conducted his inspections of the hold's exotic contents. With faltering fingers, Miquel unlocked her embrace and lightly brushed a kiss over her hands. He knew full well Conte Sordici would be waiting for them. The *Portia Regalia* was a well-known caravel in Venice. Sprite urchins would spread the news of its arrival hours before its sails expelled their last breath of air. He did not want to return with a cargo of silks and idle gossip. It was enough that they had to contrive a tale explaining her whereabouts these past months suitable for the starched Venetian puritans. Brother John had provided him with the perfect solution to their dilemma. What better refuge for an orphaned young lady than a monastery? Only he would know what she had told him between sobs of relief and joy. When she unfurled her story of rescue from the exploding city, her stay in the Spahiglani camp, and her protection under its captain, she assured him she was not ill-treated, but had lived in servitude. Miquel silenced her quickly, afraid to hear anything that would compromise her innocence. Now he was left to the dark side of his imagination that kept surfacing, despite his struggles to forget that part of Bellina's life. He wanted to know more about this man she was running from, but was afraid to discover that her heart was still his captive.

Miquel was brought out of his thoughts by the rude crack of sails and screech of departing gulls. "Bellina," a sadness in his golden eyes belied the happy tone of his words. "You can put the past behind you now," he urged, even though he suspected the horseman would ride in her night-mares or dreams. "Think of the rejoicing to come. Conte Sordici was quite funereal upon the word of your disappearance during the siege."

"Funereal, indeed!" Bellina huffed. "He would mourn only for the lost dowry." Noting his slightly surprised look, she added, "Yes, I knew of my father's plans. However, I'm quite sure the Conte has put his mark upon one of my cousins by now. In truth I pray he has, for that is all that would save me from a loveless and cruel alliance."

Bellina pulled her cape tighter, clammy fingers seemed to curl around her heart whenever she thought of the vulturous Conte Sordici. Surely he would be waiting for her promised hand, and her

168

uncle was too honorable not to carry out her father's agreement, and she worried also about her Aunt Claudia. It would be easy to beg a long engagement from Uncle Camillus, with hopes the Conte would find another with a larger dowry. But Aunt Claudia was a force to be reckoned with, and Uncle Camillus would just raise his palms helplessly heavenward in the face of his wife's unyielding resolve.

Miquel left her alone, knowing he could not disagree with her, and tried not to think how as her husband, Aurelian would ruin her. He wondered somberly if he had truly rescued her, or if he was delivering her to a worse fate.

Long after Miquel had passed under Giovanni, his first mate remained perched among the sails, a glass pressed to one eye. He stared and stared across the span of unbroken sea line—almost unbroken. His eyes watered as the wind tried to shake him from the rigging, yet still he peered, a knot of anxiousness growing in his stomach. There, upon the horizon, a puff of white showed against the sun-streaked canvas of a dusky sky. It was hard to say whether it was cloud or sail, but the knot in his stomach told him what his eyes could not determine: they had company, and it might be unwelcome company at that.

He found Miquel in his quarters, the ship's log before him and a half-chewed quill in his hand.

"Capitano?" Giovanni said, his voice holding an easy strength in its deepness.

"Yes, Giovanni?" Miquel scratched across the pages in slow curves.

Giovanni stepped into the cabin, closing the door, and when Miquel did not look up from his script, he

169

continued anyway. "Capitano, there is a sail off stern to larboard."

"What?" Miquel shoved the rutter aside. "The larboard stern you say? Are you sure?"

"I am. It is yet too far off to identify." Giovanni brushed aside an imaginary strand of hair, his brows knitting together. "It could be a merchantman."

"That it could, and it could also be pirates." Miquel took the glass from his first mate and together they left the cabin and moved to the rail. "That is what you see?" Miquel, one eye still peering through the glass, pointed, and Giovanni stood beside him stiffly.

"Yes, the white sail upon the sea line."

Miquel lowered the glass and laughed, hitting his mate upon the back. "Giovanni, you old pup, have you had too much wine? It is a cloud, just a cloud. Allie, you gave my heart a turn!"

"No!" Giovanni protested taking the glass, "It is a sail; I know it! See how the edges are firm and unmoving?"

"Friend, if you can say that distant blur is anything, you would put the eyes of a sea hawk to shame."

"Miquel," Giovanni said, "we have known each other since we were children; have I ever jumped to a conclusion without basis?" He lowered his eyes and watched the churlish water. "I can feel it. A feeling so strong I cannot rest. Something, some danger, is going to pounce on us like a cat and tear us apart with its claws, leaving our shredded remains for the sharks."

"Come on, Giovanni, you've had that same dream

haunting you since I've known you and nothing has ever happened or ever will."

"It's different this time! It's real, it won't leave me alone, ever since we left Port Solomon."

Miquel studied the face of his friend and first mate. There was a haggardness to his appearance, a shadow to his cheeks, and in his eyes, Miquel saw a hope that spoke of the trust he held in his Capitano.

"Well," Miquel murmured. "We have made good speed, a change in course should not overly delay us. If it *is* a sail, we will shake it like a flea from a lamb's tail."

However, when Miquel awoke after a fitful night's sleep and came topside, a somber-faced Giovanni pointed like the angel of doom at a ship that now was clearly outlined against the morning sky. "A galleon," was all that he said.

Miquel shrugged, looking through the glass. "She flies the flag of the Venetian levant: she probably is trying to beat us to port with her purchases. I cannot make out her name. Most likely the *Gypsy*, though."

"The *Gypsy*!" the first mate exclaimed, placing two hands carefully against the rail. "Angels in heaven! She came up fast." Giovanni critically studied the advancing galleon. "She was stuffed to the gills; I saw them load her myself. Her gunnel was her water line!"

"She's made good speed these last two hours if that be her," Miquel mused.

"It is her," Giovanni pronounced soberly.

The *Gypsy* danced over the waves like a butterfly over a field: lightly skimming, her bow vibrating, and her sails toying with the wind. Miquel gripped the cold, slippery rail with wind-burned hands, adhering his vision to the rapidly closing gap of sea between the two ships. Why was she so light and carefree? He did not like it, did not like it at all. He took the scope and scanned the decks of the galleon and could not find a soul.

"Giovanni, have you seen Bellina?" he asked, without taking his eyes from the threatening vessel.

"*Si*, I took charge of sending her to her cabin. I convinced her that we were headed for a squall," Giovanni assured his uneasy captain.

"Good, I hope she stays put." Miquel sounded detached as he watched the toy-sized galleon grow before his eyes. "But, just in case, have Marco stand outside her cabin. She knows the sea too well to be fooled for long." Then in a voice that commanded authority, he bellowed an array of orders.

The deck jumped beneath a turmoil of running and cursing. One seaman handed Miquel his cutlass while a scurry of others unfurled the topsail.

Eventually, they all stood ready, waiting as the wind howled a war cry like no trumpet could and the strange galleon gained. They all grimly gripped their weapons. A pounding exploded behind them and they shifted nervously.

The thunder that riveted through her cabin was unmistakenly cannon fire and the sea that rocked the *Portia Regalia* was far too calm. Bellina did not wish to disobey Miquel's wishes but her nature beckoned her. Surprised to meet Marco outside her door she heard herself tripping over her words. "Marco, I . . . I thought I'd . . . What are you doing here?"

"The capitano wishes you to remain inside your

cabin for your safety." Marco stepped in front of her, hoping she would comply.

"What is happening, Marco? You must tell me." Bellina became alarmed by the pallor of the youth's face. He seemed like a tightly wound spring ready to explode at the slightest touch.

"Please," his voice begged, "it is too dangerous . . . They are . . ."

She pushed passed him, disregarding stammering objections.

The galleon, closer still, loomed large and ominous, her generous hull dwarfing their caravel. Her flag dipped and fell to the deck, and like a spearhead, another rose triumphantly to snap its challenge. Miquel tore the glass away and stared at the ship as if what he had seen was only a nightmare trapped inside the cylinder.

"My God, it's the wolf's head! Put about, close to wind!" Miquel shouted above the din that had risen, and like a horse with the bit between its teeth, the *Portia Regalia* tacked suddenly and shot across the galleon's path.

Taken by surprise, the larger vessel was slow to react. Tacking also, she followed, her decks now swarming with a rough-looking lot that no one would be happy to meet. They heard an eerie howl swell like the waves until it broke and repeated in a rhythmic chant. Upon the *Gypsy*, all raised their arms and their crescent blades flashed beneath the sun.

Bellina raced to the top deck with Marco at her heels. "Madonnina, please, it is too dangerous. You are safer below. The Captain will hang me from the main mast if he sees you."

An icy wind pulled and twisted her hair until it submissively fell over her shoulders. Her fears materialized before her in the purposeful confusion aboard deck.

"Marco, there will be no safe place aboard this ship. What am I to do? Sit below and await my fate?"

Without an argument left, Marco slipped a pearl-handled dagger into Bellina's hand.

Upon the *Portia Regalia* they stood frozen. How feeble their arms appeared beside this bloodthirsty lot. How inadequate their caravel was beside this galleon that raced, barely hindered by the choppy water, while the *Regalia*'s bow slammed into them in her flight. Miquel knew their only salvation lay in speed. They were merchants and not prepared for battle, while the oaths howled by those upon the *Gypsy* gave testimony to their worship of the bastard god of war.

"It's no use," Giovanni said softly by Miquel's side. "She gains."

Miquel swallowed painfully and dug his fingers into the rail. "She will not catch us! More angle to those lateens, by God, more angle. Can't you get closer to wind?"

"But Capitano," Giovanni protested, "more angle and we'll lose the wind."

"It is our only hope. She gains, she gains."

Her men pulled at the lateen sails. The caravel, her sails holding as much as possible, bent like a willow, yet still the galleon drew up to slide neatly along her side.

"Larboard!" Someone bawled.

174

"Larboard!" Miquel echoed, "Prepare to repulse boarders."

"Break out axes!" Giovanni cried, keeping an eye upon the men that glared across the brief distance that separated the two ships.

Like ghouls, those upon the galleon began a dreadful howling that made Miquel's hair lift and a coldness settle upon him. A grapple clattered on deck and bit into the caravel, snaring her like a fish on a hook.

"Cut the line," Giovanni yelled at the men who stood closest in horror-stricken stillness. The rope that held the grappling iron was severed just as another took hold. With a swing, Giovanni attacked it. He had the look of one half-crazed as he jumped upon the lines, pulling himself along the iron until he could reach its dangling rope.

He didn't hear the whirl of metal. It turned a few times in air, hooks spreading and reaching, and digging three prongs into the deck, and two more into the rail. It also pierced the back of Giovanni as if he were nothing more than soft butter. Raking, it settled against the gunnel. Openmouthed, Giovanni laid twisted, a pinned moth, his limbs beating uselessly, bloody claw marks striped the planks as he shrieked.

Miquel wanted to close his eyes; disperse this nightmare back to hell whence it came; shut his ears to the death sounds around him; but, instead, he leaped over the injured and pushed aside the terror-struck, and with a downward swoop of his sword, stilled his friend forever.

"For Giovanni!" he screamed, meeting the first of

175

the encroaching men who crossed over with his newly bloodied blade. With a viciousness that made his cutlass hum, he joined his crew and fought for his own life as well as the hot bitter revenge that boiled in his veins.

He did not see Marco pick up Giovanni's sword, nor did he hear Bellina's screams. They were drowned in the clash of metal and the war cries that twisted together in this macabre scene.

Bellina instantly caught a pirate's eye. She didn't fail to notice the garish display of swords and knives that hung over his hips. They swayed menacingly with each ensuing step. Bellina stood stoically still, gripping the handle of the small dagger that was sandwiched between the folds of her skirt. How close should she let him get, she wondered. In her haste, she misjudged the distance between them. Her small dagger was met without resistance as it sliced through nothing. Snaring her wrist and freeing the blade from her fingers, he cruelly twisted her arm until she was forced to her knees. She felt her senses dull, the screams became hollow echoes, her vision became edged in a creeping blackness that narrowed until all before her was swallowed up by it. An arm surrounded her waist and she surrendered to it with Surek's name on her lips.

The enemy came in waves that washed over the *Regalia*. They fell upon the crew with cries of "gyaour dogs" and "Allah triumphs," and with skill they made short work of it, running them all like sheep before the slaughter. Wood splintered along with courage. Shrieks joined with the blood that sprayed into the sea air. Miquel came upon Marco as

176

he faced a sailor's hatchet with Giovanni's blade. With a heavy red fury pounding in his ears, Miquel leaped. Leaped and came full weight upon the man: hacking, hacking, hacking. The man was dead—he was ten times dead—but an insane hate flared across Miquel's eyes, blinding, pulsing through all his being; even closing his ears to the approaching steps behind him.

He did not see the mattea lifted high above his head. He did not feel the slight breeze as it was swung. He was not warned by the sixth sense that those who live by their eyeteeth develop. All he knew was that his head suddenly seemed to explode, all afire with pain and light.

Fifteen

Miquel knew the feeling well. As soon as the ship began to pitch, tossing his limp head from side to side, a feeling of anxiety and dread stirred his limbs to motion and cleared his stupor. *A storm at sea,* he cursed, and for one panicked moment he worried about his ship. Then he remembered, he had no ship. Despite his pounding head, he pulled himself into a sitting position. Nothing but blackness greeted his eyes; only his ears told him he was in the belly of a ship, probably the *Gypsy*. Massaging stiff muscles, he listened to the scratchy sounds that surrounded him. Rats. Hidden in the darkness there was also a low moan.

"Who's there?" Miquel said in a strained voice. He crawled cautiously towards the sound, tearing his pants on the rough planks, avoiding sea water and cargo. A booted foot ended his search. Stretching his hand out, a warm stickiness and a body met his fingers. "Good God!" he muttered, drawing his hand back sharply.

178

"He'll be dead soon enough," a low gruff voice said from the darkness.

Miquel's eyes strained to see him. "Can't he be helped?"

The man who spoke moved closer and Miquel saw a hefty seaman and noted the long crusted slash on his right cheek. "He's from my ship, the *Gypsy*, taken by the Osmanlis, and he chose death rather than meet his captors."

"How?" Miquel murmured, watching the dying man's breath shudder out again in another low moan.

"Gouged his wrists with a shiv of wood." The seaman shrugged. "They took our weapons but they didn't count on a desperate man and these rough-hewn planks."

Miquel leaned back, nauseous. The man grunted, "Damn coward is what he is. Not me. I want to meet those accursed heathen bastards that took my ship, killed my men, and even if it takes the rest of my life, I, Alonzo Torecelli will make them regret it!" He snarled and shook a fist towards the hatch above them. "I, Alonzo Torecelli, will recover my priceless cargo and regain my ship!" Then he stooped next to Miquel and peered down at him, his eyes afire. "I thought I would have to fight alone, but now that you are recovering from your head wound, we can get them together!"

"Get them?" Miquel asked incredulously, "More than five score men attacked my ship! From what I see there are three of us here—soon to be two. Are you mad?"

"Are you also a coward?" Alonzo spat.

"Only a wiser man. I plan on living, not dying, Alonzo Torecelli. But, I am as determined as you, for I will overcome this, even if it means cooperating with the Osmanlis in the meantime. Someday I'll make my way back to Venice. Then I'll plot my revenge with more men and another ship." Miquel fell back, wearied by the effort he put into his argument.

"I should have known," Alonzo said in disgust, "a Venetian! Of all the fine people in God's world, I spend my last moment on this earth with a damned coward and some Venetian scum."

Miquel grasped the sailor by his surcoat. "You can follow all of your suicidal plots to the end, my Genoese friend, but this Venetian has a lady to stay alive and care for."

The hatch lifted and blinding light forced their eyes closed. Shielding his, Miquel tried to distinguish the two faces that peered down. He heard the laughter that mocked their alien language. Enraged, Alonzo pitched a loose board at the opening. Falling short of its mark, it crashed to the floor and Alonzo felt an uncontrollable heat race through him.

"Do you expect to keep us down here forever in the dark without food or water? Well, I'll not let you forget Alonzo Torecelli so easily! Before I die and rot in this stinking ship, I'll see your Capitano doesn't get a night's sleep!"

The cover slammed shut, cutting off the last of Alonzo's threats and returning them into darkness once again. Stubbornly, Alonzo retrieved the length of board and began pounding the floor above them relentlessly.

Miquel cradled his pounding head in his arms, afraid to think of Bellina's fate.

Captain Fadhl Al-Sallal was finally getting a good look at his captive. After four days of overseeing the fighting, boarding, and the selling of the *Gypsy* and the *Portia Regalia*, he took pleasure in studying the rise of her plump white breasts above her gown.

Two of Fadhl's men had tied her to the bunk in their captain's cabin, thoughtfully nailing her roped feet far apart. The captain pushed her gown up, amused at her useless struggles against the ropes, and brushed his calloused hand against her silky thighs.

"You are indeed a prize fit for a sultan," he murmured, his lips following his hands.

"Please," Bellina begged, her wrists reddening as she strained against the tight bindings, "I'm worth much more if you ransom me to my very rich uncle."

Fadhl Al-Sallal laughed, releasing one of her breasts from the confines of her gown. "It is amazing how every prisoner has a wealthy relative! And wealthier than a sultan at that!" He bit her nipple gently and she screamed in fear.

"No, my pet, you are more valuable than gold," he whispered in her ear, teasing the hair around the moist crevice between her legs.

"Take pity," Bellina cried. "I am innocent of men."

"I doubt that heartily," the captain laughed harshly, giving her a probing kiss that shut her protests. "But have no fear, pet. As much as your succulent body calls out to mine, I am saving you for another. Just in case you are as innocent as you say." He beamed at her, running his fingers through her soft black mane. "Yes," he said, trying to convince his swollen manhood, "you will be much more valuable to me that way."

He left her, not bothering to fix her clothing, and she burned with shame and hate. It wasn't until much later, when a slave boy entered and untied her so she could relieve herself in a little pot, that she rearranged her dress. He left, leaving a meager meal and only one hand and one foot tied. Her thoughts were a tangle of fear and hate and a deepening ache of sorrow. Miquel was on this ship, she knew, but in what condition or where she could not know. For her sake he had come to this, and whatever would his fate be in the near future? If he were still alive, she thought with a shiver of fear.

Once the joyous novelty of her escape and short-lived freedom had worn off, she had been haunted by Surek's image whenever her eyes closed. And there lay her sorrow, for her body and her desire would hear of no other, no matter how she tried to put him behind her. She would always be his. She hated herself for running away, hadn't he warned her of this? How she longed for him now. Would he still search for her, or would he shrug her off as a problem he no longer had to deal with? No, he would find another to warm his bed. And if he did get his hands on her, it would only be to punish her for leaving him!

Quite some time passed before the hatch cover was

lifted again and moldy crusted bread and a goatskin of water was thrown to the floor. From then on, Miquel and Alonzo kept track of the passing days by the periodic lifting of the cover.

"Shut up, Torecelli!" Miquel cried as Alonzo started shouting oaths and pounding again on the ceiling. "You won't die from being cooped down here with this rotting dead body. It'll be one of those topside who hasn't slept in days. Anytime now I expect to see a jambiyyah wrenching your tongue from its roots. I just hope they know it's you and not me!"

Despite his outward confidence, Miquel truly believed that if they didn't get some fresh air soon, they'd die before their destination. The dampness of the hold made their bones ache, and the smell of oppressive death and their own bodily wastes threatened to disease them.

They used whatever they could find to make life more bearable. As they stumbled around the hold, Miquel realized why the *Gypsy* had gained on the *Regalia*. It was nearly empty of cargo. He could only assume most of it was in port being unloaded by a second pirate vessel. However, he was puzzled. Where did Torecelli and he figure in their plan? Why were they being kept alive?

"Look at them," Alonzo said in disgust, pointing at a pair of rats positioned above them on a girder. "They're just waiting for all of us to expire and then they're going to pounce right down on top of you and me and have a feast."

"Rats don't eat people," Miquel answered.

"The hell they don't! Are your Venetian rats so

183

sissified that they feast on wheat only? In Genoa they are as big as cats—nay, dogs, sometimes."

"I don't doubt it," Miquel said sarcastically, trying to find a dryer spot.

"Anyway," Torecelli said, ignoring him, "why else would they be sitting and staring all day and night?"

"I'm not going to worry about it," Miquel laughed bitterly. "It's the human rats that have my fears."

"Ha!" Alonzo sneered and grabbed up his wood again. "I'll break those Osmanli swine across my knee." He pounded at the floor above them viciously, his face a contortion of hate and the madness of an obsession. Miquel pressed his hands against his head as if to hold it together as his splitting headache worsened.

To Alonzo's horror the lid was flung aside, and he stared motionless, dropping the board as two Osmanlis climbed into the hold. Miquel's lips twisted into an ironic smile, but it was not mirrored in the eyes of the Osmanlis. One jerked his blade towards the stairs. One moved like a sleek panther to their backs, and Miquel and Alonzo obligingly climbed the crude stairs into the blinding light above. Pails of saltwater struck them, stinging their open sores and diminishing the stench from their bodies, then they were strapped to a mast. The sun wrapped them in its baking rays.

Miquel gradually opened his eyes to the searing light and studied the seamen's activities, in hopes of receiving a clue to their destiny and possibly to where Bellina was being kept. A scarred man approached and untied him, turning a stony look at Alonzo, silencing any question he was about to utter. Miquel found himself half-dragged to the captain's quarters, with only a contemptuous sneer and the biting grip on his shoulder to answer his puzzlement. He was left standing, facing a seated man with eyes and nose like a falcon. His thin lips smiled broadly while he gestured to another chair. Behind him in a cloak of shadows sat Bellina, hair and clothing disheveled, her wrists bound in red silk. Her eyes met Miquel's, still as sharp as the sunlight. Her bound hands rested calmly in her lap, but Miquel's keen eye saw the pleading message she sent him. He couldn't help taking a step towards her, but was jolted back by a crisscrossing of blades that flashed between them.

"She is the most valuable cargo aboard this ship. Don't you agree? You need not fear for her safety. Unless you do something foolish. Do you understand me?" Fadhl spoke in his own tongue and then continued at Miquel's nod. "You are a brave and strong man. I watched you and your friend take on my men and was quite impressed. Quite. It is a pity that the big one had to die. He would have been useful." Miquel flinched and gripped the chain around his wrists tightly. The captain's eyes glittered. "I see you still have the urge to fight, no matter how outnumbered."

"What did you do with the men of my ship? And those of the *Gypsy?*" Miquel demanded, watching the captain's face twist in hate.

"They were cowards and we have little use for their kind in our empire—even as slaves. That is why your world is crumbling away from you. Too many cowards who bathe themselves in wealth instead of blood, eh? And run too often to the arms of a woman for comfort instead of fighting like men.

"As for the girl," he traced her cheekbone lightly with the point of his dagger. "She has the spirit of a cat . . . and it is told to me that our illustrious sultan enjoys a good tussle." Fadhl Al-Sallal smiled and stared into Miquel's face. "But then, your mistress is no longer of any concern to you. Concern yourself with only your life, and decide how you and your friend can convince me to keep you alive."

Miquel snorted, "Surely you don't expect loyalty from us?"

"Capitano," he said slowly, his voice divested of all humor, "remember what I told you of our empire. We have little use for what will not serve us."

For the remainder of the voyage Miquel and Alonzo received daily wash downs and a short stay on deck under the watchful gaze of a guard. But their destination remained undisclosed as the captain ignored them.

"Where do you think they are taking us?" Alonzo asked Miquel after they were returned to the hold once again without glimpsing any familiar land mass.

Miquel sighed for the hundredth time, "I don't know. We could be bound for any of the Moslem states—Tripoli, Anatolia, even back to Constantinople. I overheard someone speaking of the sultan's new palace he plans on building soon. It seems Rumeli Hisari is not luxurious enough for his needs. I've already resigned myself to the fact—and I suggest that you should—that we are to be sold as slaves. Or you'll be finding yourself food for the sultan's dogs, and you'll meet your Maker being of some use to the empire, like it or not."

It was the following morning—or what they had estimated was daybreak—when they were thrown from the sacks they lay across into the sour brine that puddled between the planks of the hull's bottom. "Those fools have grounded my ship!" Alonzo shouted, shaking his fist at the hatch.

Miquel rose to his feet, his hand bracing. "Well, now we won't have to be wondering anymore."

Feet scurrying above and rope scraping, the ship shuddered as she strained against anchor. After a long silence the hatch door opened, and bound together by a length of rope, Alonzo and Miquel were shoved into a longboat. Alonzo wiped the dirty edge of his sleeve across an already sweating brow. "Weeks at sea to be brought back to this place," he grunted, his eyes narrowing as they passed the common docks of Constantinople.

When the boat was run aground upon the sands of the beach entrance of Rumeli Hisari, Miquel and Alonzo were unloaded with the rest of the barrels and trunks that made the trip with them and were pulled to the crest of the sandy shore. Miquel stretched to catch a glimpse of Bellina being eased to shore. She refused to walk humbly behind her captors, though bound and leashed to a streamer of silk, she moved purposely with her chin held high.

"So that is your lady," Alonzo said with an appreciative grunt. "She's almost as fair as our Genoese flowers." He barked one sharp laugh as Miquel scowled at him.

The captain, as bloated with self-importance as the overflowing trunks he brought, strutted across the sand. "Faithful servant!" he shouted to the janissary that approached, a merry glint jumping in his eye. "I bear gifts for our peerless sultan. Will you tell him of my arrival?"

The janissary retreated wordlessly as two others appeared on the ridge to stand, arms crossed, eyes emotionless but piercing, and their blades a sharp reminder that those who displeased were harshly dealt with. The captain waited, chuckling to himself. "Silence!" he snapped as Alonzo jabbed again at Miquel with his sarcasm.

They did not wait long. There, suddenly upon the crest, was a man which no one could mistake for anyone but the sultan he was, the conqueror—Mehmet II. His caftan blew around him in simple folds; a peasant could have worn it. The straight angles of his smooth face, the high cheekbones, proud chin, all spoke of youth, but Miquel looked into his eyes. Yes, there was one who felt the weight of an empire upon his shoulders. Miquel looked down abruptly as those eyes came to bear upon him. All the men prostrated themselves, and with a jerk upon their ropes, Miquel and Alonzo fell to their knees with little choice.

Mehmet's gaze came to settle on Bellina and she

shuddered, knowing she should avert her eyes as Miquel had done, but defiantly she forced herself not to. It was a shock to her that he was so young. She had in her imagination pictured him older, perhaps with a cruel sneer, certainly not a man barely out of youth, with a voice as clear as a monastery bell even in anger. His eyes dared her not to lower hers and when she didn't, the barest softening of a smile touched his lips and he let his gaze drop to her breasts, to caress the rest of her. Finally she could stand it no more and diverted her eyes from him.

"And what is this, Master Seaman?" His voice was low and smooth in its displeasure, as he waved a hand to indicate the three captives, and the captain rose unsteadily to his feet sputtering. "Never mind!" The sultan cut the captain's blustering off with a wave of his hand. "You and you," he pointed among the janissaries, "Take these *gyaours* away. And you . . ." he paused, frowning at the now deflated captain. "I will see you inside."

In an instant they were led away, Bellina still separated from them. Miquel and Alonzo were led down the long terra cotta walkway and through a heavily guarded gate that bridged the fortresslike wall. It opened up to another land: groomed trees and carefree fountains contrasted with the stark profiles of the janissaries that seemed to appear from nowhere. Peacocks and doves wandered freely on the expanse of carpetlike lawn. When the walkway forked, they were led away from the palace and toward the working part of the estate. They passed the stables with their silver-coated horses, passed the blacksmith, and the kitchen where the sultan's white bread was baked throughout the day and night, and still continued, passing an endless assortment of buildings that made Rumeli Hisari more than a fortress-palazzo: it was a self-contained city. They were also to discover that it had a well-fortified prison.

The citadel was located at the furthest point from the main estate, making it quite a long march. It was a barren, sorrow-filled place with dead, tortured sticks poking up from the ground instead of trees. And skulls that mocked from pikes. Worst of all, it was a soundless place.

They didn't speak to each other, even after the heavy door slammed shut behind them. They just stared at the soiled floor and the chains that hung silent against the beaten walls. Miquel circled the cell. He watched Alonzo standing motionless, staring. "At least we're not chained," Miquel laughed bitterly, but he had missed the gleam that glowed in the depths of Alonzo's eyes.

A smile tugged his mouth and he pressed a hand to his forehead. "Did you see all of that? He must be the wealthiest man in the whole world. There is not one villa in all of Genoa to compare to what we have seen! Can you imagine what the inside of his palazzo must look like?"

"I don't believe you," Miquel said disgusted. "That's just what we'll be doing—imagining! From here on in, we're not going anywhere, and especially not the palace. You Genoese slime are a greedy bunch of bastards. Is your revenge so quickly forgotten,

190

Torecelli?" He gestured at the fetid dirt under their feet.

Alonzo's fingers clenched into a hard ball, and with a primal growl, he flung himself at Miquel. Without pause he was met in kind, both of them releasing upon each other weeks of hate, fear, and frustration, until they both crumbled, exhausted and battered, but each with a new respect for the other.

Captain Fadhl Al-Sallal realized the seriousness of the situation when confronted by the stormy face of his sultan. His voice trembled with diffidence. "Your most merciful Sovereign, it is not that I wish to disobey orders, it is just that there is some confusion existing among the seamen as to what specifically are our limits? Forgive my ignorance." His hands clenched in a knot behind his back, he cleared his throat as if his words were caught there. "If we are to stop piracy altogether, it will be difficult to keep our crew under control for months at sea without promise of reward. Besides," a slight smile briefly curled his lips, "what do we care of *gyaours*?"

When he noticed the sultan's fingers choke the stem of the gold goblet, his foolish arrogance was lost and he gripped his sweating hands together in anticipation of the worst.

"Captain," Mehmet said slowly, as if speaking to a dim-witted youth. "It seems some of my seamen are not blessed with the wisdom of Allah and have to be told like children what to do, time and again. I am not patient and cannot tolerate fools that would threaten the empire with lack of foresight and direct disobedience of my wishes.

"To refresh your memory, I have issued orders to restrain the sacking of trade ships and never to use the crescent flag. This is detrimental to the exchange I wish to restore between the western world and our own. We have need of timber for ship building and iron for forging weapons, not silks and spices that are right here for us . . . or European women!" He gazed thoughtfully into the polished gold. "Though the one you brought is interesting."

When Mehmet saw the captain relax his stance, he focused again on him, quickly reminding the seaman of his serious demise. "We are at peace with the West and you are waging your own war. And what of the prisoners you have brought here? We have enough slaves to feed!"

The captain blinked his eyes against the stinging perspiration that ran down the side of his face like tears. "I beg your forgiveness, Sovereign," he whimpered, running his hand against his coat, and he felt desperation weaken his knees. He rambled, "The tall one is not much to look at, but he has stamina and courage, and the other is strong and clever. Both captains of their ships! The girl, what can I say? Have you ever seen a more tempting sweet?" He lowered his eyes and said in a final plea, "It was my intention that they would prove useful in some way to your highness."

Mehmet's face was a hard, still mask, only his eyes leaped. "Useful! What am I arguing with this imbecile for? I've had my fill of *gyaours* and I have no use for another one, no less three! Two captains and a woman—probably from a noble family! Perhaps they can clear this up before word gets back to the other merchantships and they decide the risk is not worth the voyage."

Flinging himself to the floor, rending his clothes, the captain wailed in high keening notes, "Sultan, by the beard of the Prophet, this will never happen again."

"On that account you are right, Master Seaman. It will never happen again. Now leave me." Mehmet summoned his guard and executioner. "See to Captain Al-Sallal and send the two male prisoners to me."

"Well, now, we pay for the piper's tune?" Alonzo said when the janissaries came for them. Miquel just scowled.

Upon entering Mehmet's chamber their guard forced them to the floor, then moved a few feet back to stand at the arched doorway.

"You may rise, gentlemen. Please be seated here."

Miquel couldn't avert his eyes from scanning the room; his heart sank, she wasn't there. A richly jeweled hand caught Alonzo's attention as Mehmet waved to the two cushions opposite the round table he sat behind. Mehmet drew on the gurgling water pipe as he noted their shocked expression at his knowledge and perfect execution of their language.

"You must forgive and forget the rash exploits of those who brought you here. I cannot return to you your dead friends. However, I assure you those responsible will not go unpunished. They acted specifically against my policies, for it is my concern that trade be resumed between our countries and that a healthy relationship be developed."

Contrasted against the opalescent background, an orange turban regally crowned the sultan's head, one end forming a crest while the other flowed down the back of his white and orange pin-striped caftan. He nodded his head with an easy smile.

"Please accept my hospitality until arrangements can be made to return you to your homeland. Ah, food." He waved the slaves in. "You must be famished after your unfortunate ordeal, and I assure you, you will never have tasted so fine a selection."

Alonzo's mouth drooled questionably as he watched a heavily veiled girl serve bowls of piled rice and lamb mixed with a confetti of nuts, vegetables, and raisins. Without hesitation, Alonzo plopped down upon a cushion and grinned, "Captain Alonzo Torecelli, currently of Genoa. It will be an honor and a privilege to accept your hospitality. I must confess we expected . . ."

Miquel flinched at Alonzo's incorporation of himself into "we," deciding that as long as he was included, he would also be subjected to the sultan's response to whatever fool thing Alonzo was stumbling to say.

"What he's saying," Miquel hurried to add, "is that we never thought that you were so creative with your wealth. I hail from the Queen of the Waters—fair Venice. Captain Miquel Campanello."

Mehmet's face lightened in amusement. All of Venice and Genoa would soon be whispering of the wealthy and much-enlightened sultan whose strength lay not only in the size of his armies, but the genius of his strategy—thanks to these pretentious men. Yes, and soon trade would be in full swing and gold, timber, and iron would enrich the empire while bleeding Venice and Genoa. Enjoying his game, Mehmet leaned closer to Alonzo, watching the look of uncertainty that flashed for one brief moment across the arrogance he saw there.

"What you mean," Mehmet said, his voice low, "is that you expected a tent filled with grunting barbarians."

Alonzo blanched, "No, your grace, you misunderstand."

Mehmet held up a hand to silence him. "It is quite an understandable mistake in judgment, after all of the rumors that are no doubt raging over your cities. Such stories are of no benefit to any of us. Constantinople was in decay. I would appear rather as an Angel of Mercy than a conqueror. Look around you. Is the city not flourishing? Is she not being restored to her once great grandeur of many years ago? Soon trade will be as strong as ever, eh? Enough of this talk, eat!"

They finished their meal in silence, soothed by the distant melody of oud and zils as dancers swayed and beckoned, twirled and mesmerized. Pushing back his bowl, Mehmet took a steamy towel from his slave and following his example, Miquel and Alonzo wiped their hands and faces.

"Very tasty, very tasty," Alonzo declared, his clothing straining across his thickened waist.

"Yes," Miquel agreed, "A welcome change from shipboard fare."

Mehmet laughed agreeably, but the smile on his face was suspiciously like a cat's. "Ah . . . I will make it up to you both," he promised, watching Miquel closely. "You must stay until you tire of my rich banquets and crave the hard biscuits and cheese of sea life. But until then, so much have we to talk about." He leaned closer, almost whispering, as though he was about to disclose a great secret. "Tell me of this girl one of you was traveling with. I want to know all about her."

Miquel's thoughts raced ahead. He didn't trust Mehmet, he had seen that covetous look he had given Bellina. Her freedom might depend on what he told him.

"She is Bellina Magella D'Rosallini, the daughter of a magistrate," he lied, deciding the richer and more important her connections the better, "Betrothed to Conte Sordici of Sicilia. It was fate that placed her here and tangled her in the affairs of warring empires. I was returning her to her family in Venice."

"Ah," Mehmet breathed and became pensive for a moment. "Well, then it will be so! Eh?" He leaned back, hands behind his head, "When you are ready to leave, she'll be with you."

"But, with all respect, she is probably frightened," Miquel protested. "Can I talk to her? See her?"

"She didn't look frightened to me," Mehmet laughed. "Only, perhaps angry. Believe me she will be comfortable and infinitely safer in the seraglio. Later, of course, you may see her, if you still want to.

But I warn you," laughter again rumbled through his body. "She may never wish to return to Venice once she has tasted the luxuries of my palace."

Miquel couldn't calm his heart as it flinched at Mehmet's words. Bellina was somewhere in the mazelike fortress and he couldn't protect her.

"Believe me, you can meet with her tomorrow so you will be at ease." Mehmet said smiling into Miquel's glum face. "The harem is the safest, most guarded place in my palace. She is quite safe, no man may enter there."

Sixteen

At the edge of the seraglio, the pair of janissaries waited with Bellina, her wrists still bound. Before long, two young eunuchs appeared and struck the floor twice with their staves, announcing in their strange high timber, "Aside for the Kislar Agar, Musa, Master of Females!"

A black mountain of a man ponderously approached, his eyes sweeping all sides, sharply taking in every detail. Behind him, wraithlike, followed two heavily veiled women, not even their eyes or faces visible.

As the Kislar Aga studied Bellina, listening as the janissaries related her story, she studied him. His delicately flowered silk robes sharply contrasted with the cruel set of his face. His eyebrows locked in a perpetual glower, while his nose flared over a mouth so large it filled one third of his face. As if his immense body was not enough to distinguish him as a power to be reckoned with, a two-foot cylindrical turban crowned his head.

Musa grunted to no one in particular, but as if it were some secret command, the two women turned and left. He looked at Bellina and gave her a poke with his finger. "So . . . scrawny thing, talk to Musa."

Bellina's eyes widened in a combination of surprise, nervousness, and a deep resentment at being ordered to talk like some puppet.

Musa's mouth stretched furtively, slowly exposing ivory teeth until a rumbling laugh escaped, shaking his copious belly. Sour breath reached her, then his laugh ended as abruptly as it had begun, with a snarl. "You now under my care, little bird. ALL do as Musa command. Talk!" He gasped her hair and pulled her head back, burning white hot eyes into her face.

"I'm hungry," she spat, wincing as the Kislar Aga tightened and twisted her hair around his fist.

He freed her suddenly with another laugh. "Good." He nodded, crossing his brawny arms against his chest. "Master not like puny girl." Impatiently he motioned the janissaries away. "Nefari!" he bellowed down the corridor and one of the black-veiled women returned. With a shove he propelled Bellina towards her. "Cats in kitchen think this meal! Make sure thing eat for certain. Make clean, too," he added with a sniff.

Without pause, Nefari pulled at Bellina's hand. Bellina followed her through several hallways and courtyards, entering deeper and deeper into the seraglio. Frantically she tried to memorize the way as they went, but it was of no use. It was a maze of lovely and ornate, but designed to confuse. Nefari tugged at her veil, revealing doelike eyes and a long shiny mane of coal black hair and a smile for Bellina.

199

"I think you would like to bathe first?" she asked in a delicate voice.

"Oh, yes!" Bellina said gratefully, eager to wash away the memory of Fadhl Al-Sallal's hands on her body, along with the grime of captivity.

The deeper they traveled, the more women they came upon. Here deep in the seraglio's heart they wore their veils carelessly, if at all, relaxing in a world where no man but Mehmet and their eunuch guardians entered. Some of them shouted greetings; some threw dangerous probing looks at Bellina.

Suddenly they were approached by a retinue as colorful as a flock of tropical birds, important by the respect and care others gave them as they moved aside and made way. Nefari nervously looked down. "Most gracious Sultana, lovely and beloved."

Janil was lovely indeed, if not loved. Her long red gold tresses reached almost to her knees when let free as they were now. She gazed with violet kohl-lined eyes, her delicate mouth touched by a pout. Her lavender veils were draped seductively with the studied care that ten years in a harem had given her. If Mehmet chose this moment or any other to visit, she would be at her best.

"Who is this Nefari?" Janil purred, sizing up Bellina.

Bellina instantly recognized the ingratiating voice, and memories flooded back to her of the words this one had said to Surek in the bazaar.

"I am Bellina Magela D'Rosallini," she answered.

Nefari interrupted quickly, "Delivered to our care—"

200

"Until," Bellina pushed on, "I have a word with your sultan and clarify matters."

Janil paused, closing her eyelids gently, "Nefari, tell this one that poor manners are rarely tolerated, especially from foreigners, and that Allah has sent her here to serve our most esteemed Sultan, not to teach one who is already all-knowing and all-wise."

Nefari began but Bellina spouted, her eyes flashing at Janil, "I am not deaf, dumb, and if I am rude—"

Janil dismissed her with a wave of her bone-white hand, already having dismissed Bellina in her mind. Rude, thin, and graceless, this one posed no threat, was no competition whatsoever.

Nefari and two others pulled and half-dragged Bellina to a steamy tub.

"Go away!" she tersely commanded, but someone seized her hair and kneaded it with perfumed soap.

"You should feel blessed by Allah that he has sent you here to serve our Sultan," one of them said, echoing Janil's words.

"She is some *gyaour's* mewling kitten," said another. "I think Musa errs in bringing this one here."

"Hah! Lotifa! You are just afraid that the sultan will pick her over you to share his bed!"

"Come here closer, Nefari, and say that when you are in drowning distance! I don't exactly see him pleasuring himself with you."

"How could he tolerate an anemic wretch like this?" Lotifa motioned to Bellina. "I can't understand why he has not chosen me. The man, although gifted by Allah in every other way, simply does not know a beauty when he sees one!"

She haughtily shook her ebony mane away from the water and Bellina stared defiantly at the arguing girls.

"Lotifa! You are begging to be accused of treason to talk of the sultan that way," Halida said sharply, weary of correcting her all the time. But as the eldest in the harem, who else was it left up to? If Lotifa did not learn to curb her tongue she would land in the sultan's dungeons instead of his royal bed.

Lotifa grabbed the arm Bellina had jerked away and scrubbed. "Such an old woman you are, Halida. No one but friends hear—unless we are not friends. Besides, I speak the truth not blasphemy, and no one dies for that!"

Despite Bellina's protests, they dried her with a fluffy towel and pulled her to the main sleeping chamber. Bellina's thoughts floated as listless as her body felt. Fabrics, glittering tiles, and exotic birds created a collage of strangeness she had never encountered before. What she heard could only be true: this was Rumeli Hisari, the sultan's palace. Escape from here would be impossible, and she could end up never even seeing Mehmet again. How could she even begin to make him understand her hopes? Suddenly, she had no appetite whatsoever. The piled trays were full of sweets and nutmeats and spiced balls of meat, but Bellina's stomach was a knot of turmoil. Instead, she sought the pallet they had given her and tried to numb her thoughts of despair with sleep.

Lotifa watched the strange girl curl away from her, her movement slow and deathlike and shook her head, "I don't know why Musa would be interested in you, little sister, you look half-dead to me."

Miquel paced his spacious, well-appointed chamber, oblivious to its splendor, angry in his impatience to see Mehmet. Today the Sultan had promised for the third time to take him to Bellina, but the day was passing quickly and Mehmet showed no sign of appearing. Alonzo had left early that morning to go hunting, mounted on one of Mehmet's sweet-faced mares, playfully bantering with the janissaries that accompanied him. Miquel refused the offer and instead allowed his dark thoughts to ferment.

Once evening fell, Miquel found himself herded to another of Mehmet's sumptuous banquets, shared of course with Alonzo. This time there were many of Mehmet's high ranking men attending, and Miquel found it difficult to attract Mehmet's attention, let alone accuse him of reneging on his promises. He was introduced to so many new faces and names, had consumed so many liquors and food, refused many offers of bodily pleasures from the slave girls, that by midnight his frustrations had bubbled up to a point of imminent explosion.

When he turned his head, he found one of Mehmet's men staring at him, but quickly the man turned away, refusing to catch the sharp look Miquel sent his way. That one he remembered—Surek Harum Edib. His peculiar eyes had made Miquel uncomfortable from the first time he had met him. And since Miquel was always a person who confronted those who made him uncomfortable, he was determined to find out more about Edib. Slowly, Miquel conversed his way towards him. It didn't take long for the room was emptying, many men (including Alonzo) accepting the temptation of the lovely females.

"Messer Campanello, is it?" Surek nodded in his direction. "Of Venice?"

"Yes, Capitano," Miquel answered.

"I was hoping to meet you," Surek said with a smile. "I must admit, spending most of my life on the back of a horse, I have a fascination for those of your city who live by the whims of the sea."

Miquel laughed, "It is more that we cohabitate with the sea, that is why we 'wed' the sea once a year in quite a ceremony."

"*Wed* the sea?" Surek questioned, leaning back on his hassock. "That is peculiar indeed."

"It's just a ceremony, symbolic and merry, but binding just the same. It is said that sea water instead of blood runs through a Venetian's veins," Miquel laughed. "I'm afraid we're never at home on solid ground for long."

To his puzzlement Surek's face darkened. "Yes, I know that all too well. But tell me, Miquel, you and your companion, now that you have tasted our hospitality, are you so eager for the cold caress of your lagoons?"

Miquel paused and chose his words carefully, "I must admit your plush comforts delight my insolent body well enough. As for my companion, I cannot speak for her. Nor," he added sharply, "have I seen her since we arrived here, although your Sultan advises me she is well."

"She?" Surek said, his eyebrows raising, startled. "I was referring to Messer Torecelli. I have heard of no woman."

"Ah . . ." Miquel replied, seeing his chance. "Torecelli is an acquaintance, not a friend. There were three of us taken—excuse me—brought here. The lady I spoke of is my mistress, Bellina Magela D'Rosallini, niece of a magistrate, a very wealthy and powerful magistrate—of trade," Miquel added for good measure. "I'm sure her uncle is worried beyond measure, we should really be getting back." Miquel met Surek's wide eyes, "I hope, respectfully, that your sultan's intentions are honorable."

"Of course," Surek gasped out, his wildly beating heart making his voice sharp.

Miquel looked down at his own clenched hands. "Forgive me if I worry, but I have not seen or heard from her in four days."

The Spahiglani captain leaned closely towards him. "Messer Campanello, I assure you she will be fine in the harem."

"You do not know her," Miquel protested. "She is a free spirit. Why hasn't she been here as honored a guest as I?"

Surek smiled, "It would have been unseemly for a woman to be here, it is not their place."

"Oh come, Capitano," Miquel persisted. "There are women all over here."

"Excuse me, I should have said a lady. It is unseemly for a lady to be here. However," he paused, twirling his mustache, "I will speak to Mehmet. He loves to show off his fair Sultana Janil and he would do so to a small party. Perhaps I'll suggest as a

205

curiosity to meet your Venetian mistress. Yes, he'll do it. A small party with Janil and—what's her name?"

"Bellina."

"Yes, Bellina." Surek leaned back and swallowed his strong potion in one swift guzzle, and to Miquel's startlement gave one bark of laughter and shook his head.

When Bellina opened her eyes, the first thing she saw was the gold filigree lantern over her bed. Encased in red glass, a flame flickered, its ritualistic dance waking her memory of the fire that had engulfed the camp and her then happy life with Surek. "Oh Surek," her mind wailed, remembering the hurt and anger he had felt when he had learned of her escape attempt. And now? What was he feeling now that she was truly gone? Did he feel the same pain that engulfed her whole being? If only she could feel his arms hold her just one more time. She had taken his last caress for granted. No matter how hard she tried, she couldn't hold that warmth to her. It was disappearing, slipping forever away, and she mourned like one for a dead lover.

She gazed about the room through a window of tears. It was small, a tiny cubicle that was separated from a larger chamber by a curtain of beads. Beyond she saw the sleeping shapes of many women, and within a single girl, not far from her bed, huddled in a cocoon of silken blankets. She had to get out of here. With leaded arms she pushed herself to sit, but fell back weakly against the pillows.

She felt so tired. Tired of living her life for other

peoples' pleasures; tired of "friends" who were corrupted by the rattle of gold in their pockets; tired of this barbarous land; and most of all, too tired to do anything about it. As far as she was concerned, they could do anything they wanted with her. She was beyond caring, an empty shell without the breath of life to fill it. All that mattered in her life was lost and gone forever. Her thoughts jarred against each other until her weary heart and mind accepted sleep's comfort once again.

She awoke to a stab of sunlight and the girl of the night before was gone. However, solitude did not seem to be the rule here, for Nefari, with a serenity that was very becoming, entered through the beaded curtain with a tray of food and drink.

"Ah, you're awake. Musa will be pleased." Nefari held a cherry in her hand, but Bellina turned her head away to stare at the wall. "Oh please, you must be hungry by now. It's been three days since you've eaten a thing; you'll be disappearing to nothing."

"Where is the sultan?" Bellina asked wearily.

My, these foreign women are difficult, always full of impossible questions, Nefari thought. "He is no doubt busy with the tasks that Allah has given him. Here, take some tea, too. Musa had it made with skullcap and valerian to lift your spirits."

After Bellina put a dried fruit to her mouth, Nefari spoke with bubbling excitement. "He hasn't come to the harem in many months, but I believe it will be soon!" She waited for Bellina's joy, but was bewildered when it turned to dismay.

"And I thought this was just some nightmare! How shall I ever leave? I must speak with him," she said frantically. "Do you understand that?"

"Why should you wish to leave when you are fortunate enough to be given a chance to serve Allah's descendant?"

"Fortunate! I was almost burned alive, lied to, drugged, carted here by pirates, I know not how many miles . . . Why I almost died from all this good fortune! And Miquel! My Miquel! Where is he? What have you done to him?"

Nefari frowned before her bitterness. "You are not well, perhaps you would like to rest?" It was a statement not a question as the woman, her contempt hidden beneath her veiled face, left her.

When Nefari returned the next day, Musa was with her. He checked Bellina and nodded that he was satisfied with her progress. He personally oversaw the selection and preparation of her meals. Each dish was a work of art adorning a silver platter, its savory aroma tempting the fussiest eater. Dates, apricots, and honey figs decorated roasted lamb; rice was dressed in rich saffron sauces; and instead of the simple rose-scented water to drink, she often ended her meals with a goblet brimming with almond-flavored cream. Nefari always made certain that the polished silver bowl was overflowing with fresh fruit.

Bellina knew she looked ragged. Every wall was mirrored and flashed to her a spector with haunted eyes and hollowed cheeks. She forced herself to eat. If Mehmet ever showed, she must get his attention, and if he were like every other man she had known, plainness never served that end well.

Each morsel they brought she consumed, and after

208

less than a weak, the skinny girl was on her way to becoming a voluptuous odalisque.

Just as the food was unequaled, so were Bellina's surroundings. No effort or expense had been spared in creating the gilded masterpiece that was now her prison. It could have enticed a god from his heavenly home. How barren seemed Surek's tent to its richness. After living in a tent for so long, she would never get used to the airy expanse of the harem. Although at least a hundred girls lived there, it was empty and cold and hollow. Gold and silver seemed to have been used with as much abandon as whitewash on a peasant's cottage. Gold even veined the tiled walls and gilded her tub, and threads dipped in it ran through the china blue drapery. Wooden bowls were replaced by silver, and every utensil, plate, or goblet was made of the same highly polished metal. The marble floor was spotted by fringed rugs like those in Surek's tent. Her bed was a stuffed satin couch with a mohair cover for cool nights. It was the only soft and warm thing in the room, so she seldom left its comfort.

"Poor bird," Bellina whispered to the imprisoned nightingale who called to the birds that dwelled in the gardens. "Instead of a palace, a golden cage is your prison."

So far she had not even seen her keeper except for that first day Al-Sallal had proudly displayed her. All she knew about him was what Nefari and the other slave girls told her, and that he took care of his possessions very well. Pushing aside the annoying face veil she was forced to wear while her midriff remained bare, she wondered if he was as kindly as

209

they said. But who could trust the judgment of those who dressed and lived so peculiarly? Her intuition told her that Halida and Nefari were intimidated by the wealth and power of their leader. However, Lotifa remained a puzzle, for she even defied Musa to anger Halida and upset Nefari.

As much as she tried to ignore Mehmet II, her thoughts kept returning to the enigmatic ruler. She found it hard to admit her curiosity openly, and more than that, her disappointment that he had shown no interest in her. Nefari entered, balancing a tray adorned with feathers. On closer inspection, Bellina saw a ruby-colored bird surrounded with scarlet fruit.

"I don't know if you like pheasant basted with pomegranate juice, but it's a favorite of mine." Never receiving an answer from her, Nefari kept talking as she sat next to Bellina. Picking at the glistening meat she squealed in delight. "Ummm, this is good! You can't go on like this again. If you start fasting, I'll call black Musa to carry you away."

"Humph! Musa!" Bellina frowned as she put aside her thoughts and joined Nefari, tasting the plump seeds that spilled from opened pomegranates. "I'm beginning to think he's the only man in this palace."

"Don't worry. If the Sultan rejects you, you get to live in pampered peace for the rest of your life. Anyway, few girls ever shared his bed even once."

Bellina straightened indignantly and felt her cheeks glow with embarrassment. Had her curiosity to meet the sultan been so obvious? "I've been here over a month and I've never seen the sultan—that's all!"

"That's all nothing? I do not understand you white-skinned foreign women. It is for the harmony, beauty, and perpetuation of life that we are chosen by Allah to serve man, and you want him to run to you? He doesn't, so you sulk like a child."

"What are you talking about? I couldn't care less if your sultan never comes." She hid her eyes from Nefari, afraid of their betrayal. "He's all you talk about. You go to the Sultan's bed, if he is all you deserve in life! Just go away and leave me alone." She rolled over, presenting a rigid back to Nefari.

"Oh no, you don't. Musa would punish me, not you, if you waste away in that bed. I'll show you the gardens today, you might as well get to know your home. Later I will show you how to paint your eyes the way men like them."

Even the splendor of her quarters had not prepared Bellina for the dazzling loveliness of the courtyard. Kaleidoscopic colors pleasured the eyes and cheered the spirit. The sweet honey of a million blossoms mingled with herbs and perfumed the air, rivaling any of the incenses that forever burned inside the palace.

Delighting in the plush green that stretched before her almost to the sea's edge, she kicked off her slippers and bounded across it. The few women who dallied in the shade of the apricot trees whispered furtively among themselves and sent disapproving glances in her direction. It bothered Bellina little if they thought she was insane, this was the closest haven to the gardens in her courtyard in Venice. Some of the plants were strange to her, but she recognized most of them. She would not have imagined such delicate beauty here. She rose on her toes to catch the salty sea breeze that was brought on a lazy puff of air. There it was. If she stood high enough and far enough away, the sparkle of the Bosporus could be seen over the wall.

Nefari was strolling by the many fountains that spurted awe-inspiring fans of sun-created water-jewels. Amusement lit her face as she watched Bellina. The garden had produced the desired effect; her heart was much lighter than it had been since she was brought here.

Nefari was bursting with her own excitement and fought all day to wait for the right moment to tell Bellina. She had not known when would be the right time until now. These women from across the sea were so unpredictable. At times Bellina sparkled with childish delight when they chatted about the sultan, then the next moment she would deny any interest in him. Yet Nefari knew she was at least curious to meet him, no matter how many times she denied it.

Twirling a sprig of grape hyacinth in one hand, she called to Bellina. She came reluctantly but her face glowed with the joy of being alive this sunny day.

"We must go back soon, for tomorrow will bring many more experiences for you. I have word that our sultan is indeed visiting. It is an important day for all of the odalisques." She pressed the flower into Bellina's hand. "To my people this is a symbol of acceptance. Present it to the sultan, and show him you are truly deserving of the honor he has bestowed on you."

Bellina stared at the sprig in her palm. Yes, that sort of gesture would suit her needs well.

"That is," a sweet voice said from behind them, "if you were indeed to meet our sultan, Bellina." Janil took the sprig of flowers from her hand, bringing the fragrant blossoms to her nose. "But you have not demonstrated to me that you wish to be a part of our life here. You are rude and unthinking. When our Dear One comes tomorrow, I forbid you anywhere near the pool room." And with that, she floated with immeasurable grace back with her ladies, their laughter chiming together like little bells.

Bellina felt a deep heat of resentment and anger. "She may be the sultana, but she cannot keep me away!"

Nefari placed a gentle restricting hand upon her shoulder. "Don't even think it, Bellina! She may not have the authority to keep you away, but do not make an enemy of her."

"I must see the sultan!" Bellina added viciously, "Only to make him understand I cannot live here. Then I'll be out of her hair."

Nefari tugged her away, safe from the others. "You are the first one I ever felt might become my friend. I don't want to lose you to Janil's poisons."

Bellina sighed but her mouth tightened in frustration. "I have no plans of being that whore's victim, but neither am I going to bend to her threats. One way or another, I am going to get your sultan's ear."

Seventeen

The following day the usual quiet of the harem fled with the giggling excitement that splashed as abundantly as the water from the alabaster fountains at either end of the long rectangular pool. Squeals mingled with the bubbly laughter and echoed from the mirrored walls. Even the ferns around the perimeter seemed to dance, absorbing the streaming rays of light that painted the hall with streaks of gold, creating a tableau rich in color, unsurpassed by any painter's palette. Small groups of girls, naked from the waist, spoke to each other in their native tongue. The women brushed long black and brown hair until it gleamed. They lined their eyes with kohl and chatted profusely as they periodically checked their reflections in the blue-tiled pool. A variety of languages clashed together in an unintelligible babble. A few of them, favored by the sultan, were tutored in Latin.

Mehmet was different from the rulers before him. He strove to better the Ottoman Empire through education as well as possession of land. He was powerful and ruthless, yet was saddened by the effects of destruction and pillage on Constantinople. So he set about raising the city from the ashes and rubble, and aided the Greeks and Christians in restoring their fractured lives and businesses. He held daily talks with leaders and masters of thought, discussing Arab and Persian philosophy as well as the works of Ptolemy. However, like most Turks, he viewed Europeans as generally weak, letting their women dictate their lives. They could not even go into battle without having some female waiting at camp to nourish them. It angered him that these unwashed *gyaours*, who drank too much and were impatient fools, viewed his people as ignorant barbarians. Therefore, he took much satisfaction in showing that even his concubines and the lowest slaves could speak the Latin tongue, while their ambassadors stood by in idiot muteness when Osmanli was spoken.

Halida found Bellina propped against the tufted arm of the couch, ruminating, lost in the arabesque design that covered a fine porcelain urn close by. "Well, well," Halida said, her veil not hiding the scorn upon her face. "I thought I would find you asleep; you're no doubt too excited. You should hear the wagging of tongues around the pool."

Bellina stretched, but the tightness she felt in the pit of her stomach refused to lighten. Janil's eyes had followed her from across the room with the predatory gleam of a hawk, but Bellina had no intention of being the mouse. "I don't want to keep our esteemed leader waiting now, do I?" she answered Halida's

215

disdain caustically.

Halida's eyes narrowed with the fine line of her lips. "This way," she snapped shortly, turning with the swirl of saffron silk.

Bellina almost had to run to keep up with her, slipping on the polished floor and nearly falling more than once. By the time they reached the main room, the other girls were arranging themselves in one long colorful row along the edge of the pool, their veiled heads bobbing as they talked. Lotifa and Nefari sandwiched her between them as they giggled with excitement.

She leaned her head forward in curiosity as she surveyed the young odalisques. To her embarrassment each one had only a sheer wrapper of color hanging from their waist to the floor. Long manes of hair were draped over shoulders and down backs, carefully arranged to accentuate rather than to disguise any of the girls' features. Some were adorned with long gold chains that nestled between their breasts or ornate bracelets that curled like snakes around their arms. Perhaps gifts once given to the favored?

Many of the women were strange to Bellina for she had seen little of the rest of the harem. Some were heavy and voluptuous, others were small but well formed, but all were stunning. Gone were the five little girls, Mehmet's daughters, who rounded the harem's corridors and gardens with their laughter. Their childish beauty had no place in this collection of priceless art.

It was at this moment that Bellina became aware of her own self, and noticed that time had metamorphosed her into something desirable. Something, she thought, not someone. Only another treasure to be placed beside all the rest. Yet what would happen should this porcelain doll become cracked and flawed? Poor Halida with her striking lemon-shaded hair was not old, but neither was she young, and finally Bellina could understand the look of desperation that haunted her eyes. Only Janil, in her confident role of sultana, showed none of the nervousness that touched everyone in some way.

Bellina let her eyes rove over the varying skin tones, from her own creamy white to the rich deep brown of an Ethiopian. It was obvious every corner of the world was represented in Mehmet's collection, and a quick surge of resentment flushed her cheeks. She did not see Lotifa's sidelong glance.

"Take this off!" the girl laughed, pulling on the short blouse that clung to Bellina's rib cage. "Didn't Halida tell you anything? Probably not, she would like to see the Sultan displeased with you."

The green of Bellina's eyes deepened. "This is as naked as I'm going to get. I'm not doing this for his pleasure, I just want to talk to him." She paused as a new dread entered her mind. "This is not going to be very long, is it?"

"Oh, I guess not. The sultan is just going to parade himself like a peacock, give a few appraisals, get every girl's hopes up, and only then make his choice."

Bellina snorted in derision, "Does he take a count, too?"

Lotifa laughed, "Probably."

"Are they afraid someone is going to escape from

this 'paradise'?" Bellina asked with a nod towards the line of eunuchs that stood and stared in stony silence.

"Of course not," Nefari interjected. "They are our protectors, not our keepers. Are we not all happy and content? Are we not blessed to be—"

Bellina's hand waved curtly. "Yes, yes, so you are constantly telling me." And perhaps you are right for some of you, she added in her thoughts, for it did seem some were content with their luxurious existence, even though there was nothing very stimulating or exciting, discounting one of Mehmet's visits. But that was not the case for all.

"Bellina," Lotifa pleaded. "Uncover yourself. Everyone else is. Besides, who will see you other than our sultan?"

"And those strange men? No thank you."

Lotifa gave the eunuch guards a disdainful look and shrugged at Bellina's stubbornness. It was Nefari who fretted, twisting her hair nervously. "Mehmet is not going to approve of this, you really do stand out, Bellina." But Bellina ignored her, a smile touching her lips.

Suddenly, the chatter stopped and smiles vanished. Only the fountain's splashes broke the silence with their fine tinkle, as a man, his flowing ermine-lined jibba brushing the marble, entered the room. At once the line bowed in reverent respect, leaving a hypnotized Bellina standing alone until a small hand pulled her down. The chiseled yet handsome features of Mehmet carefully scrutinized each girl's appearance as he passed from one to the other. In turn Bellina boldly stared as the ostrich plume fans waved hypnotically over him. So intent in watching their gracefulness, she did not at first notice the two dark brown eyes that took in her unguarded stare.

Again she was taken aback by his youth, surprised at how young this conqueror was as she noticed the smooth planes of his face. She stood still and indifferent, even when he gathered her hair and tossed it over her shoulders. His hands, brown and strong, firmly clasped her own as he led her from the others to the brooding Kislar Aga. He continued down the line, giving a rewarding smile and affectionate pat on the head to a few who seemed to once have been favorites; then he stopped before Janil. Her mouth had dropped in hurt surprise when Bellina had entered and caught his attention, but she quickly resumed an unreadable expression.

"You are as lovely as a flower today," Mehmet told Bellina, and he gave her the same little pat. Without another word he left as solemnly as he entered, taking the quiet with him. He did not catch all the dark shades of hate and jealousy that darkened Janil's face.

Musa motioned for Bellina to follow him through a long passageway, its darkness penetrated by glowing torches that revealed a continuation of the palace's richness. She watched the hard ebony back of Musa as he moved in what seemed like one continuous motion. Considering that he was the largest man she'd ever seen, she never ceased to be awed with the grace with which he carried himself. The corridor led to a small compartment of a room that seemed to be a private bath. A shelf surrounded a rose-marbled sunken tub that was cluttered with various jars and urns, tiny glass pitchers, and thick sea sponges. He left her standing before a pool that was quickly filling with steamy water from twisted faucets of gold. It was simply amazing. Where did the water come from? Never had she seen the likes of this in Venice.

In wonder of it all, she let her veils and pantaloons float to the floor and sunk into the calming hot water, thinking of all the trips her servant Anna used to make. All the way from the kitchens until she reached her chamber, the little maid would fret and mumble, "Madonnina, you are going to make yourself sick with all the soaking and scrubbing you do! Madonnina, what will Rosa say!"

Rose, jasmine, and the fragrances of a whole summer's garden escaped as Bellina removed the stopper from the tapered neck of a crystal decanter. With a deep sniff, she poured the richly scented oil into the water until it spread with a thick foam and faded into the steam that lingered over the top of the water. It floated about the room, shrouding it in a heavy scented mist that filmed the mirrored walls.

Lulled into a deep tranquility by the hot bath, she did not hear Lotifa's soft patter as her slippered feet paced the room. "Are you going to soak till you get all wrinkled? Halida and the Master of the Wardrobe will be here shortly."

Bellina wrapped her hair in a soft towel and let Lotifa buff her dry until her skin glowed with a pink iridescence. However, her peace was shortly disrupted as Nefari, the Master of the Wardrobe, and a procession of slaves and snipe-nosed officials followed Halida into the room. Bellina clutched her narrow strip of towel with tenacity, "What is the meaning of

220

this? Can't a person even take a bath without an audience?" I had more privacy in a camp full of Spahiglani, she thought to herself. Her complaint went unheard, just as if she were only a spectator at this bizarre performance.

Halida grabbed a corner of Bellina's towel, but she pulled away darkly scowling. "We don't have time for your famed European coquetry, young lady," the older woman chastised with annoyance as she whipped the towel from Bellina's hips. "Musa will have the soles of your feet flogged until the only position you'll want to be in is horizontal!"

Bellina tried to resign herself to it all. If this is what one had to go through to catch the sultan's ear, then so be it.

She found herself shuffled from the guardian of the royal elixirs to the curator of the sultan's jewels that lay dripping over the side of a gilt tray. But worst of all were the barbers who plucked away at her arms and legs with truculent delight until not a hair remained on her body except for her long hennaed mane.

"There, that wasn't so bad," Nefari cooed, trying to console her. "The worst is over and the best part is yet to come."

"This is the best part?" Bellina asked under a cloud of rice flour as two pairs of hands patted the powder over her oiled skin.

"This will make your skin as soft as velvet and the Sultan will not be able to resist touching you," Nefari reflected wistfully.

"He's not going to touch me," Bellina averred. "I just want to explain my situation to him. I know he'll understand," she added, mostly to reassure herself.

Bellina gasped as she caught a glimpse of herself plastered with the sticky paste. In spite of herself the sight lightened her spirits. She became less worrisome and more interested, as four girls she recognized from the harem stained each of her finger- and toenails, and one slowly peeled away pieces of the mask she wore. A sable brush whisked away the remaining flakes of mask and then a massage of scented oils were kneaded into her muscles until her skin tingled.

Nefari gathered Bellina's hair and wrapped it tightly on the top of her head in a knot and curled wisps of hair into wings that framed her face. "There, you cannot hide behind those locks!" she said triumphantly, weaving in some sprigs of grape hyacinth.

A woman stared back at Bellina from the mirror with dark kohl-smudged eyes, but its softness failed to warm her icy glare. She wondered what happened to the carefree girl she used to know. While she stood amazed at her own apparition, the room had been miraculously cleared of all the paraphernalia and people in the time it took for Musa to lower his arm in one long commanding swoop. She heard her voice echo in the empty marble and glass room. "I've been so bedraggled and dirty, weary and dusty, for so long, that I thank you for making me feel like a contessa."

"What's a contessa?" Lotifa asked, eager to learn everything about these peculiar infidels.

"Well, a contessa is like a sultana."

"And," added Nefari, picking up the small train of

Bellina's gown, "after this night you may very well become our 'contessa.'"

Bellina patiently tried again to dispel their misunderstandings, when the ominous mass of Musa shadowed the three, silencing their conversation and sending them from the room and down the corridor without any exchange of words. The solemn procession of handmaids and eunuchs snaked after Bellina in an unbearable tension that thankfully Lotifa broke. "Bellina," she whispered, "after, the Sultan will leave you alone in his room. If he has been pleased with you, he will leave presents in his clothes." Bellina blinked, not comprehending. Lotifa threw up her hands at her silence. "I give up on you, Bellina! Don't you understand?"

Bellina felt revolted and her blood began to boil. It was all she could do to repress the anger ready to explode. But the presence of the ever watchful Musa contained Bellina's wrath, as she thought of the pleasure this sadistic excuse of a man would gain from slashing her feet and throwing her tied onto his master's bed. No, she was certain Mehmet would consider the injustices done to her at the hands of his people. Although she didn't know him, she had sensed an innate sense of justice in the man.

Lotifa recognized well the stubborn set of her face. "Bellina, do not insult our ruler and shun his gifts. He may never call for you again—or worse, he may have you tied in a sack and thrown into the Bosporus!"

Before she could reply, Musa gave her a forceful nudge. She continued down the rest of the ill-lit passage alone, until she came to an abrupt halt at the foot of a trailing row of black polished steps.

Before her, seated on a couch of Venetian design, was the great conqueror of so many lands: the most feared of all men. To her he looked kindly but, she recalled in a foreboding flash, so did her old friend Naqu.

A gentle curve touched his lips. "Come, dear," he purred. But she was suddenly paralyzed until a mocha hand embellished with rings reached out to her own. Looking into his soft eyes, he could have been the bishop of Rome himself and she placed her hand trustingly in his, stepping down into the sunken room. "You tremble. Are you thinking of all the notorious tales told of Mehmet?" Not waiting for her to answer, he patted the back of her hand reassuringly. "Well forget them, you have nothing to fear of me, I don't beat women—I prefer to love them."

"It is not those tales, your highness, that have made me tremble," she murmured. She was going to add that Musa was a sadistic animal just waiting for someone to carve up, but a new instinct that she had developed in this land of ruthless men who sold women like animals, changed her reply. She let her lips part provocatively. "On the contrary, my heart is fluttering with the majesty of your presence." She lowered her eyes, afraid her falseness would be betrayed, and did not see his brows rise in amusement.

He raised her willow-thin hands to his lips and lightly kissed them before he left her to retrieve a platter of sweetmeats. His royal blue caftan, embroidered in an array of metallic threads, sparkled as he moved. Gold bracelets adorned his arms and a

224

heavy medal hung around his neck, resting upon the brown expanse of chest that escaped from the cut opening of his tunic. She smiled inwardly as she thought of Lotifa's "strutting peacock." He did not return to her but strolled over to a large divan. It was canopied by a light blue fabric that billowed with the wind floating in from the courtyard. He motioned for her to come to him, and through his eyes she watched the pleasure he took as she approached. She knew well that the gossamer veils clung to each curve and mysteriously shadowed her body, lending a seductive grace to her movements. For the first time in her life she felt the power her femininity could fire, realizing it could be as devastating to Mehmet as his own strategic genius was to the Christian fleet.

"I'm told you're called Bellina." He leaned lazily upon the divan, his eyes never leaving her. "I like that sound, so Bellina you shall be called. Tell me, my beautiful emerald, are you as cold as those green eyes of yours?"

She steamed over the casual way he indicated she was his property. It was inferred in each sentence and gesture and shook her from his hypnotic charm. For a moment he had held her captive like the swaying cobras that rose from their reed baskets in the market, but the spell was broken. She answered him tersely, "If you were in my position, would *your* eyes be cold like mine? I am here against my will at the hands of those who serve you. And my companion . . . how does he fare at your mercy?"

Taken aback, Mehmet's kind features hardened, sending a shiver up her spine. "We are not an insensitive people and we are not callous animals as

225

you seem to be thinking. It seems you are lacking the Venetian grace and manners I have heard so much of. This once will I excuse your tone, because I know our ways are yet new to you. Now come sit beside me."

She wanted to ask him how she *should* feel, when even the horses of the Spahiglani were treated with more kindness and consideration than she had been, but his words had chilled her. Perhaps she had made a grave error in her judgment of his character. She could see Musa's broad face expand with pleasure, his cavernous mouth flashing pearly teeth as he delighted in dealing with a delinquent concubine who dared to consider herself more important than a horse. Instead she bowed down and began to mend the tear in the web she wove, remembering Nefari's words. "Forgive my insolence," she murmured.

Cautiously she moved to sit upon the divan, at the same time cursing the wild tremor of her heart, for surely he would note the weakness. He did not touch her, much to her relief. Instead, he reclined upon the divan and turned his probing eyes upon her. Silently he offered the rahat lokum and at the shake of her head placed the plate on a low table.

"So," he said softly, "How do you like it here? Indeed have you found yet an unhappy soul among your companions?"

"No, my Lord. They speak of nothing but your generosity."

"Hmmm," his arms folded nonchalantly behind his head. "And what of your quarters, are you comfortable?"

"Most comfortable, my Lord."

"But you would rather be away from here? Eh? Far

226

away from this foreign devil who serves pickled babies at feasts before battles and ties the heads of his enemies upon the saddle of his warhorse." At Bellina's stricken look, he laughed. "So, that is what I am to you—a ruthless barbarian."

"No!" Bellina cried, coming to her feet, struggling to assume Janil's expressionless face. She sat with a seductive grace, her movements unhurried, and when she spoke she found it in herself to make her words come soft and low. "I mean, your Grace, that perhaps once I might have believed those words, but now that I have met you—"

Abruptly, his hand caught hers with a firm tightness and his lips thinned. "I liked you better when you showed more honesty."

Bellina's breath left her. What could she do? What could she say? Each way she jumped he was there with his swordlike words to beat her back. She felt a burning in her eyes and blinked back tears with ferocity. And then it suddenly came to her and she knew how to lay her snare.

She met his eyes forcefully. "My Lord, it seems again I must beg forgiveness. It is just that I do not know how to speak and of what to speak to the ruler of the Ottomans."

His head once again leaned back to coolly appraise her but this time she moved nearer. "If I may be so bold as to say so, you are not what I had expected."

"Indeed?"

"Yes. To find one with all the weight of the rule of half the world to be so young. . . . Well, I had not expected it."

He sighed, wearily closing his eyelids for a

moment, and when he finally spoke his voice was leaden. "I am not as young as you think, my child. When I was but thirteen I was older than most whose years were as numerous as the fleas on a dog."

"You are young to me, when I had imagined you to be a gray and wrinkled old man. Would you like me to tell you of my home, young Sultan?"

And so she told him all that she knew and some of what she had held in dreams. She spoke not of long hot nights sleeping with the shamal wind at her ear or of swords that sang death's song in the streets; but of the waters that spread like fingers, reaching and joining until they emptied into the sea; and the Doge who once each year threw a gold ring into the depths to renew the marriage of sea and merchants. Summer breezes, springtime merchant fairs, the doge's lion-headed vaults that swallowed petitions of injustice— on and on she wove her tales until his piercing eyes softened. Once she even surprised a hearty laugh out of him.

Bellina felt him lean closer and could not help but jump as his arms suddenly surrounded her shoulders.

"Your father took you with him when he came here? What was a magistrate doing here, and with his daughter no less?"

"I didn't say he was a magistrate," Bellina said, wondering how he could have misunderstood. "He was a merchant and a good one, too."

Mehmet laughed again but it did not reach his eyes. "I cannot understand your people. A woman is to be cherished, protected like the bloom of a rose, for she is fragile—a gift of nature." He held her under her chin, gazing strongly into her eyes, and Bellina tried to calm a sudden flash of uneasiness.

"My people pamper their women. Women have no thought to danger, secure in the knowledge that they are well respected and taken care of. Can life be any happier," he said with pride and total belief, encompassing the room with outstretched arms, "than here?" He gave her a gentle squeeze. "Stand!" He suddenly ordered, and before she thought about it, she followed his command.

"Tell me and look at me," he said forcefully. "Do you like my land?"

Bellina's heart leaped into her mouth, how could she insult him? She depended on his good will. "My Lord," she began, "I just miss my own home."

"But," he was quick to point out, "sooner or later every woman must leave her home." He held out both of her hands in his and pulled her towards him. His lips met hers and he seared her as he led a trail to her breast.

"My Lord!" Bellina protested, not able to hide her indignation. "Can't you understand that I want to go home? That I fear for my companion?"

"He is safe," Mehmet told her, not letting go of her hands. "He is enjoying my hospitality for the moment, while I am making the preparations for his trip back home."

"Thanks be to Allah!" Bellina praised without thinking, the time spent at the Spahiglani camp colored her speech.

Mehmet smiled broadly, "I know you will come to love it here. You were meant to be here with me, to be cherished like a jewel."

Bellina paled, stiffening as he pulled her midriff

up, releasing the rounded globes of her breasts. "Beautiful," he sighed, enraptured, preventing her from covering up. He held her arms wide and touched his tongue to a nipple, watching it harden.

"You are like a fruited garden," Mehmet said in a low voice and sighed again as she cried out at his tongue's touch. "I will not force you," he said with displeasure, releasing her arms, "but I think if you think about it, reasonably, you will realize that your life would be a utopia here."

Bellina tugged at her blouse, "You are my last hope. I am at your mercy, but I believe you to be a King of honor. I pray to your God and mine that you will not keep me here against my will, but will allow me to return to Venice with my countryman."

Mehmet smiled and stretched upon the divan like a lion. "Sleep will bring reason. Sweet slumber, my jewel, we shall talk further tomorrow."

And as Musa came to take her back, she heard Mehmet call for Janil.

Eighteen

Mehmet was an everyday visitor over the next week and as Bellina stood with the others, she could not silence her pounding heart or dispel the nervousness that weakened her knees so much that she was sure she would collapse in a heap, mortified. For certain, Mehmet must have enjoyed her discomfort. He would always linger when he came upon her, his eyes meeting hers with a painful intensity; then silently, he would pass her by to choose Janil.

Bellina sighed a mixture of relief and frustration. As long as Janil felt no threat, Bellina could eat her food without fear of being poisoned, but she was no closer to Venice.

What Bellina didn't know was that she was being watched. Two dark eyes saw the sunlight tease her eyes open every morning, lingering over every supple curve of her body as she stretched night's stiffness away. They were there again as she broke her fast, laughing with Lotifa, and later as she pressed a flower between the pages of a book. When she shed her veils and pantaloons to bathe, they languished over the soft secret places of her body. If they could have entered into her mind and looked upon every thought and desire they would have, eagerly, for those eyes were Mehmet's eyes, and he felt as if a fever was consuming him.

Eventually Janil brought him little relief. He tried to push aside the pride Bellina had wounded with her refusal, confused still, rejection was a bitter brew which he had not cultivated a taste for. It was not Janil who was called that night.

Bellina entered, soft blue veils following her curves, her black hair concealing her breasts, her eyes wary. She had no choice, she sat upon the bed where he lay.

"You should wear green," he murmured, and unwittingly his words pricked her memory and she remembered the gown she had made from the green silk that Surek had given her.

Mehmet brushed his hand across her cheek. "And you should wear a smile as well." He chuckled softly as her eyes lit suddenly in angry defiance. "Your friend, Miquel," Mehmet said lazily, "I gave him his ship today. Tomorrow we will start to load provisions for his journey. Already he has picked his crew."

"Oh!" Bellina cried, "Let me see him, please."

"Silence!" Mehmet quieted her, his body stiffening.

Bellina clutched at the silken material of her clothes, her nails starting runs in the delicate fabric.

"You like to read?" Mehmet continued, in a softer voice. "You must explore my libraries. Musa will show you. And did you see the nightingale I found for you? He is a lovely one, as sweet a singer as can be found." Mehmet's hand slipped up her arm to her shoulder and Bellina felt herself tremble.

"Sultan," she said calmly, "I am grateful for your gifts, but in truth I need little."

"That may be true, graceful one," he laughed, "but you give my eyes such a feast; you lighten my heavy heart and make the world turn golden before me; for this I must repay." His other hand touched her knee, unable to keep still, wandering over her thigh. He smiled and tried to decipher the puzzling swirl of color in her eyes.

"No matter what part of our world you and I would be, I would bring you treasures. Such things to match the sparkle of your eyes—emeralds! And ivory for your skin; rubies, diamonds, and . . ." He leaned closer and to her surprise drew a small box from his robes. "And these to match the richness of your hair."

Bellina took the box with numb fingers. When she lifted the lid her breath sputtered out of her in shocked dismay, which Mehmet thankfully took as surprise. A strand of black pearls, a king's ransom's worth, lay coiled against blood-red velvet; another unwanted gift.

She felt the brush of Mehmet's hands as he fastened the strand of pearls around her neck, and she was jerked back to reality as they fell upon her skin with a deathly chill. He kissed the tender valley between her breasts where the last one fell. "They are lovely," she murmured, and then with a sudden puzzlement, "Where did you get these? Black pearls are a rarity in such number."

"In the Black Sea, of course!" Mehmet laughed. He

nuzzled against her, passing his hand over her hair as if she was some treasured pet. "What does it matter? They are yours, my love."

"As I am yours? Then how can anything be mine if—"

"Ah, Bellina!" Mehmet sighed, pulling her even closer. "When will you stop fighting a war that has ended long ago? When will you accept life here? Is it so bad?"

She felt an unwanted flush come to her cheeks. Careful, she told herself, power would never come by alienating Mehmet with her angry words. But she was losing time, Miquel would leave soon. She smiled with what she hoped was a pleasant meekness. "Do forgive me, but I am so homesick, I fear it blinds me. This is a beautiful world that you have created, and I am happy most of the time."

She forced a timid smile and looked shyly up into his eyes. Gently her lips touched his. With a hunger almost too much for him to control, Mehmet seized her, crushing her against his hard and powerful body until she almost lost her breath.

"I know you can be happy here," he said in a voice that challenged dissension.

"But sometimes," Bellina continued, untangling herself from his arms, "I am consumed with a grief unimaginable. How my family must be half-mad with grief! They have heard nothing of me and fear the worst. I must see them one more time, to tell of my good fortune and to bid them farewell. Indeed my heart could only open if I first heal its wounds."

Mehmet's mouth thinned and set cruelly, "Never!" he said crisply, without room for compromise.

234

"They will forget you and you will forget them."

"I would come back," Bellina promised.

"I am not some stupid camel driver!" Mehmet flared.

"At least let me see Miquel before he leaves," she begged.

"All right," Mehmet agreed slowly, his handsome features stern. "You can see him, for I plan to have a last dinner with him. Yes," he said gloating in his generosity. His eyes sparkled thinking about what Captain Edib had said. How perfect! "You and Janil will grace the banquet room with your loveliness. Together you are like two gems, each trying to outshine the other!"

Bellina joined his laughter with difficulty, and although she tried to control it, her irritation showed. Mehmet's eyes danced as he grabbed her, pulling her in a tumble to the bed. He pinned her beneath him, his body hard in an overwhelming desire, and loosening his caftan, he let it part. His flesh touched hers, burning, he could feel the pounding of her heart against his chest and see the fear rise in her eyes. Virgins! Each was as exciting as a new spice, he thought, but they must be gently broken not forced. He didn't bare her breasts but bit gently at her nipples through the thin silk.

"Please don't," Bellina gasped, as his hands held her buttocks forcefully and he pressed against her, his manhood straining against her meager fabric barrier. Her body felt as if it was on fire, her heart leaped in her chest.

"Promise me," Mehmet whispered in her ear. "Promise me you will tell Miquel the truth—that you are happy and wish to stay here. Promise me!"

"You are frightening me!" Bellina cried, unable to move away from his probing hands.

"Promise! he laughed. "And I will stop." His caftan had been thrown aside and he was naked as a Greek god, brown and muscular and very hard.

Convinced that he would carry out his threat when he began to tug at her pantaloons, she forced her breath through clenched teeth. "I promise! By Allah, I promise!"

He let her clothes be, but once more held her tightly, his mouth hungrily seeking hers. "I knew you'd be happy here," he said huskily, and it was with a great effort that he let her go.

As Bellina was led back to the harem, she passed Janil. Briefly the sultana's eyes widened as she noticed Bellina's necklace. It was brief but their eyes met, and Janil's were dark with hate, and promised Bellina a slow painful death. Bellina pulled her veils closer, chilled by Mehmet's desire and Janil's jealousy. When she reached her room she heard the nightingale begin his song. Without hesitation she opened his cage and watched him soar to freedom, his notes soon faint to her ears.

Since the previous night, Bellina realized that Mehmet's gift had a strong effect on the harem, as his favoritism became clear. Every girl was aware of Bellina's new status. Some mewed at her feet like abandoned kittens, hopeful some attention would perchance rub off. Some held her in haughty disdain or ignored her. Those loyal to Janil held a dangerous silence, eyes meeting hers openly enough to show their hate. As ever, Lotifa remained a dear friend and accomplice in mischief.

Without a doubt, Bellina mused, Lotifa was misplaced in this fine gilded nest of nightingales, being the only one to beat her wings against her cage. She was a naughty child with an insatiable curiosity and an unquenchable joy of life that even Musa's presence could not temper, and Bellina could not fathom how life would be without her. Indeed the spice among the endless hours of inactivity was provided by Lotifa's escapades.

Once a guard's head was turned, both of them would disappear together for a few hours of unwatched bliss. Of Lotifa's secret places the passage through the seraglio was Bellina's favorite. They would squeeze through small hallways that were seldom used and then only by servants. They'd crouch behind the glittering mosaic that covered one wall until they finally reached the gardens. It was Lotifa's assumption that the hidden paths that wound their way through the palace and eventually through the seraglio were once used by some of the sultan's friends to gaze upon them undetected by the army of eunuchs. Bellina was intrigued by Lotifa's imagination, but would have rather believed the passages to be for servants, and since she rarely saw the slaves until they were upon her, she believed the latter.

Once outside, Lotifa uncovered a tunnel that led through the maze of hedge that sectioned the garden. Crawling through the hedge without tearing their silk pantaloons proved an impossibility, but once they lay on the warm sand with the roar of the ocean erasing their bondage, it was almost worth the lies told to Halida.

"How did the tunnel get there?" Bellina asked Lotifa.

"Who knows? I just found it one day."

Bellina turned her face into the salty wind and stared across the wild sea. "Perhaps someone had tried to escape to the sea and the tunnel was never found. It is rather narrow and overgrown, but . . ."

"Don't get any ideas," Lotifa laughed as she followed the trail of Bellina's eyes.

It was a stormy day that dawned, the day Mehmet had chosen for Miquel's farewell feast. So it passed at an unbelievable crawl as Bellina waited the hours until dinner, letting herself be primped, watching Janil do the same. Lotifa rattled on endlessly. Bellina hardly heard a word, for her thoughts were on Miquel. How happy she was that Mehmet would let him return.

It was soon time to go when Halida entered Bellina's chamber. She gave Lotifa a sharp glance but she set down two boxes. "This will dazzle those foreigners," she laughed, removing the black pearl necklace from one and fastening it around Bellina's neck. "And my Lord Sultan sends you this." Halida opened the other box to reveal an exquisite gold filigree ring holding another enormous black pearl. It matched the necklace beautifully.

"Lovely," Bellina said, awed. Halida took it out and reached for Bellina's hand. "Not yet!" Bellina said, "Lotifa hasn't hennaed my nails yet."

"Oh," Halida said, closing the box, "I'll come

back later then."

"Leave it here," Lotifa insisted. "I'll put it on her later."

Halida paused, then reluctantly placed the box upon the table, and left.

"No!" Lotifa laughed, taking Bellina's veil out of her hands. "That is not the way, look, I'll show you again." She swirled and wrapped the black veil expertly around Bellina's head, leaving only her two eyes showing.

"Surely he doesn't expect me to eat with this veil," Bellina objected. To her dismay Lotifa nodded. "If he wants to show us off, he's showing precious little."

Lotifa made a paste of henna and water and painted it on Bellina's nails. "I've heard that later, when he is relaxed, and if it is a small party, that he will remove the veil."

"Well, it is only Miquel there as far as I know," Bellina said as Lotifa turned her hands over and painted her palms also. "And he has known me all my life."

"There, let it set," Lotifa said, carefully setting Bellina's hands down on her lap. "Our Sultan's Grand Vizier is always there and sometimes his most trusted equestrian. I heard Janil say that she had been told that Captain Harun Edib of the Spahiglani will be there. Janil saw him once and has never stopped talking about him since! Bellina!" Lotifa cried, "You mustn't move! You've smeared your nails."

"I'm sorry," Bellina said faintly, a sudden ill feeling rising accompanied by a rapid heartbeat. Surek! My God, Surek will be there! She wanted to scream in horror or desire, she knew not which. That he would recognize her veiled or not was beyond questioning, and she knew his anger at her escape must have been as violent as a desert storm. Perhaps by now, she hoped, he had forgotten some of it and was over his rage. Or perhaps he would not acknowledge her before Mehmet. But, how, she wondered, was she going to last through dinner knowing he was so close, and she not able to touch his face?

Lotifa couldn't get much of a conversation out of Bellina after that, and picking up on her worry and agitation they both forgot about the pearl ring and Bellina left without it.

The music reached her ears first, an oud rhythmically singing a sensuous song that she unconsciously matched her movements to. Janil wordlessly joined her from behind, dressed in the same veils, and for the first time Bellina saw confusion in her eyes as they met hers and fell away. As they entered, their smoke-colored veils stirred in the sweep of the huge fans that the slaves used to push the air about. Mehmet conversed with emphatic gestures with his Grand Vizier, Miquel, Alonzo, and Surek. He paused and looked up with a smile.

"There are my two flowers. Come to me," he said, patting a hassock on either side of him. Janil chose first, seating herself on Mehmet's right where Surek sat next to her. With some relief Bellina claimed the remaining seat, only too happy to have Miquel next to her. Their eyes met pouring out their joy and relief, underscored by an everpresent worry.

"Aren't they matchless!" Mehmet beamed.

240

"Indeed, my Lord, they are," Surek agreed, his eyes trying to capture Bellina's.

Alonzo twisted his mustache between his fingers. "Tell me. Which one is your Bellina, Miquel?"

Before either Miquel or Bellina could say a word, Mehmet clasped her hand between his two. "My pearl from Venice. You see? She belongs so naturally to this setting, that they have trouble guessing who she is!"

Bellina lowered her eyes, refusing to meet Surek's. "My Lord, it is the veils that confuse them."

"You may remove them, my pets," Mehmet said, leaning back. "I was telling Miquel how happy you are here, but I can see the disbelief and mistrust in his eyes, even if he's too polite to disagree. I'm afraid he must hear it from your sweet lips, my dear."

Bellina's heart lurched, remembering her promise to Mehmet and his unspoken threats. In spite of herself she glanced nervously at Surek. It was a mistake, for his two black eyes forcefully grabbed hers. Although they were colored by anger, she saw they were also touched with disbelief. His face looked older, lined by pain.

Bellina felt trapped and hopeless. "My Lord, you have been most gracious; your palace incomparable; your care true and considerate, but . . ." her voice faltered. "I could never find happiness here."

All of the men fell silent, only Janil allowed a smile to curve her lips. Mehmet tried to shadow the anger in his face without success.

Bellina rushed on, "Please don't think I am ungrateful. I thank you with my heart and soul for your benevolent care, for this pearl necklace, and the ring you gave me this day."

Mehmet scowled, "I gave you no ring."

"The black pearl ring?" Bellina said puzzled.

"I gave you no ring!" Mehmet hissed, "Only my sultanas get rings." He snaked a hand around Janil's waist pulling her closer.

"My Sultan," Surek said quietly, "these foreign women are never happy. Your guest has told me this many times."

"Indeed," Miquel agreed quickly. "Some say that women are the true plague of the earth."

"I disagree," Alonzo laughed. "They are like a bitter herb. Taken in small amounts they add a refreshing bite to life, too much and they will kill you."

"Some are just better put aside," the Grand Vizier said with contempt and a harsh glance at Bellina.

"Hush!" Mehmet growled, holding up one hand. "She has more spirit than most, that is all. And she is young and confused and in need of proper training."

Suddenly, Musa flung a massive door aside to step into the room. To Bellina's surprise he fell upon the floor before Mehmet with a jumble of half-words, half-moans. No one understood what he was trying to say, but urgency was plain.

"Excuse me," Mehmet said quickly, leaving with the Grand Vizier.

They waited for an hour with their conversation stilted. Even Janil was quiet, speaking little to Surek's questions. None of the slaves appeared with food as the hour passed into another. Surek stood to pace uneasily.

Finally, the Grand Vizier returned, his face pale.

"There has been a tragedy, I fear. The beloved princess Alosha has died suddenly."

Janil shrieked, shredding at her veils and face with her nails as slaves led Bellina and her away.

A short while later, Surek found himself before the Grand Vizier and Mehmet, listening in disbelief as he was told of Alosha's death. Mehmet held the black pearl ring of death in his hand, the barb underneath the stone now cleaned of the poison.

"Bellina mentioned a black pearl ring," the Vizier said. "It was obviously meant for her."

"It was Janil, I'm sure," Surek said.

Mehmet's eyes flashed with pain. "How could she kill her own daughter! Our daughter!" he said brokenly.

"The woman is filled with poison," Surek said emphatically. "Alosha only put that ring on like any nine-year-old girl would. Janil didn't count on that, she wanted Bellina to wear it thinking it a gift from you, my Lord."

Mehmet buried his forehead into his palm. "Janil is so gentle, I've never seen her cruel or angry."

"You are blinded, my Sultan," the Vizier spat. "Edib is right. Who else could it be? Janil was consumed by jealousy."

"Or Bellina hates Janil and me so much that she would strike out at our child!" Mehmet hissed.

Surek frowned, "My Lord, let me question the Venetian. I assure you I will find out the truth."

Mehmet was silent for a long time. "Very well," he said. "Get to the bottom of this, no matter what it takes."

And so Bellina found herself facing Surek alone in

243

a tiny room not far from the harem. She could not meet his eyes, for in them she could see her betrayal of him, a betrayal he could neither understand or forgive.

By now she knew of Alosha's death and had no doubt that either Janil or one of Janil's faithful women were responsible.

"Mehmet thinks you did it," Surek said calmly, cutting through the thick silence between them.

Bellina's face drained of all color, "Why would I do it? Do you think I would jeopardize my chances to get away from here like that!"

Surek couldn't stop himself. He grabbed her by her hair, pulling her close until she was forced back and he caught her angry eyes. "Did Mehmet service you well, dear? Or did you pleasure him with every care to buy his good will? I have never seen him quite so besot. I bet you were good, very good."

"He never hurt me," Bellina accused, "the way you do."

"No?" Surek laughed bitterly. "Maybe not, but he told me I could do whatever I wanted with you."

"You're all the same," she said pommeling him with her fists until he crushed her to him, his mouth hungrily upon hers. Gasping for breath, she twisted in his arms until her back was to him.

"I'm glad you escaped from me," he said viciously in her ear. "For in truth you will be nothing to me."

Bellina felt her veils part from her struggles, falling like a soft cloud in a tangle at her hips. Surek's hands were quickly there, cruelly grabbing and squeezing her breasts. With an outraged cry she bit him. "You'll never forget me, you bastard. You'll carry scars for the rest of your life!"

Jerking his arm back he momentarily lost control, but as she lurched away he grabbed her hips. To her horror the veils fluttered away and she could feel his hard swollen manhood pressed against her buttocks. With an angry jerk, Surek released it from the confines of his clothes. "And I, Bellina," he said harshly, "will make sure you remember me equally."

She felt his hardness part her body's most secret lips to stab its fullness deep into her and she screamed in anger and pain. Again and again he pounded until her body began to betray her, smoothing his way in a flood of passion. A flash of heat that left her weak flashed through her entire being. "No," she sobbed, but found herself meeting his thrusts to drive his staff deeper and deeper until she felt he invaded her very core. Then he stopped, withdrew, and released her, so suddenly that she fell to the floor in a bewildered heap.

"You are too eager a bitch for me," he growled, adjusting his clothes.

"But I love you!" she cried, feeling her chest contract in despair.

"No, you don't," he said scornfully. "You love Venice!" And with that he left her in a disheveled heap.

In the red haze of his anger he didn't hear the pleading tone under her words that might have made him turn back. Her soft sobs didn't soften his resolve to leave her once and for all. Surek knew it was time to give up all hope that one day she would commit herself to loving him. She was the sea and Venice was her moon, the force that pulled her away from him. If he sought out Mehmet's astrologer, the uselessness of their continuing relationship could be charted. But he had proof enough.

He walked without hesitation to Mehmet's quarters. It could not be guessed, behind features cold as marble, that he reviewed images of Bellina for the last time. He let his memory bathe in visions of her sundrenched skin, her cool eyes that sparkled like the sea, her comic attempts at mastering a horse for the first time, and the frown of diapproval that preceded an argument she most often won. He imagined the smell of her skin, the softness of her hair, and then buried her forever. After all he did, she would always despise him in her heart. He gave her little reason to love him. For all her pain, she blamed him perhaps rightly. He held her when she wanted to leave. He wondered for a moment, if he had given her freedom to decide whether to stay or to leave, what her decision would have been. But it was all too late now. The last thing he could do would be to convince Mehmet to let her go, then he would owe nothing to Bellina—he could forget her and be free himself.

He nodded to the pair of guards that flanked the last hallway to Mehmet's war room. He knew he would be there, lost in the consuming strategies to expand his empire, forgetting, for the moment the deception of Janil and Bellina.

Mehmet did not acknowledge Surek's announced presence, he remained entranced in a display of miniature horsemen cast in gold, spread across a relief of hills and forest. Toy boats floated on a vein of blue past a group of soldiers hidden behind a hedge of trees.

"Edib," he finally said. "Look here by the Dnieper, the Cossacks, those crawling insects! They dare to cross my borders, raid our villages, and burn the ships that bring us timber. I want you there with your Spahiglani. Teach them to respect the pact between their Prince and your Sultan."

"As you wish," Surek bowed slightly. To be in his homeland again, though dangerous, would give him new life.

Mehmet wrapped a jeweled fist around a small band of horsemen. "They are like the Byzantines, under my thumb they will perish. One day, Edib, all of Europe will be mine. The ambassadors of Europe and Asia sought to appease Ottoman strength with their gifts and congratulatory words. The greedy Greek emperor thought 300,000 aspers and an Ottoman prince in the Byzantine court would save their empire." He laughed, dropping the gold figures one by one on the table. "But it was all for time, time to build my fortress at Asomaton."

"Fetih," Surek lifted a tiny boat from its place. "Do you compare Prince Vasili with Constantine?"

"Vasili is helping us more than he knows, that would make him less than wise. But—he will be a useful ally for a while."

"Until a trust is broken," Surek added.

Mehmet narrowed sharp eyes on Surek. "Only fools rely on trust, Captain."

"All men are fools one time, My Fetih." Surek bowed respectfully.

Mehmet crossed and folded his arms. "You sound bitter, Edib. You have trusted your heart to a woman, I suspect. That has ruined empires!"

"Precisely, Fetih. I beg your forgiveness, but that is why you must give up the Venetian."

The Ottoman ruler laughed menacingly. "I intend to do just that! She will be given up—to the Bosporus!"

Surek turned to focus on the models of fighting men, fearful his face would betray the dread he felt for Bellina. He fought to keep his voice emotionless.

"She is just a woman and you have many, but think of the use she could be of to your political image."

Mehmet's interest sparked.

"By killing her," Surek continued, "you would add credence to all the tales of murder, rape, and slavery. Send her home with her countrymen, and they would tell the world of a great Ottoman king."

Mehmet rubbed his chin thoughtfully. He liked the idea. The girl would serve him well, after all.

Nineteen

When Bellina was summoned to stand before Mehmet, she prepared to hear her death sentence. A white-robed scribe unfurled the scroll, its end still curled at his waist. Bellina kept her eyes cast down at her feet, unable to look at Mehmet directly. Certain Mehmet would have his revenge, she imagined all of her fears were about to come true. The horror tales Lotifa told her would be nothing compared to what he must have in store for her punishment. What worse crime could there be than rejecting this powerful man? To him Janil's crime had been a sin of love. Bellina doubted he saw it as a consequence of corrupted power. He had dealt with Janil swiftly, while Bellina was left to wait and wonder what he had planned for her.

At the moment she thought to be her last, she mourned the fact that Surek had left her here to face a cruel and certain death. He probably gloated over the fact that her stubborn disobedience would be finally dealt with. How could he blame her for wanting to leave the confinement he subjected her to? It wasn't her doing that she found herself in the palace, imprisoned again. He blamed her for leaving him. She wasn't running from him, the Lord knew she wanted him, but not in this place. They were worlds apart and she knew it wouldn't work.

So certain was she of the worst, Bellina failed to hear all of what the scribe said. When she did understand that she was to be sent home with her countrymen, her eyes lifted to Mehmet. He sat poised in a great chair; arms relaxed, hands curled around carved snarling wolves, looking down at her surprised face. There was not a smile on his face or a look of hatred, but a cool businesslike expression, alert to the details of her release read by the scribe. He regretted the inconvenience, hoped that she had found her stay at Rumeli Hisari comfortable, and would recall her host's generous and kind treatment to her family. It seemed like a condition of her release, but Bellina was not going to question her good fortune. She closed her eyes, bowed in respect, and hoped she would not wake from her wonderful dream until she floated safely in the waters of the Grand Canal. She was finally going home; leaving Constantinople and Surek. She would forget him as he had abandoned her and begin her life again. She had no regrets, only the excitement of going home filled her with happiness.

After an uneventful voyage, Bellina's dream came true. Its side scraping against the canal wall, her gondola bobbed before one of Andre Palladio's erected monuments—the Palazzo D'Rosallini. It loomed majestically on the canal, overshadowing neighboring palaces with its magnificence, stirring memories of the furor it had raised when the Contessa de Vicenza discovered its owner to be only a merchant. Bellina had left her home a child under the wing of her father, excitement glowing in her cheeks and oblivious to the shocked whispers that castigated such unorthodox behavior. Now she returned a woman, her clothes and appearance disheveled from her journey. Miquel squeezed her trembling hand before digging into a drawstring pouch and handing the gondolier a gold coin. Bellina climbed from the gondola, bracing her hand against the curved blade of its prow. She watched the boat slip into a gauze curtain of mist and felt her calm wane with mounting trepidation.

The quarried edifice of her home looked as it had that spring morning of 1453, its blue-gray stone bolstered against the biting salt-specked air. Her hands trembled over its solidness and she took comfort in knowing that two hundred years from this day—with the exception of a thicker growth of sottopotico—her home would be the same. It was all that was certain. Kaleidoscopic panes of rose and blue glass glittered in tear-filled eyes that lifted to the Corinthian columns of her balcony. There she had stood in the wonderment of youth and let her imagination sail to far lands, only to return to the insipid tutoring of Maestro Pavo. Until the fateful day her father granted her wish.

When a faint shadow passed behind a drawn curtain of a second-floor window, Bellina gasped.

The house was not deserted! The servants had remained! Her uncapped exuberance startled sleepy-eyed sea eagles from their perch, scattering white feathers that rocked to the canal. Grasping the hooked tail of the sea-horse knocker, Bellina banged out her presence for all of Venice to hear. The door was wrenched open and a large haughty man, obviously a high-ranking servant by his brocade vestments, eyed her suspiciously. His attention shifted from Bellina to Miquel. "Ah Captain. Come in. And whom may I say is accompanying you?"

"You may tell my uncle that Bellina Magela D'Rosallini, daughter of Gerardo and niece to Camillus Santari Poletti and his wife, my father's sister, is waiting." With a sideward glance he left them waiting in the marble foyer.

"Hundreds of miles and this is how I'm greeted at my own door," Bellina fretted. "There should be a welcoming party, not an upstart servant who certainly wouldn't have let me in if you weren't here with me."

"I'm still the old sea dog I was when I left. You should see how you've changed from a child into a woman. I haven't changed." He knew he could bring a smile to her face.

A regally endowed woman wearing a dove-colored gown glided down the spiral staircase that fanned out before Bellina and Miquel. Aunt Claudia had not changed. Three years had not ruffled her stately composure. For all her forty years, her aunt still possessed the dark beauty of her youth, except for a few silver strands of hair that softened the former hardness of her face. Perhaps Aunt Claudia had

252

mellowed a bit, Bellina speculated.

"Bellina!" Claudia gasped. "Bellina, is it really you?"

"It is I," Bellina said faintly, still feeling the rudeness of her initial welcome and wondering why she had not seen any of her old servants. "At long last I am back."

"It is really you! I thought it was some cruel prank! Never did I think I would see you again! Forgive me. But here you are, looking more striking than when you left!"

Did she sense a twinge of regret in her aunt's voice? Or was it just the shock of the striking changes in her home, once so familiar to her and now it seemed like a strange place.

They held each other tightly and awkwardly, feeling close but distant from each other. Claudia stepped back a few steps and a blush betrayed her discomfort.

"I would never have recognized you if I did not hear your voice! At least that has not changed. It is amazing what three years have done! I only hope Devota will have your beauty and grace when she reaches your age. Look at you! Even in these shabby clothes, you're a beauty. Now, you must go upstairs with Lucia." She pulled a long embroidered sash to ring the maid. "We can catch up later after you're refreshed. Lucia will prepare a bath for you and lay out some clothes. This will give me a chance to speak with Captain Campanello."

"Uncle Camillus—is he well?"

"Oh yes! And he will be ecstatic, but you must let me break the news to him gently. I fear for his heart if

253

he were to see you suddenly. My dear," Madonna Poletti paused as if struggling for the right words, then her voice flowed slow and calm. "Bellina, you must be wondering why your uncle and I are living in my brother's house. I would have been half-mad myself, if I returned home to such a welcoming."

"I don't mind, Aunt Claudia," Bellina hoped she sounded convincing enough. "I'm happy our home was cared for, and not left to pillagers and rats."

Relieved that Bellina would not contest her family's presence in her brother's home, Claudia turned to a patiently waiting Lucia. "Lucia, see that Bellina is made comfortable."

The cow-eyed girl nodded, "*Si*, Madonna," and Bellina obediently followed the servant to a spare bedroom which was elaborately furnished and always ready for guests.

Bellina luxuriated in the lightly scented water, a civilized frivolity she well appreciated after the salty dips aboard ship and what she dreamt about when desert heat pressed against her in its suffocating embrace. Would everything strike a cord of remembrance? She knew it was best to forget him and the burning sands he rode upon. He had probably forgotten her by now, and she was sure his only thoughts of her would be how he would exert revenge for usurping his dominance.

She stared at the plaster ceiling, painted to show Saint Anthony leading her grandfather Sergio Vaia D'Rosallini successfully against the Baglano family. All the great families had divine help against their enemies, she mused. Following every detail, she pondered how anyone could sleep when a battle raged on the ceiling above. A hesitant knock announced Lucia.

"Madonnina, Madonna Poletti sends these dresses for you to wear. All wait anxiously to welcome you home."

"Thank you, Lucia. I think I shall wear that green gown. You may put the rest over there." She pointed to the deeply carved armoire that stood as if it held up an entire wall and ceiling.

Once dressed, she followed Lucia down the stairs to the music room where her cousin Flavia's delicate soprano voice played across the scales. Lucia pulled the double doors apart and let Bellina step through. Abruptly, Flavia's voice failed as her mouth dropped open in disbelief. Camillus stared at Bellina as if a ghost had invaded his home and, not being able to bear his look of pain, she ran to him. "Papa is dead, Uncle, oh he's dead." It was the first time it had struck her with such finality.

"Child, you bring me joy as well as sorrow, but my heart dances once more to the sound of your voice. Put the past away, for this is a blessed day! All of you I had believed dead, and now here you stand before me, only because of Miquel's faith in finding you." He brushed back her hair tenderly and kissed her forehead. "What have I done to deserve such happiness?"

"Come, Camillus," Claudia protested. "Do not hoard Bellina all to yourself. Flavia, Devota, surely you remember your cousin? She has changed quite a bit, don't you think?"

"Did the Turks really sell all the Christians as slaves?" Devota questioned and Flavia snickered.

"Girls!" Their mother scolded. "Bellina will tell us when she is ready; do not pry. Goodness, Bellina has been with us but a short while. In time, I'm sure she will tell us all about it."

Bellina knew her aunt was just as curious as her daughters and that she would receive no peace on the subject if she did not give them all some kind of explanation. She took a deep breath and recited what she had rehearsed with Miquel on the way home. "Well, not everyone was taken as a slave, Devota," she replied with a smoothness that belied her unease. "Perhaps that is what happened to dear Rosa, but I was fortunate enough to take refuge in a monastery. The monks were like family to me and of course I could continue living a Christian life, just as if I were here."

She was amazed at how easily the lie sprung from her lips. Well, half lie. After all, she did come under the care of monks.

Camillus reluctantly let Bellina leave his embrace and stared, amazed at how the years had matured her. Blinking his eyes as if to make sure she was really there, he hid his trembling hands from view. "You must never leave again, Bellina. This is your home from now until you marry. God has been generous indeed to bring you safely to us."

Bellina moved to the harpsichord and let her fingers command a melancholy ballad. At its end she reveled at her memory. "It's so long since I've seen one." She turned to her cousins. "I fear I begin to bore you with my life at the monastery and I am truly tired of listening to my own tales. What have you been doing all these years? Surely one of you must be wed."

"Not yet," her aunt said with a huff and a glance at her husband. "Their father is a little slow in that area."

"It takes time to make a good match," Camillus protested, and he refilled his glass with a colorless liquid, handing one to Bellina. "It takes just the right suitor to please your aunt," he added with a wink. "You will no doubt want to see Conte Sordici now that you've returned. I'm afraid he's helplessly enthralled with you."

"Yes," added her aunt, "the Conte was just here this morning. Always saying he's come for some business advice, but he's not fooling anyone, is he, dear?" Claudia frowned at Bellina's pout. "I doubt the man would presume to court one of the girls before a respectable length of time had passed. After all, for all we knew, you were still alive. He hoped that one day he would hear some encouraging news, as of course he will now."

"I always remember him as being a greedy old man who thought he could buy my affection with confections and a ride on his pony."

"That was your pony, a most generous gift," her aunt reminded her.

"Yes, and I wonder what he will try to bargain with now. I've heard some talk that all he has left is his title."

Claudia gasped, Camillus stopped his glass in midair, and her cousins stiffened with anticipation.

"Well," Bellina offered quietly, regretful of her quick words, "it's just what I heard."

Her aunt puffed haughtily. "No doubt from that

257

sea captain of yours. I always told your father he would be a bad influence."

"Now, Claudia," Camillus soothed. "If it wasn't for Miquel, your brother's daughter would not be here." Camillus raised his glass high, "A toast to your return, dear!"

Bellina never favored her imperious aunt. Since her mother died her aunt felt it was her duty to advise her father on the proper rearing of a young lady. With two of her own, she was an authority on the social requirements of the time and at one point even offered to take Bellina into her charge. Thankfully her father had declined the offer, but now she found herself in the hands of Aunt Claudia who no doubt was going to try to undo all the damage of her unconventional upbringing.

At the end of a tedious week of appointments, fittings and lessons in the fine art of being a Venetian lady, Bellina began to feel as much a prisoner in her home as in Surek's tent. She had become accustomed to not having a duenna as a shadow, now she found her every move scrutinized by Maria's hawklike vision. Her only relief was when the three girls had different interests and Maria found herself in a quandary as to which girl to attend. The old woman found Devota to be by far the meekest of the three; when left alone she was happy to sit quietly with a book, but Flavia and Bellina were the devil's own. Since Flavia was like Maria's own child, Bellina was often left under Lucia's less keen observation. Had Maria not been the sole guiding light in the girls' upbringing, she would have been receptive to Claudia's suggestion of hiring another duenna. So it was that Bellina had an afternoon to herself.

Bellina stood before a palatial window that arched nearly to the ceiling. Her gown was lost in the folds of drapery that cascaded to the floor and swirled in a puddle of deep blue at her feet. Studying the scene below, she considered the striking difference between the ribbon of olive green water that wove a path through Venice for the slender gondolas and the glare of burning sand that encircled Constantinople. Venice was as calm as the canal, and Constantinople as exciting and ever-changing as the desert sands under the seductive caress of the warm wind. When her thoughts returned to the eastern city her mood warmed with memories of the tender moments she spent with Surek. She mulled him over in her mind so much that he became more of a fantasy than a real person, and at times she even wondered if he really did exist.

Devota fingered the square of half-embroidered linen that rested on her lap while she pensively observed her cousin. Sunlight filtered through the glazed window, striking up an orchestra of color that played through Bellina's hair. She thought her cousin to be more beautiful than she could ever wish to be, but was not threatened by that like her sister. Devota even liked Bellina, but wouldn't dare hint at that around Flavia. When Bellina was in one of her reflective moods, she found her to be most enigmatic. She doubted that Bellina was thinking of life at a monastery and was sure that she was hiding a dark secret. Flavia was too busy cooing over the visiting Marquis de Soubise to pay much attention to Devota's suspicions, so she was left to her own imaginings. If Bellina would confide in her, it would serve Flavia right! She huffed out loud, causing Bellina to turn her attention to her cherub of a cousin.

"Are you having trouble with a stitch, Devota? At least that is something I've had plenty of time to master!" She lifted the piece of embroidery from her cousin's hands. "Why this work is exquisite! What's wrong?"

"Tell me about Constantinople again." Her cousin's face dimpled and rosy as a Valentine, was filled with a child's inquisitiveness.

"I have," Bellina sighed. "Why you find descriptions of monasteries so fascinating, I'll never know."

"I don't want to hear about your cloistered life," Devota spouted, spying a glance at Bellina's astonished face through thick lashes. "I don't know if you really did live with monks anyway."

"What would make you think anything like that?" She laughed lightly, trying to hide her unease at Devota's doubts, and wondering if the girl was expressing the thoughts of others.

"I think," her cousin whispered huskily, "that a handsome prince whisked you away and—"

"Hush! Hush, with this nonsense," Bellina scolded, turning from Devota quickly. Her stomach dipped and her knees weakened. "If that were true," she retorted, slowly gaining her composure, "I'd still be in Constantinople."

"Perhaps, but I still think it would make a more interesting story than a dreary monastery," she flatly proclaimed, shifting in her cushioned chair like a hen in its nest.

"Well, I wouldn't make up stories, and don't you either," Bellina warned.

"What do you always think about then? Conte Sordici?" Devota giggled. Bellina joined her and soon the room was filled with raucous laughter. Wiping tears from their eyes, the girls stopped short when Claudia Poletti appeared in the doorway.

"Good day, mother." Devota stood, straightening the toppled knot of hair on her head.

"Girls," Claudia acknowledged with a curt nod that matched the sternness of her face. "Lucia." The delicate girl, a shadow behind her mistress, straightened. "Please have some tea brought in." Then Claudia turned to Bellina and Devota. "I have wonderful news. Conte Sordici has returned from Florence and will be here tomorrow to pay an afternoon visit." A silence fell over the room as though a death was announced. Claudia's beaming smile drew into a tight line. "Well, what do you have to say?"

"That's wonderful, mama," Devota looked to Bellina.

"Yes, how nice of him, but I don't feel quite ready to receive suitors yet, Aunt Claudia."

"Nonsense, child! He's waited three years! You will be presentable by two tomorrow."

"But my gowns are not ready."

Claudia's voice was frosted with impatience. "Flavia's gowns fit you perfectly; they will do until yours are finished."

A rattle of china cups announced Lucia's entrance with the tea. Claudia took the tray from her and motioned to the two girls to sit. Devota shrugged her shoulders and gave Bellina an understanding smile.

After tea the cousins were alone until Maestro Pavo arrived for their music lessons. Devota attempted to console her cousin. "Just think Bellina, when you marry the conte, you will be a contessa!"

"That doesn't matter to me, Devota. I don't love him. I detest the *thought* of seeing him, let alone his touch."

"Maybe you will like him a little. Remember, you haven't seen him in years, perhaps your memory of him is doing an injustice to you both. It is what your father wanted."

Devota's kindness was rewarded with a hug. "You are a dear, but I know I can't ever love him, even if it is what my father wanted. However, I will try to be civil, but I will not grant him any illusions. He will know exactly how I feel."

The next day Bellina sat stiffly between her aunt and Devota. If it wasn't the numerous facial expressions which she secretly exchanged with Bellina, she wouldn't have been able to smile at all. How could she possibly get out of her father's nuptial agreement, she wondered, as she studied the man seated across from her. His pasty complexion reminded her of a corpse, and his high giddy laughter at the most inopportune times added a touch of falseness to his character. Bellina was immediately suspicious of his intentions and found her childhood recollection of him to be accurate, yet her aunt could not see beyond his title.

"You can't imagine how I feared for you," the Conte continued a profession of his concern, "a flower amongst the weeds of the world. I told your father how much I disapproved of you traveling so far from home. Isn't that right, Madonna Poletti?" He leaned against the back of the settee, throwing his arm flamboyantly across the high back.

"It was indeed foolish. My brother always showered Bellina with too much freedom for a young lady. But we cannot change the past. We can only assure that her future is better than her past."

"I assure you, Madonna, I intend to give Madonnina a secure future."

Bellina felt as if she were eavesdropping the way they were talking without any feeling for her presence. And the way he emphasized "secure" grated against her already frayed nerves. Even Devota's wrinkled nose, demurely hidden behind a lace fan, could not curb Bellina's sharp tongue.

"Conte Sordici, my father would hope that I would have a happy future, not just a secure one as you suggest. I was happy to travel with my father and would not change the past. He taught me to question and explore my curiosities."

Aurelian Sordici laughed harshly, "My dear, a wife of mine would never question, let alone 'explore her curiosities.'"

"I would never marry a man who would stifle my freedom." Bellina thought her aunt would faint and the Conte would explode if the bulging veins on his neck were any indication; it was only a question of who would go first, until Devota broke the silence.

"Bellina has seen a lot of tragedy. I think she needs some time before thinking of marriage to anyone, don't you agree, Mama?"

"Devota, please, don't forget your manners," her mother warned breathlessly. "Forgive my niece's outspokenness, Conte Sordici. I'm sure it is grief clouding her senses. We all miss my brother dearly." Claudia cast a stern warning glance at her niece.

"Of course, Madonna, you are right, the child has had a terrible experience for one so young." He casually twisted a gold ring set with a tear drop ruby, then reached into a pocket of his waistcoat and pulled out a velvet sack. Catching Bellina off guard, he clutched her hand with long bony fingers. "A coming-home present, Madonnina," he cooed as he slid a matching ruby ring on her finger.

"Conte Sordici, I cannot accept such a generous gift," she sputtered.

"Your father would insist, Bellina," her aunt flatly replied, giving Bellina no chance to deny the gift but only to mumble her gratitude. She felt herself trapped like a fly in a spider's web, waiting to be devoured.

264

Twenty

Snow-frosted pines brushed inches over Surek's head as he rode through the hedge of trees towards the Dnieper River. They had traveled dangerously close to Mongol territories and far enough north to satisfy Mehmet II. Two weeks of riding and not one band of Cossacks was sighted, and now with their bold invasion, they tempted a Mongol attack as well as a clash with the Free Men.

Surek felt the bite of winter through his cotton undergarments despite a protective mantle of felt, and he knew that soon the river would be thick with ice. The towing barks at Kiev that guided boats stacked with timber through the perilous rapids would now be fighting the slippery crust of snow along the river's banks. With frozen rope they would race time until the northernmost part of the river locked them in a shackle of ice. Good sense and intuition told him it was time to turn back.

He felt the pent-up aggressions of his warriors straining to unleash at any moment. It was apparent when they encountered the roving thieves that played malice with some peasants, but his unyielding glare shot a warning that was heeded—they would take no lives. Theirs was a clear mission: find the band of Free Men, or Cossacks, who held no allegiance to prince or sultan, and who plotted to stop the flow of gold and timber between the two.

His courier, Adhemar Darr, rode silently beside him and ahead of the other horsemen. Darr had the distinction of being the only man serving the sultan with hair the color of fire and a personality to match. To Mehmet, he was a warrior sent from Allah; to Surek, he was a loyal and respected scout. Once a Cossack himself, but lured into a dual service by promises of gold, Darr sat rigid upon his mount as they approached closer to the river.

An icy wind blew around them shaking Surek's thoughts, for riding it was the scent of burning wood that could not be denied. Surek and Darr exchanged knowing glances—what they feared had happened. Mehmet would have his proof to show Prince Vasili. The Cossacks remained stubbornly opposed to trade with the Ottomans, even though the exchange of gold for timber and furs was supported by the Grand Prince of Moscow. Surek had hoped to avoid a conflict with these men who rode free; men who had not become marionettes on a string such as he and Darr had become. But the curling ribbon of smoke that rose to meet the slate sky spoke ominously; it came from the river, another mile away.

"I don't like it, Darr," Surek said in a voice as low as wind lost in the rustle of fallen leaves. "That we're so close. I feel as though we're being squeezed between our prince and sultan."

Leather creaked as Surek turned in his saddle to signal the horsemen. As ordered they remained still while their captain and Darr rode ahead. Cautiously, they weaved closer until they could see the black band of water that sliced a path from Kiev to the Black Sea. Cossacks, jubilant in their sacking of a Moslem galley, danced around a fire fueled by its planking, waving the familiar scarlet flag disdainfully. The skeletal remains of the ship, its charred ribs silhouetted against orange flames, sunk quickly into the steaming water. They were careless in the light of their victory. Surek knew it could be a quick and easy kill for the Spahiglani, and he would return a hero. He smiled regretfully.

"We'll have to change our plans. If we ride tonight those Cossacks will be far enough behind to avoid, and if they're going south, let's hope we don't meet."

Surek felt Darr's unspoken objections and even doubted himself that his men would believe the fire was only a kulak's cabin. Expecting a battle at last, they perched precariously on their mounts, some already clutching their swords. Sensing their riders' tension, the mares paced nervously.

"We go onward," Surek shouted with a wave of his hand. "It was only a peasant's shack, burning no doubt by their own foolishness."

He was met by much grumbling, but only one of his men pointed his dark eyes suspiciously towards the curling smoke. Yet the man moved in place when Surek snapped an order and returned his scowl. They rode unhurried yet swiftly for a few hours. Adhemar Darr was unable to keep his eyes from glancing back now and then. Surek, halting the troop momentarily, sought him out in private.

"And who gets careless now? I suggest you keep your eyes towards the empire, my friend."

"How far do you think we'll get, Captain?" asked Darr, his eyes piercing the skeletons of white birch around them, wary of the Cossacks they left behind. "They appeared occupied with their victory, but what if one spied us? They are as cunning as the fox and as unobtrusive as the snow rabbit. We had them back there! What difference does it make if they are our kinsmen? They hold no allegiance to the Prince and—" Thundering hooves vibrated the earth and Surek and his men were upon their horses.

"Darr! Over there—from the hill."

Dressed in fur caps, layers of clothing stuffed under leather vests and laced boots, the storming band charged the Spahiglani. The fearsome set of their bearded faces was enough to win battles.

"To think we'd be matched against our own one day," Surek said solemnly to Darr as they each unsheathed their swords and readied to lead the Spahiglani against the Cossacks.

With eyes as wild as their horses, the Spahiglani threw themselves into battle with all the violence of a volcano that had remained silent long past its time. Despite the fact that the Cossacks outnumbered them, they had the advantage in spirit, for the Winter Men were wearied by one battle already. Sharp upon the night's air, the clang of steel and the squeal of horses answered the screams of the dying. Surek was quick to notice a few Cossacks breaking away, and divining their intent, sent four of his men to stop them.

Ismeran was in the thick of it, already bleeding from a slash across his thigh. With a yell to Allah, he engaged the fierce men who guarded the Cossack leader. Surek split the remaining of his band in two with orders for one to flank the enemy while he and the others sent their horses crashing into their midst. His knees tightly clasped against Kayaska's heaving sides, he braced for the shock as she plowed into the woolly mount of a snarling Cossack. His hair, red as Adhemar Darr, was as shaggy as his horse's hide and they moved like one, each of one mind. "Sultan's swine!" the man screamed as he swung his sword in a wide arch, hoping to slash Kayaska's throat.

Any reluctance to fight Surek had felt was vanquished. With both hands holding his scimitar, he brought it down without an utterance, meeting and breaking the man's block to slice through his leather and fur and ultimately his bone. His jaw froze in shock as he tumbled, almost taking Surek's sword with him. Below he soon became indistinguishable from the bloody mud and snow, lost to the sea of pounding hooves. Kayaska reared and wheeled with a squeal, avoiding the hooves and teeth of a Tartar pony. Again and again Surek met his adversaries' blows and dodged their horse's teeth, always he strained to see where his men were. Adhemar Darr stuck to his right side, another comrade on his left, both willing to defend him with their lives. The band of four Spahiglani were lost in a flurry of red and gray as the Cossacks devoured them. Bits and pieces of bodies and clothing were strewn across the snow like some wolves' feast, their horses dying or scattered. Surek's voice cut through the din, a brief command to the band to flank the Cossacks.

They charged from tree cover, not totally in surprise, but enough to take a few of the Winter Men off guard. Their voices raised as one in a long wailing howl, even Surek felt the hair on the back of his neck rise. Soon the frigid air was heavy with the steam of spilled blood.

Adhemar Darr cried in rage as one man managed to slip past him, intent on Surek's life. Already engaged with another, Surek felt the hot sting of a keen blade dig deep into his shoulder. His arm seemed set on fire, his fingers tingled, and he almost lost his grip upon his shield. Mustering strength, his shield caught the next blow, and digging his heels into Kayaska, they leaped tightly enough to evade immediate death and to surprise his other foe. After a careless move on the man's part, Surek stabbed him through the heart.

"Adhemar!" Surek gasped. "Help Ismeran, he's almost finished!"

Ismeran's eyes never blinked, his face a mask of unholy terror, as he dispatched the Cossack leader's last bodyguard. With eagerness and a laugh the Cossack faced him, a sword in each hand. "Come to me," he called mockingly.

Surek lost sight of Adhemar Darr and Ismeran as the battle around him demanded his full attention. He slapped one man off balance with his shield, and while one of his Spahiglani finished him off, he turned to another. Suddenly he heard a dull thunk and Kayaska squealed and lashed out with her hind leg. Sticking out of her flank was the crudely hewn shaft of an arrow. Surek cursed. Another hit and the horseman next to him, clutching at his throat, fell dead. "Damned all!" Surek cried. "They've got archers!"

"There!" A Spahiglani pointed to a slight rise where three men crouched, then he and two others galloped in their direction. The archers had little trouble picking them off.

The next arrow struck Kayaska in the chest and she took two trembling steps and collapsed. Surek covered his head instinctively as he was thrown into the churning frenzy of dying animals and men. His fall didn't go unnoticed. The last thing he saw was the two spadelike hooves of a Cossack pony about to smash his brains across the frozen land.

She leaned over him, her hair a wavy field of softest black and her curls caressing his eyelids, his face, his chest. Sweet was her breath, as she placed a kiss here, there, and there. "I love you," she murmured, her voice husky with emotion, just as it had been that day in the desert, and he felt a warmth and ache spread through him. He wanted her more than anything or anybody; she was as precious as a spring of water in the desert and never would he let her go again. "Bellina," his cracked lips strained and he wanted to hold her but his arm wouldn't move. She laughed at him, leaning to kiss him one more time, and her hair fell across his face, encircling him in black, deep velvety black.

He screamed when the Cossacks pulled him from the heap of dead bodies by his mangled arm, the pain cutting into the darkness of his mind. The bloody landscape was silent now. Night would be swift upon them like a bird of prey and the Cossacks quickly picked through the carnage to claim friends to bury or injured foes to finish off. Surek, recognized as the Spahiglani leader—winning their hate, a grudging admiration, and the hope of a possible monetary reward—was thrown into the back of a wagon. Some of the Cossacks picked at his clothes, tearing off all ornamentation, eager to take home a souvenir of their coup. Surek tried to focus his eyes, strained to peer through the wagon's slats to find his men, but all he saw was bodies, and with the slightest movement of the wagon, his head exploded into black.

She was back again. This time she refused to come near him, nursing some private hurt as she blinked away her tears. "Bellina," he moaned but she turned her face from him. If he could only move his arm, he would hold her, comfort her, and never let her go. She turned her liquid eyes upon his struggles and sobbed. "You don't love me. If you loved me, you would never have stopped holding me."

He was getting angry. "Damn you, Bellina, come here!" He felt hot, hotter than he had ever felt as his frustration and rage burned him. She was turning away, leaving him. "Bellina," he shouted. "I love you!" But the fire consumed him and she was gone. He had to reach her, to make her understand he loved her. His life held no meaning without her.

Someone parted his lips and held a cup of water to them, but he smashed it away. "Where is she?" he demanded. Before him hollow eyes stared back from the faces of men clutching fragments of clothing around their freezing forms. Surek burned, his fever out of control, his arm a mass of angry and greenish putrescence.

"Petrikov!" someone snarled. "Don't waste your water on that one . . . They say he's some Turkish slime. Besides, he's almost dead, and there's little enough to drink in this prison."

Surek moaned as someone tried to pull away his torn and blood-stiffened mantle of felt. "You won't be needing it," the man stated in an emotionless tone.

"If I have any strength at all," Surek croaked in the same Muscovite tongue the man had used, "I will kill you in your sleep if you take it."

The ragged man hardly feared Surek, half-dead as he was, but nevertheless, the fire in those eyes and the perfect Muscovite speech took him aback. For Surek, the extra effort it took to react set his head pounding. He never heard the man's sarcastic reply, just a buzzing in his mind and more pain—the everlasting pain—and darkness again.

Once a week Yuri Brovik left his comfortable home and his patients (complaining more of the weather than of any ailment), and probed deep into the dark subterranean prison where pneumonia and tuberculosis ran rampant. In its bowels it held hundreds of debtors, political prisoners, and those unfortunate enough to have crossed the path of one of Muscovy's feared noblemen, Prince Stivan Stivanovich. The pitiful groans of those damned souls followed Yuri through the twisting passageways until he reached

273

Temuchin Street.

A dreary sky dispersed crystalline flakes that danced a circling ballet until settling into a cover that hid the rubble that was collectively called the Wooden City.

Yuri pushed his way past those prisoners who could still stand and beg for food outside the prison wall. He had no idea how they survived. For who would give food to criminals when those who lived here hardly had enough for their own families? His steel-gray eyes reflected sadly for a moment. They were doomed to die—all of them, and some for no crime at all. As he squinted beyond a parade of minstrel's tooting horns and jesters that led their dancing bears past pop-eyed children, he thought of the prisoner whose stare bore through him, whose eyes shone luminous like a cat's in the eerie prison light. They had been so much like Teva's eyes when struck by the flow of firelight. Had she not told him, so many times, of her brother who had disappeared six years ago? An adventurer, she wistfully called him, yearning to ride free as the wind. And it would not be unusual to find him in the irons of Red Prison, doomed to die just like the others, he surmised somberly.

"Where do you wish to go?" Repeated the sleighman a second time as he pulled the collar of his cape over his ears. "You did signal . . ."

"Yes, yes, Red Square." Yuri brushed the snow from his cloak absently and stepped into the sleigh, vaguely noting his luck at finding one at such a late hour.

"That'll be three kopecks," demanded the man

irritably. "I've got to make the trip back, and chances of finding a fare that wants to come here for the night is unlikely."

Yuri lightened his pockets and wrapped a blanket over his legs, thankful for an enclosed sleigh. He gazed in wonder over the magic effect the snow had on the foulest part of Muscovy, where the poor lived in log cabins, and opened sewers reeked and dispelled disease. After a storm, it sparkled in the sunlight with the brilliance of diamonds, becoming a pristine fairyland, in contrast to the scene of hundreds of insects that swarmed over piles of garbage in the haze of summer heat. Now snow collected in every niche, accentuating the scalloped gables and toothed eaves of the log cabins, while oil paper windows, blackened by smoke from chimneyless stoves, stared blankly.

They glided on packed ice past rows of cabins that gradually improved and changed to the grand stone buildings of the White City, to the iron gates of Red Square.

The heart of Muscovy was surrounded by a thick wall that protected it from Tartar invaders and separated it from the outer sections. Here was Kitai Gorod, the center of commerce and crafts, and also the secluded homes of the land-rich boyers.

Yuri was pushed by a strong wind to the front door of his home. His Aunt Katri met him with her plump red face and helped remove his wet overcoat.

"A day like this and you're off to that prison! You wouldn't think you had a wife!" She mumbled disapprovingly as she shook the snow from his clothes.

"Where is Teva?"

"In front of the fire where you should be before you catch your death."

"Death doesn't need catching, Katri, it does alright by itself." He left his aunt grumbling, anxious to warm himself.

Beyond the glossy oiled doors, sunk in the depths of a royal blue couch, Teva neatly folded the cloth she was sewing, unaware that her husband was admiring her beauty. Skin glowing like polished ivory rose in slight mounds above a pale blue bodice. Brown hair coiled around her head and led a trail down her back. Although she was not as dark as her mother, when she looked up at Yuri he could see the same black eyes, slightly almond in shape, that so distinguished the Melankovski children.

"Yuri!" She grasped his outstretched hands. "Ahhh, your hands are like ice, come sit with me."

After a few moments of silence, Teva sensed something troubled her husband. He was always moody when returning from the Wooden City, and at times she wished he wouldn't go at all.

Yuri combed taperlike fingers through his auburn beard and studied the light in Teva's eyes. They were so strangely like the prisoner's. At times they looked like two round mirrors, lacking a color of their own—just reflecting what they saw.

"Teva, at Red Prison there was a . . . Some say he was a Turk and others said he was a Cossack caught after pillaging a trade ship. But this prisoner, in some strange way . . ." His voice stumbled, finding a choice of words difficult. Finally he drew his breath. "He reminded me of you—your eyes."

She did not move, only her eyes grew wide.

"Surek?" she gasped, her voice filled at once with disbelief and hope. But then the full weight of her husband's words closed in on her. "No!" she cried springing to her feet. "Not in Red Prison. How would we get him out?"

"Teva, I could be wrong. There was some family resemblance, but it was hard to tell," Yuri protested, seeing the path his willful wife's mind was leading to. After three years of marriage, he should have known she would react this way, and he regretted his hasty blurting out of the man's uncanny eyes before further investigation.

She leaned towards him and pleaded with those eyes. "We must be sure." As she paused, looking intently on nothing in particular but the space before her, Yuri knew that she was devising something. "Yuri, I will go with you to this man. I will know," she said finally.

Her husband snorted like an angry, cornered bear. "You can't! The prison is afoul with sickness."

"Please, Yuri."

"No. You know I have never prevented you from doing whatever you wish, and to Muscovy's chagrin, I might add. But this! This, I cannot allow."

She settled back in the couch, tears shining as she bit her lip. "Then why did you give me false hope? You must bring him here then."

"What? Do you know how difficult it is to extradite someone from there? Teva, you're being unreasonable."

"Then I will go see for myself!"

Yuri groaned. As sure as sin, she would make good her threat and storm the prison tomorrow. He sighed miserably, defeated again by his wife's will and his own devotion to her.

"Alright, I'll think of something."

She was already upon him, shedding grateful kisses. "I knew you would, my love."

"And what if he's not your brother?"

"Then you would have saved a soul from hell, dear Yuri, in the name of Surek Alexander Melankovski."

Early the next day, before the sun topped the middle spire of Saint Sebastian's, Yuri followed the jailer into the pit of the dungeon where prisoners who were now useless and forgotten waited to die. Some showed the marks of past tortures and the doctor found himself wondering what information or confession earned them this underground peace. Too ill to beg for food in the streets, they were thrown scraps that even the rats ignored. At the end of the aisle of ragged beings, sprawled on a mat of straw, was the prisoner Yuri sought.

"How long has he been in this delirium?" Yuri demanded sharply.

"Four days, sir," replied the guard, shrugging his shoulders. "Or maybe a week."

No, thought Yuri, it isn't likely you'd remember, unless you were waiting for a new pair of boots, and then you'd be counting the days until his death. The doctor gravely addressed the jailer.

"You would not speak with such indifference if you knew who you have abandoned to the vermin that dwell here. It is a shame you did not know that you held the key to a ransom of gold."

"What do you mean? No one in here's worth more than what he's got on his back, and from the looks of

278

this one, he's not worth the trouble of throwing a scrap to. He'll be dead in no more than a week."

Yuri unwound the sticky cloth that bound the prisoner's arm and grimaced. "For your sake I hope he lives longer than that—quite a bit longer. You see, yesterday I thought he looked familiar and it kept me awake all night trying to figure out where I've seen him before. And then I remembered . . ." He looked up from the prisoner's festering arm into squinting eyes, and in his most convincing voice told the jailer he was looking down at the Grand Prince's favorite nephew, something not too far from the truth. The jailer's eyes expanded to the size of two gold coins; he was at once attentive to the doctor's every word.

"The Grand Prince himself?"

"If I were you, I'd start cleaning up this filthy hole. You can start by emptying this disgusting pail that offends my senses as much as you do."

A weight of keys jingled at the jailer's waist as he scurried about the prisoner. In these times, he did not wonder why or how a relative of the Grand Prince ended up in the Muscovy prison. It was better for a poor man like himself to remain ignorant of the affairs of officials and rich boyars, if he had any intentions of living a long life.

"You there!" shouted the doctor impatiently, "Are your hearing capabilities as dull as your sense of smell? Get me a pail of water and a bolt of clean cloth."

After some time searching, the jailer returned with a wood pail looking much the same as the one that had been used as a chamber pot moments before, only this time fresh water sloshed over its sides as he scurried to the doctor's side.

"Now get me a bottle of vodka."

The jailer looked at him blankly. "But, sir, you've not finished binding up his ar—"

"Are you suggesting that I'm going to relax with a bottle in this place?"

"It was not my meaning, sir, it just struck me as a strange request from one as refined as yourself."

The doctor turned from the jailer to wipe the beads of sweat from the prisoner's forehead. "Just see if you can scrounge up a bottle. I don't think it should be too difficult a task, certainly much simpler than finding clean cloth."

When the jailer returned with a half-filled bottle, he was astonished to witness what the doctor did. Surely he was out of his mind, he thought, wasting good drink by pouring it all over a man's arm when it could do more good in his belly.

"Do you think you could save a little?" he gulped, hopefully. "It was my last and—"

"Let's call it a superstition. Whenever I've poured vodka into a wound, it seems to heal better. Of course the rich won't hear of it, and the peasants don't want to part with their spirits, but when I can use it I do, and for your sake you'd better hope it saves this one. He shouldn't even be left here, but who am I? Only a doctor." Yuri rose and brushed the straw from his knees. "I will be back tomorrow."

He began to leave when the jailer's restraining hand upon his shoulder bid him pause and pulled him away from the prisoners who were conscious. "I suppose no one would notice one prisoner if he should be missing. That is, if no one said anything."

Yuri hid a smile. "When Grand Prince Vasili hears that his relation has been mistakenly jailed and treated as such . . ."

"Now why would you have to worry the Grand Prince with such news. Out of my own goodness, between you and I, we could have him out of here tomorrow."

Yuri paused, a frown crossing his features thoughtfully, "That would save time and Prince Vasili would be most appreciative. But who knows? If we wait any longer and he dies . . ."

"Maybe we can get him out sooner."

Yuri moved carefully towards the back of the building, each footstep muffled in the snow. It amazed him how resourceful a person like the jailer could be when motivated by greed or fear—and even more so when by both.

"Be sure to be quiet, Doctor," he had cautioned, baring an almost toothless grin. "I'd hate for you to be mistaken for an escaped prisoner."

Yuri depended on the jailer's greed as a guarantee that he'd be safe, but as he walked further into the alley his nerves grew taut and his confidence faded.

Behind the prison a snow bank as high as two men blocked his path and half hid the prison entrance. Not until he saw an outstretched arm protruding from its center, unnaturally blue, did Yuri realize that it was not a mound of snow but a pile of discarded bodies. Its hand was curled in a frozen summons. Yuri moved away from it, his suspicions growing as he wondered what kept the jailer. Not soon enough, a wheelbarrow heaped with bodies steaming from the cold rolled out in front of the jailer.

"Here he is," he grunted as he lifted the prisoner's body from the top.

Yuri brushed a hand over Surek's pale cool forehead. "He looks dead already," he said. He did not want to deliver a corpse to his wife.

"You're the doctor. I've done my part. If he's dead, it wasn't my doing. A man can only do so much in there. Now remember the favor I did for the Grand Prince."

With a little help from the jailer, Yuri managed to get the prisoner into the sleigh. After filling his hands with kopecks, he signaled the coachman. Through the Wooden City to Red Square, Yuri watched the unconscious man's chest rise and fall irregularly with a feeble rattle. He could well picture himself delivering a corpse to his wife—and, most likely a strange one at that. He tried to find further resemblance to the Melankovski family, but under the matted beard and torn clothes there was nothing that distinguished him from any of the other poor beings Yuri had seen.

Before Yuri's sleigh glided to a stop in front of his home, Teva waited at the window nervously scraping tracks on the ice-frosted glass. Hardly disguising their excitement at his return, she and Katri ran out to greet him. Coatless, Teva shivered.

"Did you get him?" she asked in a warbling voice.

As he stepped down her husband glanced at her and scowled, "You're going to get a chill, now get inside. Katri, take Teva inside!"

His wife's expression did not flicker, her eyes searching. "Did you get him?"

"Yes, yes," Yuri snapped, his nerves still tight as a

bowstring, "See?" He lifted the fur that covered the prisoner. "Now, will you please go inside?"

Tears filled Teva's eyes almost immediately as she looked at the scarred arms, the deep gray circles beneath the shallow eyes, and the sharp outline of ribs just below the torn and dirty clothing. Despite that and the strange pantaloons, she knew he was Surek, and that he was a man of importance in the life he led somewhere else. The cloth was strong and soft, not like the coarse open weave that peasants wore. And delicate embroidery circled the waistband and ran over the wide sash that she guessed once secured a fine saber. Her hands began to shake as she reached out to him.

"Yuri, it is him!" she sobbed with joy, clutching his lifeless hand in hers while Yuri carried him up-stairs. "Finally, after all these years, dear Surek's come home."

Twenty-One

From the north window Grand Prince Vasili looked loftily over his dominion while he waited. A lead sky hung heavily over Red Square, as if it were supported by the onion domes that half-disappeared in the ceiling of clouds. His eyes followed the scars of sleigh runners upon the street below as the sleds raced and crossed, lurched and slid. All kept a brisk pace against the chase of the biting wind. That is, all but the children who stopped to throw a snowball at the passing sleds. On such a day, not at all that long ago, he and Alexis Melankovski had brazenly knocked the fur cap off Baroka Tah. Ha! Even though he was only a distant nephew of the leader of the fierce Mongols, his glare was enough to send them dashing for the cover of a snow bank.

Vasili's face never left the window when he heard the clang of brass that ushered Prince Stivan Stivanovich before him. His apparent disinterest irritated the already flustered Prince, who was left to stand in silence until the Grand Prince felt inclined to greet him.

Vasili had heard well enough his consul had come to see him, "on a matter of top importance." To Stiva everything was of top importance, but this time Vasili was as curious as a chambermaid. He had heard Surek Melankovski was staying with Dr. Brovik, but could scarcely believe Stiva's condemnations. Yet, Stiva was adamant.

"Your Grace, the jailer himself has admitted to holding the Grand Duke Melankovski's son."

Vasili approached the black-robed man and dared his beady eyes to reveal the truth. "Alexis Rostov Melankovski's and dear Tatiana's son . . ." he said with infinite patience, "who has been the eyes and ears of Muscovy in the palace of the sultan? Indeed risking his life a hundred times over if Mehmet found out what he was up to, for the welfare of you and me and our people? I cannot believe that he led an attack on one of our vessels!"

Stivanovich's eyes darted from each corner of the room until resting on the pleats of brocade that stood stiffly around Vasili's feet. "I am reporting only what I've heard, your Grace."

Vasili returned sullenly to the window. "Then it is merely heresay and I wish to hear no more of these rumors. When you have tangible proof, I will see you."

Surek felt as though a herd of horses ran through his head. Even thinking pained him, but he was determined this was the last day he'd spend in bed. It was the fourth day of consciousness, and going into the second week spent in Teva and Yuri Brovik's home. Teva had sat beside him much of the time, cooling his fever and assisting her husband. He was told Yuri was her husband, but not until the third day. He smiled as he thought of his sister sitting patiently, telling him of the past six years like peasant folklore, and then ending happily with her marriage. He folded back the down blanket and slowly raised his body from the bed. His limbs felt as though they were tied down as he moved to free himself of the stuffed mattress that clung to him possessively.

"Surek! You can't! How do you expect to get well?" his sister cried, as she bustled into the room with Katri not far behind.

"Aren't I allowed a moment's peace?" he growled, still struggling despite her attempts to push him back. "How can I expect to get well if I let the two of you coddle me like a child?"

His impatient tone was met by Teva's own angry words as Katri kept her distance. "See, you have nearly fallen already. If you would listen to me—"

"To you! My baby sister! Teva, you have not changed. Although more beautiful than when I left, you still are as headstrong as any man."

Forced to compromise, she smiled in half-defeat. "I'll get you a cane, and I'll not hear any arguments!"

After she left, Teva felt somehow tricked but filled with such love for her brother it didn't matter. Returning, she found him standing by the fire, using a poker to lean on.

"Here, you'll find this a little better than that, and you won't have to be so close to the fire." She scanned

286

the room, hands on her hips. "Where is Aunt Katri?"

"I think she's afraid to stay alone with me, she left in your wake."

"And no wonder, with your sharp words. Your temper has grown even shorter since you've been away."

He embraced his sister tenderly. She smiled devilishly, her eyes piercing his from under a bristle of lashes.

"There are many people anxious to see you, dear, especially the ladies you left behind like a trail of unstrung pearls." She felt his muscles tense beneath his shirt. "And what lady has caught your fancy? I sense a prisoner still, under all that armor."

"If all my enemies knew my moods as well, dear Teva, I would have been defeated many times. You will just have to wonder."

And wonder his dark-eyed sister did. She wondered of the girl that haunted his fevered dreams in the weeks past, remembering his dull eyes that stared unseeing, and his breath calling Bellina. His screams for water to drown the fire—for the burning fever or for another fire? Now that Yuri and Katri were not here to silence her, she dared to ask the forbidden question.

"Surek, brother. Where were you all these years? To just show up so suddenly like this, and no explanation . . ."

Surek's head dropped and he stared at his hands. He had hoped she would accept his return without questions, but how much he had forgotten about his sister. He shifted, and then coughed, and then drew a long breath.

"Teva, how can I hope to make you understand? I did not abandon my family or country as you must think. Now, I am here, and that's all that matters."

"Father is anxious to see you, but his pride will not allow him to come here. He thinks you have become a Cossack," she replied flatly, watching his eyes narrow. "A simple answer such as you want me to accept will not do for him. You will have to do better, Surek."

Surek sighed. She would know, even if it meant going to Stivanovich himself for the answers. Yet perhaps it was better this way, for it was hard enough having his father believing the worst, but his sister . . .

His eyes met hers pointedly. "How can I begin to explain when I am beset by confusion myself? Torn between two rulers who are expanding their boundaries, each suspicious of the other?"

Teva looked perplexed but waited silently while he paused to assemble his thoughts.

"Six years ago Prince Stivanovich and the Grand Prince secretly devised a plan to watch the Ottomans, whose empire was expanding further into the East by the passing of each year. Prince Vasili feared their gaining strength would threaten his own plans and so, some others and myself came under the scrutiny of the sultan by an elaborately planned scheme. We were sent in the disguise of Slavic traders to Constantinople. Some of us were to attempt the assassination of the sultan, while four of us were to come to his aid. In the name of patriotism, the sultan would have lost his life if it were not for myself and a few colleagues eager for the Grand Prince's adventure! And so, coming to Mehmet II's defense, we placed ourselves into forever grateful hands, just where the Grand Prince wanted us."

Eyes like saucers, Teva balanced on the edge of her seat. Surek gave her a questioning glance. "This is a true story, dear sister. Doesn't it concern you that your brother has killed many men?"

"I only know you did what was right."

Surek continued, hands clasped behind him and his eyes focused outside where snow fell heavy. "After three years as a Spahiglani horseman, I was promoted to Captain Surek Harum Edib." He paused, then turned towards her, his eyes blazing, and for a moment he did not seem to be her brother, although he spoke her name.

"Teva, I tell you I could have forgotten my true identity. I became Edib. I grew to respect and even like Mehmet. No," he said at her gasp, "he is no more a barbarian than our Grand Prince and all the rest of the world's scheming rulers. My troop, my men, were like brothers. I would have forgotten but for two things: the taking of Constantinople and the numerous messages sent to Stivanovich. For the former, I agreed totally with Mehmet; the city was being ruined by the mismanagement of the corrupted Byzantines. However, Constantine was able to stir up the fears and suspicions of the people to support his shaky rule and the city fought a hopeless war against the Ottomans, knowing it would go all the harder when they fell.

"But Teva, the children, and the women and old people . . . they had to pay for the greed and ruthlessness of both sides. It is one thing to meet your enemy face to face and fight for what you believe. But how can Mehmet or Stivanovich or the Grand Prince—or anyone else—expect me to use the innocent like expendable pawns in their game? And always, always, came Stivanovich's missives eager for every detail."

Teva frowned with annoyance. "That carrion! To think of how many times we've seen him and not one word of you! Letting us think all this time you'd run off!"

"You were not to know, and if you should see the prince again, do not even hint at your knowledge."

But it was as if she had not heard his warning. She jumped to her feet and came to him, her lips brushing his cheek. "Oh, Surek, father will be so proud of you."

"Surek is right, Teva, leave matters to him."

Teva and Surek turned, startled to see Yuri standing in the doorway, his coat and hat still in hand.

"Yuri! How long have you been there?" exclaimed Teva.

His eyes met Surek's piercing eyes with silent sympathy. "Long enough to understand how Surek has grown wise and weary of killing in the name of princes and sultans." Yuri's beard still sparkled with melted snow as he brushed a kiss across his wife's forehead.

Her lips made a slow warming smile. "I'll have Katri bring in some chocolate to warm you." In a rustle of silk she hurried from the room, leaving the two men alone for a rare moment.

Yuri and Surek exchanged formal pleasantries,

awkwardly at first, until they touched the subject of Teva. Each had a common ground in the beautiful but iron-willed girl. Surek learned how his sister had not lessened her ardent admiration and loyalty to Prince Vasili, but how, unlike their father, clearly saw the danger of the influential Stivanovich. Yuri described the Red Prison as tripling its fold since Stivanovich's commanding presence in the palace became more frequent.

"I have tried unsuccessfully to convince your father the danger Stivanovich poses, hoping he'll warn the Grand Prince. As his longtime friend, the Grand Prince might hear him, but your father refuses to see the corruption."

Yuri leaned closer to Surek, continuing in a voice that was barely above the frenzy of flames that snapped in the fireplace. "Perhaps you could speak to him and tell him of the—"

Before he could finish, and before Surek could tell him that he was the last person his father would listen to, Teva and Katri returned, balancing a tray of steaming chocolate. After filling their cups, Katri tried to get Teva's attention to take their leave, but she ignored the plump woman. Katri marched away shaking her head in disapproval. She had all but given up on Teva's insistence in meddling in men's affairs.

Teva's lashes brushed over the edge of her cup as she noted how handsome her brother had become. Even though his cheeks were hollowed by weeks of illness, his face still revealed the strong lines of their father's heritage, their Mongolian mother's black eyes that now sparkled, and hands that clearly fit the sword. He was still the most exciting man in Muscovy.

"Yuri," she began in a voice thick with sweetness that he had come to know preceded a request. "Let's give a party for Surek. We can invite those he hasn't seen in years. It would be much less exhausting than traveling about Moscow to see everyone!"

Yuri paused to consider the request, then nodded. "Yes, Prince Stivanovich will be asking of you, Surek, and it would be better to meet him here."

"Oh must we invite him?" Teva whined. "He always puts a chill over everyone."

Surek knew that soon enough, as long as he remained in Muscovy, he'd have to face Stivanovich. In fact he was surprised he had not come already.

"If it's agreeable to you, Surek," Yuri continued, "I'd rather not argue with my wife when she's got her mind set."

Before he could reply, Teva was gone from the room calling for Katri.

In a week the Broviks opened their door to friends and family, all eager to hear of Surek's mysterious disappearance. Left to their own imaginations, men huddled together arguing in hushed tones over whether he was involved in some secret affair or had returned to his mother's Mongol camp. Ladies whispered behind screens over how much more handsome the intriguing Melankovski had become—all to the delight and amusement of Teva.

It wasn't until some of their guests began to call for their sleighs that, to Teva's relief, Prince Stivanovich arrived.

"He was no doubt detained by some very important business with the Grand Prince," whispered an admiring guest.

Yuri left Teva with Surek and cut through the clusters of guests to greet Stivanovich. The sleek, would-be handsome Prince piled his cloak, gloves, and hat in Katri's arms, otherwise ignoring her presence as if she were a household servant. Seeing the burning glare in his Aunt's face, Yuri quickly whisked the prince from the doorway.

"My Prince, it's an honor having you here, especially knowing of your busy schedule."

Sensing he said something wrong by the Prince's downcast look, Yuri quickly changed the subject. "Surek is looking forward to seeing you again. That is, if you can pry his attention from the ladies." Yuri chuckled alone as they slowly made their way through the room. Guests parted, leaving a path for the Prince. His eyes darted back and forth and his head nodded slightly to a few of the lady guests.

Teva could feel rather than see the Prince's presence; it felt like a cold draft had swept through the room. To her dismay, Surek displayed a dangerous arrogance and turned an ignoring back to him, continuing his conversation until someone made an introduction. Stivanovich's eyes settled on her instead, sending a chill up her spine. A short full beard failed to soften the sharp lines of his features and cruel twist of his smile. In his blackness he reminded her of a vulture ready to swoop down on a victim.

Yuri's voice rumbled in his throat. "Surek, you remember Prince Stivanovich?"

Surek turned to the all-too-familiar face, one that he had envisioned many times during his exile—an exile imposed and lengthened by the Prince under the guise of duty.

"How could I have forgotten?" he said, bowing with an exaggerated sweep of his arm that twisted Teva's stomach when she saw the glint of warning in the prince's eyes.

Stivanovich's words met Surek challengingly. "Baron, at long last. I feared you would not return. You know, you are quite a lucky man to fall into the hands of Yuri Brovik. That sword you caught nearly cost you your life."

So, he knew. Did the attack come from Stiva's own orders? Surek's eyes never left the prince. "It isn't like you, Stiva, to be so concerned," he parried. Stivanovich motioned for Surek to follow him, away from the others.

"What happened?" Stivanovich demanded when doors closed behind them in Yuri's library. Surek grabbed a flagon from among the doctor's assortment of decanters and filled two glasses with vodka. After pouring his own down his throat, Stivanovich's voice seemed to be afire with the liquid.

"What were you doing so close to the border?"

Surek looked at him pointedly. "What are you suggesting, Stiva? That I arranged my own capture?"

"I'm suggesting you've been less than enthusiastic about your mission in the Osmanli army of late. What am I to think after receiving messages from you requesting release from your services, and then *this!*"

"I was following orders! For six years! A promise of only four turned into six. My father thinks I have become a Cossack, my sister was but a memory—a child when I left, now a woman. Think what you want, Stiva, but I'll tell you this—I could think of easier ways to return to Muscovy then by the vile cells of Red Prison."

Surek cooled his throat, emptying his glass in one long gulp and filling it to its lip a second time before turning on the prince.

"Do you know why it's called the Red Prison? Because of all the blood that flows through its corridors and drips down the backs of men beaten to death. And many only because they stole a piece of bread to feed their starving children!"

"Surek, I've upset you," Stiva purred, his lips curled back in a self-righteous smile. "Perhaps we can assign you to some other duties more to your liking."

Shrouded in black, the prince posed an evil figure. He walked over to the window and let his eyes scan over the line of carriages and sleighs, their lanterns glowing like jewels in the dark hour of midnight. Unseen by Surek, his mouth twitched nervously. The one man other than himself who the Grand Prince would honor as counsel, the man he himself had hoped would die, had returned as arrogant as ever.

"I'm finished with you and your treachery, Stiva," Surek vowed.

"Your refusal would be treasonous." Stiva let his pleasure at baiting Surek show brazenly in his unshielded smile. "As are the circumstances of your arrest."

"Ahh, now I see. The rumors that I've joined the Free Men. You'd like that, I think. But it so happens I was their prisoner before they were ambushed by the Muscovites, which, you seem to forget. Treason!

That is ridiculous and you know it!"

"There's little I'd have to say to convince Grand Prince Vasili of your treason. And what do you think would happen to those who helped you? Your little sister, the good doctor? Why, they were hiding and giving aid to a traitor." He smiled, pleased at the hard stare he aroused in Surek. "I think a trip to Venice would please the Grand Prince. Yes, when you are settled there, you can purchase some ships, keeping their appearance Venetian, of course. Venice and Genoa are taking too much trade from Muscovy."

In Surek's silence, the prince gloated in his victory. "Don't look so gloomy, Surek. You'll be back in society, your father will forgive you, you'll have your life. As long as you stay away from Muscovy."

"Stivanovich, I know nothing of sailing."

"But you know the Ottomans and Constantinople. You can find some Venetian sea dog to do your sailing."

Surek stared intently at Stivanovich until the prince could no longer face him. "And what I have learned from the Ottomans is that the path to a man's soul is through his eyes. Why don't you send one of your faithful pups? What good is this plan of yours other than to fill your own pockets with Venetian gold? Or is it to keep me far away from your plots?"

"One day, Surek, we will be so strong and united that that gluttonous Sultan would not even amuse himself with the idea of adding Muscovy to his empire."

Surek gave a bitter laugh. "And what of Tver? There is a province that has no wish to become part of Vasil's Empire. Mehmet is not the only one who is gluttonous."

"Tver? Tver needs us and is too foolish to realize it. She refused to acknowledge the supremacy of Moscow now, clinging to Lithuania, but it is only a matter of time before they collapse as Kiev did." The prince saluted Surek with the last of his drink.

Surek returned a menacing grin. "You've forgotten quickly about the Ottoman Empire."

"As long as she keeps her distance . . ."

"And what is to guarantee that? A few informers? Hardly. But don't worry, the sultan has no time to waste on Muscovy now. At the moment he is as involved with other affairs as Prince Vasili is with Lithuania and Tver. Besides, Mehmet needs the timber for his ships, the ships I might add, that may one day sail up the Dnieper and—"

"That will never happen!" the prince cried, his voice barely controlled and filled with warning. "I suggest you leave for Venice as soon as possible, Surek, before such talk sends you back to Red Prison, and this time with company!"

He marched stiffly from the room, and no sooner had he left then Teva stood in the doorway facing her brother, her forehead creased with worry.

"I couldn't help it. When I heard voices and I knew it was him and you, I . . ." She looked down at her feet and Surek instantly was reminded of the child she once was.

"I'm not angry with you, Teva, but what if he saw you?"

"When are you leaving?"

It had been Surek's intention to defy the hailstorm of threats issued by Stivanovich and remain in

Muscovy, perhaps approaching the Grand Prince, who at one time had been as close to him as any uncle. But he had not returned home as a hero and he had to admit, that however unlikely the circumstances surrounding his return to his beloved country, it reeked of treason. As the prince suggested, this new directive would restore his honor. And it would place him in Bellina's city, where he would be the foreigner. A slight curve pulled at the corners of his mouth.

He could not ignore Stiva's threats, he had no doubt he'd wield his power for his own gains and destroy anyone in his path. Suddenly he remembered Teva and feared for her. He knew that Yuri and Teva would suffer any injustices brought upon him by the prince. He took his sister's face in his hands.

"I'll be leaving soon, but not for long this time. I promise you."

"You will see father first?" she asked in a pleading voice.

"Yes, tomorrow."

Twenty-Two

The sound of a thousand bells diminished into the whispering pines as Surek's sled left the Wooden City. He pulled the cape that had once covered the back of a black bear around his shoulders. The open sleigh provided little protection from falling snow and the wind stirred by its movement.

Iced with gingerbread gables, his father's house appeared magically through a gossamer veil of lacy flakes that swirled into snow devils in the sweeping winds. As the sleigh came closer, Surek could see the toothed eaves, curved balconies, and crisscross panes of glass that sparkled even in the gray of winter. It looked strangely like a palace with its teardrop dome piercing the low hanging clouds.

Surek wondered what would be said after all these years. It would be better if his father remained thinking he had gone off in search of adventure. He had no desire to debate his allegiance (or lack of it) to the prince, to discuss Stivanovich or Mehmet II, but he knew the questions would come, along with his father's infernal gaze. Lifting the bronze knocker, he let it fall, violating the quiet and stirring a squirrel from its nest.

Alexis Rostov Melankovski greeted his son with contained emotion, his face hard, resembling the same carved features of his son's, and refused to show the joy that spread through him when they embraced. "It has been a long time. You must have many tales to tell. And look! You left a lanky man, restless as ever, and now you come back strong like a bear. And," he added gruffly as he studied his son, "I see Yuri has taken good care of your wound."

So, Surek thought, as he followed his father, he knows of Red Prison.

Later, Surek told his father all he wanted to hear. He told him of his life as a prestigious horseman in the world's most elite army: the battles he had won, the lives that were lost, and all in the name of the Ottoman Empire. His father beamed with pride but regretted that his longtime friend, Vasili, had left him to wonder of his son. "But the Grand Prince has his reasons for secrecy," he said finally, and with that simple statement his father forgave and reaffirmed his support of their ruler.

His son continued the recounting of his secret service through the afternoon and into dinner. When they had finished the last ounce of borscht, Surek risked turning all of his father's joy into outrage. He looked down the long table gleaming in the candlelight, reflecting each goblet and plate, to where his father headed the table. "I have been proud to serve the Grand Prince many times, father, but also have I many times been ashamed. No, hear me out!"

he said when words began to sputter from his red-faced father. "I am through with killing, through with the careless attitude my leader and others hold toward the poor populace!"

"Where have such thoughts entered your head? Certainly not under Mehmet's lead!" his father shouted, bringing his fist down on the table. "Certainly not from me! Surely the masses deserve a man's pity, but not his loyalty! That, my boy, belongs to the Grand Prince and no one else."

Surek's head shook slowly, "I can follow what the Grand Prince wishes, only if first my heart follows."

"You are a fool. And worse, a sentimental fool! Why didn't you become a poet?" he asked in disgust. "That is more fitting for you!" Wiping the grease from his walrus moustache, Alexis Melankovski pushed aside his plate and cleared his throat in one vibrating rumble. From then on a distant air of formality prevailed.

"What will you be doing now that you are finished with the prince?" Alexis asked bitterly.

"I have one last journey to make for Stiva before—"

"Before what? It is time you claim your inheritance. If you have given up on Muscovy."

"Father, please, I will never abandon Muscovy."

"Let me finish! Since Moscow will not be of your concern, then this household should be. You will bring an heir to this family. I will not have a rebel son rampaging around the countryside. You'll take your place here!"

Surek poured the rest of his drink down his throat, bowed to his father, and left for his room. It would be useless to argue against his recurrent threat to sever his inheritance if Surek did not marry during his father's lifetime. There was no one he could think of with a faster temper or stronger will than his father's—except for Bellina. The thought of bringing her home to meet his father brought a smile to his lips as he imagined how they would get along. Yes, he knew his father would approve of Bellina. He had not raised his own daughter to be content to sit and sew beside a warm fire. Teva was a match for any young man who would be foolish enough to challenge her in a sled race. How Alexis would hide a smug smile when his daughter won. She was as good a rider as any Mongol and would often take to the hills on the back of her high-spirited mare.

Surek stared deeply into the leaping flames and disintegrating ashes, visualizing a mirage of tents wavering against the burning sands. An angry heat crept over him as he thought of the lives lost one way or another, directly or indirectly, because of the greed for land and power over others: the circumstances that drove a wedge between him and Bellina.

"All right, father, you shall have your heir," he said with an oath and taking another glass of vodka, raised it in salute. "To the continuation of your empire," he vowed.

"To the beginning of yours, Surek."

The next morning his father seemed more agreeable, convinced that his son would find a bride and return home to lift the burden of the estate from his shoulders. "Well, Surek, tell me where it is you're off to this time. A place where there are a lot of available ladies, I hope."

Surek's fork lay still on the edge of his plate as he

contemplated his father's reminder. "It would please you to know that 'I'm off' as you say, to Venice."

"You will be staying with the Visconte, I presume?" he said with a knowing smile that tightened as he tried to check the obvious pleasure the news gave him. The Visconte led quite a string of ladies, and it was his hope that his son would find at least one to his liking.

As they walked to the sleigh, a whip of wind lashed around them, fluttering wool capes behind their backs. A whirlpool of snow caught in the gust, swirled in miniature tornadoes. With a final Ho! followed by the awakening of bells, two stocky mares plodded away from the mansion and the sleigh vanished in the mist as mysteriously as it had appeared.

It was nearly spring when the majestic galleon and its passengers from eastern Europe and Asia docked in Venice. The last remaining chill of winter rode on the sea breeze that tousled the ship's rigging and grabbed at passengers' clothing as they departed. With the wind behind him, Surek headed for the River Piave, now filled with slender gondolas.

Venice was teeming with bargain hunters whose loud voices were carried on the lacework of canals that followed the tide and ran their way out to sea. They awaited the returning vessels, cramming the docks of the lagoon-city until they bowed from the weight. Palazzos as dark as night were planted precariously on floating islands, huddled together as if to offer support against the sea-born storms. Moss clung relentlessly to their dark exteriors and moisture dribbled in tiny waterfalls along the walls until trickling into the canal. "So this is Bellina's Venice," thought Surek. "Then she must truly be a water-child to find comfort in this city of rivers."

Before seeking a gondolier to ferry him to the Sile, Surek paused below the *Fortunata*, its size dwarfing him. A feeling of inadequacy advanced as he watched the man aboard her wrestle with canvas, toss ropes from one end of the deck to the other, and climb rigging as deftly as rats.

"You're welcome to come aboard if you'd like," shouted a shabbily dressed man, younger than himself, in a dialect less polished than the noble class of Venice, yet educated more than most. Surek squinted into the glare of sunlight that had shoved its rays through a parade of clouds. What had moments before been visible was now washed in a blinding light. Miquel Campanello extended a hand to Surek as he fought to keep his footing on the slick planking.

"Sure your captain won't mind?" Surek's smile faded when he recognized Miquel. For anyone here to remotely connect him with Mehmet and his armies would mean a death sentence. He studied Miquel's face sharply but did not detect a glint of recognition.

"If I did, I wouldn't have invited you. I'm Miquel Campanello, captain of the *Fortunata*."

Surek formally bowed. "Baron Melankovski of Muscovy."

"It was not Muscovy," thought Miquel, "where I have met you before." Miquel did not like strangers aboard his ship, but when he saw this man, there was something so familiar about him that he was compelled to invite him on deck to get a closer look. He had seen those eyes before and heard his voice, but the clean-shaven face was unfamiliar. "Muscovy!" Miquel exclaimed out loud. "A long way off, sir, and what would you be doing here in Venice?"

"Visiting a family friend by the name of Cagliardi. It's been so long, I don't know if he still resides on the Sile."

Miquel shook his head. "I know no one of that name, but if your friend is no longer there, I will be glad to help you find a place among my skeleton crew." Miquel watched his face for a clue that would spring this man's identity to his mind. If the stranger stayed long enough, Miquel knew it was a puzzle he would solve.

"Your offer is most generous, but I've been looking for a ship of my own." Breaking away from Miquel's scrutinizing frown, he gave a sweeping glance over the *Fortunata*. "In fact, a good ship and men to sail her."

Pulling the end of his rope taut securing the half hitch, Miquel draped the long chain over his knee. He had a mind to kick this impudent Muscovite down a slippery ramp, if it were not for his vexing familiarity. "I am my own master, Messer Melankovski. This is my ship and crew. If you are looking for a good vessel, I can tell you who may have one to auction."

Miquel might remember him, Surek thought and he wanted to be close by when he did. "I know nothing of the sea. In fact, I prefer the back of a horse. But," he paused a moment, "I'm willing to learn."

"But to captain a ship without knowing the sea first?" Miquel laughed heartily. "I may as well make my cabin boy captain! He would fare better than you I'm afraid, Messer Melankovski."

Now confident that Miquel had not yet recognized him in his European clothes and beardless at that, he dared propose an offer that would catapult Miquel's small enterprise into one that could profit. "My father has not left me to struggle too much. I could easily buy my own galleon but you are right. If you will teach me, I will prove very grateful financially." Surek looked at the scant crew. "And I've been in and around the eastern ports."

Now Miquel knew! It was Constantinople. Of course. But why was Mehmet's man here in Venice, and under the guise of a Muscovite? Miquel was intrigued enough to want to learn more of this adventurer who was as mysterious as the sea.

"I do not want a part of the *Fortunata*," Surek continued. "It would be like having a silent partner. All I would expect would be half of the profits and—"

"Thirty percent and either party can terminate the agreement at any time."

"Agreed."

The two stood, each giving the other a congratulatory pat upon the back, as canvas slapped the approach of a rising gale. Scurrying about them, all hands worked to secure any loose objects against the threatening sky.

Twenty-Three

It seemed like more than a month had passed since Surek had made his pact with Miquel and had insisted on signing up as part of the crew for the *Fortunata*'s first voyage. Also the first voyage since she had been a gift from Camillus Poletti. Miquel would not say what circumstances prompted such a generous gift, and Surek did nothing more than wonder. They respected each other's private thoughts and concentrated on a profitable trip.

During their short stay in Port Solomon, Surek proved his worth in his fluency of the local dialect and knowledge of customs. They quickly made their purchases, filled the hold until its sides bowed, and set sail again only a few days after their arrival.

Covered in veils of fog, the tall campanile that rose before San Marco was barely visible to the *Fortunata*. In daylight and even on moonlit nights, its gilded angel sparkled like Polaris, guiding each ship to its berth. However, this was a night as thick and dark as black velvet. Venice was shroud-wrapped, its waters slick and oily. To Miquel, the slap of each wave as the *Fortunata*'s bow dipped and rose, was like a blind man's tapping cane. Without a star to guide him, he abandoned his astrolabe and blindly steered his ship ahead. His senses were acute: his skin tingled with the brush of an easterly wind, his ears peeked at the jovial singing of a drunkard minstrel, and his nostrils flared as the city's refuse flowed by them.

At Miquel's command each man struggled to lower all but the jib sails. As the *Fortunata* glided through the pitch of night, when sea and sky meet as one, a sensation of floating through space prevailed. After what seemed like a journey into infinity, Miquel could finally make out the faint yellow glow of torches melting into the inky night; they were but a few yards from port. Miquel's muscles readied for the crash and splintering of wood as the *Fortunata* edged into the crowded harbor, but the only sound was the gentle lapping of waves. Sails furled, a tense quiet reigned as the ship silently made its berth.

By noon the holds were empty. The men had returned to their wives and babes and even the ship's cat had gone in search of food. Miquel and Surek, the only ones who remained, leaned over the ship's side to gaze into the flotilla of bell-shaped coelenterates and pieces of churned-up seaweed.

"You fared well for your first voyage as a merchant seaman," Miquel said, silently congratulating his own ability to know a good man. "With one such voyage a month, we and our purses will fare very well indeed."

Yes, thought Surek bitterly, and so will Stiva's purse. Mehmet would eventually receive gold to buy the timber for his growing fleet, and Venice and all the other city-states would be blinded by rich silks, their brains clouded with perfumes. "Now that Constantinople is stable, and trade is favored more than ever," Surek said, once again staring into the bobbing water. "Tell me, Miquel, were you as unlucky as some to be swept up in the war?"

Miquel dug his hands deep into his pockets, hoping to pull out the right words with as much flair as a magician. Since their first meeting, he had been nagged by an unrelenting sense that they had met before. It was in Constantinople, that he knew for sure, and now, after nights of turning his thoughts over, he could keep them silent no more. It seemed to him that Surek wanted to stop the charade as well. Why would he ask about the war? He must have sensed how Miquel studied him when he thought he would not notice.

"How long do you intend on avoiding Bellina?" Miquel prepared to face off a steely glare, but Surek just studied the rhythmic slapping of water.

"When did you know?" His voice was even. It was no surprise to him that Miquel had surmised this much.

"Almost from the start," Miquel confessed. "But not definitely until I placed you in the right surroundings. Besides, you have the look of a lovesick pup."

Placing a heavy hand on Miquel's shoulder, Surek met his eyes squarely, "She is not the reason I am here. Besides, I doubt she would be too pleased to see

309

me. I am grateful you have seen her safely home."

Miquel pursed his lips as though to prevent his thoughts from slipping through them. Since Bellina had returned to Venice, more observers than he had noticed her detachment. Part of her was back in Constantinople with Surek. Perhaps Surek didn't care for Bellina in a real sense, and it wasn't up to Miquel to throw the two together, though he knew, sooner or later, time would. And if she was not the reason he was here, what was? Was he still loyal to the Ottoman Empire?

While Miquel's thoughts tumbled around in his brain like leaves whipped up by the wind, he did not hear Camillus's voice calling him or see him standing on the pier. Squinting in the light, Camillus searched along the top deck for Miquel while his family waited.

"Really, Mother," Flavia whined as Devota nodded her agreement. "Must Papa bring us down to the docks like common folk?"

Not attempting to disguise her irritation, Bellina answered her cousin. "Must you always whine? It does grate on one's nerves."

"You're just jilted because Papa wouldn't let you go with him to see Miquel," she snapped, then added in a honeyed voice, "I'll bet you even shared his cabin on the way back."

"Flavia!" Claudia gasped. "Enough of this bickering."

Flavia had not changed since they were children. She had always had a way of injecting the most biting insults. There was no one she didn't look down upon, unless they were of title and their wealth was beyond measure.

Like her mother, her eyes were shallow and deeply set, as though the ancients had carved them in stone, a prominent straight nose perched haughtily above lips curved down into a perpetual pout. The same age as Bellina, she possessed a questionable worldliness that attracted the men of Venice.

"You knew all along if you wanted to see Andre for a fitting today you'd have to wait for your father. He should be coming back soon. It looks as though Miquel is not here." Claudia leaned against a smooth pylon and sighed, distressed herself that Camillus had spotted Miquel. "You may as well relax, dears, it looks as though Miquel is here, and someone is with him if my eyes are correct."

Flavia, so intent on making out the broad figure standing with Miquel and her father, nearly fell from the narrow walkway to a cold splash in the sea as she leaned forward for a clear view.

"Now we will have to wait even longer, won't we, Flavia?" Devota teased.

But her sister was intent on trying to see the stranger. She had never seen him with Papa or Miquel before. He was taller and huskier than any of the men she knew, and even at a distance he had a pleasing tingling effect on her. His skin was bronzed even deeper than Miquel's. She shuddered with excitement and blushed with thoughts she dare not reveal. Why, with all the new foreigners who came to Venice since Constantinople's fall, he could even be an Ottoman prince! The thought of sharing a real man's bed made her abdomen quiver and her nipples tighten, pressing against her binding bodice.

"Mama, who is that man talking with Miquel and Papa?"

Her mother studied the man for awhile. "I don't know, probably one of Miquel's men." As if knowing her daughter's thoughts, Claudia added, "He certainly would not be a proper suitor."

Flavia was not the only one who had taken notice of the stranger. Bellina stood frozen, watching the pantomime of the three men as they talked. She wished, like Flavia, to get a closer view of the man. His silhouette ignited a racing desire in her, that she once had thought she would never feel again.

It seemed like a week had passed before Camillus finally climbed from the ship and headed towards them. Trying to sound vaguely interested, Flavia waited until they reached the market before mentioning the man on Miquel's ship.

"How is Miquel doing, Papa, now that he is on his own?"

"He was always on his own, dear, always of his own mind when it came to the sea. His first trip has been a profitable one, he tells me. And with his partner, a baron from Muscovy, quite astute in the ways of the Ottomans, there will be no limit to their success."

Flavia's eyes sparkled, surpassing the flicker of interest in Devota's and even the aroused concern creeping along the lines of Claudia's mouth. "Was that the baron you were talking to?" Claudia asked, adjusting her hennin over her hair as though already under the scrutiny of the baron's royal eyes.

Camillus regarded his wife and daughters under a humorous smile. "And why all this sudden interest? I

312

dare say, you've never been so concerned about Miquel's affairs."

"It's that man!" Devota burst like a spiked blowfish. "The one who was with Miquel." She shrank under Flavia's glare.

"Devota! Be still! I was just curious as to Miquel's new life."

"Hah! I saw you hanging out over the water trying to get a better look," Devota said into Flavia's rising fury.

Madonna Poletti looked despairingly at her husband. "Girls!" He chastised sharply. "Messer Melankovski, as he wishes to be addressed, will be formally introduced to you within a week at your mother's yearly spring festival. Then you may fight over him all you wish. Now! We will go about our day as planned—a peaceful outing." His daughters' exuberant hugs nearly toppled him over.

The next week was spent in preparation as though the doge was to be their honored guest. Flowers were placed in every corner, and garlands of mint, rosemary, and oleander were draped over each entranceway until the dining room looked like a garden. A table laden with fruits stretched invitingly, their fragrance mingling with the sweetness of fresh herbs.

Devota and Flavia tittered gleefully over meeting the wealthy boyar from Muscovy. Bellina matched their avidity with mute indifference. Another dinner to suffer through Conte Sordici's puffery. Her only consolation was that Miquel would be there this time to offer her some refuge, and perhaps this Muscovite, who had peaked her interest, would prove more entertaining than most of her aunt's guests.

As excited as her daughters, Madonna Poletti had even ordered the famous frozen cream once served at Nero's banquets. Packed in snow from the top of the Alps, it was an impressive dessert only the very rich could afford.

"He's here! He's here!" announced Devota, startling her mother into a near faint.

"Devota, remember you are a lady. Where's Flavia?" It distressed Claudia that her younger daughter did not possess the same cool loftiness as Flavia. Devota just bubbled over with emotion, leaving nothing to the imagination. "Best you take notice of your sister's conduct," chided Claudia as she prodded back tendrils that fell in disarray over the girl's eyes. "And do tell Bellina not to keep Conte Sordici waiting this time. Now walk slowly or you will ruin your hair. Anna will see to the door. Go upstairs until you are sent for."

Camillus almost regretted inviting the Muscovite, it had caused such a commotion, but he knew his wife would never forgive him if he had not. She gave him a smile from her favorite chair, nodding her approval of their gracious guest. He was splendid in his wine-colored doublet, cutting a magnificent figure. Bouffant sleeves with marquise slashes of white silk accented his broad shoulders, and creamy tights were molded to thighs muscled by years of riding. Camillus flushed; his wife could be as bold as her daughter.

Surek smiled lightly, causing a ripple of raised flesh to run over Flavia.

Bellina tarried as long as she dared, feigning

314

dissatisfaction over wisps of stray curls. A gush of breath released some of her tension over the long evening ahead.

"You wouldn't be thinking of becoming ill again, Madonnina?" fretted Lucia.

Bellina slapped the creases from her teal gown. "Don't give me ideas, Lucia. Just the thought of Conte Sordici makes me ill."

"Madonnina!" gasped Lucia.

"Don't worry. Besides, Flavia has peaked my curiosity about this Muscovite."

Lucia rolled her eyes in exasperation and followed Bellina to the top of the balcony for a last-minute smoothing of her gown. Midway on the staircase Bellina paused to study the knot of people to one corner of the ballroom. Her Aunt Claudia on the outskirts of the hub glanced nervously in her direction. Bellina felt her heart sink to her stomach when Conte Sordici picked his way through guests to greet her. Though he cut a foppish figure in his creamy white doublet—accented with far too much lace for a man—she felt a dangerous aura envelop her whenever he was near.

"Bellina, you grow more beautiful by the setting of each sun," he flattered her relentlessly while guiding her past the approving nods of guests, stopping just beside her aunt. Claudia seemed less agitated now that her niece had made her appearance. Her headstrong niece would be the death of her if she did not marry soon. She made a mental note to speak with her husband on the matter.

"Bellina dear, before you and the Conte dance away," she smiled teasingly, "you must meet Captain

Campanello's associate and our honored guest, Baron Melankovski." Although Surek insisted on being addressed as Messer Melankovski, Madonna Poletti insisted on using the title he chose not to associate himself with.

Bellina didn't hear her aunt's introduction or her own animated response. Her thoughts scrambled around in her head. The blood drained from her face, leaving her skin as white as the circle of pearls around her neck. There was no mistake about his identity, though he called himself Baron Melankovski of Muscovy. She could trace no surprise in his face, only a knowing smile as he lifted her hand to his lips.

Flavia squirmed, watching Surek's intent interest in her cousin. After all, she saw him first and she wasn't about to give him up to her. Curling a mahogany tendril around her finger, Flavia cooed. "Bellina is betrothed to Conte Sordici, isn't that so, Bellina?"

"My congratulations, Madonnina," Surek bowed stiffly. "May I offer you and the Conte a toast to your happiness?"

Aurelian's arm curled like a serpent around Bellina's back to circle her waist in a claiming gesture. She tried to pull away, but his fingers dug painfully into her side. Flavia gloated like a cat in cream.

A crop of musical notes popped up like mushrooms after a summer rain, luring the younger guests to the dance floor while others made their way to the banquet tables lining the walls. Surek watched Aurelian and Bellina join the parallel rows of dancers, then took his place in line, returning Flavia's flirtatious smiles. He laced his fingers with Flavia's, the effect was deliberate and it melted her instantly.

Claudia could not be more pleased as she watched Flavia and Bellina paired with such unrivaled men. Doting more on her daughter, she failed to notice the tightness in Bellina's face, the strained smile she offered the Conte out of politeness, or the sidelong glances at Surek and her cousin.

To Bellina, Surek seemed to be thoroughly enjoying himself. Flavia was obviously enchanted by him as she had been not so long ago. They made an elegant couple, each movement complementing the other's. It seemed that Flavia's feet never touched the floor, that she just floated around Surek and the other dancers. When Bellina was noting how charming her shrewish cousin could be, Surek caught her eyes in his and a consuming smile made her blush with embarrassment. Before she could turn away, he let his hand run slowly up Flavia's bare arm, until finally wrapping his hand over her fingertips. Bellina felt a profusion of goose bumps roll over her skin as she remembered Surek's touch. Now she watched as he displayed his affections towards her cousin. Is this why he came back to her, to punish her for the rejection he felt when she left him?

It was like her dreams come true when she first laid eyes on him, standing unbelievably at her aunt's side and in her own house! Now she watched her dream turn into a nightmare as he leaned closer to her cousin. She felt a rage growing in the pit of her stomach, unaware that the same feeling had strangled

Surek when Flavia announced her engagement to Conte Sordici.

Dancers bowed and weaved through the line to turn around and face a new partner until at last Bellina and Surek opposed each other. After a humiliating bow, Bellina lifted her chin and stared into the waving flames of the wall sconces just above his shoulder, but when his warm hand folded over hers, she could not maintain her detachment. She felt her flesh tingle and face warm with a blush that she feared would be obvious. He bent his head beside the coil of braided hair that rested upon her head. She could smell the exotic blend of oriental musk that drove her back to the burning sands of the desert.

"It seems as though fate has placed us together again," he said smoothly, despite his inner turmoil. His words reached her on a warm breath that stroked her neck.

"Has it really been fate? Or is it some order that has sent you to Venice, 'Baron' Melankovski?" She smiled sweetly, satisfied that her barbed words had displeased him, not knowing how close she had guessed his reason for being there.

"I merely wished to see the city you lamented for and," his gaze moved to Flavia and their smiles joined, "I'm glad I have, it is truly beautiful."

When she moved back from him, he clasped her hand painfully tighter and drew her towards him. "If you don't release my hand," she said, her voice scorched with anger, "my duenna will not be slow to crack her cane across your knuckles!" She pulled her hand back sharply. "Furthermore, my uncle will be especially displeased to hear of our first introduction."

Surek bowed in mock respect. "In that case, he would be compelled to marry us immediately, so I would be careful of such threats, Madonnina. Don't fear," he assured, the look in his eyes stabbing her, "I have no intentions of standing in the way of your becoming a contessa."

The dance ended with a final tap on a drum but before she could retreat, he blocked her way. "Until tomorrow, Madonnina," he said politely, just as Flavia graced his side and put her arm through his.

"Baron Melankovski," Flavia rolled his name over her tongue, "has Bellina been entertaining you with her tales of the East?"

"Oh? I had no idea your cousin was so well traveled." Bellina caught a satanic gleam in the flash of his smile. "I've not been so honored to hear them, but perhaps one day Bellina would do me the honor. I'm sure she has fascinating stories to tell."

Flavia laughed, her voice tinkling like bells blowing in a gentle breeze. "Oh, they're not so fascinating, unless you think monasteries are that interesting. I do believe Bellina has the calling." She coquettishly fluttered her lashes. "Oh, don't look so glum, Bellina, I'm only teasing."

Surek's face lit up with amusement. These two beauties could not live under the same roof peacefully—that he knew! "A monastery?" He raised an eyebrow. "I always wondered what went on in the cloistered mountain retreats."

"I would certainly be honored to enlighten you, Baron Melankovski." Bellina's voice matched her cousin's in sweetness, though she was aware of the flame of color that rose to her cheeks. That seeing Surek again was exactly what Flavia didn't want

Bellina to do was evident by the pout on her face. Bellina twirled around, leaving her sulky cousin hanging onto Surek's arm. Spying Miquel in a corner, seeming as forlorn as she felt, she threaded her way through the maze of guests.

"Miquel, it's so stuffy in here. Would you mind escorting me to the garden for some air?" Before he could answer, she folded her arm in his and led them into the stone-walled courtyard.

With all the concern of a brother filling his expression, he took her chilled hands in his and looked into eyes that were like two dark saucers. "Bellina, is something troubling you?"

"No, I just needed some air." Knowing he wasn't convinced, her mood lightened. "Oh Miquel, I never could fool you. Don't look so worried." Her hands began to shake, as all the pent-up emotions sought release. Sensing his alarm, she tried to dismiss her own shaky feelings. "Goodness, I'm just being silly. We'd better go inside now before we're missed. You know how Flavia likes to talk."

Miquel was not going to let her slip by so easily. "Bellina, as you said, you cannot fool me for long. Has the Conte overstepped his bounds?"

"With Aunt Maria in constant pursuit? No, bless her watchfulness." Bellina fretfully twisted the pearls in her necklace. "Remember the Spahiglani camp I told you I stayed at?" Her voice faltered. "The Muscovite you brought was the captain who . . . protected me." She could not look at Miquel any longer.

Now Miquel understood the extent of Surek's kindness in helping to secure Bellina's release from Mehmet's palace. Although Bellina pleaded with him, Miquel would not give her any more information about Surek than she already knew. If she loved him—which Miquel was sure of even if she wasn't—she would have to go to him herself to resolve any differences they once had. Only then would she be free to admit her love.

The couple did not see a thin specter of a figure leaning against a cyprus. As they were veiled in moonlight, Aurelian Sordici was cloaked in the shadows of the garden. He could barely make out their hushed voices, but their tone and the familiar closeness they displayed were indicting enough. As Bellina and Miquel approached him, their arms entwined like lovers, they were startled by the conte's accusing stance.

"Evening, Aurelian," Miquel said matter-of-factly. He nodded to them both and disappeared under the archway. It didn't matter what words of explanation he could offer, Aurelian would think what he wished no matter what.

Bellina found herself quite vexed by the threatening pulse that beat at the conte's brow. She pulled her arm from his hand with such suddenness that for a moment he was taken aback. "How dare you spy on me!" she snapped.

His composure regained, Aurelian lifted a slice of hair from her shoulder and wrapped it around a bejeweled finger. "My dear, you forget, soon you will become my wife, and then I shall dare do anything."

"And I shall do everything possible to delay that day," she replied with equal coolness. "If you'll excuse me, Conte, my aunt must be wondering where I am."

Her plan to evade him quickly was stopped by a hedge of people. Aurelian was at her side and guiding her indoors before she could seek refuge among the guests. Her aunt's smile broadened when she saw them approach. It was obvious to Bellina that she thought of them as a royal couple already, the conte and his future contessa. Knowing her aunt too well, she knew her matchmaking plans extended to Flavia and Surek. Perplexing as it was, this bothered her as much as her own nuptial dilemma.

Standing together, not far from Claudia and her two daughters, were Miquel, Surek, and Camillus, absorbed in conversation. Bellina could not help staring at Surek as though to prove to herself that he no longer mattered. However, his presence still had the power to unhinge her knees and take her breath away. Unconsciously she leaned toward Aurelian and felt his breath violate her ear.

"Your lover has quite an effect on you, Madonnina. You should be more careful, especially in public. It is not uncommon for men at sea to have accidents. I hear Captain Campanello will soon be sailing again and is looking for extra men. I know a few I could recommend." His muffled laughter sent a chill through her body. He would go as far as killing Miquel to attain her dowry, that she was sure of.

Claudia smiled sweetly in Camillus's direction. "Husband," she spoke softly, hiding her impatience, "are the three of you going to speak politics all evening, when two lovely ladies await your attention?"

"My dear lady, I assure you, your daughters and Bellina have not gone unnoticed," Surek replied.

"They are indeed as lovely and alluring as any sea siren found in the journey of Odysseus."

Claudia beamed and Miquel flushed crimson when Camillus wrapped an affectionate arm about his shoulders. "We owe Miquel a lot. Without his herioc efforts, we would not have Bellina here tonight. He is like a part of this family."

Flavia shifted, a frown touching her lips slightly. "Messer Melankovski, will we be seeing more of you in the future?" she asked, trying to divert the direction of the conversation and provoking a warning glance from her mother for her forwardness.

With little choice of response, Surek bowed graciously. "If your parents will have me."

"Of course!" Claudia's voice leaped with enthusiasm. "You and Miquel are always welcome in our home." A warm glow began to spread over her cheeks at the thought of the handsome baron calling on Flavia.

"It has been an honor, Madonna, Messer Poletti, Madonninas . . . and one I wish to return."

"We would be pleased to have you and Miquel as our guests on Saint Joseph's Day," Claudia added quickly before Miquel could hustle Surek from the courtyard. "Of course we hope to see you again before then. Perhaps for dinner next Friday?"

As Miquel and Surek walked back to the *Fortunata*, Miquel could keep his thoughts no longer silent. "Beware of the spider that weaves her jeweled web to snare a poor morsel for her fair daughter," he sang teasingly. "Madonna Poletti is not that friendly to strangers unless they are viable suitors."

"Devota, she is too plump. But Flavia . . . I could

323

have her too easily if I wished."

"And Bellina?"

"She has promised herself to the Conte Sordici."

Miquel detected a note of bitterness in his voice. "Her father made that match. Bellina has no choice but to marry him."

"And if she had her choice, Miquel, would you be one of her suitors?"

Miquel laughed softly. "No, not now. Her heart is promised to another." He skipped off into the fog, leaving Surek to wonder.

Twenty-Four

The blue Adriatic sparkled like a giant turquoise in the Italian sun. Venice adorned it with its richly colored buildings that boasted flamboyant architectural styles. The whole city was a statement of the wealth collected from the merchants' trading routes. Even some of the gondolas boasted some artist's touch in their gold trimmings.

The muffled sound of a donkey's hooves clip-clopping against a marble chessboard that spread out in front of the doge's palace and the lilting voice of Flavia barely touched the edge of Surek's consciousness, as he was deep in thought. Here he sat next to this beautiful seductress and Maria, an ever-present shadow behind them. The duenna thought his intent to be honorable, but actually seeing her mistress was the only way he could see Bellina. It was outings like this that he tried to avoid. At least at the palazzo Bellina was there. It amused him to see Flavia's frustrations when Bellina refused her hints and remained steadfastly present. Claudia would sense the tension when he and Bellina engaged in too much conversation and would diplomatically steer Surek and Flavia together. Was it only his imagination that saw fire light Bellina's eyes during those moments? Soon the opportunity for them to be alone would arise, and he would have his proof one way or the other.

"Surek, Surek!" Flavia repeated, using his name whenever they were out of the Polettis' earshot. The stiffness of Maria's silk skirts rustled like raven's wings at the impropriety. "You're not listening!" she pouted.

"I'm sorry, please go on," he answered, looking into her eyes deeply, trying to wash away the rising anger he saw in them. He could not help feeling a little guilty at using her, but then reminded himself of *her* motives.

"Never mind! Go back to your thoughts." She set her eyes straight ahead, focusing on the plumed headdress of the donkey. She glared into the feathers that shot up like a colorful fountain.

Surek motioned for the driver to stop. "Since you are not speaking, then we will take the gondola back to the palazzo."

Flavia, who could warm as quickly as she could turn into ice, cradled Surek's arm in her lap. "You have the same look as Miquel when he stares into the sea." Then her voice became edged with urgency, "You're not thinking of leaving, are you?"

"A minute ago you would have set me sailing," Surek replied with amusement.

"That was a minute ago. I don't want you to leave unless you take me with you." She straightened uickly as if struck by Maria's cane. "Show me the *ortunata!*" Her excitement eased some at the gasp of .er duenna whom she had forgotten. "Of course, Maria would like to see her, too."

"Flavia, you surprise me, I thought you despised hips." He recovered his arm from her hold and tried ɔ put a distance between them. "If you want to see he *Fortunata*, it is Miquel you should ask."

"I wouldn't ask him for anything." She had turned ɔol again, and for now that suited Surek.

Devota kneeled on a stuffed cushion that covered he top of a window seat and peered out over the anal. "They're here!" Her shrill announcement sent Bellina leaping from her bed. She was next to Devota ɔefore the little gondola bobbed close enough for Surek and Flavia to disembark. She cringed when 'urek lifted her cousin lightly from the vessel and ccused his hands of lingering too long at her waist. Her face burned with jealousy at the pouty look on Flavia's lips and she was close enough to kiss him. Bellina had no doubts she would have if Maria were ɔot in need of assistance.

"Watch how the gondola lifts from the water ɔow," giggled Devota when Surek had reached for heir duenna's hand. But Bellina was not in a mood ɔ be amused by the unsteady rocking of the gondola. nstead she rushed from the room to the first landing ɔnd crouched between wide fans of greenery that sprouted a concealing screen from clay urns. From ɔer secret perch she could hear voices from below.

Claudia gaily greeted her daughter and escort,

327

hardly noticing the tight lines around Flavia's mouth. "You two had a beautiful day for sightseeing." She looked to Maria for a hint of how the day went and was given a look of consternation. However, Claudia tossed it off. Maria had been displeased with the visits of Baron Melankovski and had not attempted to hide her dislike for him. "Well, I hope Flavia hasn't bored you with too much of our city in one day."

"No, Madonna, Venice is indeed the gem of the Adriatic." Surek watched Flavia become annoyed with her mother and wondered who could ever totally please her.

Claudia was not anxious to see Surek leave. "You must be hungry after being out all morning."

As anxious as Claudia was to keep him, Surek was just as determined not to stay another night for dinner. "Madonna, your kindness is always generous, but I must return to the *Fortunata*. Miquel is charting our next voyage and I—"

"All right, but I insist you must stay for a piece of Grazia's bread. The loaves have just come out of the oven, and Miquel would never forgive you if you did not bring him some."

Bellina left the landing as swiftly as a breeze. Her slippers were silent against the hard steps of the servant's staircase that spiraled to the kitchen. She startled Grazia so that she dropped the crust of biscuit from her fingers. "How did you . . . What are you doing in here, Madonnina?"

The thick warm air in the kitchen was so suffocating she felt faint from the effort to breathe. Her heart pounded a dull, vibrating rhythm that sounded in her ears, driving out Grazia's mumbling. The few minutes she waited seemed like forever. She began to wonder what craziness had gripped her. Giving way to second thoughts, she rose to leave, but it was too late, footsteps moved closer to the kitchen door.

Flavia, accustomed to always charming the men she chose into bending to her every desire, stiffly grimaced under the thought that Surek was still unaffected by her advances. That made her want him even more. He was unlike the rest; any other man would have met her advances with passion. When she began to doubt his reasons for accepting her mother's invitations, there was always that devilish smile or warm kiss on the back of her hand to subdue her frustrations and put him back in control Now if he wanted to keep a hold on her, those gestures he threw to her would have to come more frequently, and not resemble the small affections of a brother. Deliberately leaving without any parting remarks, she heard her mother ask her usual question as Flavia climbed each step to the floor above.

"Will we have the honor of your presence tomorrow, Baron Melankovski?"

Surek's attention to Flavia's leaving was misinterpreted by Claudia, who felt assured that her plans for her daughter were going smoothly. His thoughts were well concealed behind the emotionless mask of a Spahiglani. Flavia was becoming impatient, and he knew he could not keep her satisfied with bits of his attention for much longer.

From the doorway he spied Bellina snacking at the marbletop table that spanned nearly the length of the kitchen. Grazia had such a foreboding look that he doubted this was a chance meeting and smiled with self-satisfaction. In two strides he stood opposite her, pulled out a stool from under the table, and straddled it. She posed such a fake look of surprise, that he had to fight back the urge to laugh. So, this was going to be an interesting day after all.

"Good afternoon, Madonnina. Do you often have lunch in the kitchen?" He tore a thick piece of crusty bread from a round loaf that lay between them.

"This is my house Baron Melankovski, and I eat where I wish." Though her voice was strong and unwavering, her hands trembled. She met his eyes coldly but was forced by his hard returning stare to look away. He had not lost any of his appeal. He was as handsome, as alluring, and as arrogant as ever.

He reached across the table and pulled her hand free from the crook of her arm where she had shoved it to quell the trembling. It had been so long since she felt his touch and so often had she dreamed of it, that she could not force herself to release his hold. A silence fell between them. Bellina knew that Grazia was watching from the corner of the kitchen with sidelong glances, and if not threatened or bribed would set the house afire with gossip that would eventually find Aunt Claudia's and Flavia's ears. She should draw away from him, but could not. He traced each finger with his, sending tingling sensations rolling over her skin. He molded her hand between his, as a reminder of more intimate pleasures. Bellina was motionless and breathless while his hand, calloused from leather reins, trailed under the flowing sleeve of her gown to her forearm. He pulled

330

her to him and whispered in a low, almost growling voice.

"You desire me, Bellina, as much as I want you."
Shocked by his presumptions, however, struggled against his grip. "How dare you make such a conceited conclusion! Release my arm," she choked. Why did he have to spoil everything with his surly remarks, she fumed. He leaned back, his arms folded over his chest, watching her try to regain her composure. "Grazia, isn't it time to bring in the laundry?" she announced finally.

"Yes, Madonnina," the cook answered quickly and almost seemed grateful to leave the hot kitchen. Bellina wondered if she would listen at the door, but now it didn't matter. She had seen enough to imagine the best bit of gossip the household had ever heard and was probably on her way with it already.

"You conceited fool! What makes you think I would desire you? The way you kept me prisoner and forced me to please your erotic pleasures. You kept me from my family. What if they knew of that! Don't fancy yourself that your secret is safe with me." She knew she had stumbled dangerously into the fire of his anger with her threatening and regretted some of her words. He stepped around the table that divided them, his voice strained to whisper.

"I *forced* you! Hah! It was you who begged with your eyes, your movements, and your words. I thought you a child. You reminded me you were not. When I moved away, you moved closer. I would have put you on the first ship to Venice if I could have." For every step he took towards her she moved back, trying to keep the safe barrier of the table between

331

them. When he saw her white skin and wide eyes, he realized how frightening he looked and then let a satisfied smile break the hard lines of his face. "You talk of being kept prisoner. Try to remember all the freedoms you really had and compare that to here. You are as much, if not more, of a captive in your own house!" Now the sparks flew back into her eyes, giving life to the Bellina he knew.

"I am not a prisoner here. I am free to do what I please." Bellina hoped her voice did not betray the doubt she had. She stood her ground and swore she would not be intimidated by him. There was no table dividing them now, they stood face to face. "I am here with you, am I not?"

"Yes, and who knows of it besides the cook? I'd bet you sneaked down here." She hated it when he mocked her, and he knew he could wield her stubborn pride to his own advantage.

"Bellina, you are as much a prisoner here as in a guarded Spahiglani tent. Your aunt and uncle, Maria—and let's not forget your elegant conte—are all your keepers. Can you escape them?"

The ruby ring she had gotten so used to suddenly tightened around her finger. She tried to pull it off, but it would not even turn. What he said was true, but she would not admit it to him. She had waited too long to answer him, she knew he must suspect her doubts, but despite his look of triumph she would not let him glory in it. "I am not a prisoner here. I can go and come, as I please."

"Really?" he said slowly, a glint in his eye. "Then if you are truly free to do as you please, come back to the *Fortunata* with me."

For a moment Bellina was struck speechless. She

332

should have guessed he would trick her so. He knew she would go with him to prove her words. If she refused, it would be a victory for him, and if she went with him, it would still be his coup. With a smug grin he walked past her to the back door, and without a glance to see if she was following him, held the door open.

"Oh, Bellina, don't forget Miquel's bread."

Bellina was proving to herself as much as to Surek that she was not a prisoner in her own house. For awhile she walked haughtily, but when her anger wore away, she began to doubt the wisdom in what she was doing. Devota would surely look for her. Hopefully cook's gossip would be kept among the servants. If anyone recognized her alone with Surek, and word of it got back to her aunt and uncle, they would marry her to Conte Sordici in a week. Surek was right, she fretted, she was as much a prisoner in her own land as in Constantinople.

Bellina scanned the row of merchant ships, their masts and rigging weaved together across a cloudless sky, but she could not find the *Fortunata* among them. Out a distance, midway between the horizon and port, on a sea so calm it resembled a china blue plate, posed a handful of ships.

"It appears we need a sandolo if we are to board her. I've made your point, Captain, or Baron Melankovski. I don't see any reason to go further." Bellina held out the basket of bread to Surek.

"Indeed, Madonnina, you must return before your absence is noticed. But first, I have promised to deliver this to Miquel. You may wait here if you like."

She pulled the basket from his hand. "I'd like to see

333

Miquel myself,'' she huffed and silently followed him into the small craft.

A few yards from the *Fortunata* she heard some of the crew sing out Surek's name and from their excitement and the scurry on deck to prepare for their boarding, it was obvious he was well received on Miquel's ship. Once aboard, Bellina greeted the men she was introduced to and tried to ignore their obvious stares when Surek left her standing apart from them while he spoke to a bewhiskered old sailor. When he came back to her, he took the basket and gave it to the sailor who gave her a sly grin before he scurried away.

"That's Vasco, a leathery old sea dog who's sailing adventures include battles with monsters as big as a caravel. But now his adventures are mainly in the galley whipping up meals stranger than his stories. He's told me Miquel has gone ashore to celebrate the birth of Leo's firstborn,'' he announced as he closed a heavy door behind him. Bellina whirled to face him.

"This isn't Miquel's cabin. How could I have let you trick me like this?'' She paced the floor like a caged lion. "Wait until Miquel hears of this!''

"Miquel? Bellina, you are such a child. Why don't you admit it to yourself that you've enjoyed this outing? This is the first time you've felt like your own person since you've come under the Polettis' roof.''

"*My* roof.'' Bellina corrected.

Surek uncorked a crystal decanter and poured two glasses of wine. Bellina readily accepted one to ward off a penetrating chill. He settled into a walnut chair with wide arms that wrapped around in a near circle. By the second generous glass, she had warmed considerably and had no thoughts of returning home. However, she did think of Flavia and with that thought, a smile dimpled her face.

Surek smiled back, pleased with a softness he had not seen in Bellina's face in a long time. "What has caused this rash outburst of glee? It looks as though you have just plotted some devilish plan and can't wait to execute it."

"Perhaps I have already." Her eyes sparkled even in the subdued light of the cabin as she thought how furious her cousin would be if she knew she was here alone with Surek. But then she reminded herself that he had brought her here on a dare.

"Am I the object of this plan?" He swung his leg over the edge of the massive desk, bracing his elbow against his thigh, he leaned toward her, his chin resting in the palm of his hand.

Bellina almost squirmed under such close scrutiny. Avoiding his eyes, she studied the creases in the brown leather boot that hugged his calf, the same riding boot that crushed desert sand and rode across the plains of Muscovy. "How is it that you've come all the way from Muscovy, Baron Melankovski?" she wondered out loud.

"That is a simple question." He moved away from her now, stretching like a big cat.

Bellina turned to look at him as he paced the perimeter of the small room. "I doubt anything about you is simple."

"My home is in Muscovy. And I am not a mercenary, if that is what you have been thinking. I am loyal to my prince, and at one time would do anything to protect my country from the encroachment of the powerful Ottoman Empire."

"Such as becoming a respected leader in Mehmet's army?"

He stopped to face her. "Even if it meant the loss of respect of those dear to me. But that is all past history. Soon I will be returning home to my family."

"Will Flavia be going with you?" Bellina shocked herself at her boldness. His broad smile further humiliated her. She quickly retreated to the cabin door, only to be caught by the sweep of his arm.

"I would take you, if you were not so intent on being the conte's wife."

His hold on her was less than tender and became tighter the more Bellina pushed her arms against his chest in an effort to free herself. Being unsuccessful, she realized how foolish it was to follow him here. Now that he had her alone, she was at his mercy, for it was doubtful any of the crew would respond to her screams.

He did say he would take her with him if . . . How could he think she wanted to marry Conte Sordici? She burst with an indignity that took him by surprise.

"You think I would marry that pompous fool to be a contessa! That is an arrangement of my family. One that does not please me in the least." His look of astonishment made her laugh. "All this time you thought I wanted Conte Sordici?" At the risk of infuriating him, waves of giggles bubbled over her lips. He let her go so suddenly she whirled and fell onto the bunk. He turned his back to her, placing his hands on his hips and his feet solidly on the planked floor. Bellina wiped the tears from her cheeks and began to sober.

'I'm sorry. I didn't laugh. It's just that the conte is so repulsive to me that the thought that anyone could think— Even Miquel knows how I detest the man. I'd do anything to somehow free myself of this obligation to my father.''

When Surek finally faced her, the storm cloud that had darkened his face was gone. He knelt beside her, resting on one knee and grasping her hands between his, kissed them passionately, drinking in their perfumed softness. "Then come with me when the *Fortunata* leaves in two weeks."

Bellina felt like she was living one of her dreams and that soon she would awake only to find herself alone in her bed. She had to reassure herself somehow that this was real. "But what of Flavia?" she dared to ask.

"Flavia means as much to me as the conte means to you. She was the only way I could see you." He put a finger across her lips to silence her protests. "You would not see me and that you cannot deny." He twisted the thick rope of hair that lay over her shoulder in his hand. "You will come with me in two weeks then?"

It sounded like more of a command than a question, but Bellina did not mind this time. She would leave *now* but she could not bear the thought of hurting her uncle. Two weeks would give her enough time to collect some of her things and bid a farewell to her family. "Yes. Yes, I will go anywhere with you. Even if it is back to the heat of the desert. Uncle Camillus will be upset, but—"

"You must not tell anyone. If they suspect, they will surely stop you. You may think you are free in your palazzo, but you are not." Bellina opened her mouth to protest but was silenced by a firm kiss. She weakened and fell against the soft pile of blankets that covered the bunk. It seemed like an eternity had gone by since the last time he had wrapped her in his embrace. His hand stroked her slender neck, resting where he could feel the pounding of her pulse. Letting his fingers weave through her silk gown, he traced the form of her body, pleasingly fuller now than before. Without resistance, he slowly pulled the gown away and felt her smooth skin grow hot beneath the palm of his hand. Holding her breast in his hand, he lowered his head and pressed his warm lips against her skin. His tongue flickered teasingly over the white mounds that rose slightly with each breath she took and trailed down the center of her abdomen. Spreading her thighs apart with his knee, he cupped the velvety mound between her legs in one hand and slipped a finger through the moist folds until he felt her shiver in ecstacy.

She rested her hands on his shoulders as he lowered his head to drink of her passion. Inebriated with desire, she watched with glazed eyes as he pulled off his shirt and shed the pants that strained under the swollenness of his longing. He covered her with his body, his hardness pervading her soft interior. Joined as one, they moved as one in a rhythmic consummation of their love. When they were satiated at last, Bellina twisted her arms around Surek's neck and pressed her cheek against his. "Let's stay like this forever, joined eternally in love."

"That is a tempting thought, and I promise to join with you in love very often, but for now you must leave. If you stay away from your palazzo much longer, there will be too many questions you would not be able to answer. And Miquel should be returning soon. I do not want him to discover us like this without some preparation." He had finished dressing and cast a stern look at Bellina. "Come, get dressed. In two weeks I shall lock you in my cabin without a stitch." A rosy blush spread over her as he teased.

The position of the sun told Bellina that it was late afternoon. As she raced to keep up with Surek's long strides she tried to think of a plausible excuse for her absence. She led Surek through the back alleys and avoided the busier parts of the city whenever she could. Lines dripped with patches of white, gray, and black clothing that formed a canopy between the stone buildings. The bright sunlight filtered through the day's wash that hung overhead, casting them in shadows. This was the poorest part of Venice, and it surprised him that she knew the area so well. He stopped on a small bridge that spanned a still, foul-smelling canal. "Bellina, how do you know this shortcut? Surely you don't venture this way alone?"

"Don't worry. As a child Miquel would take me home through here, with my father of course. This is where he grew up."

"I see. There are even more depressed streets in Muscovy. You would not believe the conditions in the Wooden City. It is no wonder Miquel escaped to the sea at such an early age."

Bellina gripped Surek's hand as they moved through the slick and narrow walkways. Without the warmth of the sun, she shivered in the icy shadows of the parallel rows of buildings. Soon they emerged from the dim interior of Venice and were bathed in rays of light unopposed by the impenetrable stone facades. When they were within a short distance of the palazzo Surek left her to return to the *Fortunata,* forming the words he would speak to Miquel.

Entering the palazzo unseen was easier than Bellina had thought. No one was in the kitchen when she peered in, so she quickly used the servant's staircase to reach the second floor without fear of encountering her aunt. She was filled with such an exhilarating feeling she thought she would burst with happiness. She smiled into the mirror as she pulled a brush through her tangled hair. "Conte Sordici, I will be so charming you will not know what to think, and in two weeks you will be courting cousin Flavia, no doubt."

Twenty-Five

It had been four days since Bellina had seen or heard from Surek. He hadn't even called upon Flavia, which made her cousin about as pleasant to be with as a snake with a pinched tail. Like the servants, Bellina made herself scarce, slipping into the back courtyard and the comfort of the newly opened roses. Had it all been a dream, she wondered. Her heart had thumped a frantic beat of hope, happiness, and disbelief. Almost, she was afraid to believe that Surek loved her, for to do so would fan to fiery life a whirl of overpowering emotions. Bellina cupped a delicate bloom in her hands and inhaled its sweetness.

With a sigh she settled by the fish pool that Claudia had built with stones from the Alps. Where, her restless, weary self kept asking, where was Surek? Her body ached for his, and if sleep came at all, it came with nightmares of Surek leaving on the *Fortunata*, smug with the knowledge of her admitted love, leaving her heart in a shatter of bitter pieces.

"Madonnina Bellina!" She heard Lucia call, and

for a moment Bellina childishly thought of hiding before she was discovered.

"I am here," Bellina answered, heavyhearted.

"Madonna Poletti says that Father Masalia has arrived to hear confessions."

"Tell her I will be along," Bellina said, dismissing Lucia, reluctant to leave her sanctuary. Instead, she let her eyes follow the golden carp that darted beneath the water. Flavia should keep Father Masalia's ear for half the afternoon, Bellina mused, that is if she told everything. I may not be any better, she admitted, but at least only one man has claimed my body and soul.

Abruptly she left the pool, glancing at a peaking sun. If she was quick, she could be the first confession heard, then could easily slip away while the others followed, and since Father Masalia always said a mass afterward, the house would be occupied the rest of the day. Another minute I will not wait! *I will come to you, Surek,* her mind spun with the weaving of her plan.

Conte Sordici pulled his velvet hat further down, trying to shelter an already burned nose from the sun. "Can't you move faster?" He shot his clipped words at the silent gondolier. "Can't you see I'm beginning to blister?"

The man braved a halfhearted smile and tried a quicker pace as Aurelian's eyes darted, following Bellina as she negotiated a narrow walkway. Her steps were agile like a goat's, her attention purposeful, never faltering. Aurelian had been on his way to visit her when he realized it was confession day at the

Polettis', but then much to his surprise he had caught sight of Bellina entering an alley. It was his duty to follow her, for mischief, no doubt, was her mistress.

"Curses of Hades!" Aurelian snarled at his man. "Let me out, you slug! I'll make more progress by myself!"

Aurelian crawled out of the boat onto the walkway and followed her, careful to keep to the shadows.

Occasionally she darted quick little glances behind her and Aurelian's heart raced with excitement. How I would love to crush her, he thought, crush her between me and these stones. He paused to sink back against a niche between two buildings as Bellina turned once more to look back, her brows knotted in worry. As Aurelian felt a familiar excitement building in his loins, he forgot the uncomfortable damp coolness of the twisting walkways that crossed Venice's dark heart. Occasionally they passed others; a curious assortment of half-clothed children, men sleeping off their sport of the night before, uncaring of the bugs that quested across their prone bodies.

"You slut!" he cursed, his eyes losing sight of Bellina. He stepped up his pace and came to a crossway. Which way had she taken? Convinced there could only be one place Bellina was going, Aurelian turned left and continued towards the docks.

Sure enough she appeared ahead of him. Momentarily she stopped as she wrestled a corner of her hem from the grasping hand of a drunk. Aurelian felt a sudden heat of anger flash across his face. He knew it. She was a guttersnipe. No decent woman would traverse these alleys even in daylight. Could she not wait another day to see her sea rat lover? The thought of Miquel and Bellina naked, entwining their lusty limbs around each other, swelled Aurelian's manhood painfully and consumed his heart and mind with black rage.

He had always known deep in his heart that there was something between the two of them. Miquel was always overfamiliar when it came to Bellina, and she, like a cat in heat, encouraged him.

Aurelian's hands cried out in pain and he unclenched them, trying to relax as he closed the gap between himself and Bellina. "Nowhere will she go today," his mind raced. "I'll stop her! I'll grind her into the stones of this path. Let her blood run and pool with the rivulets of water from the cracks in these crumbling walls. No one will care—not here," he laughed.

The hand that had delayed Bellina clutched at Aurelian's boot. "Pity me, kind sir, the gods have placed curses upon me," his quivering words barely rose from his chest.

Aurelian, in even less of a compassionate mood than usual, kicked the hand away without pause and without losing sight of Bellina.

She leaped over a puddle, pulling her skirts away. The alternating dark and light of the alley was pitched into darkness when three men formed a barricade in front of her.

"Bellina!" One of the men sputtered in alarm.

"Miquel!" she cried, suddenly shy, her hands betraying her nervousness as she confronted Miquel and two of his sailors.

Aurelian flattened against the wall. He could see

Miquel's hand angrily grab Bellina's arm as the four of them walked away.

"We're not children anymore!" Miquel scolded. "And even then I told you never to come here by yourself. Cristos Sanctos," he gestured heavenward. "But come, I'll take you the rest of the way."

"Witch!" Aurelian spat, watching them disappear. His mind whirled into a dark storm of wicked ideas. "Let them have their fun, until she is wed to me." As much as she turned his stomach, he could stand her for a wife for as long as it would take to claim her fortune. Indeed, she would bring him much pleasure as he basked in her wealth and pounded his frustrations into the soft recesses of her body. Then, he would kill her.

Bellina's lips quivered as Surek closed his cabin door behind them, but she met his eyes and matched his anger with indignation. "I knew perfectly well what I was doing. After all, wasn't it you who said I lived in a prison?"

Surek motioned her to sit on the bed. "Stop leaving the subject. You know quite well what I think of your shortcut to the docks, and I won't have you doing anything so foolish again."

"Well, I wouldn't have needed to do it, if you had cared anything at all about me!" She sat on the bunk hard.

Surek eyed her pointedly. "And what is that supposed to mean? It's only been four days," Surek said. Bellina knew by the surprised look on his face that she had overreacted, but it was too late now, for

345

anger raced with the blood in her veins.

"I spend my life waiting for you. Couldn't you even send someone to bring me word that you'll be by soon? I heard you were sailing again. I'm finished waiting."

"Did you want me to send word to your aunt that I would be calling on you or Flavia? Bellina, be realistic! Every day at the palazzo I am reminded you are to wed Conte Sordici." He stroked her hair rhythmically until she was calmed like some wild horse under his hand. "And besides, how do you think I *should* react," he grabbed her squarely by the shoulders. "You are always getting into trouble. What will I have to do when you are my wife? Hobble you like some wayward horse when you're on your own?"

Bellina's eyes widened, "You, sir, do not take me seriously, and I assure you I am not jesting."

"Bellina, you have to be patient for a little while longer." He gave her a squeeze. "I'm sorry. I should have sent word to you, but the four days went by before I knew it."

His last words hurt her. How could he not be as anxious as she had been to see him! She was a mere convenience. He was not happy to see her, even when she had risked coming here. She was only met by his anger, not his joy. "Well," she fumed, "I'm glad you can do so easily without me, for you'll never see me here again, I assure you!"

"Bellina!" He grabbed her arm painfully as she turned and wrenched toward the stubborn door.

"Let me go!" she ordered, but instead he pulled her into his arms and crushed her against his mouth. His

346

kiss was a hungry one while his hands greedily wrapped around the curve of her hips.

She pushed away his hands and his mouth bit at her swollen nipples through the fabric of her dress. Without even thinking, her hand smacked against his head. If she could have retracted the slap she would have at the hurt expression on his face, but instead she turned from him and stomped away from the cabin.

"Miquel!" Surek's voice boomed. "Have an escort see Madonnina D'Rosallini home."

"Stay where you are, Miquel," Bellina said with a burning glare at him and Surek.

As she fled from them, Surek turned to Miquel. "Follow that little vixen and see that she gets home safely in spite of herself."

Miquel laughed, "Didn't she believe that you've been busy these last days making arrangements for your wedding?"

Surek rubbed his face with his hand. "She didn't even give me the chance to explain."

Bellina made it home with no difficulty and she was certainly aware of Miquel trailing, no matter how he tried not to be seen. So be it, if it made them feel any better.

She had been gone for such a short time that nobody had missed her at all—or so she thought. However, Flavia, her rosary clutched in her hands, but her eyes wandering, betraying a mind not on pious prayers but on a whirl of speculations, was gazing out a partly open window watching Bellina enter a servant's stairwell. "Now where has she been?" she wondered with wicked curiosity about what she might have missed while listening to Father Masalia's nasal voice drone on. And then she saw Miquel, not far behind and obviously following Bellina.

Flavia's hands stretched the rosary tautly. Her first emotion was surprise that Bellina would be so audacious in taking a lover. Then a flash of jealousy loomed that Miquel had never in these years made any advances towards herself! Then elation, for this was an opportunity. Yes indeed, this was how to shake that sparkle from her father's eyes whenever he looked upon Bellina in a way, Flavia thought angrily, that he never looked at her. All she had to do was wait and watch and the chance would come when she could reveal the shameful lovers to everyone. Flavia kissed the cross on her rosary and Claudia smiled, catching her daughter's pious action out of the corner of her eye.

For the next two days, Bellina seethed like a tightly lidded pot. By the third night she felt empty, her anger boiled away into despair. But with despair came the realization that she couldn't live without Surek—whether or not he truly loved her. She had admitted it to him before, and now she finally accepted it herself without further protests from her pride. He was her happiness, her sorrow, her reason for living. She would follow him to the ends of the earth or wait for him here, forever.

Bellina moved to her balcony to watch the fingernail slice of moon rise. It threw glittering streaks across the moody Adriatic and fluttered its softer light amongst the leaves of the vegetation below. It shimmered through her night dress, revealing all the curves of her young body, and it lighted her tears, turning them into jewels. Around her the wind sighed and whispered its secrets to the trees and Bellina moaned and breathed deeply of its rose-scented sweetness. Her numb despair drained away, pushed aside by something primeval. Something that was found in the wind and the water and the whispering leaves.

She didn't know how long she remained there, but eventually her eyelids and knees felt heavy and she retreated to her soft bed kissed with the chill of the night. She let the balcony doors remain open and the drapes danced with the light breeze. She fell asleep knowing deep inside that Surek loved her and that he would come for her. She knew because the wind had told her so.

She woke up with a start, trying not to breathe with startled loudness. It was much later, for the moon had set and clouds now covered the stars. Something must have woken her, she thought, her heart pounding. Yet no harm revealed itself as she lay still, ears and eyes straining in the darkness. The wind snapped the drapes, biting in its chill, and she now wished she hadn't left the doors open. She started to leave her warm cocoon when she heard it. A complaint from an overstressed piece of wood, a creak. It must have been that sound that had warned her senses. She felt the hair on her neck and arms lift and remained still, listening. She could neither see nor sense anything. The wind?

She waited until finally a shudder wracked her

body and the wind whipped to blow one of the vials off her dressing table. That was it. She left her bed and grabbed each of the doors to shut them. It was then that she felt an arm encircle her waist and found a hand across her mouth. His breath came ragged. He pulled her so forcefully against him that she felt the hardness of his erection in her back. Before he even spoke, she knew it was Aurelian, smelling the familiar goatish pungency of his body beneath the cologne he wore.

"Thank you, Madonnina," he whispered in her ear. "Thank you for your invitation." He pulled her back towards the bed despite her struggles. "Such a beckoning sight it was, too. You in your night dress, and those convenient vines and opened doors. But what is this?" He said looking into her face and her fear-widened eyes. "I think you're a little surprised to see me." He laughed, the weight of his body forcing her into the soft mattress. He gasped as her knee finally hit home and for a moment he lost cover of her mouth, but it was just a moment. When she opened her mouth to scream, he stuffed his handkerchief into it. While she struggled, choking, he secured the gag with a sash. "Not yet," he said, panting from the effort. "You can scream for the guards all you want later. For I want them to find us together, my body deep inside of yours. And then what do you think your stalling uncle will do?" Aurelian laughed at his own clever plan. "Why he'll marry us! He'll have little choice if he wants to retain his family honor."

Bellina shuddered, for he just might be right. Rape would bring a destroying shame upon this household. Claudia would force Camillus to marry Bellina

350

to Aurelian to solve that problem and the future problem of an unexplainable pregnancy.

Her hands strained and her legs lashed out whenever they could under the weight of his body. "Stop it!" He shouted louder than he wanted, and he hit her in the head, dazing her. "Don't be so explicit with your disappointment, Madonnina." He lay over her to crush her struggles. "I know I'm no brawny seaman like your Miquel. But I assure you, my staff will prick you just as deeply. You might just as well enjoy it."

Unfortunately Bellina had already pulled her nightdress up in her struggles to expose her well-shaped limbs, making it easy for Aurelian. He covered the mound of hair between her legs with his hand, probing until he could stab two fingers deep inside of her. "Just like that," he growled and continued, mesmerized by the rhythm he set.

At first she continued to fight him, succeeding only in grazing his nose with her nails. In exhaustion she became still, letting her breast pound, feeling her flesh shrink away from Aurelian's hands.

"You enjoy it, don't you?" he said softly into her ear. He had both of her arms pinned beneath her back, always keeping his weight upon her. "You're going to have a wonderful time—a day to remember, as our wedding night will be," he promised, pulling a nipple with the edges of his teeth, causing her to cringe in pain. "I will make all of your nerves scream with life. You will find out the joys a Sordici can bring a woman to."

He spared one hand to release his throbbing organ from the confines of his pants. Taking him off balance, Bellina arched her back, gaining enough freedom to free her legs. She kicked with the last ounce of her strength. His stomach, his chin, one shoulder, all suffered her blows before he realized what had happened. Bellina was out of the bed tearing at her gag. Aurelian, clumsy in his half-dressed state, seized her by her flowing hair and managed to get one of her arms under his control.

Bellina grabbed at the bedwarmer and swung, but with only one hand the blow was feeble. She had more success with her legs, almost delivering a debilitating kick to his genitals, when Aurelian twisted her arm behind her back with a curse. Pain brought swift cooperation.

"On the floor, bitch! Where you belong," he cried through a red haze of rage. He forced her to her knees, pleased as she shivered in her torn clothes. He continued to tear at them until every inch of her was exposed to his eyes and hand.

"Is this the way you and your sea dog lover do it?" Aurelian laughed, pushing her down before him in a prostrate position. Her heart and mind froze in terror, bracing for the pain physical and mental that this rape would bring. Instead, she heard Aurelian's muffled cry of pain.

Someone had entered the darkness of her room and was beating Aurelian with his fists. Aurelian groveled for the sword he had carelessly left by the window. The stranger was quicker, grasping Aurelian's leg, he pulled him off balance and they rolled like clawing, biting cats onto the balcony.

Bellina followed, grabbing the poker from the hearth, intent on smashing Aurelian's head. To her disappointment she was just in time to see the stranger rip Aurelian's grasp from the railing and send him hurtling to the ground below.

"No!" she cried. Amazed eyes, Surek's eyes, turned to her, soft in the gentleness of night's darkness with the poker held menacingly in her hand. She couldn't stop the flow of tears, frustration born of the terror she could not avenge.

Surek gathered her close in his arms, his warm body a refuge of love and warmth. "Don't fret," he said. "I saw him crawl away. When I encounter him again, and I assure you I'll find him, I'll let you do whatever you want to him." Bellina couldn't help but shiver as Surek's voice became deadly cold. "And then, I'll kill him."

He carried her inside, gently placing her on the bed, but she would let go of him. "Hold me," she cried, "Oh I need you to hold me so much!"

He lay beside her and she buried her head against his neck, inhaling the sweet comforting smell of him, pulling him as close to her as possible to block out the memory of Aurelian's vileness.

"Are you hurt in any way?" Surek asked, brushing her hair back from her face with his hand. She took a while to answer.

"No," she said finally. "A few bruises will show, I'm sure, but fortunately he didn't get to do the damage he wanted to."

With a resounding thunderous noise, the door flung open, and it seemed a hundred lanterns poured in an accusing blaze of light. Surek grabbed for his sword, but halted as a rapier came to a threatening rest upon his chest. His light-blinded eyes adjusted, showing eight guards and Camillus standing before him. Camillus saw the unclothed niece he loved like a daughter, shamelessly entwined in the clasp of a man she wasn't wed to, and could have cried.

"Hussy!" Camillus roared, throwing Bellina a blanket. "Cover your shame!"

Surek followed the motion of the rapier's tip and backed away. "And you," Camillus turned his eyes to Surek, "You were a guest in my house! A man of honor, so I thought!"

Bellina rushed to her uncle but he pushed her away. She clung to his feet. "Forgive us, Uncle!"

"Forgive the shame you bring upon yourself, on me, on this house? That is too much forgiveness to ask of me."

At his words, Bellina was stricken to the heart. To hear such from her beloved uncle, to know she had hurt him so, was more than she could bear.

"I love her," Surek said, piercing Camillus with his angry look. As Bellina was crying hysterically, he stepped towards her.

"Another move, Baron Melankovski!" threatened the guard hopefully with an eager smile. Two of the others had worked their way to his back and he knew they'd pin his arms. Surek seemed to ignore them but held the tensed guards in his peripheral vision.

"It is not what it seems," he started, hearing how ridiculous his words sounded in the light of their situation.

"We are to be wed," Bellina cried.

"Wed?" Camillus raged, "Wed you say, girl? By who's decree? Your own? And what of the matter of your dear deceased father's wishes?"

"May my father forgive me, I'll hang first before I'll wed that vile Sordici," she vowed.

All turned at a faint gasp to see Flavia at the chamber's entrance, her eyes wide in disbelief as she saw it was Surek not Miquel held in the guard's gasp. Camillus blindly swung an arm at her, "Are you here to gape in self-satisfaction, daughter? Go to your room. You've done enough mischief for one night."

Surek pulled one of his arms loose with an angry glare at one of the soldiers. "Messer Poletti," he started, but a fist ended his words and he found himself bent in pain, unable to defend Bellina.

"Take him below and chain him," Camillus ordered. "Until I decide what is to be done with him." He shook a cringing Bellina off his sleeve. "Retain some shred of dignity, girl. I leave you to your maids. Until you are dressed and calm, I have no desire to speak to you."

Bellina watched the guards drag Surek away, her uncle following, leaving her in despair. Lucia and Maria entered, Lucia's eyes as wide as a startled cat's and Maria's face taut with disapproval.

"Leave me," Bellina sobbed into her pillow, unable to face them.

"Ah no, Madonnina," Maria said without compassion in her voice, "your uncle wants you dressed and in his study."

The bristled duenna chose a somber dress from Bellina's wardrobe while Lucia tried unsuccessfully to unwrap the blanket Bellina clutched around her.

"I knew you were trouble," Maria huffed prying Bellina's fingers back. "Right when I saw you. And who knew what bad habits you acquired in that

355

heathen land! Well, now we know, don't we! A monastery, indeed!"

"Leave me be," Bellina lamented, curling the cover around her like a cocoon.

"Madonnina," Lucia said gently, her hand brushing Bellina's forehead. "You must speak to your uncle. They've taken Messer Melankovski into the dungeons."

"I know," Bellina said in a hopeless voice, letting free of the blanket. Her thoughts were black thoughts, deep and deadly, as she silently cursed Flavia for calling the guards in hopes of dishonoring her and not saving her from a rapist's attack. If she told her uncle now of Sordici's attack, it would be highly unlikely he'd ever believe her. All he would see was a foolish lovesick girl out to slander the suitor her family had chosen for her. Gone were any means she had in her battle to change her betrothal to Aurelian. How weak and base a person Surek must seem in his eyes.

"You two minks play roughly," Maria clucked. Bellina followed the duenna's eyes. Ugly red spots upon her breasts were turning into angry purple bruises. In the mirror she saw more on her neck. Uncle will be turning Surek over to the doge's condottiere for sure, she worried.

As if reading her mind, Lucia was searching her trunk, and found a lace mantilla to drape artfully around her head and shoulders. Then she was led to the study and left to ponder and curse the fate that awaited her with her uncle's return.

The moon was beginning to set before he finally entered the somber room. Bellina, although exhausted, was seated in a dark corner, tense and wary. He sat down heavily and spread his hands apart. "Why, Bellina?" he asked in a heavy voice, as if all the problems of the world were his burden.

She looked at her hands folded neatly in her lap. "I love him, Uncle, with all my heart. I could never be without him. And although I didn't always know it, I would follow him anywhere, for his path is mine."

"I am bound by honor and by law to see that your betrothal to Conte Sordici is honored," her uncle said gently.

Bellina's eyes snapped and her lips thinned, "I will go to my grave before a marriage bed if that were to be!"

"There is no need for that," Camillus said, stretching his cramping legs. "I have had a long talk with your baron. He has agreed to pay quite a large fee to Conte Sordici to annul your betrothal. Knowing the Conte, the money will be more than enough to change his mind. Of course, he will be convinced that your dowry is not as substantial as he thought."

"Oh, Uncle, thank you!" Bellina cried, bounding across the room to give him a hug. "All the happy years of my life, I will remember this and never forget your kindness."

"Mind you," Camillus said sternly, "I am still disappointed in you. Your actions were sinful and until your wedding with Baron Melankovski, I expect you to act as the lady you were taught to be." He scowled when Bellina kissed his cheek. "Your Baron, he's not so bad, I think." And to himself he added, "I never did like that Sordici anyway."

Twenty-Six

The Genoan splashed water on his face and neck from the shallow bowl on his nightstand. A small cracked mirror hung precariously from a rusted nail that poked through the old plaster wall. In it he regarded his meager accommodations: a once discarded straight-backed chair rested near a slit of a window that afforded dim light from the adjacent alley; a scanty mattress pushed to a corner of the room, on it lay the malnourished form of a young girl. She was company enough and all he could afford, on his meager allowance, to pass the time while he waited.

He slipped a short dagger into the top of his boot, straightened, and patted the bulge of gold in his pocket. It had been lucky meeting him, and so soon after Miquel Campanello had refused his offer. That scum of a Venetian had no right to slight him. Go back to Genoa, he had told him. But there was nothing in Genoa. His ship was all he had had, and that was taken by the thieving Ottomans. The

Ottomans Campanello had bargained with, with nothing in it for him. How much had the scheming devil profited behind his back? It was Campanello and the horseman who arranged the details of their passage behind closed doors. He would have extracted more compensation than a mere wisp of a girl for their losses. After all, he had lost a ship and a crew— his whole life's savings. Be happy with your life, Campanello had told him as he ushered them hastily from a palace dripping with enough gold and jewels to make all of Genoa happy for a lifetime.

When he was shown the *Fortunata*, his heart froze, gripped by the fingers of avarice. The *Fortunata*, he could almost see the red and gold flag flying atop its mast, for surely this was the gift of a sultan.

A slight rustle quieted his breathing. "Alonzo," a thin voice called in sleepy perplexity.

Alonzo Torecelli turned the knob and pushed the complaining door open. "I'm going for some food." He forced a smile. "Man cannot live by passion alone."

"Promise to come back," she said faintly, knowing he would soon leave her like all the others.

"Sure, sweet," he said, less than convincingly, and closed the door behind him.

Alonzo melted into the shadows, slipping through the alleys unnoticed. Yes, it was lucky he met him, he smiled to himself. After he left the *Fortunata*, or rather was rudely escorted from her deck, he sensed a presence following him. A presence that turned out to be Conte Sordici. He was later to learn, after a bottle of wine had warmed their bellies, that they had much in common. Joined in revenge, they made a pact in gold that would bind them in blood.

Sordici laughed often at his own secret jokes that rattled Alonzo's sanity. Alonzo demanded gold now. "All right, here," the conte pushed a purse of gold coins across the table, laughing. "It's his own gold that will seal his death," he cackled. Alonzo stared at him suspiciously. "Don't worry, friend, there'll be more where that's come from. Just make sure you do a good job."

"You don't have to worry about my end," Alonzo vowed. "But you'd best think twice if you have any thoughts of crossing me. I'll be looking for a lot more of this," he weighed the purse in the palm of his hand, "when the deed is done."

"Don't leave any loose ends. When Campanello and the Muscovite are reduced to bait, I'll bide by my end. The *Fortunata* will be yours to rule, and with a healthy chunk of the profits."

Alonzo became part of the fog that rolled over the quay. He slithered unnoticed onto the *Fortunata*. His hope was to find the two men asleep and silently slit their throats one at a time. The crew he knew would be no problem, they would still be cozying up to a bottle and a warm female far away from the *Fortunata*.

He budged the heavy door to Miquel's cabin a fraction and scanned the dark shadows in the room. His bunk was empty. Sordici said he would be there. There was still the Muscovite, the one who had looked on in amusement when Campanello showed Toricelli the end of the gangplank. He would not regret ending his life, but he had hoped to neatly take care of both men together. This would compli-

360

te matters. Sordici would pay dearly for this convenience.

The Genoan smiled. The Muscovite was asleep, a half-empty bottle of vodka rested on his desk. He hoped he was in a deep sleep. He moved silently, avoiding loose floorboards. His fingers gripped a dagger tightly, too tightly. A board creaked out its complaint under Alonzo's step. He crouched like a cat stalking its prey and dared not breathe.

Surek turned, pulling his cover of muslin over his shoulders. He was lying on his back facing Alonzo. Satisfied Surek remained asleep, Alonzo moved forward, every muscle in his body tight as a spring. It was not like him to waste time on a victim, but there was something curious about this man he was about to kill. With a growth of beard shadowing his face, it was apparent. Shocked by his recognition of the man, Alonzo stood rigid, a move he would later regret. It was he who had counted on the ally of surprise, now it played against him.

Unnerved, he slowly crouched, leveling his knife, preparing to assassinate his unwary victim, when his wrist was suddenly crushed in Surek's hand. His dagger clanked to the floor. Alonzo would not be doomed, he had come prepared. Backing away from Surek, he regained his balance but had lost his advantage.

"I have two choices, you conniving servant of Mehmet; to let you hang for all to witness in front of the doge's palace for your crimes against the Byzantines or to have the satisfaction of killing you right now," Alonzo breathed heavily with excitement. "But being that I'm a greedy son of a bitch, I'll take

361

you for myself now."

"What have you to gain by risking your life?"

"It might please him to let you know who ha
sealed your death . . . and Campanello's."

"Who has sent you?" Surek inched closer, keepin
the back of his hand turned to conceal the blade in hi
palm.

"A friend of yours—Conte Sordici. He'll pa
nicely for this favor."

"Leave while you still can," Surek warned.

"And miss my chance of revenge for my los
livelihood, my ship, and crew, lost to your sultan,
Alonzo spat.

"Don't be a fool! You will not be avenged b
killing me."

Alonzo lunged for Surek, but was soon startled b
the point of his dagger opening a deadly woun
across his throat. Using all of his strength, he counter
pressed Surek's arm, and in one movement rolled of
him and slipped the dagger from his boot. Crouche
and ready to strike, Alonzo leaped at Surek, his knif
successful this time. An aggressive fighter, h
charged again and again with no thought to his ow
life.

The close confines of the cabin left little room fo
maneuverability. Surek rolled away Alonzo's thrus
but, with little time to recover, felt the second jab o
his dagger pierce through his chest. His visio
clouded, Surek made vain attempts to gain control o
his opponent. Taking a last gamble, he jumped a
Alonzo, surprising him with his effort and managin
to dislodge the deadly weapon from his hand. Now i
was his advantage, if he would only fight the pain i

is chest that threatened to swamp him. His strength
axed, Surek gave way to Alonzo's strength and was
catapulted across the floor. His head slammed with a
splitting crack against the wall; his body lay limp
nd bleeding.

Alonzo stood over his victim, a stream of blood
owing down his heaving chest. He lifted the bottle
f vodka from the floor, uncapped it, and took a deep
rink. The rest he poured over Surek's sprawled and
feless body.

"How you people defeated us, I'll never know," he
aid. Too weary to drag Surek's body and dump him
verboard, he added whatever gold he could find to
e bulge in his pocket and left. He would search for
e other one after Aurelian came up with some more
old. Yes, it was his lucky day.

"Three more days, Miquel! Three more days and I
ill be wed!" Bellina rambled on. She dangled a
and in the cool waters of the tiny fish pond and a
ungry carp nibbled at her fingertips. "And who
nows if it will be for better or for worse . . . But that
how things will be, they cannot be changed, nor do
. . ." She grew silent and pondered the lily pads.
Do you think he truly loves me?"

Miquel turned his face away from her and stared
ard across the lavish D'Rosallini gardens, to where
he sea stretched beyond the wall. His breath came
low and heavy, for as often as he tried to prepare
imself for this day, he could not join in her
omplete happiness.

Sitting down on one of the iron chairs, Bellina

smoothed imaginary wrinkles from her skirt. "D[o]
you think—"

"Yes!" Miquel almost snapped, then continued i[n]
a softer tone. "It is expressed in his every word, ever[y]
movement when he's by you. Do not fear, little one. [I]
know the signs very well. He will be yours forever[.]"

"I only hope what you say is true," she sighe[d.]
"There will always be pretty faces to turn a man['s]
heart when I have withered like this rose." Sh[e]
plucked the weary flower and sniffed it for life.

"But you are not a flower, foolish child. Do yo[u]
give men so little credit? Beauty is transient and neve[r]
to be relied upon for choosing a wife. No . . . Sure[n]
chooses well and he knows it. He will never b[e]
careless with such a treasure."

"I hope you are right," she mumbled into he[r]
hand.

The lone tree, carefully nurtured with its ancien[t]
gnarled trunk and bitter olives, hung low over th[e]
man-created pond that held a fascinating array [of]
vibrantly hued fish. It was a place to settle problem[s.]
Here, listening to the contented chirps of the well-fe[d]
chicks that nested in the drooping boughs, or th[e]
rush of the sea against the wall, one could think.

Finally Miquel sat next to her, his brow moody. I[n]
silence they watched the fish feed on the stale brea[d]
she threw them. When she spied the worm that fe[ll]
from its silver thread to Miquel's curly nest of hai[r]
she gently brushed it off. He jumped to his feet s[o]
suddenly she half-expected him to be swatting at a[n]
offending bee. "It is only a worm, Miquel," sh[e]
laughed.

The sun outlined his dark looming form and h[is]

asted back a stray curl from his sweaty brow. "It is
too hot out here for me! Perhaps Grazia can be
convinced to fetch a bottle of wine from the cellar.
With your uncle's permission, of course."

"Since when do you ask permission? It has been
whispered you have been drinking more than wine.
Really, Miquel!"

"I'll bring you a glass if you'll stop nagging. Poor
Jurek, how I pity him!" he teased.

His laughter was like the rush of a waterfall upon
parched ground. She watched the ferns close around
his body, wincing when he hopped through Aunt
Claudia's delicate phlox. Lately he brooded too
much. If he wasn't dragging himself about the docks,
or aimlessly poling along in a gondola, he was
moping among the statues and flowers of the
D'Rosallini garden. He was not himself at all, and
she worried. Perhaps one of the maids had spurned
him? He had never mentioned a girl, but then that
was not his way. How she wished he would pay
attention to Lucia; the poor girl mooned after him.
Bellina let a smile overcome the frown that had
controlled her features all morning. Perhaps, just
maybe, she could ask Miquel to help Lucia with the
boxes containing her trousseau. Whether he liked it
or not, he was going to see more of Lucia.

A limp breeze rippled the pond's surface while the
carp eyed her with bulging eyes, blowing bubbles.
Spring had ended too abruptly, dying in the
suffocating grasp of a sweltering humidity. She
wished she could entice a magician into changing
her into a fish for awhile. Then she could have
sought out the cooling, calming waters to cease the

endless pounding that raged inside her head. Instead she urged her slippers from her feet, pulled her skirt out of the way, and, confident that she would hea Miquel before he glimpsed her abandoned behavior and let the waters take the burning from her feet if no her head.

She did not hear him. As she tangled one foo around the lemon grass and water lilies, he cam silently and stood behind her. She laughed when th carp returned to poke at her toe. Diving, the fish fanned a spray of water at her, disappearing unde the greenery and leaving behind echoing rings upo the mirror surface. When the water cleared, sh searched for him. Suddenly, the shadows that she ha taken for leaves merged into a grim visage that stare at her with hollow eyes from their dark depths.

"Conte Sordici!" She pulled her naked feet from the water, tucking them under her skirts. Her spike glare brought a shallow curve to his lips. His fac still bore paper-line scars from his fall a few week back, but his limp was almost a thing of the past.

"My sweet innocent betrothed," he stated deter minedly. "Is the water cool?"

"I am not your betrothed. You have accepte Baron Melankovski's money."

"What you say is of no importance," he paused savoring the flush that rose to her cheeks. "I have n use listening to raving, so still your harlot's tongue. put faith in contracts that have been made betwee two gentlemen. Melankovski is no gentleman." H smiled wickedly, sending an icy shiver up her spine

"Do not waste your words, Sordici. I know m uncle has spoken with you. And will you bring

Surek's anger again upon yourself, fool?" She stuffed her still-wet feet into her slippers and stood to leave. A crushing hand grasped her shoulder painfully; he laughed at the shocked look in her eyes.

"Leaving so soon? And you have not even heard what I came to tell you." A vein pulsed madly on his forehead, matching the frenzy in his eyes.

"I'm not interested in anything you have to say."

"Do you think I am fool enough to come here when Surek is around." His face twisted in cruel laughter.

"What have you done? Where is Surek?" She felt a rush of panic take hold and smother any rational thought.

"It's my right to have you," he answered, ignoring her questions.

"You bear me no love. Take what you were given and leave me."

"Love has little to do with it, my sweet. It is simple. I want the D'Rosallini wealth that comes with you, too."

She stared at him. Could he truly be serious? "That you will never have!" she hissed, ignoring the threatening chuckles that rattled from his throat.

"I met a friend of yours by the name of Alonzo Toricelli. Do you remember him and that long voyage home? Fascinating story he had to tell. Not every girl gets to play the harlot for a sultan."

She clawed his hand away and stumbled back, her face ashen. If Alonzo were in Venice, than it was possible he could have connected Surek with Mehmet. Aurelian was up to something. Where was Miquel?

With an effort, she focused her voice to an even

timbre. "And do you have proof of this lie?"

"Why should I fret over proof when just a whisper in the right ear will ruin you and your 'Baron' forever." He raised his brows at her and gave a light laugh. "Would you believe they all think you've been in a convent these past years! But still, once they hear you've actually been the whore of the man who crushed Constantinople, why that convent story will be scattered like a rose thrown to the waves. No one will accept you, wherever you go! You will need me to save you from the condottiere, or a prison will be your palace."

Bellina shrugged as carelessly as her pounding heart would let her. "My uncle's words will set your vile mutterings back to the dirt where you first found them."

Aurelian started at her words and anger flashed across the sallowness of his face. "I am a Sordici!" he snarled. "And a conte. They will believe anything I say before they believe a Poletti!"

Bellina laughed in both bitterness and digust. "If I am so tainted as you would have others believe, then why would you be so eager to take my hand? I can only conclude that the D'Rosallini money is of more value than," she inclined her head in mock respect, "the honorable name Sordici."

His fingers dug into the olive tree's wearied bark. "You are a slut and deserve no better than that Ottoman whoremaster."

A crack of the hedges and a voice savage in its hate brought them both to a start.

"Mind your tongue, dog! Do you imagine slander is taken so lightly in this house?" Miquel's face was

368

dark and lined in a way Bellina remembered when men had clashed in the streets of Constantinople.

"Miquel," she said breathlessly, "he is mad!"

It was as if neither were aware of her. Aurelian met Miquel with a thin smile as if he had invited him.

"Slander, Miquel? Hardly."

"Bellina would sooner die than pleasure that accursed Turk! I should have killed you long ago."

"No!" Bellina screamed, hearing Miquel's sword hum its eagerness as it slid from its scabbard. He flung her aside as she grasped his arm.

"Go away, get away from here—" His words ended in a grunt as he met Aurelian's polished blade with a crack that splintered the lazy tranquility of the garden. Carefully, yet with an agility that defied his healing leg, Aurelian sidestepped Miquel's hasty lunge and, with a flash of metal, opened his cheek to the bone. Bellina's scream sent the nesting birds to flight.

Sobered by the stream of blood that ran from his quivering flesh, Miquel parried with a ferocity born of skill now instead of blind frenzy. Each impact wracked Aurelian's arm painfully. Each thrust backed him into the tangle of shrubbery as Miquel hewed with deadly determination, raining mutilated leaves around them. Fear leaped into Aurelian's eyes. With a whistle past his ear the sword tangled for a second in the ruffle about his neck. Dodging sharply, he slipped, and Miquel directed his steely harbinger of death at his heaving chest. With a shrill shriek Aurelian rolled away, the blade glancing off a rib with a sickening grate.

He kicked out, his leg catching Miquel full in the

knee. "Bastardo!" Miquel gasped, limping back as Aurelian sprang to his feet. Yet it was not enough to prevent him from catching the edge of Aurelian's sword which sliced obliquely into the muscles of his arm. Miquel's sword fell upon the bloodied dirt with a thud.

It came as no surprise that Aurelian took that precise moment to fling himself upon a helpless man. They both fell to the ground a confused mass, with an angry glitter of metal and Aurelian's sword arm twisted between them, their clothes sticky with blood and the conte's cape tangled around them both.

Miquel's fist smacked into the Conte's head. Pulling away, he caught up his sword and stood swaying, but just as quickly Aurelian faced him, his eyes mocking.

It seemed like a clutch of hours had passed as they stood there staring and heaving like two stags matching antlers. But then, in one tremendous effort, Miquel lunged with deadly accuracy.

Bellina closed her eyes, ready for Aurelian's death cry. It did not come. Instead, the shatter of wood cracked in her ears, and when her eyes flew open, she saw to her horror Miquel's blade protruding from the tree's trunk. With a macabre leer, Aurelian sunk his rapier deep into Miquel's chest.

"My God, no!" Bellina screamed, backing away from the nightmare before her. As Aurelian withdrew his blade, Miquel clawed at it, his eyes dilated and a bloody foam bubbling from his mouth as it opened in a soundless scream. Bellina clasped a hand over her mouth when Aurelian's eyes, dripping murder, turned on her. He clutched the wound at his side and advanced painfully.

"If I did not need your wealth, I would dangle your worthless heart from this tip," He raised his blood-slimed sword to shine dull and crimson in the afternoon sun.

However, her eyes flew past Aurelian. "Miquel," she moaned, watching his still form, wanting to go to him yet repulsed by the gash that pumped blood over the foliage and ground. Aurelian twined a fist into her mane of hair and pushed her forward.

"He is no better than food for the vultures. That is all he ever was good—"

His words ended in a strangle as she grasped his neck, raking his flesh under her nails. "You would not even be fit for the vultures, for you are poison!" He flung her from himself, but not before his face was scarred with welted lines from his eye to his neck.

"Be warned, my sweet betrothed," he wheezed. "There is no one to help you now. Such rebellious-ness will not be tolerated in a wife of mine."

He was weary and hurting. Like a striking hawk, she saw her only advantage. As if reading her thoughts, Aurelian locked eyes with her, his dark look promising reprisal. With a screech she swooped upon him, gashing his delicate blouse, and ripping the skin on his face and chest before he crushed her to the ground. Her arm still in his grasp, he twisted it cruelly, forcing a cry from her lips.

"Such a pair we'll make, you and I." He jerked her arm tighter and she felt the blood trickle down her throat as she bit the inside of her cheek. How they had all underestimated him. "You will be a good wife,"

371

he promised in his ragged breath. "Much have I learned from the condottieri. Things that cannot be appreciated until you need to quell a rebellious mate." He hurled her viciously and watched her crash into the sharp angles of the marble fountain.

With a snap Miquel's blade was wrenched from the tree, freezing Aurelian's wheezing to silence. It bit into the dirt at his feet with a soundless shudder of its hilt. Stricken, Aurelian's gaze lifted to see Surek at the tree.

"Surprised?" Aurelian stared at him as though he were a specter from the afterlife. "Take it!" Surek commanded without any of the hot emotion that had pushed at Miquel. "You need that sword and your own if you count your life any worth."

Aurelian back away from Miquel's chipped sword, his hand resting upon his own. Surek's black eyes glanced from Miquel's twisted body to circle and find Bellina, crouched and dazed beside the fountain. The eyes turned back and Aurelian's stomach knotted.

Quickly, cunningly, the conte gave a gracious smile. "Good sir, put down your arms. There is no need for rash actions. It was a quarrel between myself and this treacherous sea rat. And you will thank me, for I have uncovered a vile treachery, this girl has been warming the bed of the Ottoman King himself and," he added quickly, "this scoundrel was in conspiracy with her."

Surek plunged Aurelian into confusion with a thunderous laugh that could have hailed from Zeus himself. An uncertain smile quivered at one corner of Aurelian's lip. "Yes, yes, you see how I have prevented her from throwing your name in disgrace," he rambled nervously.

"I know you are lying, Sordici," Surek pressed the point of his sword into his breast. "Do you know how I know? No, I suppose you don't." A satisfied smile broadened his face. "Torecelli did not have time to tell you."

"Torecelli? The fool, to let you off so easily, but I see he has left his mark." Aurelian noted Surek's wounds.

His words ended with startling abruptness as he felt rather than saw Surek's sword arch across his chest. A spreading pain told him without lowering his eyes that the blade had left a thin line of encouragement to draw his weapon. He did not need another.

Aurelian lifted his sword in a wide arch, but with a clatter and spray of sparks, Surek sent it whirling from his hand. It skipped and landed in the fish pond. With a jerk of his sword, Surek motioned at Miquel's battered weapon.

Aurelian pulled it from the ground with unsteady hands, stabbed a hundred times by the two metallic eyes. With a cry he swung again and with a numbing blow Surek set him back.

"Lord," Aurelian whined as he took a limping step. "I have no quarrel with you! Would you fight a man who is disabled as you have made me?"

"That did not stop you from murdering Miquel," Surek growled, striking one jarring blow, then another in answer. Aurelian brought his own blade around in defense.

From the corner of his eye, Surek saw Camillus's ashen face from the balcony. He tightened his hand about his sword and with sudden viciousness the blade slid through Aurelian with ease.

In the end, after much debate, Camillus decided to let Surek have his way. As much as he was sure the authorities would be sympathetic to his and Surek's problems, he finally let the Muscovite take both of the bodies in a Poletti gondola under the night's care to God knew where. Of two things he was certain: Aurelian's final resting place would be among sharks, and no one would ever learn of what happened in the Poletti courtyard this day.

Camillus walked the garden now, wrapping the fractured branches of his olive tree. The heavy odor of blood rose about him, despite the fresh sand his men had scattered. Regardless of the nauseous feeling it gave his stomach, he did not go and seek the comforts of his bed.

He needed time for thinking; one day had seen the deaths of two men he had known. It had been almost too foolish for Aurelian to have challenged Surek. Although Camillus was all too aware of how angry Aurelian Sordici had been over Bellina's coming marriage to Surek, no one thought he was mad enough to engage in a fight which could never have had any other outcome but his death. In fact, he could not even imagine him attacking Miquel. True they hated each other, but Aurelian was a fop and had more concern for his own skin than any young shipmaster's. He would have taken the easier way and had him assassinated.

The fact that Miquel attacked Aurelian was unthinkable. Miquel had always kept a cool regard, if not respect, for the power of the aristocrat. Bellina had told her uncle not to waste any thoughts on Aurelian, and then disclosed the truth about the night he came to her. How he wished she would have told him that night! All of this might have been avoided.

Camillus gave a final twist around a branch and then tied the ends of the rag so it stayed in place. The wind was stirring, whipping the sea in the distance to a white-capped fury that swelled hauntingly in the moon's glare. The old man sighed.

To be sure, the wedding would not be canceled, it might give rise to unwanted rumors, but Camillus could not help but wish the ceremony postponed. To consecrate a marriage beneath the shadows of these murders chilled his blood. It would be an ill omen, his superstitious self thought in dread; but then all the teachings of his childhood insisted otherwise. Surely a holy joining by the bishop of San Alfredo's could not help but be a blessed one.

Bellina crept out to the balcony and let the wind dry her tear-wet face. Below, the lush courtyard held no beauty, only the horror of the day before. The garden with its harsh bloody secrets, like this, her father's home, would hold only pain if it were not for her uncle and Surek.

The bushes below shook suddenly, setting her pulse pounding. When the dense foliage parted, Surek's eyes caught the shimmer of the sun's rays and glowed up at her. Carefully finding a foothold, he pulled upwards while she watched, hypnotized by the play of his muscles beneath the silk of his blouse. When he topped the rise, a thousand moist kisses tickled and blinded him.

"Bellina, let me get in," he said, grasping the railing. "Do you want your uncle to find me?"

Instantly she halted, tugging his arm in haste. "Oh come, come. They will see you."

He laughed and shook his head at her fleeting moods. But once inside he remembered from where he had come. "It is finished," he sighed, falling heavily into the well-padded chair beside her bed. "I did not know Miquel long, but I feel his loss sorely."

"Oh do not talk of death and funerals to me. I cannot bear it any longer!"

Surek cast a wary glance towards her, sensitive to the throbbing in her voice. Like a violin strung to a wracking tightness, she wavered first at high pitch then low. He pulled her tightly to his chest, longing to vanquish her pain.

"What is this?" he whispered. "New tears? I was sure every bit of moisture had been wrung from you."

"You knew it, didn't you?" she asked with a sudden intenseness.

"Knew what?"

"Knew that Miquel loved me."

"Of course he loved you." He smoothed her hair back with a hand.

"No," she said impatiently, determinedly. "I don't mean as a sister, I mean he loved me and I didn't even know." Her voice climbed higher. "But it suddenly became clear in the end! Oh God, when I think of how he must have suffered all these years."

"Hush, Miquel was happy for us. And how could he expect you to know? You didn't even know you loved me!"

Surek came up behind her, wrapping his arms securely around her waist and burying his face in her hair. "Enough of this talk of death," he said softly.

"This is not my home any longer," she murmured.

"I should say not," Surek said lightly. "After tomorrow we will be on our way to Moscow." He saw her innocent surprise as she turned to face him.

"To Muscovy!"

"Of course. I promised my father a bride," he chuckled as he thought of Yuri faced with a daughter-in-law as headstrong as Teva.

Of course! Why hadn't it crossed her mind? But she had never once thought he meant to return to Muscovy. Uncannily, he read her thoughts.

"Did you think me so enthralled by your fair Venice that, like a fly in honey, I would stay? No, I am here only to spread the Grand Prince's greeting to his neighbors, and perhaps raise a profit or two with an established trade line in the meanwhile."

Muscovy, her mind stirred. What was it like? Cold and dreary she had heard, but what did that matter? It was away from here and she would welcome it with joyful arms as long as Surek was there to hold her. They would start their own life, away from the past that reeked of death and sorrow.

"I shall love your land," she smiled, hugging him.

He kissed her, lingering, despite the alarm in his head that said it was time to go. Tomorrow she would be his for all eternity. However, as he turned to go, he felt a hand bid him to pause. "Stay with me tonight," Bellina whispered, and all his willpower and better judgment fled. Wryly he hoped he could wake to leave in the morning before her maid came to prepare her for her wedding.

Twenty-Seven

That Saturday arrived with dark swirling clouds that pelted the richly clothed guests as they crowded into and on the fringes of San Alfredo. Yet, however cold and cutting the weather, the atmosphere was one of celebration, for here was the powerful Poletti family giving away the last of the D'Rosallini's to a man of royal blood. The fact that he was a Muscovite did little to dampen their awe, for had not the doge himself walked with this man? Would not the doge have attended the ceremony if his gouty leg had not acted up? What did Venice care if he was foreign; they had made their wealth with those who were foreign.

Bellina dashed into the cathedral as quickly as the heavy silk gown would allow. She would hear a low whispering rise and fall like the waves of the sea. Her eyes sought no one. As water dripped from the orange blossom wreath upon her head and beaded like dew; as the folds of her dress clung damply to her knees; as the pages of the Bible in her hand stuck together; she wanted to leap and flee from all the ceremony and staring faces.

How could she have agreed to this? Deep within
the ancient bowels of this church, two hundred and
fifty people waited, their faces masks of joyous
anticipation. She felt like a pagan sacrifice before
them. All she wanted to do was find Surek and hold
him, far away in some private place.

Lucia arranged the folds of yellow silk artfully so
that they brushed the floor with a sculptured grace.
"Oh my Lady," she chirped. "You are lovely. Baron
Melankovski surely has never see one so beautiful."

Bellina let the girl coo and ah and arrange her
hands as if she were a doll. They told her in hand-
smothered giggles what the night would bring, but
she felt far away, not a part of this at all. . . . She could
see the land spread out before her like a yellow-
clothed table. The brush speckled it like crumbs and
stood stoically against the hot breath of the desert
wind. The sun lengthened their shadows until they
joined those of Kayaska and the black stallion.

His arms were wrapped tightly around her and she
relaxed against his chest. They had the scarlet and
gold tasseled blanket upon the sand, and for once the
colors that marked him as the sultan's captain did
not flash anger across her eyes.

"We must start back," he said in a voice heavy with
emotion.

She stretched lazily and yawned. "Just a while
longer, please?"

"My men will be sending a scout if they do not see
me soon." He stroked the curve of her hip and lifted
her face to him. "I love you."

"Oh Surek," she whispered, reaching a hand to

aress his cheek.

"Bellina!" Maria said impatiently. "Did you hear me? It is time."

Flavia pinched her cheek. "Smile! After all, this is what you wanted, isn't it? You don't want Surek to think he made a bad choice, do you?"

Bellina grimaced at her cousin. Camillus gently folded her arm over his, strains of music reached out possessively to guide her towards her destiny.

Someone gave her a nudge. Camillus gave her a parting smile. Woodenly, she followed her cousins in a processional down the cold stone of the center aisle. And then she saw him. So alone next to Father Masalia and the bishop, his black eyes a mirror to his soul and his smile a radiant sun.

Away fled her fears, burned back like a weedy field before it could take hold. Nervously he waved a hand across his hair. A smile so fleeting only she was sure to see, kissed her lips. Here happiness would be abundant, Bellina thought with a contented sigh and, taking courage, she found herself kneeling beside him.

If she had not been familiar with the wedding mass, having attended more than she could have counted, Bellina would never have known what the bishop had questioned or what she had responded. Dazed by the opiate of happiness, she was suspended, distantly aware that all was as it should be.

Suddenly, two broad arms, strong yet tender, pulled her close and she could feel Surek's breath, heady, ethereal, and then he kissed her. It was an awakening. Just as firmly, betraying the passion that fanned into flames, she returned it without reserva-

tion. "Husband," she murmured, and Surek only
smiled. They both turned, hand in hand, the bishop's
blessings at their back and the good wishes of family
and friends before them.

After all the feasting and merriment, the wine and
the music, the teasing, a thousand toasts, and the
scattering of wheat grains of fertility upon the waters
of the Grand Canal, they happily retreated to their
chamber, a lifetime of passion and love before them

FIERY ROMANCE

CALIFORNIA CARESS   (2771, $3.75)
by Rebecca Sinclair

Hope Bennett was determined to save her brother's life.
And if that meant paying notorious gunslinger Drake Fra-
zier to take his place in a fight, she'd barter her last gold
nugget. But Hope soon discovered she'd have to give the
handsome rattlesnake more than riches if she wanted his
help. His improper demands infuriated her; even as she
luxuriated in the tantalizing heat of his embrace, she
refused to yield to her desires.

ARIZONA CAPTIVE   (2718, $3.75)
by Laree Bryant

Logan Powers had always taken his role as a lady-killer
very seriously and no woman was going to change that.
Not even the breathtakingly beautiful Callie Nolan with
her luxuriant black hair and startling blue eyes. Logan
might have considered a lusty romp with her but it was apparent she was a lady, through and through. Hard as he
tried, Logan couldn't resist wanting to take her warm slender body in his arms and hold her close to his heart forever.

DECEPTION'S EMBRACE   (2720, $3.75)
by Jeanne Hansen

Terrified heiress Katrina Montgomery fled Memphis with
what little she could carry and headed west, hiding in a
freight car. By the time she reached Kansas City, she was
feeling almost safe . . . until the handsomest man she'd
ever seen entered the car and swept her into his embrace.
She didn't know who he was or why he refused to let her
go, but when she gazed into his eyes, she somehow knew
she could trust him with her life . . . and her heart.

Available wherever paperbacks are sold, or order direct from the
Publisher. Send cover price plus 50¢ per copy for mailing and
handling to Zebra Books, Dept. 2884, 475 Park Avenue South,
New York, N.Y. 10016. Residents of New York, New Jersey and
Pennsylvania must include sales tax. DO NOT SEND CASH.